# Praise for ~~Warwick Downing~~ and His Previous Mystery
## *A Lingering Doubt*

**Books by Warwick Downing**

Choice of Evils
A Clear Case of Murder
A Lingering Doubt
The Water Cure

Published by POCKET BOOKS

*April 1995*
*For Bobby—*
*This is my best.*
*WD*

# CHOICE of EVILS

## WARWICK DOWNING

**POCKET BOOKS**

New York    London    Toronto    Sydney    Tokyo    Singapore

This book is a work of fiction. Names, characters, places and incidents are products of the author's imagination or are used fictitiously. Any resemblance to actual events or locales or persons, living or dead, is entirely coincidental.

An *Original* Publication of POCKET BOOKS

 POCKET BOOKS, a division of Simon & Schuster Inc.
1230 Avenue of the Americas, New York, NY 10020

ISBN: 0-671-76035-1

First Pocket Books printing October 1994

10  9  8  7  6  5  4  3  2  1

POCKET and colophon are registered trademarks of Simon & Schuster Inc.

Cover design by Irving Freeman

Printed in the U.S.A.

To John Dunning, my partner in crime, for his invaluable suggestions, comments, sarcasms, dire predictions, and steadfast encouragement.

To Janet Fitch, who—in an earlier novel—crafted Frankie's voice, and in this one, gave it back to me.

To Mary Halloran, who endured—not always quietly—the daily inflictions and assaults of a demanding ego, patting it and kicking it constructively, as required; but mainly for her love.

To Alice Price Knight, who saved me from the embarrassment of having to explain how the Nile River could flow from the Mediterranean Sea to Lake Victoria.

To Sam Rosen of *Securus,* for his guided tour through the hi-tech world of surveillance equipment.

To others, for their information and trust, who choose to remain nameless.

# Prologue

Hours had gone by since Rick Adamson had folded his long body into the spacious trunk of the large sedan. He waited in total blackness, except for the luminous face of his wristwatch. He watched it helplessly, his chest tightening with each passing second.

He couldn't stop the clock. The time came: 1:15 A.M.

With trembling hands he edged up the lid of the trunk, letting in light. His eyes contracted with its sudden assault. Was anyone watching him? he wondered, fearfully peering into the well-lit underground parking garage. Seeing no movement, hearing no sound, he opened the trunk lid and forced himself to climb out.

His face, hands, and arms had been darkened with charcoal. His clothes were black: a short-sleeved cycling shirt, running tights, old-style tennis shoes. Closing the trunk, he touched the right rear pocket of his cycling shirt, feeling for the heat-treated plastic knife. It hadn't fallen out; he still had it.

Crouching, he ran to the stairwell in the center of the cavernous room and jammed himself against the wall. His legs shook and his eyes pounded with tension. Wild-eyed, he started up the stairs.

At the landing, he heard sentries talking in Arabic—when

the panic he'd been fighting surged through him, freezing his mind. Nothing made sense to him. An inner voice urged him to run. Forget her and get on with your life! it commanded. Powerful hands seemed to grab him and turn him around. . . .

Then he saw her face. It glowed with love, for him. Torn by conflicting emotions, he begged muscles that wanted to flee in terror for the courage to stay.

He stayed. Slowly he peered around the corner of the wall.

Two Rashidis, in tailored dark blue uniforms, sat with their backs to him in a circle of light, guarding the main entrance of the embassy building. They faced tinted glass panels that opened onto a cul-de-sac for cars. Rick had to reach the hallway behind them, on the other side of the darkened lobby.

He crawled on his belly, inching his way across the thick carpet, completely exposed to view. One of them turned his head, glancing backward. But then he leaned toward his companion, said something Rick couldn't understand, and laughed. A lifetime later, Rick slithered out of sight.

He could breathe again! Gulping air, he felt huge, super-human. He ran noiselessly down the hall to a back staircase. Leaping up the steps three at a time, he came to a wide hallway. Large, brilliantly colored murals of land and sea hung from the walls. He sped past them, then crouched in front of an exquisitely decorated glass door: the office of Faris abu abd al-Rahman, the deputy ambassador.

Trust within the circle was a way of life to the Rashidis, and the door had not been locked. Slipping inside, he let it close behind him. A sliding glass door on the south wall of the large room was covered with drapes. He reached behind the drapes, opened the door, and squeezed through onto a balcony.

Thick vines covered the wall of the building, but a fire-escape ladder, hidden in the tangle of growth, could be seen by those who knew it was there. He balanced on the balcony railing and grabbed for it, pulling up until his feet reached the bottom rung. Cautiously he began the climb— when the thin, intense figure of Abd al-Hafiz jumped through the door onto the balcony. Al-Hafiz and Rick had been friends, but when he spotted Rick, grim determination registered on his face and the gun in his hand jerked upward.

Rick pushed off the ladder and dropped. His knees smashed into the smaller man's chest. The palm of his left hand skidded across the cement surface and pain blew through his right foot. The pistol clattered to the deck. He grabbed al-Hafiz under the chin, choking off sound, but al-Hafiz fought to his feet. Rick yanked out the knife, pricking him with its tip. "Cool it, man," he hissed, but al-Hafiz wrenched violently. They fell against the wall.

The blade jammed between al-Hafiz's ribs. A strangled cry pushed out of him which Rick couldn't stop. Terrified, he forced the knife deep with the heel of his hand. Pulling on al-Hafiz's chin, he held him, held him, held him—until a final tremor was replaced with the slackness of death.

An awful feeling of despair spread through Rick's chest. The men had traded stories of their lives. Cupping the still head tenderly in his hands, Rick eased the lifeless body to the deck. Without feeling, seemingly without thought, he picked up the pistol and dropped it in a pouch of his cycling shirt. As though moving through a dream, he regained the ladder and began the climb.

By the time Rick reached the roof, his mind had cleared. He stole across it softly, knowing any creaks would be heard in the rooms below. He opened the door to a small brick structure that stood over a stairway. The stairway dropped from the sundeck into the women's living area.

A realization of his nearness to the woman engulfed him. Before, we were two, Sahar had said. Now, we are one. And as one soul, each of us forever will know love. For a moment he had the illusion that he had stepped inside a bubble large enough to hold a piece of time.

A feeling of ecstasy radiated through him: an inexplicable gratitude, like the miracle of shared love. He was so thankful he hadn't turned back! The blood of Abd al-Hafiz would forever be on his hands, but at that moment he knew he would succeed.

The hallway in the *hareem* was dimly lighted. Many doors

3

opened onto it, and her apartment was at the end. He crept down the hall until he stood in front of her door, then tried the knob. . . .

Locked. He tried it again. . . .

The knob turned against his palm. He snapped his hand away and pressed into the wall. Slowly the door opened and the profile of a woman's face, her head covered in an *abaya*, appeared. As though pulled by magnetic current, she turned toward him and smiled.

It was Sahar. "I know you will come for me," she whispered, taking his hand. "I know I will go away with you."

# 1

## Tuesday, July 30, 1991
## Washington, D.C.

As Frankie Rommel emerged from the underground depths of the Judicial Square Station, she squinted at the sun and tasted the mid-morning air. It was cleaner than the last time she'd been in the District, but the heat was the same. At first you didn't feel it. Then you became aware you were drenched. Then you vaporized.

The tall, wide-shouldered woman, in her mid-forties, had flown in from Denver that morning and dropped her bag at the downtown Embassy Suites Hotel. Sorrel-brown hair hung loosely down her back. She wore a silver-gray pantsuit, a silk shirt, and flats: comfortable attire to travel in, but all the women she saw were in dress suits. Her jewelry had been given to her by the man who made it: a Shoshone Indian she played with as a girl, on her grandfather's ranch near Lander, Wyoming. The copper bracelet on her left arm was a serpent and warded off evil. A watch, on a silver chest washer, hung between her breasts. Her earrings were tiny golden aspen leaves, on sprigs.

She moved easily through the crowd of suits and ties. Frankie lifted weights and jogged for exercise, and her trim figure looked younger than it was. Turning right on Fourth Street, she walked toward the U.S. Attorney's office, one block away.

She hated reading on planes and had barely skimmed the file she'd been given the night before. The killing had occurred in the embassy of the Kingdom of Rashidi. The story had been splashed over the newspapers and the late night news. She hadn't learned much from the documents faxed to the National Association of Special Prosecutors that she didn't already know. The thin file, two novels, a portable desk, and a small purse had been jammed in her roomy briefcase and hooked over her shoulder like a handbag.

A barren lot spread to the west of Fourth Street. Mounds of brown dirt, excavations, wooden guardrails, and debris gave it the appearance of a war zone. The large brownstone building she wanted had slits for windows. It looked like a fort in an occupied country. So this is my nation's capital, she thought ironically. The land of the free.

Pushing through a glass door, she was funneled by ropes and stanchions toward the security checkpoint. She tossed her briefcase on the conveyor belt and nodded at the uniformed woman who read the images on the screen, searching for weapons. She walked through the door-frame-shaped electronic metal detector, feeling like an Indian from a warring tribe who'd been given safe passage.

Another guard telephoned to confirm what Frankie told him, then hung up. "Mr. Grantland is on the second floor, Miss Rommel," he said. "The guard at the top of the stairs will direct you, if you need help."

"Thank you." Frankie spoke in a soft growl, partly the product of fifteen years in the courtroom and partly the result of her one major vice: she smoked.

She was directed to a cavernous waiting room filled with benches, fold-up chairs, and people. The ceiling was twelve feet from the floor and seemed to sag. She left her name with the receptionist and found a seat on a bench along the wall.

It was eerily quiet, as though everyone was a suspect who knew that whatever he said would be used against him in a court of law. She found a cigarette in her purse and was searching for her lighter when a short black man, with skin light enough so the freckles on his high forehead showed, entered the room through a door she hadn't seen. He wore a tie but no coat. "Miss Rommel?" he asked, looking around.

Frankie quickly put the cigarette away and stood up. She walked with confidence; a gift from the man who had raised her. She thought of her grandfather often, grateful for the old man's firm but gentle guidance and his willingness to let her make her own mistakes. "Hi," she said, approaching the man by the door. "I guess you're Grantland."

"Yeah." He held the door for her but did not offer to shake hands. His quiet eyes held a quality of sadness. "Follow me, okay? Kind of a maze back here."

Maze was right. They rounded several corners and might even have doubled back on themselves, but the terrain didn't repeat, and the solemn faces they passed were never the same. They reached a room that had been carved out of a larger one, with walls no thicker than the plywood they were made of. He opened the door.

The room was big enough for a large desk, two bookcases, two chairs, and a line of boxes along one wall. The desk was clean, except for a thin file, a notepad, and a telephone. "Have a chair," he said, indicating. He plucked the file off his desk and sagged tiredly onto a chair next to her. "How was your trip?"

"Great," she said. "I love flying, especially into the sun."

"You like working for NASP?" He sounded wistful. "Travel all over the country, try cases in different cities. Is it as good as it sounds?" He handed her the file.

"It doesn't get boring." She looked at it: *United States* v. *Richard Adamson, Jr.* "Like this one. Arabs, oil, embassies. The son of a prominent doctor. It should be fun." She smiled, but didn't drum up any enthusiasm. "I get tired of the bodies."

"Tell me."

"Is that your beat, Roy?"

He nodded slowly. "Felony murder, you know, plus all the baggage goes with it. Like burglary, robbery, and rape. I try one a week."

"Oh, my goodness!" she drawled sympathetically, looking around the room. The dreary, slate-green walls were barren, as though he had just moved in and hadn't unpacked. "Doesn't anybody plead out?"

"Most of them do. But like last year? I still had to try forty-four." His hands, laced together in his lap, were still as a dead man in a coffin.

Frankie wondered if he'd just come off a loss, knowing how it can leave you feeling. "Do you win or lose around here?"

"We stack 'em up," he said. "I got convictions in forty-two." He got up, pulled an ashtray off a bookshelf, and stuck it on the desk between them. "Go ahead and smoke if you want."

"Thanks." She lit up, careful to avoid blowing smoke in his direction. He interested her. Small, unimpressive in manner, a personality—unless he was holding back—as exciting as a wet towel. Who would think of him as a trial lawyer? Yet he had to be good at what he did. You didn't win forty-two murders out of forty-four because you were lucky.

"Looked at this thing yet?" he asked, indicating the file.

"Reading on airplanes gives me a headache." She also preferred staring at sky, and clouds, and vast expanses of land. "Where are you with it?"

"Did *Gerstein* yesterday. Preliminary hearing got set for August eighth."

"'*Gerstein*'?"

"What we call it the first time the bad guy goes in, you know. Enough probable cause to satisfy the hearing commissioner, hang on to the dude a few days without bond."

She wondered how much of this stuff she needed to know. "Don't you use a grand jury? Why a preliminary hearing?"

"You know. We have to make sure all his rights are protected." The muscles in his jaw flexed. "We do a preliminary to hold long enough for the grand jury."

"What about bail?"

"This kid'll argue it, he comes from money, but no chance." He snapped his eyes shut suddenly, as though blotting out an unwelcome vision. "It's a felony murder hold. Our judges don't let them out if they get charged with felony murder."

Frankie tried not to notice his oddness. "So the preliminary goes on August eighth. Then how long before he's indicted?"

"You'll get another ten days, unless you get an extension."

Frankie tapped her chest. "Moi?"

"Oui. Vous." He smiled, rubbing his eyes. "Somebody's working up your appointment as special prosecutor. You're supposed to do the preliminary—nothing to that—then take it to the grand jury, do the indictment and the trial."

She glanced inside the file, then thrust it in her briefcase. "What's in here?"

"Autopsy, police agency summaries, lab results, witness statements. Clippings from the *Washington Post.*" Suddenly he looked pitiful, like a little boy who'd been bucked off a horse and whose daddy made him get back on. "Hard to get excited about murder in the District," he said, gazing at her with pain-filled eyes. "But you don't get a killing in an embassy every day, even in Washington. Practice your smile. Your picture will be in the paper."

What was troubling him? she wondered. Or had he just had a sleepless night? "I've been down that road," she said. "What I hate is when they follow you to the toilet. What's this about an Arabian princess?"

"You hear about her?"

Frankie dug in her briefcase and pulled out a newspaper clipping. She handed it to him.

"Where'd you get this?" he asked.

"One of our lawyers is from California. He takes the San Francisco *Chronicle.*"

He read through the article quickly, then laid it on his desk. "Smoke and mirrors, you know. She doesn't exist. That won't stop the press." His eyes snapped shut again, then opened, like someone who couldn't stand the light. What was his problem? "California probably do more with a make-believe princess than the District," he said, trying to sound conversational. "Here, you got Beltway gossip which the locals like better. What the prez had for breakfast, and how it impacted on the collapse of the Soviet Union."

According to the story in the *Chronicle,* Richard

Adamson—a Marine from the Bay Area who'd fought in the Gulf War and who was the son of Dr. Richard Adamson, a prominent heart surgeon—was innocent of the murder. His sister Tami, eighteen, claimed her brother had been involved with an Arabian princess and was being framed. "Has his sister been interviewed?" Frankie asked.

"Yeah. She told the cops she made it up."

"Do we have motive?"

"Disgruntled employee. Adamson worked at the embassy, got fired, then did the man who fired him." He picked up the article, glanced at it again, then set it down. "Good-lookin' guy," he said, referring to the high school yearbook picture of Adamson in the paper. "They all look like movie stars, you know? Even the poor ones. Kids don't care what they do anymore, if they look good doing it." He gazed at Frankie like a soldier, tired of war. She wanted to hug him. "When you see the cop pictures, you'll see how he looked when he took the Arab out. If the papers had them, they'd run them on the front page. Dashing, you know. A commando on a raid. Black tights, muscles, white teeth."

"Would he do that?" Frankie asked. "I mean, why would he risk breaking in? Why not wait for the man to come out?"

"Good question."

"We could let the Rashidis have him," she suggested.

"Yeah." He grinned, making a motion with his hand across his throat. "I wouldn't mind giving them my whole caseload."

The press had made the most of what they termed a fascinating legal issue. Because the killing occurred inside an embassy, did the Kingdom of Rashidi have the legal right to try him for murder? The Rashidis wanted to take him to their country for trial. "Will there be an extradition hearing?" Frankie asked, butting her cigarette.

Grantland nodded wearily. "Yeah, a big waste of time. They'll say, Judge, our embassy is part of the sands of Rashidi, so the crime occurred there. We'll say, hey, we only pay attention to legal fictions when we feel like it."

"Do we care, Roy?"

"I don't know." He looked at the bare wall behind her.

"He's one of ours, you know, an American citizen. He's physically in this country, so I guess he's entitled to due process." The words seemed to stick in his throat. "Presumption of innocence, reasonable doubt, in Rashidi? Forget it. Maybe they're right." He looked at her. "But removing a defendant's head with an axe, that's cruel and unusual. I guess I wouldn't want to see that."

"My goodness," she drawled, "is that what they do?"

"They don't mess around."

His deep brown eyes continued to search the empty wall, as though looking for meaning. Frankie wondered what he would do if she were to tell him there was hope in the world. "Do you have children?" she asked suddenly.

"Yeah. Three."

"Can I help you with something?"

A ripple of surprise washed over his face, but didn't last. "Kind of personal, isn't it?"

"That was dumb of me. I'm sorry." She pushed back in her chair.

He looked at his hands, as though he couldn't trust them any longer to do what was right. "Six hundred forty-four murders in the District last year. A war zone in half the town. Kids, wives, old people hidden all over the place, afraid to go outside or sit near a window." He looked at her. "It doesn't work, Frankie. The system doesn't work. Man, I thought after five years of this shit my hide would get thick and I'd quit feeling the bullets. But they're tearin' me up."

Slowly, he got up and opened the pedestal drawer of his desk. He pulled out a thick file. "Look," he said, showing her a portrait-size picture of the face of a hauntingly beautiful girl. Her eyes were closed and her mouth was open slightly. A bead of blood had formed on one side of her mouth. "Here's the rest of her." The second photograph was ghastly, showing her slashed, mutilated, nude body. One of her breasts had been sliced off. The cavity stared at Frankie like a huge eye socket. "I start this one tomorrow."

"God."

"One of the killers is her older brother. He's not on trial. Probably the only decent thing he ever did in his life was

11

plead out." He sat down. "So the defendants are all blaming it on the brother. You know. He copped out, so now they all point the finger at him. The truth? A little coke party, you know, that got wild." His voice became soft and far off, like from another room. "Freedom. Is this what it does to people? Is it a virus like some kind of disease, or like cancer, that kills?"

Frankie thought of putting her hands on his shoulders— and what? Telling him to keep a stiff upper lip? "Don't beat yourself up, Roy."

"Yeah."

She reached for his hand and gave it a squeeze, then let go. "If you need to get your trial ready, I can come back."

"How'm I gonna lose this one?" he asked. "When the jury sees those pictures, I'll be lucky if I can stop a lynching."

As they talked, the picture of the girl's mutilated body stayed in Frankie's mind. What an awful, useless way to die. Are people animals, only fit to live in cages? she wondered. Who keeps the cages? Who feeds the animals?

"You got some exotic twists," she heard him say. "Yours won't be slam-dunk, like mine." The cigarette she'd butted still smoldered in the ashtray, like something that wouldn't die. She put it out. "Adamson's background, the way he was dressed, and nobody can figure out how he got through their alarm systems. The victim's body was hammered too, like he'd been hit with a truck. Then Richard buries a plastic knife in the Arab's lungs. If the princess gets in the script, you know—especially now that Slasstein has it—show-time."

"Brooking Slasstein?" Frankie asked, sitting up straight.

"Filed an appearance this morning. You know him?"

"I've heard of him.

Grantland smiled, for the first time as though he meant it. "Brooking'll do anything. A Watergate caper that went sour, blame it on the adminstration."

"How do District juries go for that kind of crap?"

"A white defendant, ex-Marine, all he did was kill one Arab?" He shook his head no. "They might buy it if he was black. You'll have at least eight blacks on the panel, and they are tough. They are pure hell on drive-bys, drug killings, and gangs. . . ." He shrugged. "But who knows? What if the kid was a DEA cop, saving America from drugs?"

Frankie felt better, watching him smile. She liked what he said too. Against a man like Slasstein, it translated into the kind of game she loved. She would have to be ready to rebut—who knew what?—in the way of bullshit. "Do the Rashidis know the prosecutor will be a woman?"

Grantland scratched an ear. "I don't think so. Nobody's said anything. Why?"

"My boss wanted to send one of the men. What do you think? Will they care?"

"Fuck 'em." He shrugged. "I mean, you know."

She started putting things in her briefcase. "Thanks, Roy. Where's the Capitol P.D.? If gender is a problem, they might have some ideas."

He told her. His face began to close. Frankie wondered if he'd started thinking about his trial. "I'm glad you came by, Frankie. Thanks for listening." She nodded at him. "Watch out for the cops."

"What?"

"You've got Lamar Gleason. He kind of crowds the line."

She got up and looped the belt to her briefcase over her shoulder. "Thanks for the warning," she said. "Break a leg."

"Yeah."

# 2

Lieutenant Lamar Gleason, Capitol Police Department, wore the kind of cynical sneer Frankie had seen before. It said, "What's *your* scam?"—clearly assuming that everyone had one. She guessed him to be in his late forties, and, from the red lines that webbed his fleshy face, a boozer. He had thick shoulders, a deep chest, a stomach that surpassed both, and hair the color and texture of steel wire.

His first reaction on meeting her in his office was to smile with male appreciation. Then his expression changed. "So you're the lawyer from NASP," he said, still standing behind his desk. "I'll be damned." His smile shifted into an unpleasant leer and his eyes flickered with recognition.

"That's me," Frankie said, meeting his eyes and wondering who, or what, he saw. "I'm the big, bad prosecutor." She started to sit down.

"You mind terribly waiting in the lobby for a few?" He glanced at his watch. "A call I gotta make. Afterward we can go eat, if that'd work for you. Okay?" He reached for the telephone.

Frankie felt her ears wriggle, like a wild horse at the scent of a lion. She'd just arrived, he'd asked her into his office, and now this. "It can't wait?" she asked testily.

"This won't take long. One I forgot to make. Okay?"

"Whatever." As she walked back to the lobby, she told herself not to get paranoid. Finding a bench, she sat down, lit a cigarette, and pulled out the file Grantland had given her.

The first report was the summary of the officer in charge of the investigation: Lamar Gleason. She'd seen it with the material faxed to NASP. This time she read with care. It was easier to read after meeting the slug who wrote it. She could hear his voice.

He wrote in a salty version of "cop talk," describing the actions of the first officers on the scene.

Corporal Johnson, Corporal Bronson, and Sergeant Gore—while guarding the perimeter of the Rashidi Embassy shortly before 0200, July 26—were alerted to the possibility of trouble inside the embassy, because of obvious commotion inside. The officers observed floodlights which lit up the grounds of the embassy, also the legation, immediately behind and adjacent to the embassy. Persons could be observed running every which way, yelling and screaming.

Officers next observed an individual, later ID'd as Richard Adamson, departing the legation grounds. Adamson was dressed entirely in black attire, and exposed skin portions were smeared with charcoal, arousing the suspicions of the officers. It occurred to them that there could be a connection between Adamson and the commotion. They therefore stopped the man and questioned him.

Adamson stated he had stopped to take a leak. A 9mm HK with 13-round clip, known to be standard police issue to certain agencies, was seen in his bicycle shirt, which further aroused the interest of the officers. Adamson was detained, pending further investigation. At that point, he refused further comment.

Frankie quit reading long enough to take a deep drag and knock the ash off her cigarette. The uniformed woman at the intake desk was looking at her. "Hi," Frankie said.

"Are you waiting for the lieutenant, Miss Rommel?"

"Yes."

"I'll ring him if you want."

"That's okay. He knows I'm here."

The humor in Gleason's report matched the sneer on his face, Frankie thought. It had an undertone of arrogance.

Officer Gore called the embassy, offering assistance, and advised of contact with a person who identified himself as Rick Adamson. Faris Rahman, the deputy ambassador—in a state of great agitation—asked for a physical description, which was given. Rahman then advised that the suspect was a former employee at the Rashidi Embassy who had just murdered Abdul Hafiz. Adamson was placed in custody and transported by Officers Zwicker and Melrose to the Federal Detention Center, where photographs were taken. His clothing was removed from his person and seized for evidence.

Officers at the scene requested permission to enter the embassy to conduct an investigation. At 0237, they were admitted. They were taken to the second floor, the office of Faris Rahman, where they observed the body of an Arab male on the floor. The deceased was identified as Abdul Hafiz, who was in charge of internal security at the embassy. This fact was verified by Corporal Bronson, who had known the deceased prior to his murder and recognized him on the floor.

Frankie stuck a yellow Post-It on the report, to remind herself to talk to Bronson about Hafiz. She would want to humanize the victim: especially in this case, because of his Arabic heritage. She continued to read.

When officers attempted to conduct an investigation, it generated a heated discussion conducted in Arabic, beyond the comprehension of the officers. It was explained to Rahman that evidence would be needed to prove Adamson was the murderer. A mo-

16

bile crime lab unit from the FBI would have to process the scene of the crime, he was told. Evidence could be anything: fingerprints, blood smears, hair, clothing fibers, impressions of a person's feet. There would also have to be an autopsy of the deceased. Pending any investigation, the crime scene should be sealed off in order to keep it as free of contamination as possible.

Rahman—who spoke good English—could not see the necessity of a crime lab unit or autopsy, stating it was obvious what had happened. Nevertheless, he agreed to seal off the crime scene, but did not author- ize the entry of the crime lab unit or removal of the body until 0318, when presumably he received the order to cooperate fully.


"Ready?" Gleason asked.

Frankie jerked up her head. "What?" She had not heard him come up. For a big man, he moved softly. "Yes!" she said, standing. "I'm starved." She started to stuff the file in her briefcase when Gleason yanked it out of her hand. "Hey!"

"Might as well leave this here," he said. "No sense carrying it all over the place. We're coming back, right?" Before she could stop him, he was gone.

When he reappeared, she could still feel steam coming out of her ears. "Why the hell did you do that?" she demanded.

He looked perplexed, as though he would like to help her. She didn't believe it. "Hey. I didn't think you'd mind. If it bothers you, I'll buy your lunch." He smiled at her. "They don't do Mex food very good around here, but you'll love this place."

"Don't ever do that again."

"Hey. Sorry."

She still burned when they left the building, but held herself in. He assumed the role of tour guide as they walked down Massachusetts Avenue, talking easily about all the things to do in the District, including where you needed a bullet-proof vest and how to use the Metro. It was a monologue, not a conversation. The restaurant was called Carlos; a stereotypical pub, with sawdust on the floor, wooden tables scattered around an arena, big-breasted waitresses, and checkered tablecloths. They sat near the middle, next to a wooden pillar. The waitress gave them menus and, in no hurry, wandered off.

Gleason spread his beefy arms on the table and smiled at her. "You don't remember me, do you?"

Frankie opened her briefcase, found her handbag and pulled out a cigarette. "No." She lit it.

"I remember you, gorgeous. I've seen you in court."

"Where?" There were empty tables, but the noise level was high. Still, she knew she would have no trouble hearing him.

"Remember *People versus Hansen,* eight or nine years ago, in Bridger City, Wyoming?"

"Sure do," Frankie said, recalling the case. Hansen had been chief of police in the town of ten thousand people. While under investigation for the unlawful conversion of public property to private use—a cheap paper-trail case, typical of the politics of small towns—he shot and killed his accuser, a man named Davis who had been the city auditor. Davis had a gun in his hand, and Hansen claimed self-defense. But Frankie proved Hansen had provoked a duel. It was a mismatch; like the Denver Broncos playing against Evanston High School. "Were you a witness?" she asked.

"Only a spectator. I stayed as close to the old chief as I could. He was kind of like my idol."

So that was his problem, Frankie thought as their waitress plopped tortilla chips and salsa on the table, then left to take someone else's order. "What do you want from me? An apology?"

"Yeah, that would be nice."

"Sorry. The jury was right. The man had it coming."

Gleason jammed a chip in his face and chewed it viciously, as though flexing the muscles in his mouth. "The hell he did. He was a good cop."

Gleason wanted to stare her down, so she let him. They were not getting off to the best of starts. "He wasn't

18

prosecuted for being a bad cop, Lamar," she said mildly. "He killed a man."

"Davis wasn't no man. He was a snake. He had a gun. If he'd been a man, he'd've used it."

"That gun in Davis's hand was about as useful as a darning needle against a grizzly bear." She inhaled deeply. "Let's forget it. We need to work together."

"Hansen got out of the joint a couple years back. Did you know that?"

"He didn't stay long, did he?"

"Long enough." Gleason picked up a chip and swirled it around in the salsa. "Committed suicide." He balanced a chopped pepper on the chip. "What happens to cops in prison, either they kill 'em outright or fuck 'em to death. I don't need to tell you, do I?" He popped the chip quickly in his mouth, before any of the salsa dropped off. "Nobody'd hire him when he got out. After bein' fucked by everybody in the Wyoming state pen, he couldn't look at himself anyway. So he ate the barrel of a shotgun."

Frankie dropped her cigarette on the floor and crushed it. She felt ill. "That wasn't my fault, Gleason. I don't need this."

"'Gleason.' What'd I do, get demoted? A second ago it was Lamar."

She challenged him to a new staring contest. "You don't like me. I can deal with that. Can you? Or do I get another investigator?"

He smiled. "Lighten up, right? Where the hell is our waitress? I could use a beer." He glanced at his watch. "I'll go get her," he said, jumping up. Frankie watched him go over to the bar. But he didn't bother with the waitress. He spoke to the bartender, who handed him the telephone.

"Somebody should be here in a minute," he said later, smiling with satisfaction as he sat down. "Hey." He peered at her, twisting his face into a grimace somewhere between a smile and a sneer. "You know the definition of a perfect woman?"

"I don't think I want to know, either."

"She's three feet tall, with three legs and a flat head."

19

Frankie stared at him coldly. "The reason she's perfect is, she's perfect for a man to put his beer on."

Frankie had all she needed from the creep. She unhooked her briefcase from the back of her chair. "You'll hear from me, Gleason." She started to stand, but he reached over. His large hand on her arm effectively held her in place. "Get your hand off me."

"Official business, Miss Rommel. I need answers to a couple questions, won't take long. How much of the file Roy-boy gave you did you read?"

"Your hand is still on my arm." He moved it. "What's this official business crap?"

"You're off the case, Miss Rommel. I'm making an official demand on you for any and all information you have relevant to the case in your possession. I'm prepared to arrest you for obstruction of justice if you don't give it to me."

Frankie got up. "You do, and you'll wish you hadn't."

"Lady, I'm the one with the badge and the gun."

She realized how quiet the restaurant had become. Everyone seemed to be watching the unfolding soap opera. She was furious, but wasn't about to let herself be the center of attention. "If you want to accuse me of something, we go outside." As she walked toward the door, he marched behind her, as though she was under arrest.

In the hot sun she turned on him angrily. His hands hung at his sides, like a gunfighter waiting for his enemy to make a false move. She recognized the adrenaline boost that worked its way through him, and for a moment felt fear. But only for a moment. "I am not going to give you my file," she said evenly. "If you want it, you will have to take it from me with force. Are you prepared to take that risk?"

He stepped forward, and Frankie steeled herself against the infliction of pain by a man who obviously knew how. But he stopped and grinned at her. "What are all those people in there thinking, Frankie? The way you walked out, all stiff-legged and hot, like a woman who'd rather fuck than eat lunch."

She backed away slowly, keeping him in front of her. "You're sick."

"A sicko'd get mad, Frankie," he said affably. "All I do is get even." He touched his forehead with the tips of the fingers in a mocking salute. "Later, cunt." He swaggered as he walked away, obviously pleased with himself.

# 3

Frankie sat in her hotel room glaring at the telephone. She couldn't believe it! Instead of hanging Gleason's hide on the wall, she was being stonewalled!

She had stormed the U.S. Attorney's office, but could not get past the guards. She tried to talk to Roy Grantland, but he was out. No one would talk to her! What kind of community of silence had suddenly sprouted into existence? What was she faced with? Why?

"This is not happening." Hot tears of anger and frustration burned down her cheeks and she jumped up, stalking the bathroom. A glass on the washbasin counter appeared in her hand like a baseball. She heaved it at the lamp that dangled from the ceiling across the room. She missed by inches, but it smashed into the heavy plastic window and shattered. "God damn!"

She splashed water in her face, then—calmly and with determination—picked up a hand towel and blotted the moisture off her face. She looked at herself in the mirror and got busy, repairing the damage created by her anger.

Frankie no longer had the radiant beauty of youth, but the cowboys in Lander still whistled at her when she was in town. There were crow marks at the edges of her eyes, and thin lines like parentheses surrounded her mouth. But her skin had the vitality of a woman who loved life and could handle whatever it dished out. So did her wide-apart eyes and firm mouth.

That wasn't what the cowboys whistled at. They couldn't help it, they said. Her jeans were packed, she'd been told. So was her shirt. Most of the time she liked it when they whistled. Brushing her hair in front of the mirror and tossing it out of the way, she would have enjoyed hearing the long, drawn-out call of a two-legged wolf. A hit of Wild Turkey would go down too.

Later, she thought, dropping the brush and marching down the aisle between the double beds. Lighting a cigarette, she watched the smoke climb a straight line to the ceiling, then picked up the telephone. The hotel operator got her a long distance line, and she punched in the numbers needed to reach Jim Trigge in his office in Denver. She waited for him to get on the line, and when he did, she wanted to yell at him. "Have you heard anything about me?"

"About ten minutes ago. I was afraid something like this would happen, Frankie. How are you doing?"

"Who did you talk to, Jim? What were you told?"

"Her name was Jennifer Marten, one of the lawyers for the U.S. Attorney. She thanked me for all the trouble, said she'd been trying to call you, but the thing has changed and they don't need NASP. The Rashidis think the prosecutor should speak Arabic, and they have a line on one."

"What difference does that make?" The line of smoke began to wobble. "Do they want an Arab jury too? I'll bet everyone at the embassy speaks English, or they wouldn't be over here!"

"Yeah, but they speak Arabic better." It took long enough for him to pick up on her anger. "You don't really care, do you, Frankie? Take a couple of days. Go to New York. We'll bill them for it. She said they want someone who knows the customs of the country and can relate to the witnesses."

"Bullshit," Frankie said. "God damn it."

"What's going on, babe? It isn't like you to take things personally."

23

She took a huge wad of smoke into her lungs. "Did I ever tell you about a case I tried in Wyoming, a police chief who killed a guy?"

"I know about it. It's why I hired you. What about it?"

She told him: who Lamar Gleason was, what he'd done to her in the restaurant, and now what he was getting away with! She spoke with the kind of intensity her opponents in the courtroom hated.

"What are you going to do?" Trigge asked.

She touched her face with the fingers of her left hand. "I don't know yet." Humiliation and outrage possessed her, and for a moment she couldn't breathe. "File a complaint. Demand an apology. Make as much trouble as I can. Go to the newspapers, if nothing else works. Get him fired." She heard Trigge sigh. She knew how protective he was of NASP, and that his first reaction would be to take care of his baby. She waited to see which was more important to him: his baby, or the people who worked for him.

"I'll help you any way I can, Frankie. Tell me what you want me to do."

"That's not good enough!" She knew she was being completely irrational. She didn't care.

"How can it be any better than that?"

"You *know* what to do, Jim. You're a politician. You *know* people! Don't ask me what you want me to do. *Do* it!"

He was silent. Finally: "Look, I can't force the U.S. Attorney to appoint you. If I could, I would."

"God damn it," Frankie said, grinding her cigarette in the ashtray. "Do you know what I mean, Jim?" Once again she heard him sigh. "I mean, goddamn it."

Frankie sat at a table in the bar at the Embassy Suites Hotel, jotting down ideas and trying to let the smoothness of a snifter full of Wild Turkey mellow her out.

There were members of Congress to contact; the Civil Rights Commission; the U.S. Attorney. She would confront Jennifer Marten, and talk to Roy Grantland. She would lunch with acquaintances and pick their brains. No one wins them all, she thought; but you can't—you simply cannot—let anyone walk on you.

That evening, the concierge got her a ticket to *Faust*, playing at the Kennedy Center. She changed into a dress and heels, tied her hair into a ponytail, and tinted her eyelids with green. At the Hors d'oeuvre—the cocktail lounge on the top floor of the Kennedy Center—she left her name with the maître d' and was soon guided to a round table in the middle of the room, between red velvet banquet booths. It was like a Gay Nineties house of joy. She admired the elegance, although her grandfather—bless his soul—would have wondered pointedly where the girls were.

She ordered the shrimp salad and red wine. A huge window overlooked the Potomac, and jets seemingly flew through it as they landed and left Washington National. How did they manage it without shattering the glass or making waves of sound? Yet she could hear nothing. Apart from her, no one in the room seemed aware of the miracle.

"Miss Rommel?" the maître d' asked.

She faced the graying, distinguished-looking man. "Yes?"

"You have a telephone message from a Mr. Slasstein," he said, handing her a slip of paper with a number written on it. "When it's convenient, he would like you to call."

"Thank you," Frankie said, standing and instantly intrigued. What did the hotshot who'd been hired to defend Rick Adamson want with her? "It's convenient now. Can you tell me where the telephone is?"

A moment later she dropped a quarter in the coin slot of a public telephone and dialed the number. "Brooking Slasstein," an abrasive male voice said.

"Hello. This is Frankie Rommel."

"Frankie! You don't waste time. How you doin'?"

"Well enough. Yourself?"

"Wonderful. You don't know me, I don't know you, except by reputation. We need to meet."

Frankie had trouble believing a high-profile lawyer like Slasstein would have heard of her. She wondered what he really wanted. "How did you know where to call?"

"What you told your hotel. I like that in a government lawyer." He made a sound, as though biting off the tip of a cigar. "Heard some things about you, Frankie, pays to be a snoop in my business, you had a flap with one of my favorite cops. Lamar Gleason, big wind out of the West. Want to take him on?"

"The great Brooking Slasstein wants a sexual harassment case?" She watched the people walking toward and away from the restaurant. Some of the men wore tuxedos, but a couple of them had on hand-tooled leather boots. She didn't see any of the green stuff on them, though.

"Nah, Gleason's too bad for that. Man needs to be torched. Abe Fortanier. You remember Abe?"

"I sure do." She smiled at the memory of her silver-haired, angelic-faced tormentor from Atlanta.

"Abe's got class, Frankie, how he wins. I got no class whatever, just balls. Trouble is, I got a case I need help on, right up your alley. Abe says you're the best, I got the balls to see if you'd like a piece of it."

How serendipitous, Frankie thought. Slasstein could help her too. "I'm flattered, Mr. Slasstein, but I don't need a job."

"Brooking. You can call me. Fact is, you do, babe. Need a job. I talked to your boss, Jim Trigge? Tell her she's fired, what he told me to tell you."

"Just like Jim. He forgot to mention it when I talked to him."

"This was ten, fifteen minutes ago we talked. Maybe he just decided, I don't know."

She looked at her reflection in the mirror behind the telephone and decided she needed more practice with eye shadow. It was a smidge heavier on the left eyelid than the right one. But she liked her hair. "All right. I'm looking. What have you got, Mr. Slasstein?"

"Brooking," he insisted. "It's okay. Wife tells me I got an ego, I'm in everybody's face, the truth is, nobody understands me. I'm just friendly. Brooking."

He waited. "Right," she said. "Brooking."

"That murder case, the embassy kill. Richard Adamson."

26

"You're kidding me. I can't—"

"Choice of evils, forget I said that, Abe says you could write a book. The big gas, Gleason. How'd you like to take him on the stand? A chance to take a big bite out of his ass. I took the case because they paid my fee, never thought I'd get what I asked, but I got more'n I can do, and besides, this case needs someone with class. Fortanier says you got class."

"Brooking, there is no way. I came here to prosecute the case. I can't do an about-face and defend."

"Where have you been, Frankie? Happens all the time. I mean, this is the 1990s, some sleazeballs even do jingles for clients. You seen the yellow pages?"

"No."

"Listen to me. Maybe some things I know, you don't. Meet me tomorrow morning, my office, seven o'clock, okay? What have you got to lose? Have breakfast at a classy joint, get a close-up of a Washington original. What's to lose?"

"Nothing," Frankie said. "I'd love it. Where is your office?"

He gave her the address. "If you forget, just look in the yellow pages."

The shrimp salad was crisp, and the wine bold and rich. It could have been her mood, which the conversation with Slasstein had done wonders for. She arrived at the center stage in time to watch the opera buffs file in, which the concierge had told her could be better than the show. It impressed her as a real people's theater. She felt better in her dress, but—from some of the costumes—realized she could have worn nice, comfortable blue jeans and boots. Her seat was on an aisle on the main floor, and she let herself soak in the musical drama. She knew the story, but didn't know German, and loved it when the translation of the dialogue flashed above the stage. She had never before been able to follow the tale as it happened.

On the way back to the hotel her cab driver told her how the purists hated the English translation. His kids didn't, though. "Never thought kids of mine would take the plugs outta their ears long enough to hear real music." He scoffed at the story, however. "Faust, for his moment of bliss, goes to hell. Margarita, for hers—even after drowning her own sweet little baby—goes to heaven! I ask you, lady, who's in charge here? Gloria Steinem?"

The message light on the telephone in her room blinked on and off. She tossed her coat on one of the beds, sat on the other and dialed the operator, who gave her the message: "Call me tonight when you get in. Urgent. Jim."

He could have been at the office, but she tried him at his home in southeast Denver. He answered. "It's nine o'clock here," he said. "What time is it there? I thought you'd be out until midnight at least," he shouted. "You sober?"

"I'm fine. You?"

He laughed loudly, a dead giveaway that he was two sheets down. "Did you talk to Slasstein?"

"You don't talk to the man, Jim. You listen." She lit a cigarette. "He's buying my breakfast tomorrow. I think." She inhaled deeply, loving it and hating it. "He said you'd fired me."

"That's right. I don't want you prancing all over Washington, looking into closets where there are skeletons and upsetting people. Not as one of my troops. So—you're history."

"Are you serious about this?"

He laughed more loudly than the first time, indicating his true state of mind. "Slasstein wants to hire you. I think it's a lovely solution to our problem. It's time you took a sabbatical from NASP and did a defense. It'll give you some perspective," he shouted boisterously into the telephone.

Frankie kicked off her shoes and crossed her legs. "Our" problem? she thought. She might have to give Trigge the news. If it meant letting Gleason go, it wasn't a solution to "our" problem at all. "I don't see how I can do it, Jim. There is obvious conflict."

"Slasstein says you can. All you did was look at the file." He tried to cover a belch. "A defendant has a Sixth Amendment right to the lawyer of his choice, and if Adamson wants you on his team, it's a balancing act. What's more important, a constitutional right or a minor conflict of interest?"

"You make it sound easy."

"*Slasstein* does. Says he's been through the drill before, and it doesn't worry him."

She could smell her feet. She wriggled her toes and leaned her head back, wishing someone—a man—would materialize and rub them. "Is this the urgent message?"

"I made some calls on Gleason. Be very careful of the man. Don't underestimate him."

Frankie sat up. "What is he, a serial killer?"

"He's a power broker. A small potatoes Hoover. He won't go down easily."

# Wednesday, July 31, 1991
# Washington, D.C.

Brooking Slasstein's office was on the fifth floor of a gray stone building on Indiana Avenue, within easy walking distance of the courts. Frankie prepared for the ostentatious display of a typical defense lawyer; a garish, glowing painting on satin cloth. Instead the decor in his office had the nice, friendly touch of someone who wanted people to be at ease. A cheerful lobby off the elevator took full advantage of the available light. A wall of windows looked toward the Washington Mall. They were broken into small panes, like old-fashioned French doors that opened into provincial countrysides. Small, colorful rugs were splashed here and there over the stained oak floors, and a tropical ceiling fan spun lazily overhead.

The man himself met her expectations. She had dressed as she would for a job interview, in a blue suit, hose, and heels. Her hair was pinned behind her ears with tortoiseshell combs. She towered over him. He was no more than two inches taller than Danny DeVito, with thick, black hair that curled and twisted around his head like a storm cloud. His nose, ears, chin, and mouth looked too big for his face, as though sculpted by a political cartoonist. He was flawlessly dressed in a dark, expensive suit, complete with bouton-

29

niere and matching pocket handkerchief. "How are you, Frankie," he said, strutting toward her with cocksure arrogance, extending his hand. "Brooking Slasstein."

"Nice to meet you," she said. The fingers on his hand were thin and strong, like her grandfather's. She liked his grip.

"Let's go eat."

The restaurant—around the corner, in the basement of another elegant stone building—had thick red carpets, linen tablecloths, crystal water goblets, and sterling silver place settings. A waiter helped them into their chairs. "Poached eggs are awful," Brooking told her. "Lox, bagels, and cream cheese better than New York."

"How's the coffee?"

"Out of this world and clear into the next one."

He leaned on his elbows, forcing his short body even lower, creating the impression that he was even smaller than he was. Somehow he turned it into an advantage. "Class," he decided, staring up at her. "Abe was right."

"How is he?"

"Don't change, Abe. Still fightin' the wars like a courtly southern colonel, off a Southern Comfort label. Cracks me up. Great lawyer, Abe, says you dumped his ass. I got some history on you, he said I wanted you on my side. Not theirs." He started to say more but closed his mouth.

"What else?"

"You double-crossed him. He thinks he knows why, he'd have done the same thing, says give him a call. You got secrets?"

Frankie smiled. There weren't many people whose opinions mattered to her, but Abe Fortanier was one of them. "Thanks for the message. I'll never forget him, or the case." Or the man he represented, she thought.

"Choice of evils, right? What he tried to fly by you, but you shot it down?"

"In Georgia, they call it the law of justification. But it's choice of evils."

The waiter—elegant in a white dinner jacket—reappeared, poured coffee, and took their order. Frankie

30

asked for the lox, bagel, and cream cheese, and wondered how Brooking, or anyone, could stomach whitefish on toast with hollandaise sauce. "Don't tell my wife, hollandaise sauce, she worries. How much you know about this case, Richard Adamson?"

"I read Gleason's case summary, looked over a diagram of the crime scene, and thumbed through the autopsy report." The aroma from the coffee filled Frankie's nostrils with a pleasure that was sensual.

"You keep anything?"

"I still have the file they faxed to me." She sipped from her cup and it tasted as good as it smelled.

"Don't even look at it. Mail it back, certified. Who you talk to?"

"Roy Grantland and Lamar Gleason."

"How long?"

"Probably half an hour with Grantland. The extradition—"

"I don't want to know what, just how long. *I* could get disqualified. Gleason?"

"The time together couldn't have been more than twenty minutes, and we didn't even talk about the case." She settled her cup in the saucer. "Mind if I smoke?"

"Go ahead, kill yourself. What did you talk about, then?"

She lit a cigarette and crossed her ankles. "I was a county prosecutor in Wyoming. He recognized me. I tried a cop friend of his for murder."

"You win?"

She shrugged. "A draw, but he went to prison. I guess he got raped a few times." Slasstein stared at her. "When he got out, he couldn't wait to kill himself." She showed him her palms. "So I feel bad about it. But he thinks I should kill myself too."

"Okay, here's what I want you to do. Grantland, no problem, he won't lie. Gleason, write down everything you can remember. What you said, what he said, who heard, where you talked, what it looked like. Stay in his office?"

"We went to a Mexican restaurant on Massachusetts Avenue."

31

"Good. People see you there. Got a picture of yourself?"

"I can get one." She exhaled away from him. "What's all this about?"

"I hope nothing. But you don't know, Gleason. Give it to Beacon, you'll meet her, my secretary. I call her Chuckles, don't tell her, I'll kill you." He frowned at his hands, as though wanting to make sure he didn't forget anything. "How does two hundred thousand sound to you? Plus expenses?" He looked at her quickly, for a reaction.

Frankie wasn't sure she understood him. "Is that what you're offering me, Brooking?"

"Yeah. You are perfect for this case, babe, I gotta have you, I'm willing to pay. Of course this business you never know. You could get bumped on a motion to disqualify, then just your time, I find somebody else is perfect, maybe Abe. Make it two and a quarter." He watched her carefully, as though for signs of greed.

"Why am I perfect?"

"That's part of it, Frankie, you know what questions to ask, I can't tell you the rest. You gotta make it through the hoops first." His fingers worked the top of the table. "I'd be lead counsel, that's for show, but you'd try it, every now and then I do something looks good but won't hurt the case."

It occurred to her that this was for real. As a trial lawyer for NASP, she earned eighty thousand dollars a year. "Will I survive a motion to disqualify?"

"You should, but who knows? What the judge has for breakfast." He drank coffee, chewing on the cup. "We force the issue, get a quick answer. When you file your appearance, we list your qualifications up front, demand the government file objections right away if they have any." Some hair had worked out of the comb over her left ear, and she brushed it back, listening intently. "What you know about the case doesn't bother me. Get that out of the newspapers. But the fact you worked for NASP, came to Washington to try it for the government, could be a problem." His strong fingers started to hammer the tabletop, hard enough to rattle the ice cubes in their water glasses.

"Adamson's right to the lawyer of his choice should out-weigh that. The government says you're not good enough because you don't speak Arabic. Okay, they don't want you. That mean Adamson can't hire you?"

Frankie barely heard him. She was thinking of what she could do with $225,000. "Let's get back to the fee," she said, staring at him with what she hoped was coolness.

"I can go higher, you want, give you more to do. Abe said don't start too high, might scare you."

She butted her cigarette and unlaced her ankles. "The expenses?"

"You don't stay at the Watergate, but I got some nice places you can. We can work that out."

The waiter appeared and spread food in front of them. All the talk of money made Frankie hungry. The difference between eighty grand and two hundred twenty-five was the difference between a week at Mesa Verde and a month at Monte Carlo. It felt to her as though her cheeks were on fire. She hoped her skin hadn't changed color. "What will you make?"

"Fair question." He forked a piece of fish. "The problem is, the feds. Let's make sure you're on the case before I give you that."

"Ballpark. I don't want to have to renegotiate, Brooking."

He grinned, enjoying himself. "I been paid seed money, you know, enough to try it and make wages. If I walk the kid, there's a nice bonus." He watched her face. "For discussion, we'll say a mil."

Frankie could feel her heart pounding. She smeared cream cheese on a bagel, then loaded it with a slice of lox. "Did you promise an acquittal?"

"Never do that. Totally unethical."

Frankie laughed. "Like, bonus pay is ethical?"

He opened his hands. "It doesn't bother me. What doesn't bother me, as far as I'm concerned, is ethical."

"Would my fee depend on the result?" She took a big bite and chewed hungrily.

"No. You take it on, you get paid. Isn't that the way the government works?"

She swallowed. "If he walks, I think I should share in the bonus."

Slasstein's eyes measured her carefully. His heavy lips formed into a smile. "Money can mess with a person's judgment, Frankie. You want that?"

"I can handle it."

His eyebrows hung over his face. "Okay, a quarter mil."

"That's bonus pay, right? The other I'd get paid, even if they execute him?"

"Right."

Frankie thought: I like it up here. She looked down at the two of them from the ceiling. "Make it a third and you've got a deal."

He laughed, loud enough to turn a few heads. "You been working the wrong side of the street, babe." He shrugged. "What the hell. Deal. Want to know something else?"

"Sure," Frankie said, feeling wonderful.

"I just won ten thousand dollars, Abe."

# 4

## Thursday, August 1, 1991
## Approaching Washington, D.C.

Husam al-Din let his imagination turn the carpet of clouds, spread beneath him, into the Nafud Desert. The light from the sun, which had dropped under the horizon, glowed red on the clouds, creating the illusion of the crimson-colored dunes of his homeland.

His imagination would only take him part of the way. The air he breathed in the pressurized passenger compartment of the Eastern Airlines jet could not compare with the dry, pure desert air of his youth. The ventilator over his head blew treated, perfumed gases that coated the skin of his face and forehead with a film of humidity. He longed for the cleansing of the pores afforded by immersion in desert climate. The heat could purify a man's soul as well as his skin. The lowering of the sun brought the cool currents of the clean, unscented air, which washed over the Nafud like ripples in a stream, unseen, like the breath of God.

But his memories may have softened the harshness of the heat. In truth, he had no desire to exchange his memories for the reality. He enjoyed life in America, in spite of the softness of luxury.

The speed of the aircraft slowed as it dipped toward his imaginary desert. "The captain says we'll touch down in fifteen minutes," the cheerful voice of a stewardess announced. "Please buckle your seat belts. As we descend toward Washington National Airport, we'll go through a cloud layer and could experience some choppiness. Temperature at National, eighty-three degrees Fahrenheit. The humidity is about the same. So enjoy your last few moments of comfort."

The woman sitting next to him closed her book and buckled her seat belt. She was younger than Husam by several years, and he had appreciated her nearness: the accidental touchings of thighs and shoulders, her soft blouse, which tugged his eyes toward her breasts, her provocative scent. "At least we're on time," she said. "I hope it doesn't get *too* choppy in there."

Her name was Emily Scot. She was a professional dancer, doing a "gig" in Chicago, but her mother had been in an accident and Emily had taken the night off to see her. Husam looked toward the window, dragging his eyes from her blouse and trying to elevate his thoughts. "The sky is magnificent," he said.

She leaned toward the window; toward him. "Yes."

He admired the pale turquoise-green at the rim of the world and its abrupt shift into dark purple-blue. "The bedouins of the desert enjoy such skies every evening," he said. "Here, it is only when one is in an airplane, high above the cities and the pollution."

"Husam," she said, mocking him gently. "Sixty percent of that pollution comes from Arabia."

"So. Do you blame me for your dirty skies?"

"I hold you personally responsible."

The aircraft lowered itself into the mists. He saw her smiling at him in the reflection of the window, and smiled back. "Will you be returning to Chicago?" she asked.

"Yes, I have business there to finish. Odds and ends."

"When will you start prosecuting that poor man?"

"So. The poor man who stabbed to death the Arab?"

"That's the one."

"At once. I will see him in the courtroom and will jump on him with my feet. I will grab him around the throat and shake him until his head falls off."

As he talked, Emily reached for her purse. "Here," she said, pulling out a card. "When you're in Chicago, call me, okay? I know you don't drink, but we could still do something exciting, like have a Danish and coffee."

Other women had made approaches. Husam had become adept at declining with grace, but was surprised and appalled by the brazenness of American women. He took her card and put it in his pocket, knowing he would never call. It saddened him. There had sprung between them an instant camaraderie, perhaps based on some mysterious rapport of body and soul. But that which can lead to the forbidden is itself forbidden, and Husam knew he would remain faithful to Islamic law.

They broke through the clouds. Even though it was not yet dark, lights were on below, and he watched the beams from automobiles draw lines along the highways. The Potomac cut through the landscape like a thick black belt.

She turned her face toward the window. Did she watch the ground come up to meet them? Or did she watch him? She leaned forward, enough to see his reflection in the window. Their eyes met once again. She smiled and waved. "Hi."

Minutes later she walked through the enclosed ramp into the terminal alongside him, as though they were together. They made a handsome couple: the tall redheaded woman of thirty years, in form-fitting trousers and soft yellow blouse, with her smart-looking carryon over her shoulder, easily keeping stride with the six-foot-four-inch, dark-eyed man in a custom-tailored suit. He could not help but be flattered by her attentions. "I have enjoyed our conversation," he said with politeness, anxiously scanning faces for his wife, who would be there to meet him. "It is not often I have the opportunity to meet a dancer."

She hooked her arm in his. "Are we like those ships that pass in the night?" she asked, looking up at him.

Her warmth startled him with its force. It was as though she wanted to break through a barrier or open a door that was stuck. "Please." He moved to disengage his arm. "I am made uncomfortable by this situation. You must understand."

She clung to his arm, then abruptly let him go. "I won't hurt you, Husam. What are you afraid of?"

"Allah."

Abir sat quietly beside Husam as they drove toward their home in Arlington. She had seen him with the tall, flame-haired woman, and Husam could feel her reproach. It angered him because he had done nothing wrong. "How is Kawthar?" he asked, speaking in English.

She answered in Arabic. She would do that when sad or disheartened, as though wrapping herself in the comfort of the past. "Your daughter has changed much in the two months of your absence, my husband. She works at a pizza parlor in a short skirt, her face painted with lipstick."

"Kawthar does this?" Husam asked, feeling a stab of both fear and anger.

"Yes. You must speak to her, Husam. She does not listen to me."

Husam watched the road. Why would Kawthar do this thing? For the money? He would raise her allowance. She would listen to reason. He knew of men in the Muslim community with similar problems, although they were rarely talked about. Perhaps he could get advice from someone. "I sat next to a woman dancer," he said, not conscious of which language he spoke in. "Tall, with red hair like a lioness."

"She held your arm as you deplaned," Abir said. "As though it belonged to her."

"The poor woman," Husam said, a lofty smile on his face. "She could not keep her hands from me."

"Of course not." Abir moved closer to him and put her arm over the seat cushion. "What woman can keep her hands from playing with you?" Her warm fingers played with the back of his neck.

Husam forgot about his sixteen-year-old daughter and thought only of his wife. At forty-three, four years younger than Husam, Abir no longer had the lithesome grace of youth, but was still quite attractive. "Perhaps when we are home, your hands will wish to continue with their play?" he asked hopefully, slowing down to accommodate a driver who needed his lane.

"My hands have waited for two months for this day," she said. "But Kawthar will be home from her job. She wishes to greet you."

Husam sighed, then gripped the wheel tightly. "Kawthar grows like a weed," he said, "without discipline. I do not think she wishes to see me, Abir. She wishes to replace me as the head of our house."

Husam could not believe his eyes. Kawthar looked like a woman of the street. Already taller than Abir, with the same luxuriant skin and dark eyes, the costume she wore struck him as a blatant, sexual, provocative display of breasts, hips, and legs. Her face was marred with rouge, lipstick, and eye shadow. Bracelets rattled on her arms, drawing attention to their bareness. Her eyes had the disquieting look of sophistication. "Is this how you dress for me?"

She tried to put her arms around him and to give him a kiss. He pushed her away with disgust. "Daddy. Hi. It's me. Kawthar."

"You will go to your room at once. You will change into decent clothes."

Kawthar backed away. Her eyes swelled with moisture and grew red with pain, but she defiantly stood her ground. "This is my uniform, Daddy. It's what I wear to work. I wanted to show it to you."

"You no longer work there," Husam said, advancing toward her. "I will not have my daughter seen in such clothes. It is a disgrace!"

"It doesn't mean anything, Daddy. Nobody touches me!"

Husam grabbed her by the shoulders. It was all he could do to keep from hitting her. "I will touch you, Kawthar. With open hands, I will strike you. Someday you will thank me. Leave my sight!" He pushed her roughly toward the stairs. Stumbling and crying, Kawthar ran up them. He heard the door to her room slam shut.

Gradually he became aware of Abir's hand on his waist. "You have done well, my husband," she said softly. "She will listen to you."

Husam saw something else in Kawthar's manner. His worst fears as a father may have come to pass: a daughter who would not submit.

Why had Allah denied him a son?

## Friday, August 2, 1991
## Washington, D.C.

Husam al-Din had spent years living near the District, but had never been to the embassy of the Kingdom of Rashidi. He had emigrated from Iraq. The countries had much in common: language, custom, religion, and intertwining histories, but—like the children of jealous brothers—the people were not close. As he was admitted into the embassy, he admired the rich tones of the carpets, the tasteful tapestries and exhibits on the walls, and the clean lines of the furniture. Much of it was covered with ornate designs and Arabic calligraphy, and all of it made a statement that appealed to Husam: Arab dignity.

He was guided to the second floor by a modestly dressed woman in high heels and skirt that hung over her knees. She was attractive without being sexual, which Husam appreciated. She had greeted him in English, although Husam suspected—from her general appearance—that she was Rashidi and fluent in Arabic. A receptionist seated behind an expensive-looking executive secretary desk made of dark wood was turned toward the typewriter pedestal and working on a letter. "This is Mr. al-Din," his guide said.

The other woman rose from her chair. Walking to an elaborately carved door, she opened it. She too was attractive without flaunting her sexuality. "The ambassador is expecting you," she said, smiling modestly and ushering him inside.

Husam was surprised at the size of the office of Prince

Umar ibn abd al-Rashid, the ambassador to the United States from the Kingdom of Rashidi. It was huge; as large as the lobby downstairs, and more richly decorated. The thick carpets, luxuriant furniture, and exquisite murallike photographs of vast desert scenes were befitting of royalty. It would be impossible, in this room, to forget that the prince was a brother to the king.

Husam walked beyond a huge desk toward the comfortable circle of chairs, near a deep window that looked over the lawns and gardens of the embassy, where two men were standing. A silver pitcher, smelling of coffee and surrounded by gold goblets, was spread on a glass-topped table. It was not difficult to distinguish between the prince and his deputy. Faris abu abd al-Rahman, whom Husam had talked with on the telephone, showed deference and respect toward Umar ibn abd al-Rashid. *"As-salaam 'alaykum,"* the prince said, bowing slightly. "Do you speak Arabic, Husam al-Din?"

*"Wa-'alaykum as-salaam,"* Husam replied. "Yes," he continued in Arabic. "I would speak my language more, if there was opportunity. It rings in my ears."

The prince, whose sturdy body was tightly wrapped in an expensive Italian suit, had the nose of a hawk. "Please," he said, gesturing with his hand and sitting down. "Be seated." Faris waited until Husam was comfortably in a chair, then also sat down. "This one looks like a prosecutor, eh, Faris? Big. Like a mountain."

"But not as wide. He is trim, like the sails of a boat. He has the proportions of ibn Saud, as a young lion."

"I would rather have his checkbook," Husam said.

"Ah!" Prince Umar reached for the coffee. "Your name: Husam al-Din, Sword of the Faith." He poured thick, black liquid into a goblet. "It is a good name for a prosecutor. Where do you originate, Husam al-Din?"

"The Nafud. My father, peace to his memory, was a bedouin of the clan of Ruwalah."

"Then are you a Saudi?" He handed the cup to Husam.

"No, Prince Umar. I am an American."

"Of course. But before?"

41

Husam held the cup in both hands, smelling its aroma. "Officially, I emigrated from Iraq. But the men of my clan never agreed with the Englishman who drew the line between Iraq and Saudi Arabia."

Both men leaned back in their chairs and laughed. "May I ask?" the deputy ambassador asked the prince.

"As you see fit, Faris. We are in this together."

"Your allegiance now, Husam al-Din. How is it?"

Husam did not waver in his reply. "My primary allegiance is to Allah. And in His name, I have sworn temporal allegiance to the United States of America." He straightened his back, sitting taller than either of them. "I am firm in my faith—which in this land, with all the temptations so easily at hand, is a matter for the conscience, rather than the law."

The prince and his deputy glanced at one another, then nodded. "So. We do not entrust you with secrets of state, eh?" Prince Umar asked.

Husam smiled. "No. But I assure you, I am not an operative for the CIA." He saw that Prince Umar had taken a sip of coffee, and permitted himself a taste. "This is superb," he said, closing his eyes with enjoyment. "It reminds me of my youth."

"Then you miss your land, even though you are now such an American?" Umar suggested, his tone of voice good-humored but teasing.

"I miss the coffee." They laughed. "And I miss the land, and the sky, and the language. I would truly love to see my father's father, who still lives."

"How long have you been away from your homeland?"

"Twenty-seven years. I was twenty years of age when my father and I arrived in New York."

"Truly! I had thought of you as my son, but we are practically the same age! Why do you stay so youthful in appearance?"

"In this country, it is an obligation," Husam said, sipping coffee. "One can take pills."

"You know of a pill?" Ambassador Umar wanted to know.

"A bad joke," Husam said swiftly. "It is my love of running that keeps me thin. As a boy, I ran as much as I was allowed through the sands of the Nafud. Now I run on bicycle paths along the Potomac. It is an addiction I choose to keep."

"Have you traveled to our land?"

Husam thought of the desert kingdom, south of Saudi Arabia, with coastal access between Yemen and Oman. The Rashidis and the Saudis had fought bitterly for centuries over the land, even though the tribes were related through marriages many times over. "My father was once in Qahtan. He spoke with reverence of the Mosque al-Rashid. But I have not been to your country." He held his nearly empty goblet to his nose, breathing in its scent, hoping his host would take pity.

"More coffee?" Umar asked, lifting the pitcher.

"With pleasure!"

Faris looked toward the ambassador for permission to continue with the interview. The prince nodded. "What is the agency you work with for the Americans, Husam al-Din?"

"I am a litigator with the Department of Justice. But I have done much criminal prosecution, and miss my criminals."

"Do lawyers in this country have dealings with criminals?" Faris asked, his eyes wide with interest.

"It is quite common." Husam allowed his body to soak up the simple pleasures he experienced from the exhilaration of the coffee. "Perhaps it is my Arabic heritage, or that I am truly named, but enforcing law gives much satisfaction. There is also excitement in the criminal courts of a kind which is not found in civil litigation."

"This disposition of criminals is the prerogative of the king, is it not?" Faris asked.

Husam understood Faris's confusion as he tried to make sense of the American legal system. "I work for the executive branch of government, which stands in the place of the king," he said. "Comparisons can be made."

"Were you this prosecutor here, in Washington, D.C.?"

"Yes. I was five years with the United States Attorney's office, but transferred a year ago to the Department of Justice."

"Why, may I ask?" Faris requested. "If you enjoyed the prosecution of criminals, why did you transfer?"

Husam plunged ahead with information they might not wish to know. "There were threats against my life. I prosecuted Imam Ibn al-Mathrib, and a Shi'ite sect. . . ."

"You?" the prince asked.

"Yes, Excellency."

Once again the prince leaned his head back in laughter. It sounded like applause. "Not everyone in the Muslim community was offended, Husam al-Din. But tell me," he said, his manner changing, "where is your allegiance as between this infidel Adamson and Abd al-Hafiz? Did you know he was the nephew of Faris?"

Husam bowed his head toward the deputy ambassador. "My heart opens to you, Faris. I am sorry for your loss."

"He was an excellent young man. He should have been named Jesus, for he gave far more than he received. He is in the garden."

Husam leaned forward, touching the man's knee. "Believe me when I tell you I will do all within my power to bring this American to justice."

"'Justice'?" Umar asked. "For such a senseless, brutal murder, in Rashidi there would be justice." He nodded his head emphatically. "But here, in this land of the free, I have grave doubts. It is my understanding that the criminal will be allowed to live!" He spoke in an incredulous tone of voice. "Is it true that the most severe punishment is prison?"

"It is, Prince Umar. In the District, there is no capital punishment. But he faces a sentence of imprisonment for the rest of his life." Husam knew of the value of freedom of movement to the Rashidis. "For a man to be confined to a cell, within prison walls, for life! Is that not a most severe punishment?"

"They do *that* to men?" Faris asked, his expression

moving from awe, to repugnance. "And they regard Arabs as barbaric?"

Prince Umar also appeared to struggle with his imagination. "Would not it be far kinder to bring the matter to an end? Until the family of Abd al-Hafiz can see the man's blood, how can they cleanse their minds and emotions of the natural vengeance that will otherwise disturb and twist them?" Then his voice took off, sailing around the room, filling it with the sounds of the magnificent Arabic language. "Is it the law, in this Christian country, that families must live out their lives, each day knowing that criminals live while their sons are dead?" he asked rhetorically. "And what must it do to the soul of any man, even a murderer, to lock him in a cage for fifty years! Is it not better to cleanse the wound before applying the bandage?"

"I do not disagree," Husam said, feeling their reactions as a fellow Arab. "I merely wish to point out that the consequences to this man are most severe."

"Can you promise even *this* result?" Umar asked.

"Sir, I cannot."

"Would it not be justice to deliver him to Rashidi?"

"Do you refer to the extradition hearing?"

"Of course! In Rashidi, this man would be compelled to stand before the king, next to the family of Abd al-Hafiz!"

"I have no comment," Husam said. "The extradition hearing will take place in another courtroom. I have nothing to do with it."

The prince jumped up. "I mean no disrespect to your law in America, but how can this be?" he asked in agitation. "Is this a question for a *qadi*, to be answered in a lengthy *fatwa*? Where is the need for lawyers in something so obvious? The man Adamson killed Abd al-Hafiz, here, in this building, in this embassy of the Kingdom of Rashidi." He leaned toward Husam, his hands extended in an imploring gesture. "Give him to my king! He will not 'punish' him for the rest of his life as a child for his misdeed. He will let the father, the family, of the man he murdered dictate his fate." He straightened his back and turned away in thought. "It is probable they will say 'kill him, as he did our son.' But there have been instances of mercy. In any event, the pain is in the heart of the father of Abd al-Hafiz. Isn't it 'justice' to alleviate his pain?"

"I can think of no adequate reply," Husam said. "It is a different system. In this country there is a complicated procedure that must be followed."

Prince Umar sat down. "I am sorry, my friend. I rail against you as though you are responsible, and I know you are not. Answer me truly. At this extradition hearing, is there any possibility that your adopted government will give this person to us?"

Husam slumped forward, aware of the fact that the hunch in his shoulders said it all. "There is always the possibility. Your lawyers will be listened to with respect. But I must tell you I would be astonished by such result."

The prince wearily glanced at his deputy. "Faris?" he asked, a twisted smile on his face.

"Is it true there will not be a trial for at least one year, and possibly two?"

"That is true." Once again Husam felt himself in the awkward position of admitting an absurdity.

"Need I point out that in Rashidi this matter would be concluded within one turn of the moon?"

Husam opened his palms and shrugged.

"Why, may I ask, will it take such lengths of time for"—he rolled his eyes expressively—"justice?"

Husam tried not to smile. "There are procedures. There are always delays. There is the condition of the court calendar, which means the number of trials to go before this one. All of these matters use up the clock."

"These procedures. Can you explain?"

"There must first be a preliminary hearing, then a presentment of the case to a grand jury, then an indictment, then an arraignment, then various pretrial motions, then—"

"Please, my brain cannot work so quickly," Umar pleaded. " 'Grand jury'?"

"That is a collection of people who decide in case after

case whether the government has sufficient evidence to take an accused person to trial."

"Where do these people come from?"

"From all walks of life," Husam said. "Their names are drawn by lot, from lists."

"Common people? Uneducated people? People with no training in law?"

Husam heard amazement and disbelief in their tones. He could stand in their shoes; and from where they stood, he too found it strange. "As a matter of fact, persons with legal training—a *mufti* or a *qadi*—are often not allowed on grand juries."

Umar smothered a laugh. To show disrespect for the ways of others was the height of crude behavior, but this was too much. "And this is the most enlightened country on earth?"

Faris too choked back his mirth. "Indeed, Your Highness. We in Rashidi are trying to catch up to them."

Husam could not control himself. He broke up in laughter, opening the gates for the others. "Shall I tell you what happens next?"

"Please tell us of this next sign of progress!"

"This grand jury will listen to the testimony of witnesses who have seen the body of the victim. It will hear the coroner who examined the body and found the plastic blade inside it. It will hear from others who captured the intruder Adamson as he fled from the embassy with the blood of the victim on his clothing. They will stroke their chins and ask questions of me and then decide: this, indeed, is suspicious!" The three men shouted with laughter. "They will say to me, Husam, you may proceed with this case. You may file an indictment in court against this fellow, charging him with murder!"

"Allah be praised!"

"And then, after the passage of a week, I will return to court and Mr. Adamson will be there with his lawyer. I will read the indictment to him, and ask him if he wishes to plead guilty. 'If you do so, you will admit that you murdered Abd al-Hafiz. Or is it your wish to plead not guilty, which is to say you deny it?' And the judge will give Mr. Adamson and his lawyer another week to consider how to answer my question!"

Husam continued with his explanation. It was impossible for him to say anything they did not find uproarious. "If I should kill my wife's mother," Faris declared, "I will seek a trial in America!"

The explanations should have taken five or ten minutes, but took half an hour. He described the motions and hearings that would probably occur before the trial could begin. Each pause was like a punch line, greeted with hilarity. "And where is Mr. Adamson during this travesty?" Faris asked.

"He will remain in jail—unless, of course, bail is authorized and he is released!"

They shouted with laughter.

"It is the simplicity, and the certainty of result, of the laws of your country that recommend them!" Umar declared through the tears in his eyes. "One knows precisely what to expect!"

When Husam left the embassy a few minutes later, it was with a warm feeling. The Rashidis were good fellows, and he would enjoy working with them. Among other benefits, it could return him to the good graces of the Muslim community. He skipped down the steps as though on vacation, loosening his tie. Before meeting with the officers of the Capitol Police Department, he would go home, change clothes, and go for a run. . . .

Across the street, standing with a brown-skinned man, he saw Kawthar, dressed provocatively. She wore a revealing summer outfit of shorts and tight blouse. Her swept-up hair did not even cover her naked shoulders. An assertive expression that he found intolerable shone in her eyes. "Daddy? Come meet my boss. Please."

The man, wearing a short-sleeved sport shirt that had only been buttoned part of the way up, bristled with muscles, but Husam barely saw him. Heat surged in Husam's groin, stomach, and face, raging through him like fire. "You defy me!" he shouted, storming across the street, barely aware of the car that swerved to miss him. He reached back with his hand to hit her.

Somehow the man got in the way and caught his wrist. "Hey man, don't. She's your daughter."

"Who are you?" The fellow was three inches shorter, but unexpectedly strong. Husam could not tear his hand away.

"Her employer, Mr. al-Din. Kawthar works for me." He laughed with nervousness. "This is crazy."

Husam wanted to kill him. He tried swinging his briefcase at the man's face, but nothing happened. He couldn't get leverage. Dropping it, he tried to hit with his left fist, but the punches were muffled. "Kawthar does not work in such a place! You leave her alone!"

Pain exploded in his stomach. "I don't need this shit," he heard the man say. He couldn't breathe. The man helped him sit down next to a tree. "This didn't work out, baby. I got to let you go."

"Daddy!" Kawthar knelt down, her face white, one hand reaching out for him. "You didn't have to hit him like that, Robert."

"Huh! Did you see what he tried to do to me?"

A feeling of intense humiliation filled Husam. He glared at his daughter with hatred. "Get out of my sight," he commanded. "You are not mine." He saw his briefcase on the grass, near the sidewalk. "You wish for freedom from my protection? Go!"

# 5

Frankie could not remember when the practice of law had filled her with such a wonderful sense of power. After breakfast with Slasstein she'd gone back to his office, where she dictated and signed her appearance as co-counsel in the case of *United States* v. *Richard Adamson, Jr.* Then she and Brooking sketched out the details of their agreement on a legal pad, which they signed, made copies of, and gave to Brooking's secretary to formalize. Grinning at her like a Christmas elf, he picked up the telephone, called his bank, and transferred twenty thousand dollars to her account in Denver.

She had plenty of questions, starting and ending with: Why her? Didn't he know other lawyers who could do it better? She wasn't after compliments. She didn't get it, and didn't believe in Santa Claus. What was the catch?

Her suspicions didn't dampen her enthusiasm, however. On the flight to Denver later that morning—first-class with all the trimmings—her lists of things to do somehow turned into things to buy. A new barn for Bozo, pastured in Indian Hills; new saddle and tack, Fox Saddle Shop, Cortez; horse trailer; pickup truck, to drive to Cortez to get the saddle; gravestone for Victor Hand, a Shoshone Indian artist in Lander who died of alcoholism; presents for the troops at

NASP; wardrobe; piano. She loved it, but couldn't quite believe it. There had to be a catch. It was as though she'd won a million dollars in the lottery, but the payoff was in marked money.

That afternoon she caught Trigge at NASP headquarters in Denver. His barrel chest had sagged toward his belt line, and his frame contoured comfortably into his desk chair. But his eyes still had the spark of an old, seasoned warhorse. She found herself measuring him as she would an adversary, and decided she wasn't ready for him yet. "You be careful," he growled at her from time to time.

Keane Williams, the cherub-faced Boy Wonder from California, was staring at himself in the mirror when she broke in on him to say good-bye. She had the impression that he could hardly wait for her to leave because he wanted her office. Davey Reddman had left early for a training ride on his bicycle, up Squaw Pass. Frankie left him a note, telling him if he got in her way on the highway, she would run over him. Rachel Stone wished her luck, gave her a hug and a message from Stu VanOchre. It had been faxed to Frankie from Anchorage, where Stu had been for the last month on an environmental prosecution. It had been marked, *Personal, to Frankie.*

"You read it, of course," Frankie said.

Rachel shrugged. "It's very short. What's he like?"

Frankie read the message: *I hate this. Please. Come see me. Don't laugh. Just do it.*

"Great lawyer, Rachel," she said, realizing she had all she needed of Stu VanOchre. "He should make some mother a nice little boy."

On Friday she rode Bozo up Parmalee Gulch, trying to miss all the weekend riders and watching his ears flatten as grim-faced mountain bikers grudgingly yielded the trail. The next time she rode the big red, she would be mounted on a J. Fox hand-tooled, handmade soft leather western saddle. She started packing that night, working into Saturday morning, with occasional interruptions where she would write out a line of questions in a furious burst, or a strategy, or some ingenious legal scenario that would result in dramatic victory for the defense. She savored scenes of herself breaking Lamar Gleason into bits and pieces on the witness stand. Part of her deal with Slasstein was that she had to forego her personal vendetta against the slug, except as a weapon to be used in an overall strategy of defense. But the time would come when she could crucify the bastard on the witness stand.

Her energy level was huge. She mowed through all her personal business: storming through bills, answering letters with exuberance, arranging for the watering of her plants, the shipment of her things—without even having an address. Her house on South Humboldt, near Washington Park, was close to the old 1880s mansion on Capitol Hill that housed NASP. She trotted back and forth over the weekend, leaving instructions in files and tying up loose ends. Her desk had been moved into the hall the last time she saw it, and Keane's furniture shoved in what had been her office. She found a note from Davey, on a Post-It, stuck to her door: *Hey. Who do I call when I choke? I'm gonna miss you!* She scribbled a message on the bottom of it, and stuck it on his chair: *Try Rachel. Save her from that asshole Keane.*

It was too late to take Bozo for a ride when she finished, about one o'clock Monday morning, but not too late to drive up to Indian Hills to wash and comb him. The elevation at the ranch where she boarded him was over seven thousand feet, and she could see her breath. The stars to the west were buried deep in the vastness of the Colorado sky, but lights from Denver glowed dully to the east. It looked like the sun had gotten stuck on its way up. The air was clean and scented with pine, with only an occasional whiff of gasoline fumes from the occasional teenager or new yuppie resident who ripped along the winding mountain highway nearby. She knew she would miss the country and her old horse.

Slasstein wasn't in his office Monday in the early afternoon, when she came in from Denver. He had left a note for her with Miss Beacon, his secretary and office manager:

*Check the contract, I made a couple changes, see if you're sharp enough to find 'em. Beacon will get you started, call me tonight, BS.*

BS, she thought, smiling. Very appropriate.

Miss Beacon was a tall, angular woman with hollow cheeks and deep eye sockets, whose face looked like a skull fitted with a tight brown balloon. She had already moved a desk, a telephone, and a laptop computer into a small conference room for Frankie. She gave her a set of keys to the office, as well as keys and a key card to an apartment north of Dupont Circle. "Mr. Slasstein has told me that your work has priority, Miss Rommel," the severely tailored woman with metal-framed glasses said. "Please feel free to ask me any time for anything you need." Frankie decided to keep her questions to a minimum.

She had crammed two bags full of clothes and essentials, and moved them into the apartment and unpacked. Washington was not like Wyoming. It might have been nice to have a view—a reason to open the drapes—instead of thousands of reasons to keep them closed. But she couldn't complain. Five large rooms, an ultramodern kitchen, an okay library, and food in the fridge. After a quick jog around the neighborhood, she called Brooking. "You like the digs?" he asked.

"They're fine."

"Belongs to a friend, a car lobby, one of those guys who's kind of against clean air. Don't get attached, okay? I got friends all over town, when he comes back we move you to another."

Instant heat flowed through Frankie's face. "Not acceptable," she declared. "I've got a ton of stuff coming from Denver. I do not move on five minute's notice. Get me a place where I can move in."

"A dig is a dig, right?"

"Wrong. I need a safe house, Brooking. A bed I can get used to, a place to store my saddle, and a closet for my teddy bear. I won't take anything less."

"Okay, babe, I'll work on it, gotta go."

*"Don't* hang up on me. We need to talk!"

"Yeah, sure, not now, okay? I'm juggling fifty zillion things. See you late—"

*"When,* Brooking?"

She could hear him clear his throat. "Thursday, meet me here, breakfast. You need anything, use Beacon, she'll figure it out. She won't leave you in stitches, but she gets the job done."

Frankie glared at a hole in the carpet. "Great. Any words of advice?"

"Yeah. You got the preliminary on Thursday too. Don't fuck it up."

## Tuesday, August 6, 1991
## Washington, D.C.

Richard Adamson, Jr. was an enigma to the reporters in the Bay Area, Frankie discovered from the newspaper. She sat behind the desk in her new office and bent the stem on the lamp down, for better light. The San Francisco *Chronicle* had done an in-depth feature article on her client.

He had it made. From a prominent family, he had money, girls, good looks, country clubs, cars, a superb pitching arm, and—so everyone thought—the heart of a champion. As a junior in high school, he'd been named to the Bay Area all-star team as a starting pitcher. Four major league teams had let him know they were interested, and three large colleges were in active pursuit, offering scholarships and alumni association perks. A representative from a name-brand athletic sportswear manufacturer had contacted his father's lawyers, offering guidance. "Rick" didn't need his father's money. He would make more than his old man by the time he was thirty.

"So what does he do the day he turns eighteen?" his coach told an interviewer. That had been in March of his senior

54

year. "Joins the Marine Corps, to see the world. Never even suited up."

Frankie stared at Adamson's picture in a baseball uniform, delivering the ball. It was as puzzling as if Carl Lewis had decided not to compete in the Olympics two days after he'd qualified. "Don't ask me," his father said. "The boy is whacked. He's too big for his own britches. Way too big for the big leagues."

A nice fatherly sentiment, Frankie thought, staring at the photograph of Dr. Adamson. A full head of gray hair, his eyes glared at the camera with the tough harshness of a man who has it, and intends to keep it.

The first Mrs. Adamson—Richard's mother—could not be located, and the current Mrs. Adamson had no comment. Richard's sister provided the kind of explanation that added to the mystery. Tamara, named after their Jewish mother, was two years younger than Richard. She wore a wide smile and had beautiful dark, doe eyes. "He hated being rich," she said.

Frankie ran her fingers through her hair and massaged her scalp. Hated being rich? What was horrible about being rich?

Tami's statements in earlier reports, to the effect that her brother was being framed because of an Arabian princess, were repeated. However, in later reports, the girl denied making those claims.

Reading on, Frankie wondered what she was looking for. As a prosecutor, when she put a man on trial, she focused on two things: his defects, like his callousness and greed, and the victims left in the path of violence. Was she supposed to turn the equation around, a standard defense ploy? Did Brooking want her to portray Adamson as some kind of misunderstood but true-blue knight in shining armor, who either didn't do it or took out Attila the Hun?

Several high school students and teachers were quoted, giving their impressions of Adamson. Their comments justified the reporter's conclusion that either he was ten different people or no one knew him. He was cocky, undisciplined, warm, generous, arrogant, cold, sex-crazed, respectful of the rights of others, conceited in the extreme, a poet, spiritual, wonderfully sensitive, larger than life, a pain in the ass like a boil.

Who was this guy? She reached for a cigarette, then changed her mind. A country-club nut case with a major league arm, or a spoiled brat?

He joined the Marine Corps in March 1988, the article continued. Boot camp at San Diego, infantry training at Camp Pendleton, MSG school—for Military Security Guard—at Quantico. His first duty post was Costa Rica. From there he transferred to the United States Embassy in Qahtan, the Kingdom of Rashidi. In dress blues, at parade rest, he looked better than the Marine on the recruiting poster. His hitch in the Mideast started in February 1990, a few months before Saddam Hussein invaded Kuwait.

She lifted a piece of hair off her forehead and put it behind an ear, where it belonged. She wondered how much of the article she could accept as fact. Adamson had been reassigned in November to a training unit in Saudi Arabia. He fought in the Gulf War, was discharged from the Marines in Washington, D.C., and immediately went to work for the Kingdom of Rashidi as a security guard. "They treated him like one of them," an undisclosed source reportedly stated. "In a way, he was."

The article concluded with a quote from Richard's sister. Somehow, Frankie had known it would finish up with something yuckie. "Rick should be in college, not in jail," she said. "People don't know him. He really has a vision. It's all so sad."

Frankie glanced at another of the photographs in the piece, this one from his high school yearbook. He was photogenic enough: clear-eyed, easy smile, nice jawline, even teeth. She'd prosecuted a dozen punks who photographed just as well, however. She stuck the article in her briefcase, turned off the lamp, and pushed her chair away from the desk.

Beacon gave precise directions to the Federal Detention

CHOICE OF EVILS

Center. Frankie had dressed in a casual safari-cut pantsuit that morning and coiled her hair. She arrived at the jail at ten o'clock and was ushered into a small attorney conference room, where she waited for Adamson. A plastic glass plate separated lawyer from client with a voice-amplification system stuck in the glass, below eye level. Frankie put her briefcase on the floor and pulled out a legal pad. She opened it and spread it on the shelf. A uniformed officer brought Adamson in, took off his cuffs, and left the steel-walled room, shutting the door behind him.

He wore an orange jumpsuit and didn't look any older than his high school photographs, until he got close. Six feet two inches tall, wide well-muscled shoulders, and no waist, he looked like all the cowboys in Wyoming thought they looked. He was way too handsome to make a decent defendant. Jurors liked to dump on movie stars. His face had thinned and lines had grooved around his mouth. There was also something startling about his pale green eyes, and Frankie tried to figure out what it was. They gave the sense of someone who either felt too much or couldn't feel anything. He could be a murderer or a priest.

He rubbed his wrists, sat down, and looked at her with a nice, well-mannered reserve. "Hello."

"Hi," she said, continuing to eye him critically, then catching herself at it. "Did they tell you who I am?"

"They said my new lawyer was here." His voice through the speaker, though low and soft, carried well. She liked the sound of it. "What happened to the old one?"

"He's still on the case. I'm Frankie Rommel. I'll be working on it too."

He nodded, with courtesy. "Will another lawyer do me any good?"

"It won't hurt."

His eyes swept through the cage he was in, as though searching for a crack in the wall. "Who's paying for all this?" he asked, mildly ironic. "My insurance company?"

The question had not even occurred to Frankie. She assumed his family. "Don't you know?"

"I know who isn't." He looked tired. "My old man. 'Rick my boy, if you'd listened to me, this wouldn't have happened, right?'" His face took on the aspect of the photograph Frankie had seen of Dr. Adamson. "'Right, Dad.' 'Do I finally have your attention?' 'Yes, sir!'" The statement was delivered with a salute. "'Excellent. I've decided to give you the freedom and independence you've always wanted.'" He wiped off his nose; a mannerism perhaps that belonged to Dr. Adamson. "'You've managed to get your butt in a crack. Let's see if you can get it out. Without, of course, any help from me.'" The young man grinned. "Great guy, my dad. You'd love him."

Frankie pulled out a cigarette and lit it. "Oh dear," she said. "Well. Somebody is. A rich uncle?"

"Ha."

She told herself there was probably a simple explanation. "I don't know, then. Brooking hired me, and I didn't ask." Thoughtfully, she took a drag. "I'll find out."

"Okay."

She made a note on her pad. "The preliminary hearing is Thursday. It won't amount to much; they never do. But it'll give me a chance to ask some questions."

"What is there to ask? I mean, I did it."

"Rick. You don't know what you did at this point, and neither do I."

"What's that supposed to mean, Miss Rommel?" he asked sardonically. "'Leave everything to me, Rick.'" She heard her voice through the amplification system, and saw her expression on his face. "'Your father may have deserted you, but I haven't. I'm going to get you out of this awful mess you're in.'"

"That's very good," Frankie said, lifting an eyebrow. "You don't trust me, do you?" He smiled and looked at his hands. "What is it, Rick? Who do you think I am?"

"I don't know."

She dug the file out of her briefcase. "Here's the entry of appearance of Brooking Slasstein. You know who he is, don't you?"

She was looking at a caricature of Brooking. "'I'm your

lawyer, kid, don't worry my size, hard to hit,' " Adamson said. " 'Ask anybody.' "

When Dr. Adamson declared his son a wacko, he didn't go far enough, Frankie thought. "He's also the best criminal defense lawyer in the District." She pasted a document against the glass. "Here's my entry of appearance. He signed it. Compare the signatures."

Adamson looked at them casually, then shrugged his shoulders. "So?"

"Damn it," Frankie said, annoyed. "What's wrong? I'm here to help you."

His expression softened. "I hope so. What do you want to know?"

She took a deep breath. "Are you okay? That's the first thing. Is there anything of a personal nature that's bothering you, or anything you need that I can get for you? All your stuff, your clothes, car, what do you want done with them? Any bills that need to be paid. In other words, what can I do to make you comfortable?" She felt like an agent, hustling a property.

"You can get me out."

"Rick, listen to me." She tapped the ash off her cigarette. "I hope you don't mind if I call you Rick."

"As long as I can call you Frankie."

She blushed. With pleasure. What was *that* all about? "You'll be charged with felony murder. They don't set bail in the District for felony murder. You can forget about getting out until after the trial."

He nodded slowly, dropping his eyes. "I've got an apartment in Hyattsville." He gave her the address. "I'm paid through August, but they read the papers. My stuff is probably in boxes, in the garage. Can you store it somewhere?"

"Who are 'they'?"

"Atwalter. The managers. A husband and wife."

Frankie wrote the name down. "What about your car?" She felt ghoulish.

"It's on the street," he said, then paused. "I don't remember where."

"Can you describe it?"

"Sure." He did.

"But you don't remember where you left it?" she asked incredulously.

"No."

She made notes, not certain that she believed this. "What do you want done with it if we find it?"

He shrugged. "Give it to my sister. She'll be here as soon as she can talk Dad into letting her come."

"Does she need help? Maybe we can send her air fare."

"Why would you do that?"

"To keep you happy." He intrigued her, but he made her nervous too. "Is there anything else?"

"That's really what this is all about isn't it, Frankie?" When he wasn't entertaining himself with mimicry, his voice had that gentle quality designed to make a young girl swoon. "The anything else?"

"I don't understand you," Frankie said, smiling.

"You want to find out where she is, right?"

"Who, your sister?"

A look of disgust spread across his face. He got up. "You guys are more obvious than Dad. Go away."

Frankie's mouth opened with surprise. She shut it, dropped her cigarette on the floor and stomped on it. "Poor little rich boy." Angrily she pushed things in her briefcase. "If that's what you want, fella, that's what you get."

He stopped, turned around and watched her. "Wait. Please." He frowned, trying to assess her. "I want to trust you. But I don't know what's going on."

She folded her arms over her chest and tried to understand his problem. Then she glanced at her watch and realized what time it was. "Let's do this. I've got an appointment with the U.S. Attorney in half an hour. We'll try again before the preliminary. Okay?" He nodded cautiously. "A word to the wise. Don't discuss this case with anyone. That includes your sister, and it especially includes any 'buddy' you meet in jail."

"I know. They could be a plant."

"Brooking already told you?" she asked.

"So did the public defender. Before he found out my old man was Daddy Warbucks."

Frankie didn't understand him, but decided she liked his eyes. They were flecked with brown; enough so they didn't have that metallic, alien-from-space sheen that often afflicts pale eyes. She snapped her briefcase shut.

"Will you be the lawyer at the preliminary hearing, or will it be Mr. Slasstein?"

"Me." But there would be photo opportunities, so Brooking might do it. "I think."

"You're not sure?"

"No."

"But you'll be back to talk to me before we go to court? You need to know what to ask, right?"

That film of mistrust had dropped over his face. "Rick, what's eating you?" She looped the belt over her shoulder and stormed to her feet. "You act like you think I'm working for them!"

"Aren't you?"

Frankie had about given up. She'd been sitting half an hour, waiting for Roy Grantland to appear. The waiting room for the U.S. Attorney on the second floor of the Judiciary Center Building was as crowded as it had been before, and as eerily quiet. Her hair felt dirty, and no one would look at her. She was on her third cigarette and her throat felt like a smokestack when the door she'd been watching opened and his face poked through. She stood up quickly, catching his eye, and he waved and beckoned. "Hi," he said, holding the door for her. "How you doin'?"

She hadn't known what to expect. He seemed so genuinely nice that she wasn't sure if he knew what had happened. "You were right about Gleason."

"I heard you had a little flap." He didn't mention her calls to him that he hadn't returned. He guided her through the maze to his office, let her in, shut the door, and beckoned her toward the chair in front of his desk. "You really quit NASP?" he asked, sliding into the high-backed chair behind his desk.

"Call it a vacation."

"Shoot. Denver sounds nice. Maybe I could move there."

"How did your trial go?" she asked, sitting up straight. His desk was as clean as the last time. But she could still see that awful picture.

"One squirrel on the jury. It hung up."

Frankie could feel his disappointment. "Will you try them again?"

He shrugged. "I don't know. It'll cost the taxpayers a hundred thousand dollars if I do. Is justice worth it? Where will it fit in my trial schedule?" He laughed. "I'd have to deal somebody to make room, you know. Due process for the animals."

"I know how you feel."

"Yeah." He smiled wryly at her. "So now you're gonna inflict some due process on the system, right? Might as well make some money!"

A tic under her eye felt as though it were shaking off the whole left side of her face. She had watched it in the mirror and knew it was barely visible. "Do you see a problem?" she asked, referring to the conflict of interest possibilities.

He shifted his weight and leaned toward her. "If it was mine, I'd look pretty hard, but I don't think I'd push to get you off. I'd just want to know if there was something I had to do about it, like what to tell the judge if there was a question."

Frankie relaxed. "Will you be trying it?"

"You don't get so lucky. I'm buried." She brushed her hair back with her left hand. "We found an Arab. The guy's name is Husam al-Din." Grantland grinned at her. "He's tough. He doesn't lose."

"Nobody wins them all." She pulled out a cigarette and lit it. "What else can you tell me?"

"He was a trial deputy here before moving over to Justice. Born prosecutor, you know, shines with decency. The women love him because of his looks, the men respect him because of his size." He let his arms hang like a gorilla. "Big. But by the book. When it comes to discovery, all you'll have to do is ask. He'll make sure you get everything you're entitled to. Might even do it before the preliminary."

"Should he get a medal?" Frankie crushed her cigarette in the ashtray. It tasted awful. "I don't make the defense jump through the hoops. Do you?"

"Sometimes." He gave Frankie a funny look. "If I ever go into private practice, though, I might not remember it that way. Never met an ex yet who wasn't anything but perfect when he looks back on his long and distinguished career."

Frankie cocked her head, closed one eye and stared at him with the other. "Moi?"

"Vous." He picked up the telephone. "Now I've described this paragon, want to meet him?"

"Yes."

He dialed four digits. "Husam, how busy are you? . . . Someone here you should meet. The lawyer you replaced, only now she's on the other side." He listened, laughed, then hung up. "He'll be right down."

"What was funny?"

"He said, 'What a country.'"

Frankie liked Husam al-Din, whom she thought of as an Arab hunk. The three of them ate lunch at the Greek Café on the garden floor of the Stanton Building, and Husam's manner throughout was reserved but unpretentious. There was even a hint of gallantry in his attitude toward her, which might have been residual chauvinism, but after her experience with Lamar Gleason, she was charmed by it. He ate a small Greek salad and a gyro, eating the lamb in a pita bread sandwich with his hands, kind of like the way a man should, the woman from Wyoming thought. They did not engage in the oneupsmanship games lawyers often play, even when talking about the case. He told her to send a letter requesting discovery, but promised to show her what he had after lunch.

While she picked through her salad, he gave her a bare-bones outline of the case. He drew a diagram on a napkin showing the embassy grounds, the legation behind it, and an iron fence that ran between them. "This is how Mr. Adamson got in." He drew an X at the approximate location of the gate in the fence. "He carried with him a pistol of the kind issued to Rashidi guards. He was captured here." He drew another X, near the main gate of the legation. "Abd al-Hafiz had been the head of security for the Kingdom of Rashidi. He made the mistake to discharge Mr. Adamson, for which he was murdered."

"When was he discharged?"

"Perhaps a week before the murder."

"Did Adamson use the pistol?" Frankie asked.

"No." Husam frowned, as though to himself. "He stabbed with unbelievable force with a very lethal plastic knife, known as a CIA letter opener."

When they returned to Husam's office, Gleason was there. Frankie nodded at him coldly, and it pleased her when his jaw dropped through the floor. "Husam, my man, got a sec?" he asked as both he and Frankie waved off the tall man's effort to introduce them. "We need a fast conference."

Her teeth ground, but she would look foolish if she tried to get between the prosecutor and his investigating officer. She sat in the chair Husam found for her, along the wall in the hallway near his office. "I will be with you as soon as possible."

He was alone when he saw her a few minutes later. "I am sorry," he said. "I cannot give you discovery until I receive from you a request in writing." His attitude had changed. "Even then there may be a difficulty."

"I see." Frankie stood up and stared at him with anger and frustration. "Something Gleason said?"

"Yes."

She took a deep breath. "Do you want to hear the other side, or will that matter?" she asked, hooking her bag over her shoulder.

"Of course there are 'sides' to all things. At another time, perhaps it will matter. But for the present, please send to me the standard letter for discovery."

She walked away quickly, overwhelmed with anger. She did not want him to see her face.


# Wednesday, August 7, 1991
# Washington, D.C.

Frankie had just stepped into the shower when the telephone rang. She ignored it, then remembered there was no answering device. Dripping water on the carpet, she found the nearest extension: by the bed in the bedroom. "Hello." She glanced at the time on the clock radio: 6:42 A.M.

"Hi, babe, Brooking, we got a problem." He sounded serious.

"It'll have to wait while I get a towel."

"Hey, don't bother on my account!"

She trotted to the bathroom, grabbed a huge towel and wrapped it around her. Then she stood by the bed and picked up the telephone. "I'm back."

"Bad news. The bastards filed a motion to disqualify. Against both of us."

After running into Gleason, Frankie wasn't surprised. She found a cigarette, stuck it in her mouth and lit it. "You too? What's their basis?"

"Two-pronged attack. Your unethical conduct takes you out. Me—wait a minute." She heard the rustling of paper. "'Material information received by Rommel, which must additionally be imputed to Slasstein.' What a shot in the ass. That's how they get to me."

"That bastard Gleason. I met the prosecutor yesterday, and—"

"Hold it. I don't want to know what happened yesterday, you met al-Din."

"What difference does it make? They—"

65

"It could be imputed to me, Frankie. Didn't think they'd do it. Nothing personal, but I got to keep space between us until after the hearing."

"I'll be down as soon as—"

"Damn it, no! Stay out of my sight. You're a leper to me, babe. Until the hearing. I can't take the chance."

"What are you talking about?" Frankie asked angrily. "Don't give me any leper crap, God damn it!" Viciously, she sucked on her cigarette.

"Chill out, Frankie," he said mildly. "Listen, babe, it goes with the territory. I have to be able to testify I got nothing from you. Absolutely nothing. You need to be able to testify you gave nothing to me. See what I mean?"

The towel fell off her body, leaving her naked. She inhaled deeply. Her professional reputation was being challenged, and all she heard him say was, "Chill out." "What am I supposed to do? Send you a bill and walk away? Oh no."

"Don't send me a bill. Don't walk away either. Just stay away until I get this taken care of. That's all. Shssh!"

"There's a preliminary hearing tomorrow, Brooking. Who will do that?"

He took a deep breath. "Me. Shit. Be up all night."

"I don't like this. At all."

"Babe, criminal defense is war. I thought you knew. The Government has a bigger army, so the defense has to have more heart." She heard something in his voice she hadn't heard before: commitment. "David and Goliath. They pull shit like this all the time, they can afford it, turn the screws, turn up the heat. They go after lawyers now, if the poor slob has a good one. Make him get rid of the good one, take a schlock. They wear you down, rub your face in dirt."

"Dirt doesn't bother me. I've been bucked off plenty of horses. But this isn't dirt. It's filth! God damn it. How did I let you talk me into this?"

"All it is is dirt, babe, washes off, trust me." The money, she thought. It was the money. "Listen. Show up at the hearing on this bullshit motion to disqualify, hasn't been set yet, but Beacon will let you know when. Maybe a week from now."

CHOICE OF EVILS

"I can't sit here and do nothing. You are messing with my life!"

"It's Rick Adamson's life." She heard it again: commitment. "What's best for him right now is all that matters. You mix in now, they'll use it against us."

Angrily, she picked the towel off the floor. "Us, or you?"

His voice grew loud. "Maybe you prosecuted too long. When you go balls to the wall for a client, you don't think of you. I don't think of me. I do whatever it takes as long as it's legal, and I'm not real careful about that."

Frankie realized her hands were as shaky as her voice. "Would you sacrifice your own reputation? That's what you're asking me to do!"

"So, what's a reputation, the tag line under a picture in the paper? Listen. If the court denies the motion, the kid keeps both of us. But the judge might kick you off. I want him at least to keep me."

She could hear determination in his voice. "Do I get a lawyer to represent me, Brooking?"

He thought a moment. "Up to you. The way I see it, there is nothing inconsistent in our positions, you'll have me for your lawyer. When I fight for me, I fight for you." He seemed to rethink what he had just said. "Yeah, you need your own lawyer, babe. But for the kid's sake, I hope you'll trust me." He hung up.

# 6

## Thursday, August 15, 1991
## Washington, D.C.

Frankie couldn't sleep. Her conscience—her grandfather's face—would not allow her to take a sleeping pill. She thought if she could wear her body out with exercise, she might be able to drift off, so she jogged in the morning until she was drenched with sweat, joined a health club and lifted weights in the afternoon, and jogged in the evenings before going to bed. She talked on the telephone with anyone she could think of—even VanOchre was a relief—watched bits and pieces of trials, cleaned her apartment, started four books, went shopping, visited museums, and daily fought back the urge to storm Slasstein's office. Beacon called and told her the hearing on the motion to disqualify was set for Thursday, 3:30 P.M., in the Superior Court.

She started dressing for her day in court at eleven o'clock. The lack of sleep showed in her eyes, and her face looked thin and hard. She softened it with cream. As she brushed her hair she tried laughing at herself for taking her problem so seriously. She was not Joan of Arc, on trial for her life. Whatever happened, she could deal with it. After three beginnings she settled on her soft gray suit, a silk blouse, and high heels. She gathered her hair in a wide brooch and let it hang luxuriantly down her back. You look terrific, she said to herself as she called a cab.

At 3:15 P.M. she was funneled through the security check system of the Superior Court Building, one block south of the U.S. Attorney's office and two blocks away from Brooking Slasstein's. The pounding of her pulse in her ears was so loud she wondered if anyone else could hear it. She found Room 146 down a wide hallway with marble flooring. A plaque hanging on the door in front of the courtroom proclaimed: QUIET, PLEASE. COURT IS IN SESSION. It probably hung there all night. Bolted under a small window, another plaque was emblazoned with the name of the judge: Barbara Clardy. Frankie pushed open the door, which led to a small vestibule, then through another door to the courtroom.

The courtroom was shaped like a fan, with the elevated bench at the apex and an arc-shaped railing—the bar—framing the stage in front of the bench where the lawyers performed. The props were familiar to her, although her perspective had changed. As a prosecutor, she thought it only right that the prosecutor's table be the closest one to the jury box. Didn't the prosecutor represent the people? But as a defense lawyer, she didn't like the arrangement at all. Why should the defense be stuck against the far wall of the stage, like a useless piece of furniture, to fill up an empty space?

Husam al-Din and Lamar Gleason were sitting at the table for the plaintiff. As she came in, Gleason's voice tailed off like an echo. "Hello," she said to Husam. "Has Brooking showed up?" She put her bag on the floor under the table for the defendant and sat down without looking at Gleason.

"He is always on time, with seconds to spare," Husam said.

They waited in silence. At twenty minutes after the hour, the court reporter struggled through a door behind the bench with her equipment and adjusted the small black box on top of the tripod. She smiled at Husam, who smiled back, then perched on a stenographer's chair in front of the box and pulled through a ribbon of paper. She whacked the keys a few times, enough to satisfy herself that everything worked, then settled back in her chair, pulled out a nail file and perfected her nails.

At 3:29 by the clock on the wall, Brooking blasted through the door from the hall and rolled down the aisle to the stage in front of the bench like a bowling ball. Frankie hadn't seen or talked to him for a week. He said hello to Husam and sat down. "You look great, babe," he said, winking at her. "For a leper."

The bailiff and clerk came in at the same time, from the door behind the bench. They sat at their desks: the bailiff, out of the way, behind the defense table, and the clerk next to the bench. The door opened again, and the judge—a small, attractive black woman the same age as Frankie— swept into the room and trotted up the steps to her thronelike chair behind the bench. Frankie started to stand, but no one moved. "Where is the defendant?" the judge asked, sitting down. She peered at the people assembled below her as though she was their queen and they were petitioning for royal dispensation.

"I called, Judge, and what happened is they took him to the wrong courthouse," the bailiff said. "Over to District. What we have here is a failure of communication." He grinned. "He'll be along."

"Very well." The judge turned toward Husam al-Din and smiled. "Have you returned to us from the Department of Justice, Mr. al-Din?"

Husam stood up. "I have, Your Honor, for the present. I hope it will be permanent, but one never knows." He sounded tired. "The flight between the District and Chicago is now a boring experience."

The door to the courtroom opened and Richard Adamson, Jr., handcuffed and shackled at the ankles, shuffled in. Frankie stared at him with a concern she had never felt for a defendant before. The guard with him shut the door behind them and led Richard past the railing to one of the chairs at the defendant's table.

"I certainly hope you are Richard Adamson Junior," the judge said, nodding at the court reporter. "For the record. Are you?"

The court reporter sat up quickly and went to work. "Yes

I am," Richard said, looking past Slasstein to Frankie. He smiled at her.

"Good. Please be seated, Mr. Adamson."

"Can the iron come off, Judge?" Slasstein asked, jumping up. "There's a bailiff and a guard behind him, they're packing pistols. What's he gonna do we're afraid of?"

"Perhaps you can remove the handcuffs and leg bracelets, Officer," the judge suggested. The guard removed them and sat down in front of the rail, directly behind his prisoner. Rubbing his wrists, Richard also sat down. "It's twenty minutes before four o'clock. Shall we get started?"

Gleason pulled a yellow pad in front of him, like one of the lawyers. The court reporter checked her tape. As Husam walked slowly to the lectern, his manner suggested there were only two people in the courtroom of any significance: himself and the judge. "May it please the Court, this is the Government versus Richard Adam—"

"Yes, I think the court reporter can be relied on, Mr. al-Din. Can you give me the status? Just where are we on this little adventure?"

At first Frankie had liked the idea of having a woman judge. But her imperious air and droll sophistication had started to grate on her nerves. She listened to the prosecutor.

"On August twelfth, 1991, Mr. Adamson was indicted for murder," Husam said, "and certain related counts, concerning an incident that occurred in Washington, D.C., at the Rashidi Embassy, on July twenty-sixth. He is scheduled for arraignment on those charges tomorrow, at two P.M." Husam's voice had a nice urgency, lending a tone of importance to whatever he said. "Gerstein hearing held in Courtroom Ten on July twenty-ninth, the Monday following the incident, which took place on a Friday. Brooking Slasstein appeared for the defendant at that hearing. No bond was allowed and the preliminary hearing was set for August eighth. Before the preliminary, on August second, Frances Rommel filed an appearance as co-counsel with Mr. Slasstein."

Clardy, with the file in front of her, slowly turned its

pages. "What happened to the preliminary hearing?" she asked. "I don't see an order."

"If it please the Court, it was taken off the calendar when the Government filed its Motion to Disqualify on August sixth. Since that time, the Government has obtained an indictment from the grand jury, muting out the necessity for the preliminary."

Clardy watched Brooking, who sat at counsel table for the defense, hunched over a legal pad. "What's done is done," she said. "And so today, with all deliberate speed, we'll hear the Government's Motion to Disqualify. Have you anything to add, Mr. Slasstein?"

Brooking popped up like an empty bottle in water. "No, Your Honor." He sat down.

"Very well," Clardy said, watching the court reporter's fingers float slowly above the small box. "I've read over your motion, Mr. al-Din, and understand it as it relates to Frances Rommel, but it's a bit of a stretch, isn't it, to cover Mr. Slasstein with the same net?"

Husam al-Din, from his position behind the lectern, appeared actually to be looking down at the judge. "We believe information obtained by Ms. Rommel, and the tactics employed by her, must be imputed to Mr. Slasstein." His attitude spoke to the gravity of the situation. "It is our position, respectfully submitted, that he too must be disqualified."

"Isn't Mr. Adamson the subject of an extradition hearing in District Court?" Clardy asked. "Let me suggest that this unpleasantness may not be necessary. If the defendant is extradited, the problem will disappear." She made a slight tossing gesture with her hand and smiled.

"It will not disappear," Husam said in a voice that sounded like the call to prayer. "I have been informed that the Kingdom of Rashidi will withdraw its warrant for the arrest of the defendant."

The judge's smile died. *"That* is a disappointment. Apparently, then, there is no good reason to avoid the dilemma you wish me to resolve?"

"The Government does not believe so, Your Honor. It is

our belief the disqualification, should it occur, should take place before the defendant enters his plea, so that he may make suitable arrangements to engage new counsel. As previously stated, his arraignment is set for tomorrow afternoon."

"We'd better hurry along, then," Clardy said, glancing at the clock on the wall. "Mr. Slasstein and Miss Rommel, are you representing yourselves?"

Slasstein jumped to his feet. "Judge, I'm representing both of us."

She favored him with a regal smile. "Certainly you are aware of the folk wisdom surrounding that arrangement?"

"Something about a fool?" Brooking asked loudly. With a savage grin he turned toward Frankie. "Makes *me* a fool, don't know what that says about you, Frankie."

What kind of shot was that? "Speak for yourself," Frankie said angrily.

Clardy smiled with royal amusement at the antics of her subjects. "For the sake of clarification, what is the issue here? Mr. Slasstein, I'll hear from you first."

"Whether the Sixth Amendment means what it says." Brooking spoke with the rapid and forceful clarity of a machine gun. "Bill of Rights gives defendants the right to choose who they want to represent them. Sixth Amendment says a person charged with a crime can have the lawyer of his choice!"

He bounced around behind Frankie and Richard like a kid on a pogo stick. "This man has chosen me, and this woman, to defend him against a murder charge." He rested a hand on Frankie's shoulder and on Richard's, showing how the three were connected. "But the Government"—he extended a hand toward the tall prosecutor who loomed above him—"wants to deprive him of his constitutional right! The issue here is whether the Government can yank the teeth out of the Constitution!" He popped into his chair, sitting straight up, his feet barely touching the floor.

"Mr. al-Din, perhaps you will be so kind as to give me your version of the issue?"

The tall Arab had been watching his opponent with

amusement, from his station behind the lectern. He faced the judge. "Let me say at the outset, Your Honor, that the issue has nothing to do with teeth." Frankie was impressed with his ability. Even his barbed arrows were launched with dignity and composure. "No constitutional right is absolute, and that includes the right of a defendant to be represented by the lawyer of his choosing. What if Mr. Adamson wishes to be represented by me, for example? Or by the Court? Or by some person who does not wish to represent him? As with all other constitutional rights, there is a balance to be maintained." His calm demeanor epitomized the sought-after balance.

"Obvious," Slasstein hissed. "Be here all night."

Except for the court reporter, who recorded the comment, no one seemed to have heard it. "The public has an interest in maintaining the integrity of the judicial process," Husam al-Din continued. "The issue is whether this defendant's right to counsel of his choice must give way, because the integrity of the judicial process has been compromised. The evidence we offer at this hearing goes directly to that issue."

Frankie watched the tall prosecutor lean forward. He used his height advantage like Indians of old used lances; as props, to enhance their argument. "Our evidence will demonstrate that Miss Rommel—an attorney for the National Association of Special Prosecutors until the very day of her appearance in this case—took unfair tactical advantage of her NASP affiliation to obtain material information. We will show that she was sent to the District by the National Association of Special Prosecutors, an agency of the federal government, to prosecute this man whom she now represents! She resigned from that agency *after* using her position as prosecutor to gain material, nondiscoverable information, only to be hired, immediately, by the defendant!"

His outstretched arms rose slightly, expressing disbelief. "The integrity of the judicial process cannot tolerate such an assault."

Judge Clardy peered at Husam with regal amusement. "It

is apparent to the Court that this matter will be what is euphemistically regarded as 'hotly contested,'" she said, her small mouth pursed in a small smile. "Do we need a day? Two days? How many witnesses are there?"

Husam al-Din glanced at Brooking, who held his head down. "I have only one witness, and one exhibit, but will reserve the right to call both Miss Rommel and Mr. Slasstein, as adverse witnesses, under the Rule."

"Mr. Slasstein?"

"Depends on their evidence, Judge. We'll be calling witnesses, about all I can say."

"Why does this happen to me on the night when I have tickets to the opera?" Clardy asked, apparently of God. "Well. We will work until six o'clock. Mr. al-Din, it is your motion, and the burden of proof is yours. Call your first witness."

Husam nodded at Gleason, who rose majestically and marched to the witness stand. His manner was that of a crusader for truth. He would not look at either Frankie or Brooking, as though his outrage might spill over and cause him to lose control of himself. He was sworn in, then settled in his chair.

"Give us your name and occupation, please?"

"Lamar Gleason. Lieutenant, Capitol Police Department, an agency of the United States headquartered in Washington, D.C."

With a minimum of questions, Gleason testified as to his background and experience. Husam went on to another phase. "Lieutenant, as a part of the jurisdiction of the Capitol P.D., does it provide any special services for foreign embassies?"

"Yes it does." Gleason leaned back in his chair and looked toward the judge, aiming his gravelly voice in her direction. "Our officers guard the perimeter of all the foreign embassies in the District, to aid and assist any embassy in the event trouble develops inside, or a threat of trouble develops from the outside."

"In other words, you keep them under surveillance?"

"We do."

"Are the embassies aware of it?"

"They are. They appreciate it. Many of the smaller ones depend on it. We stay in touch with their own security guard personnel."

"Does your authority extend internally?" the tall prosecutor asked. "By that I mean this: Can your officers go inside an embassy without invitation?"

"No sir." He shifted his weight and stared directly at Husam. His chin was so high he had to look down his nose. "We can't even get a warrant. The inside of an embassy is privileged."

"Privileged!" Brooking said loudly. "What's that? A legal opinion? No objection."

Clardy smiled. "What was it, Mr. Slasstein? If it wasn't an objection, why did you make it?"

"Couldn't help myself, Judge. Every now and then something inside me pops." He glowered at Gleason with satisfaction.

"Mr. Slasstein," Clardy said firmly, "please refrain from not objecting, then. We don't have the time."

Brooking nodded an apology. Husam had the ability to ignore Slasstein as he might a beetle crawling on his pant leg. He continued as though there hadn't been any interruption. "Direct your attention to July twenty-sixth of this year, sir. Were members of the Capitol Police Department on duty near the embassy of the Kingdom of Rashidi?"

"They were."

Quickly, Husam established that at approximately two o'clock in the morning a homicide occurred inside the embassy, and the suspect was apprehended by Capitol P.D. officers outside it. Gleason further identified himself as the officer in charge of that investigation.

"Now direct your attention to July thirtieth, 1991. Did you have the occasion on that day to see a person who identified herself as Frances Rommel?"

"I did."

"Is that person in court today?"

76

"She is." Gleason frowned with distaste at Frankie, identifying her as "that person," then testified about their conversation. She told him who she was: an attorney with NASP, assigned to prosecute Richard Adamson, Jr. "We talked, must have talked, three hours about the case. I showed her everything the Government had up to that point: diagrams, notes of the officers in charge—everything."

Frankie had put hundreds of people on trial, but had never before been the subject of one herself. As she listened she struggled with her rage at the lies. On a legal pad, hard enough to poke holes in the paper, she wrote *What a crock!* and shoved the message under Brooking's nose. He nodded and pushed it out of the way.

"As you talked with her and showed her your file on the case, what did Ms. Rommel do?"

"Took notes." Gleason glared at her, his lips trembling. "Copious notes. Photostatic copies until the copy machine broke down. So she took some original documents with her, said she'd make copies and send the originals back to me. Far as I know, she's still got 'em. I laid out our hunches, theories, conclusions. She gobbled it up, asked some real tough questions, I thought we had us a real fine prosecutor."

"And then?"

"She hadn't been gone more than five minutes when I got a call from the U.S. Attorney's office. Don't know who. I was informed—"

"Objection," Slasstein said, bouncing to his feet. "Hearsay."

"This isn't a trial, if it please the Court," the prosecutor said, calmly and coolly. "The rules of evidence are relaxed at these pretrial hearings."

"I'll allow it."

Gleason described a conversation at which he was informed that Ms. Rommel had been pulled off the case. "The Kingdom of Rashidi, the way he said, wanted a prosecutor who could speak Arabic. Because many of the witnesses are Arabs, the Rashidis didn't see how someone who couldn't talk the language could prosecute the case. They'd complained to the State Department and—"

"Objection, Judge. Hearsay on top of hearsay, and opinion on top of that! One thing to relax the rules, another to demolish them."

"I agree. Mr. Husam, please tighten up the reins."

"Of course. Mr. Gleason, in this conversation, was anything said regarding the knowledge of Miss Rommel? Let me rephrase. Did this person tell you whether or not Miss Rommel knew she—and NASP—had been pulled off the case?"

"Yes sir."

"What was said?"

"I distinctly recall being told that Miss Rommel had personally been informed of the decision not to bring NASP in."

"Personally informed?"

"Yes sir."

"Then I take it she knew of that decision before coming to your office?"

"Yes sir."

Slowly, the tall prosecutor picked the legal pad off the lectern. "I have no further questions," he said, walking to his chair.

"Mr. Slasstein, cross-examine?"

Brooking approached the lectern with hesitation. He could barely see over the lectern, but refused to come out from behind it, as though it afforded him protection from the righteous sword of the witness. "Let's see, Gleason, Lamar, a lieutenant, right?"

"That's right."

"Been with the Capitol P.D. how long? I know, you said, I missed it." He seemed to sweat over his notes.

"Four years, sir."

Frankie sat up straight, appalled at the transformation that seemed to take place before her eyes. The great Brooking Slasstein? As she listened helplessly, she slumped in her chair. He was timid and hesitant and appeared to get caught in seeming blunders. No wonder he had to have help in the trial of a case. He was awful!

Worse than awful, she thought, listening and staring at the grain of the table. He was making their case. Like a hammer, pounding down nails in her coffin that had been missed the first time around, Slasstein found out even more about the mass of material Frankie had uncovered. "How did the two of you do all that in three hours?" he asked, as though impressed.

"She knew what she wanted," Gleason said, trying manfully not to snarl at her. "She knew exactly what to ask."

"Okay. So you testified she got there in the morning and you worked right through into the afternoon?"

"That's correct, counselor."

"Take a break for lunch?"

"No sir . . . Wait. Seems to me . . . I'm not sure. We might have."

"You don't remember? Everything else you got down so pat, but you don't remember a break for lunch?"

"Yes sir, we did, I remember now. Actually, we had a very short lunch before we started." His face seemed to darken with color.

Brooking emerged from behind the lectern. His manner had changed. "The fact is, Ms. Rommel arrived at your office just before lunchtime. Isn't that right?"

Gleason shifted in his chair and appeared to think. "That sounds about right, sir."

"And you had her wait in the lobby, you had to make a telephone call. Remember that?"

Gleason cleared his throat. His eyes darted toward Husam al-Din, who was obviously interested. He smiled. "Wouldn't surprise me. Things come up."

"You can do better than that," Brooking demanded loudly. "Do you or don't you remember asking Ms. Rommel to wait in the lobby while you made a telephone call?"

"I don't remember."

"You know Corporal Donna Larson, Capitol P.D., don't you, Lieutenant?"

"Yes sir."

"Who is she?"

"She's intake at our department. Works the intake desk."

"She's the receptionist, right? The first officer a person meets, they come in the police station off the street?"

"That's right, sir." He smiled affably.

"She keeps a record, all visitors, arrival and departure times, right?"

"Yes sir." He laughed with apparent good nature, but had started to sweat. "You know more about this than I do, sir."

"That's very possible, Lieutenant," Brooking assured him. "So you're telling me Larson does the telephone switchboard too, right? Corporal Larson?"

"I remember now, sir. I *did* ask Miss Rommel to wait in the lobby."

"Fine. Corporal Larson has her desk there in the lobby too, isn't that right? So she'd know if someone was sitting there?"

"Corporal Larson has her desk there, but—put it this way—Donna has a reputation. She's where she can do the least amount of damage."

"So you figured out where I'm going, now you'll paint Larson as a dim bulb. Okay. When you made this telephone call, who was it to?"

Gleason looked at Husam, as though for help. Husam sat with stiffness, waiting for his answer. "I don't remember."

"The Rashidi Embassy, right?"

Frankie felt the life rushing back into her soul. "No. I'd remember if it was them."

"So it was somebody else, you don't remember who?"

"That's correct, sir."

Slasstein made a point of making a note. "After your call, you went out to lunch, right? At"—he looked at the photostatic copy of an official-looking document— "11:52?"

"To the best of my recollection."

"You went to a Mexican restaurant, Carlos, on Massachusetts Avenue?"

"I don't think so. My recollection, we went to the Green Thumb, just a block from my office."

"That is your recollection?"

"It is."

Slasstein nodded. "Then you came back to your office"— he frowned at the same document, searching—"at 12:27?"

"That would be about right."

"You were alone at that time. Ms. Rommel was not with you, was she, Officer?"

"That is wrong, sir," he boomed, offended. "She was with me."

Slasstein bounded toward the clerk with the document in his hand. "Ask this be marked for identification as Defendant's Exhibit One."

"So ordered," Clardy said as the clerk pasted a small blue label on the document. She handed it back to Slasstein, who lunged with it toward the witness. "Officer, take a look at Defendant's Exhibit One." He shoved it at him. "Tell this Court what it is."

"All I can say is what it looks like. I don't know what it is."

"Good start. What does it look like?"

"Sort of like the visitor log we keep, Corporal Larson keeps, at the station."

"The woman who makes mistakes," Slasstein sneered. "You recognize her handwriting, Corporal Larson, don't you?"

"Yes."

"Her handwriting, the entries there, the times and people and destinations, right?"

Gleason kept his composure. "It appears to be her handwriting. But this is a photostatic copy and you can do anything with a copy."

"You accusing me of something here, Officer?"

"No sir. Stating a fact."

Slasstein looked at the clock on the far wall. It was five-thirty. "Request permission to call a witness out of order," he said.

Clardy did not appear thrilled by the prospect. "Wouldn't

it be more convenient to stop? Or, if it's Corporal Larson to authenticate the log, perhaps Mr. al-Din can be persuaded to stipulate. He's been known to do that."

"Corporal Larson is under subpoena for tomorrow, Judge. Someone else."

"Are you through with this witness?"

"Yes," Slasstein said impatiently. "No further questions of this witness," he added contemptuously. "Would work a real hardship on my witness who's in the hall if she has to come back."

"Can you finish with this person in half an hour?"

"Easy."

"Very well. Step down, please, Officer Gleason," Clardy said.

"Judge, I have some redirect," Husam al-Din said, standing. He peered stonily ahead.

"I'll allow you to recall Officer Gleason, but we'll hear this mystery witness now. Mr. Slasstein?"

Brooking bounded through the rail, down the aisle, and disappeared momentarily into the vestibule. A moment later the door opened and a dark-complected, blue-eyed stoutly built young woman with dyed red hair was ushered in. She was sworn, took the stand, and faced Slasstein, who moved away from the lectern so she could clearly see him.

With a few quick questions she was identified as Elvira O'Donnell, a waitress at Carlos, who had been working in that capacity on the day in question. She identified both Frankie and Gleason, whom she remembered seating. "What did they order, if you recall," Slasstein asked.

"They didn't order anything," the woman said, moving around in her chair, getting comfortable. "They were hardly there at all."

"But you remember them?"

"Yes sir."

"Describe to the judge what happened, Miss O'Donnell, just what you saw and heard."

"Just what I saw and heard," she repeated. "I was on the floor working tables, and just the usual buzz? You know, people talking and stuff. Then it just got quiet, you know, like there was this tension, and you can feel it and everybody kind of has their ears pointed at it? It's like you're afraid to look but don't want to miss anything, so you do."

"Where did you look?"

"At him and her." She smiled at them both, tentatively.

"Record reflect the witness identified Frances Rommel and Lamar Gleason, if it please the Court," Slasstein mumbled hurriedly.

"So ordered."

"What did you observe about them?" Slasstein asked.

"Their voices were kind of high, you know, like there was this real edge on them."

"Did they appear to you to be angry about something?"

"Yes!" She looked at Gleason, who slowly shook his head at the witness, as though in disbelief. She switched her glance to Frankie, who smiled back. "It was like they got *very* angry with each other. Then the man—he stayed cool—he told her if she didn't give him something, he'd put her under arrest."

"Did you hear the word arrest?"

"Yes sir."

"Who said it? The man or the woman?"

"The man did."

"Then what happened?"

"She could—like, she got self-conscious? Like she could see everybody in the place watching? So she got out of her chair—I think he kind of held her with his hand, but he let go—and she had this big purse, and put it on, and said, 'If you want to talk, we go outside.'" She was vaguely imitative of Frankie. "So that's what they did, him following her like he was a policeman."

"What did you do?"

"I—Well, I wanted to see what would happen? I thought, you know, like this is a drug bust, but the lady looked so nice, so . . ." She blushed. "I watched them. There's a little space between the doors. The foyer? I watched from in there."

"What did you see?"

"She just really looked angry. She faced him and I couldn't hear anything, but like she dared him to go ahead."

"What did he do?"

"Said something, then like he tipped his hat and walked away."

"Did she follow after him or go with him?"

"No! I wanted to go out, you know, see if I could help, but it wasn't any of my business." She glanced at Frankie, as though hoping for understanding. Frankie smiled back.

"How long did you watch?"

Her head leaned to one side. "Until both of them were gone."

"Did they go the same way, or different directions, or what?"

"The lady went down the hill toward the Capitol, the man went east, along Massachusetts."

"Do you know where the Capitol Police Building is?"

"It's just off Massachusetts?"

"Right," Brooking said. He sounded satisfied. "Did the man head in that direction?"

"Yes sir."

"Thank you. She's your witness, sir," Slasstein said, plopping in his chair.

Gleason had a grip on Husam al-Din's arm, whispering violently in his ear. The mask had slipped off his face, exposing purple rage. Frankie loved it. Husam pulled himself away and got up.

In a mild tone of voice, he tested Elvira's answers. He made her describe exactly where she had stood, suggesting she might not have been in a position to see anything. He also challenged her interest, asking whether she'd been paid to testify—she had not—and whether she knew Frankie from some previous association. There had been none. He finished by asking her to describe other things she had witnessed that day, such as what other customers had talked about or done that was unusual. She had to admit that she couldn't remember much of anything else. Staring coldly at Gleason, Husam announced he had no further questions, and sat down.

"Mr. Slasstein, do you have any redirect?" Clardy asked.

"No, Your Honor."

"Very well. You're excused, Miss O'Donnell. Thank you for coming." They watched her climb out of the box, smile uncertainly, and leave the courtroom. "We're adjourned until ten tomorrow morning," Clardy said. "You might try getting here a few minutes early, in case my docket clears." She stood up. Looking at the frowning prosecutor, she said: "Mr. al-Din, if there is a change in your position, please let me know as soon as possible. Will you do that?"

"Yes. Of course."

Slasstein loaded his briefcase with two scoops of his arms and blasted his way through the gate. "Got to run, Frankie," he said, before she could even stand. "See you tomorrow, kid," he said to Adamson.

"Wait a minute!" Frankie's heels tangled together when she tried to get out of her chair. She wanted to catch him, but he was already out the door. "Rick, I'll explain tomorrow," she said, mobilizing her energy to chase after Slasstein—when she saw something in Adamson's attitude. He looked too relaxed. But his eyes were on the guard and the bailiff and his body had coiled into a spring. "Don't!" she whispered tersely, then planted herself in front so he'd have to run over her too. She put both her hands on his shoulders. "Don't even think about it."

His green eyes registered surprise, then agony, then nothing. He settled back in his chair, refusing to look at her.

Frankie kept a hand on his shoulder as the guard snapped the bracelets in place. Only the two of them were in on the drama. "I hope you won't give anyone a reason to shoot you, Rick," she said, as though teasing him. The guard smiled at her. "I need you alive so I can defend you."

She had to sit down as the guard and Adamson shuffled down the aisle. She and the bailiff were alone in the courtroom. "I'll be just a minute," she said, trying to look busy.

"No hurry," he said, looking at his watch.

At nine o'clock that night, as Frankie watched the evening news, Slasstein called. "Don't go to court tomorrow ten, come down here seven, buy your lawyer breakfast, okay? We got to get busy on this case."

"What happened?"

"Husam just called. The Government will withdraw its motion."

"*You won it!*" Frankie shouted, coming off the couch. "God!" She took a deep breath. The tightness in her chest disappeared.

"Shssh!" he said. "What'd you expect?"

At three o'clock that morning the phone rang again, pulling her out of a deep, satisfying sleep. A mechanically altered voice, like a series of bad chords, reached out at her. "Cunt. Bitch. Cop killer. Know who I am?"

She waited.

"Chief Hansen's ghost, cunt. I'll see you in hell." The line went dead.

# 7

## Friday, August 16, 1991

The brass plate on the heavy double doors read BROOKING SLASSTEIN, ATTORNEY AT LAW. At fifteen minutes before seven that morning Frankie tried her key. The door was unlocked and she pushed it open, walking in.

She found Brooking at the large table in the law library, scribbling on a yellow pad, bunkered behind a stack of books. He sparkled like a jewel, in a gleaming silk white shirt, large black onyx cuff links, dark blue tie, and red suspenders. "Some fun, right?" he asked, not looking at her. "How often you get to rip the asshole out of a cop like Gleason, this business?" He traced words in a volume in front of him with the fingers of his left hand, wrote with his right hand, and talked with his mouth. "What you'd like to do every day of the week, but ain't it sweet when you get one? Be a couple minutes."

"He called me last night."

"Who?"

"Gleason."

Brooking jerked his head up. "Tell me."

She did. "He scares me."

"That's good. Stay scared. The man's dangerous." He leaned back in his chair, thinking. "You can't carry a gun this town, he can."

87

"I can carry a fish knife."

"Whoa, podnah!" He swallowed. "Can you use it?"

"I've cleaned enough fish."

He stuck a finger in his collar and loosened it, then thought of something. "What I'd like to know, is how he found out where you're staying. Anybody follow you?"

"I don't know." She plucked a hair from her skirt. "I don't spend my time looking over my shoulder."

"You're too normal, Frankie, need to be paranoid, your problem." He tapped his fingers. "We'll fix phones, record everything, get something on the bastard. Might do us some good." But then he lost interest. He picked up his pen and found his place. "We'll talk about it, make some plans," he said, concentrating on something else.

Frankie thought, whatever was done, she would have to do herself. What else was new? She shrugged off her mauve-colored coat and walked into her office to hang it up.

Her office had changed. The furniture had been upgraded: a large desk, worktable, high-tech modern chairs designed for comfort and efficiency, and computer keyboard, screen, and small printer on a credenza behind the desk. A small vase with flowers had been placed in the middle of the desk, next to the file: *United States* v. *Richard Adamson, Jr.* There were even respectable abstract paintings on the walls. Frankie was admiring them when Brooking bustled into the room, shoving his arms in his coat. "This is wonderful!" she said.

"Beacon must like you," he said. "She did all this, she don't even do it for me, I'm the one who pays her. Let's go."

As they walked down the street, Frankie had to lengthen her stride to keep up. His short legs moved so fast they blurred like spokes on a wheel. They turned off Indiana Avenue into the restaurant where he'd taken her before: Queen's Bench, an elegant hangout designed for well-heeled lawyers. "Only greasy spoon I trust in this town," Slasstein said. "Plus they run a tab on me."

"I'm buying this time. Remember? So you will tell me why it had to be me."

"Oh. Yeah. What you'll make on this case, you can afford it."

The booths were wood-paneled high-walled cubes with linen-covered tables and chairs, lined with leather upholstery. A waiter, dressed like a colonial period coachman, led them to one. After seating them, he brought coffee. "You know, you could have done a lot of things, that little trial by fire," Brooking said, shifting in his chair and leaning his arms on the table. He looked up at her. "You could have hired your own lawyer, or kicked it all over and run back to Denver, or shot Gleason, pushed me out a window, and slit your wrists. But you stuck it out."

Frankie smiled at him, watching the vapors rising from their cups and enjoying the scent. "It's the money," she said. "That, and the chance to watch a Washington original in action."

He beamed at her. "Want to know the definition of a perfect woman?"

"No!" She glared at him. "I want to get started. You've hired me to defend this kid, remember? I'm perfect for it?"

"Touchy. You heard it?"

"From Gleason."

He poured coffee. "Is that where I heard it?" He dropped a cube of sugar in his cup. "The extradition hearing is off, by the way, we don't need to worry, the Rashidis withdrew their warrant. Too bad, would've been a carnival, right?" He stirred in the sugar. "Arabs and feds fighting over who gets to tear Li'l Abner to shreds? But you know how it is, this business. Half the time, the fun stuff never happens."

Frankie picked up her coffee and tasted it. " 'Li'l Abner?' You mean Richard?"

"Who he reminds me of. Big muscle, brains of a fence post, can't figure out why I like him. Except he don't come from Dogpatch, an old man who's a fucking heart surgeon, works three days a week, makes millions. Sheesh."

"Is that what you see?"

"What else is there to a guy like that, silver platter syndrome I call it." He slurped down some coffee. "Arraignment is scheduled for today; great photo op, but I'm in District on a deal that'll take two seconds, the same time," he said, holding the cup near his chin. "You take it, make sure they ask about me, spell my name right, okay?" He glanced at his watch. "How you and Abner getting along?"

"He almost ran yesterday."

Brooking looked startled. "No shit. What happened?"

She told him, watching him frown, letting her own questions build. "He thinks we're working for the Rashidis."

"When did he tell you that?"

"Last week."

"I'll be damned, didn't think he had it in him." He put the coffee cup down. "You shoulda told me, Frankie."

"I couldn't. You wouldn't let me talk about the case."

"The dumb shit. He's supposed to trust you." He peeked at her. "*I'd* trust you, put my life in your hands, everything I got in your . . ."

He assessed her expression and changed his mind.

"Are we working for the Rashidis?" Frankie asked.

"Everybody is, thought you knew, they own the world." The cup rattled in his saucer as he picked it up again.

"Brooking, if we are setting him up for something, I quit."

"You care that much? Come on, he's a parasite, we kick him loose he'll sail around the world on his own yacht."

Frankie folded her arms and stared at the man who had hired her. "Are you going to tell me what's going on, or aren't you?" she asked. "Start with who's paying for his defense."

"Don't you know?"

"Don't play games with me, Brooking," she said angrily. "I know his family isn't. Who is?"

Brooking smiled. "Good. You're perfect this case, like Abe said." He looked as though he was trying to see if anyone was behind him without moving his head. "We aren't setting him up, Frankie, trust me. We are totally on his side."

"He needs to know that."

"Yeah." His fingers worked the linen tablecloth but his mind was somewhere else. "This morning, before the arraignment, see if you can get discovery."

"What are you waiting for, Brooking?"

"The waiter. I like knowing where everybody is."

She poured more coffee in her cup, smelling it. "While we wait, can you tell me why I'm so perfect?"

"Finding the right lawyer, you know, it's like casting actors for a movie, everything's got to fit. Schedule, background, looks, heart, ability, you got exactly what this case needs. You'll see. Wait'll we order, I start, I don't want some creep behind my back, okay?"

"I've waited this long. What about Husam. Is he any good?"

"The trouble with the Arab, he's relentless. He's also decent and fair, another problem." The waiter appeared and hovered over them. "Juries see it, they know he believes in his case, they love him." He looked over the menu. "You're buying, right? I'll take the steak and eggs," he said to the waiter, grinning at Frankie. "Fifteen dollars. What costs is the eggs."

Frankie stayed with lox and bagels. "I don't know." She watched the waiter move away. "His workup on the motion wasn't that great. He relied entirely on Gleason. Not to take away from your brilliant performance, but doesn't he have an investigator? Why didn't he check out his own facts?"

"Don't underestimate him," Brooking said. "He could be playing games with Gleason, Husam."

"Seriously?"

"If I know Gleason, he came on like J. Edgar Hoover, telling JFK how to run the government." He took his coffee cup with his long fingers and drank from it. "So Husam let him run the motion. Who do you think is in charge now?"

Frankie thought about it, leaning on the table. "I won't underestimate him." She watched his hand play with a crease in the linen.

He turned his head, as though to make sure no one was behind him, and leaned forward. "We could be in the eye of a hurricane, this case," he said, his eyes trying to protect his back. "Major culture clash, Mideast politics, billions of dollars, and God swirling around in the storm system."

Frankie straightened her back, hoping this was it. "Really," she said, brushing her hand along her thigh. "A melodrama?"

"No good. Melodramas work out in the end. The rent gets paid, the sweet little virgin keeps her purity, thank God. But who knows how this will play out? What do you know about Rashidi?"

"Not much." Brooking's hands were lean, strong, smooth, and pretty. Hers were scarred, tough, and stained with nicotine. "Only what I've read. An oil-producing Arab kingdom in the Mideast, like Saudi Arabia, only not as big."

"Ever hear of Nuri ibn abd al-Rashid?"

"No."

"The king of Rashidi." His expressive hands seemed to add: Da-da. "A Muslim, not like the Ayatollah, though, this guy's the enlightened monarch type. He makes noises about bringing his country into the modern world, you know, like establish a parliament, give women some rights, not too many." He provided her with a smug, male smile. "He ain't stupid. But for that part of the world, he's a revolutionary."

"Isn't the same process going on in Kuwait?"

"Has to there, we fought their fucking war, they better not forget. But the king of Rashidi isn't under pressure. Why give away power? Who the hell knows why he's doing it?"

"A good guy?" Frankie asked skeptically, spreading her fingers and examining her nails.

"There are good guys this world, you know," Brooking said.

"Sure there are."

"Okay. He's a Muslim, I'm a Jew, you're a Christian—maybe."

It was a question. She shrugged, but nodded in the affirmative, as though to say, more or less.

"So, the three religions connect, the Muslims say. We're all 'People of the Book.' But what they have in Rashidi is a theocracy, based on Islamic law. Like Saudi Arabia and Iran, some other places too. The way those people think, if the law comes from Allah, what do you need a parliament for?"

"So King Nuri has a problem."

"Serious. His subjects are very fundamentalist in their approach to religion and politics, like over here if the religious right took over, wouldn't *that* be a shot in the ass!" His eyes opened wide. "But the king has all this money, instead of building up an army to protect himself from other countries want to take it away, what any sane man would do, he wants to give it away to his people! Crazy." His head jerked, punctuating the king's craziness. "He sees how his people live in comparison with the West, wants to raise them up, but he's on *his* knees five times a day like everybody else. Very explosive, very tricky situation."

"Does this have anything to do with Richard Adamson Junior?" Frankie asked.

He crowded into the table, as though trying to touch her knees with his. "You wanted to know the money, right? Adamson's defense? It doesn't come from his old man, you found that much, here's the rest. Very confidential, Beacon don't even know, lives are at stake. You ready?"

Suddenly Frankie wasn't so sure. She put her hands in her lap. "How bad do I need to know?"

"You gotta know. So you can explain to the kid. We are totally on his side, he needs to understand, keep him from doing anything dumb." Frankie nodded her agreement. Brooking let his voice drop even further. "King Nuri's daughter-in-law is paying the bill."

Frankie tried to fit this information in its proper place. "Brooking. Is there really a princess?"

His eyes glittered as his head rocked in the affirmative. "Why I hired you, babe, why you're perfect for this case. The kid broke a princess out of the embassy, killed a man to save her life, they were gonna take her back to Rashidi and execute her. Choice of evils. Abe says you wrote the book."

It took a moment for Frankie to absorb what Brooking

93

had said. Without thinking she pulled out a cigarette and lit it. "The Government doesn't know?" Then she remembered why this was the first cigarette of the day: she had quit.

"I don't know what they know. You read the papers. The Rashidis won't talk about a princess, the feds deny it, but if they *do* know about her, bet your sweet buns they're looking."

"Wheee!" Frankie said, her mind churning with excitement. "This is marvelous! An Arabian princess!" He frowned at her, as though warning her to keep her voice low. Questions flooded through her brain. "Except I didn't think Arab women were allowed to own anything."

"You got to get the players straight." Brooking barely spoke above a whisper. "The princess with the money isn't the one the kid busted out. Nuri's daughter-in-law, in her early forties, Hanifah, she's the bank. Her husband, the king's son, got killed racing speedboats or some damn thing. Hanifah's loaded, got her own Swiss bank account, Sahar is Hanifah's daughter, a seventeen-year-old kid. Sahar's a princess too, and she's the one Richard liberated."

"Brooking. I should be paying you to try this case."

He grinned. "You want, we can renegotiate."

"Does the king know what his daughter-in-law is doing?"

"No. What happened, I got this call, London, Princess Hanifah. We dance around, she's trying to figure out if she can trust me, I'm trying to figure out who the hell she is. She calls again, says something she has to do for her daughter, all she wants to know is how much. I don't want the case, but let's see how high she'll go, she doesn't bat an eye, I can't believe it." He waved his hand at Frankie's cigarette and she moved it out of the way. "The money's in an escrow account, we get paid like I told you, the source isn't named in the instructions, but it's Hanifah. She says the king, nobody else in Rashidi, must ever find out."

"Then who knows?"

"You, me, Hanifah, Sahar. We're it."

Frankie let the possibilities soak in. A lawyer's dream, if they could prove it. "This is wonderful!" she said. "I'll be defending Robin Hood! Where is Sahar?"

"I don't know." Slasstein pushed himself back, glancing over his shoulder.

"I'll have to talk to her sometime. We'll need her at the trial." She knocked a long ash into the ashtray.

Brooking stroked his chin: a mannerism Frankie hadn't seen. "We do?"

"Of course! She's the one he rescued. What about Hanifah? Can I talk to her?"

"No way. She's out of the picture."

Frankie inhaled deeply. "Brooking, how do we prove this great case without witnesses?"

"Why I hired you, babe. You'll think of something."

"Does Hanifah know where Sahar is?"

"Yeah, but she won't say. If she was a good daughter-in-law, she'd tell the old man. Then they'd snatch Sahar up and haul her butt back to Rashidi." He shuddered. "Instead, she's a mother first, what I hear that's rare in that part of the world."

"Mothers are mothers, for God's sake!"

Brooking lifted his shoulders and showed her his palms. "The way I get it, in the Arabic world, tribal loyalty outweighs motherhood. Everything they do is for the good of the family."

"Who decides what's good for the family?" Frankie wanted to know.

"The patriarch, babe. The men are in charge."

Frankie butted her cigarette and looked at the stains between her fingers. "What would Nuri do to Sahar?"

He shrugged, then drew a finger across his throat.

"Brooking! Good King Nuri? For what?"

"Look, I don't get these people, they take all the fun out of sex. Hanifah said they got caught in the sack, you know, a couple of kids. Big deal."

The waiter set a tray on a folding platform and served them their food. The steak and eggs smelled wonderful to Frankie at first. She had broiled lots of beef in Lander, and her grandfather would smear his breakfast steak with ketchup. But the garlic and blood on Brooking's platter made her nauseous instead of hungry. She watched Brooking's eyes turn greedy with lust.

"Allah doesn't allow hanky-pank," he said, picking up his fork and knife. "The family is dishonored."

Slowly, Frankie folded a thin slice of lox over the toasted bagel. Her grandfather would have laughed at the things she ate. "Why is Hanifah doing this?" She watched him cut through the steak. "Why doesn't she just give Sahar the money she's paying us, so the girl can run off to Venezuela or somewhere?"

"You got me. That's between them." He stuck a piece of red meat into a bright yellow egg yolk, swirled it around, and plopped it in his mouth. From the expression on his face, Frankie knew he had just been transported off the face of this earth and into a better one. "Needs some ground pepper. Where is that guy?"

Frankie looked for the waiter, caught his eye, and motioned him over. Brooking made grinding gestures with his hands as he chewed, and the waiter scurried off. She played with her food. The thought of executing Sahar sickened her.

The waiter appeared with the long pepper grinder, and Brooking pointed at his whole plate. Before letting him go, everything on the plate was coated with coal dust. "Perfect." He waved the waiter off, cut off a large piece of meat and shoved it in his mouth. "Be a hotshot defense lawyer, tell me. How bad do we need Sahar, we gonna win this thing?"

"I don't see how we prove it without her." She watched him chew. "I don't feel well."

"Eat. Put some meat on your bones." He cut off another large hunk of steak and speared it with his fork. "Sahar has to testify what would happen, they take her to Rashidi, right? How our hero saved her neck from her nice old grandpa?" He shoved the fork in his face.

"Yes," Frankie said, thinking of all the colorful alibis that defendants had paraded before juries, which she had shot out of the saddle. "If we can't do that, she's just another fairy tale."

* * *

The air was still cool when they walked back to the office. The sky, a deep blue, gently touched the abundant foliage—grasses, leafy trees, and shrubs—like a caressing hand, providing nourishment. Frankie couldn't get her grandfather out of her mind—not that she wanted to. He had brought her to his ranch after the highway death of her parents. With a firm, steady, wonderfully masculine hand, he had guided her through the perils of childhood: school, boys, vastly important questions, idiot small town attitudes, life's cruelties. Somehow he had filled her with a sense of the wonder and beauty of life beneath the bullshit.

In the process, he had provided her with a sense of her own worth. What would it have done to her soul, or psyche, or whatever "it" was, to know—if she crossed over some cultural line—he'd have killed her?

At shortly before ten that morning she was on the street again. The air had warmed and thickened with humidity, like soup. She thought of calling a cab, but it was only three blocks to the U.S. Attorney's office, and she liked listening to the sound of her high heels clicking along on the sidewalk. Entering the fortress on Fourth Street was welcome relief, like climbing inside a refrigerator.

Husam al-Din, wearing a neatly pressed blue pinstripe suit, waited at the top of the stairs for her. With grave courtesy he escorted her toward his office. "It is nice to see you after the unpleasantness," he said. "Lamar Gleason is my witness, but not my most trusted companion."

She hadn't known how he would receive her after the hearing on the motion. "I'm glad we cleared that little hurdle too," she said, brushing hair over her shoulder and smiling. "Now, if you'd just dismiss . . ."

He lifted an eyebrow and opened the door for her. "Please, sit down. You may smoke if you wish."

She sat in the government-gray-metal chair in front of his desk and watched him circle around to his desk chair and sit down. His room was more cheerful than Roy Grantland's tomb, she thought, crossing her legs and pulling her skirt over her knees. There were landscapes and seascapes on the walls, diplomas, and certificates proclaiming the courts Husam had been admitted to practice before.

"I have made inquiries about you," Husam said. "Unless, now that you are defense lawyer and have changed the stripes, I am told you are a very pleasant person to try a case with. You handle yourself like a man."

"Is that supposed to be a compliment?" Frankie opened her handbag and yanked out a cigarette. She didn't see the ashtray.

"My apology. I meant only you are professional, and do not attempt to take feminine advantage."

"Husam, I'll take any advantage I can get," she said, lighting the white stick in her hand. "Fortunately, most men are too dumb to know it. Where's the ashtray?"

"So." He jumped up and grabbed one off the top of the bookcase. "The men you have battled in the courtroom are dumb. I shall tell them what you say."

"Good."

"Coffee?" he asked, putting the ashtray down and pushing the file toward her. "I will train for this trial, like a dumb man. I will wait on you with my hands and feet."

"I'd love a cup. Is it okay to look in here?" she asked, touching the file as he walked toward the door.

"Yes," he said. Frankie couldn't tell whether he was enjoying the exchange or not. "We have secret cameras. I will know if you steal anything."

The discovery practices in the different courts where Frankie had practiced were as varied as their geography and location, and she didn't know quite what to expect in the District. In Colorado it was a statutory right, and in most of the state was as wide-open as the sky. But in Georgia and California it was buried under the weight of case law and available only to those defendants who could figure out how to get it.

In the federal courts, pursuant to Federal Rule 16, it had been turned into the greatest game of all. When the government gave it to the defense, they dealt it out like face cards in a game of stud poker. The defense could never be quite sure what was in the hole card, which the government wouldn't show until the trial. Also, a quid pro quo ingredient had been grafted on to the procedure. By asking for discovery, the defense opened itself up to the prospect of having to give it.

"Can I get copies of reports I want?" she asked Husam when he returned with coffee.

"I am sorry, but office regulations do not permit." He cleaned off a metal worktable along the wall. "However, you are entitled to copy anything in the file in longhand. Please." He looked at his watch. "Take your time."

Frankie moved her chair, ashtray, and coffee to the worktable. She would not be pressured by any nonverbal messages he might choose to send, and fully intended to take all the time necessary. Quickly, she was engrossed in the file.

She made notes and sketched the meticulously drawn diagrams: the first, an overview of the embassy and legation grounds, showing the position of the high fence between them and a shrub where a climber's rope and grappling hook had been found; the second, a floor plan of a portion of the second floor of the embassy, keyed to the first diagram and showing in greater detail the area immediately surrounding the balcony where the crime occurred; and the third, focused on the balcony itself, locating the body of the victim, scuffle marks, and the smears of blood on the railing and the deck.

DNA test results on the blood had been ordered and were pending. However, preliminary indications showed the blood had come from two sources: the victim and the defendant.

Husam waited patiently at his desk for her to finish, occupying himself with paperwork. The regulations required him to stay in the same room with the file while the defense lawyer went through it, and when she turned around, he was watching her. "Can we talk?"

"Of course."

"Do you have any photographs?"

"They are with the exhibits at the Capitol Police Building. When you wish to see them, I will give you a letter."

Frankie made a face. "Who do I give the letter to? Gleason?"

"Yes." He raised his shoulders. "There is no other way."

It will be interesting, Frankie thought. "What else is over there?"

"The pistol your client was carrying when he was arrested. The climbing equipment used to climb to the balcony. The knife. It has been cleaned and no longer drips blood." He smiled ghoulishly, for the first time showing what might be characterized as humor. "The clothing of the victim and the defendant is still at the FBI lab. You may view them there and talk directly with the technician. I will provide names."

"Has the climbing equipment been matched to Adamson?" Frankie asked, glancing at the scenes on the walls of his office. Leaves and trees, mountains and beach—no portraits or people. "Fingerprints or anything?" He wore a ring on his finger. Shouldn't he have a picture of his wife or family somewhere? She didn't see one.

"Not at this time."

"What about to the balcony? Any transference?"

He made a note, as though to remind himself. "I do not believe it has been checked for such purpose."

"I've been sitting too long," Frankie said, standing and stretching her back. "So Adamson climbed up to the balcony and waited for the victim to come out?"

"Yes."

"How did he know Abdul Hafiz would do that?"

"His name was Abd al-Hafiz," Husam said, correcting her. "With sacred meaning in Islam. He was Servant of Allah the Guardian. Abdul Hafiz could have a blasphemous meaning."

"Oh." Frankie filed the knowledge away. She might use it on cross-examination to get under the skin of a witness. "My question?"

"Mr. Adamson had worked for the Rashidi security force. Abd al-Hafiz was the head of the security forces. He discharged Adamson from employment. Abd al-Hafiz ap-

100

parently was in the habit of checking that balcony, a routine of which Adamson obviously was familiar."

"Why was he fired?"

"A sexual impropriety, I do not know yet the details."

Frankie sat down and crossed her legs. "'Apparently' in the habit of checking the balcony?"

"Yes."

"Old American proverb, Husam," she said, swinging the top leg back and forth. "When prosecutor says 'apparently,' it translates to 'best guess.' Do you have evidence of such a routine, or are you guessing?"

Husam smiled. "At present it is of speculative nature. But at trial time, I am confident of proof."

"You will of course make the evidence available to me in advance?"

"You may expect from me all matters which I am bound to provide you, under the law."

"I hope you don't mind if I wander around," Frankie said, getting up and going over to his window.

"I do not mind."

"So he sneaked on the legation grounds, went through that gate in the fence between the legation and the embassy grounds, around the corner of the building"—she drew her finger around a corner—"to the balcony, and waited for Abd al-Hafiz?"

"Essentially, that will be our proof."

"Wouldn't he have set off an alarm?" She stared out the window, across Fourth Street, at the rubble in the vacant lot.

"There was in place a very simple electric circuit alarm system along the fence between the grounds." Husam swiveled in her direction to see what she was watching. "It was made deliberately simple because the gate between the buildings was used with such frequency. Opening the gate would break the current and set off an alarm in the embassy. Our investigation shows that someone—obviously Adamson, meaning best guess—strung a wire between the posts of the gate. When your client passed through the gate, there was no break in the circuitry."

101

"Okay. Then he climbed on the balcony with the grappling hook and rope, waited for Abd—the victim—stabbed him when he came out, jumped off the balcony, threw away the grappling hook and rope, and ran out the way he came in?" She faced him and tried to read his expression. It told her nothing.

"So it would seem." He smiled pleasantly.

"Did he do anything else?" Frankie asked, fishing. "Or was he just satisfied with killing Abd al-Hafiz? Did I get it right?"

"You sound like Arab woman. There are rumors, started by Mr. Adamson's sister in California, of the swashbuckling liberation of an Arabian princess. The girl has been questioned by officers and admits she made such stories up. Perhaps you have other information?"

Frankie shrugged. "No." She walked back to the worktable and picked up her notes. "Another question. If Adamson waited for Abd al-Hafiz on the balcony, then stabbed him when he came out, how did the two of them get so banged up?" His head leaned to one side. "I'm talking about the autopsy, and Adamson's condition when he was arrested."

"I am aware of what you are talking about." He seemed to catch the severity of his voice, and forced himself to sound pleasant. "Cuts and bruises on knees and hands, blood smears everywhere, the broken collarbone—the victim, not the clean, wholesome defendant, of course."

"A fight, don't you think? What I don't understand is, why didn't they spill over the edge?"

"I suggest that you ask your client for the answer," he said sardonically. "Unfortunately, I cannot."

"What about pistols? The reports don't indicate it, but I assume the victim had one too?"

Husam frowned. "I had not thought of that," he said, making a note of his own. "Thank you. With two heads, we arrive at the truth, don't you agree?" He smiled at her with satisfaction. "I will make inquiries."

Frankie realized her mistake. She might have embarrassed him with questions about another pistol at the trial, or even claimed something helpful to her case, such as that the weapon on Richard really belonged to the victim. But he would have thought of it. "Yes. Truth will out," she said ironically. "Isn't that what the system is all about?" She handed him the file and stuffed her notes in her briefcase, snapping it shut. "I'll see you in court," she said, looping the belt over her shoulder and looking at the clock on the wall.

Time flies when you're having fun. The arraignment was less than an hour away.

# 8

Frankie cringed at the performance taking place in Judge Barbara Clardy's courtroom. She watched from a seat in front of the bar, near the empty jury box. "This offends the whole concept of justice!" the public defender—a young, sincere, carefully groomed black man proclaimed.

His client—a small white man with large horn-rimmed glasses—was scheduled to be tried for illegally possessing drugs. He had been arrested for murder, and when the police searched him following his arrest, drugs were found in his pockets. The irony was that the police had arrested the wrong man. "Probable cause is required to make a valid arrest," the lawyer begged. "Without that, any evidence seized by the police is tainted. How can there be probable cause to arrest a man for a crime he didn't commit? If there is such a thing as 'justice,' the only conceivable answer is: it can't happen!"

"It does seem unfair, doesn't it?" Clardy spoke with sympathy, but Frankie heard a suggestion of malice. "Unfortunately, your client matches the description of the man the police were looking for. I must therefore find there was probable cause to make the arrest." She smiled at the obviously crestfallen young man. "Your motion to suppress the evidence is denied."

"But—"

"No buts, Mr. Terry. You can appeal if you wish— assuming your client is convicted." The lawyer obviously had more to say. His mouth remained open and his right index finger continued to point toward the wall behind the judge. Clardy glanced toward her clerk. "Call the next case."

*"United States versus Richard Adamson Junior,"* the clerk said. Her small desk was attached to the bench like a turret, and she handed the file to the judge.

Frankie waited for the lawyer and his client to give up their places on the legal stage. They limped away, and she moved to the defense table, wondering if her client would be Clardy's next victim.

Several court watchers had come into the room. Four conservatively dressed men with dark complexions and dark eyes were bunched together in the second row: the Rashidi contingent. A casually dressed young woman, her blond hair in a large Afro, sat directly behind the bar with a shorthand notebook in her lap. Probably a reporter. A small woman with dark eyes and intensely black hair sat on the prosecution side of the aisle. She wore a full dress, low shoes, gloves and a hat. She reminded Frankie of a nun on vacation.

"Good afternoon, counsel," the judge said. "I hope this won't be as involved as our last encounter. Aren't we missing someone?" She sounded businesslike but bored. "Ah. The defendant. Didn't we go through this little charade yesterday?"

"Perhaps he gives bad directions," Husam suggested.

The rear door opened and the shackled prisoner, in the company of his guard, shuffled down the aisle. Frankie took a deep breath, glad to know Rick hadn't been killed, trying to run. "Please remove the ankle and wrist bracelets," Clardy said.

"We don't like to do that, Judge," the guard said. The beefy, reddish-faced white man had the attitude of an old salt. "He won't be here that long."

Frankie liked Rick better in irons too. Clardy wouldn't get

any help from her. "Officer, this is a court of law, not a chain gang," the pint-sized woman judge said. "Take them off."

"Yes ma'am." Everyone waited until Adamson was seated next to Frankie. He rubbed his wrists and scratched his ankles.

"Proceed, Mr. al-Din."

Husam spread his file on the lectern. "Present is the defendant Richard Adamson Junior, with his lawyer Frances Rommel," he said matter-of-factly. "This matter comes on at this time for arraignment. An indictment was returned by the grand jury on August twelfth, 1991, charging the defendant with one count of murder, one count of illegal possession of a firearm, and one count of burglary."

Clardy turned toward Rick. "Will the defendant please stand?" Frankie and Richard got up. "You've heard the United States attorney, Mr. Adamson. Would you like me to read the indictment?"

He looked questioningly at Frankie. "If it please the Court, we'd like a copy of it, but we'll waive the reading of it," Frankie said.

Husam handed her a document. "The record should show I've given counsel a copy of the indictment."

"Noted," Clardy said. "Mr. Adamson. To Count One of the indictment, how do you plead, sir?"

"Not guilty."

"To Count Two, what is your plea?"

"Not guilty."

"And to Count Three, what is your plea?"

"Not guilty."

"I must say this matter is so far without surprise. The clerk will set the cause for a trial to a jury and advise you of the date." She looked at the clock on the wall. "Ms. Rommel, I'll allow you thirty days to file pretrial motions. What can I expect?"

"I don't know at this point, Judge. We won't waste your time."

"I hope not. Anything further?" She held the gavel in her hand, ready to whack it on the marble plate in front of her and call the next case.

"Yes, Judge." Frankie leaned on the tips of her fingers as she spoke. "Mr. al-Din gave me some discovery this morning, and I learned that the firearm allegedly carried by my client is at the Capitol Police Department. I'd like it examined by our expert, but want to make sure no one touches it until that can be arranged."

"What do you want from me?"

"An interim order, giving me time to work out the details. The weapon needs to be examined for fingerprints, and I'd request that the Capitol Police Department be instructed to carefully bag it until a proper motion and order can be submitted."

"So ordered. Mr. al-Din, please see to it."

Husam, from his position at the lectern, peered down at her. "Yes, Your Honor." When he was pissed, he went into neutral.

"Anything else?"

"I'd like to talk to my client before he goes back to the detention center," Frankie said. "Is that possible?"

"Use one of the witness rooms." Clardy smiled at the marshal. "You will assist, sir."

"Judge, my orders is—"

"You have a new set of orders. Anything else?" She smiled around the room. "Going once, going twice . . ." She tapped the marble plate with her gavel. "Call the next case."

"We're done until three o'clock, Judge," the clerk said.

"Really!" Clardy stood imperiously and descended from her throne. "I actually have time to go to the rest room!"

Frankie kept her eyes on Rick. "What do you think of the judge?" she asked, ready to grab him if he tried to bolt.

He couldn't seem to look at her. "I thought judges were like generals," he said. "I didn't think they had to use the rest room."

"Stay where you're at, Adamson," the guard commanded. With the judge gone, he was back in charge. "Miss Rommel, you'll have to wait in the witness room. I'll bring him to you, soon as the courtroom is cleared."

"Whatever you say." Relieved, Frankie picked up her briefcase and met Husam at the gate.

He opened it for her. "Fingerprints?" he asked. "What do you expect to find?"

"You never know until you look."

Husam glanced at the small, overly dressed woman with the black hair, then seemed to dismiss her. The woman with the notepad stood expectantly, listening to them as they started down the aisle. "I'm from the *Post*," she said. "Is there some question about the pistol? Like, did it belong to some other person?"

The lawyers exchanged glances. "I have no comment," Husam said.

"Ms. Rommel?" Her pen was over her notebook.

"Mr. Adamson is being represented by Brooking Slasstein, and me. We have serious reservations about the Government's case."

"What are they?" she asked, writing it down.

"We've only now started to look into it, and can't say anything more at this time without jeopardizing Mr. Adamson's situation."

"Was he looking for a princess?" she asked.

"I don't even know what you're talking about," Frankie said, turning away.

"We have no indication of any such nonsense," Husam added emphatically.

The woman with black hair hesitated a moment, glanced toward Husam, then walked out of the courtroom. "Do you know her?" Frankie asked as they moved away from the reporter.

"She is my wife."

Frankie glanced at the Rashidis as they walked by. Husam said something to them in Arabic, then insisted on taking Frankie to the witness room. They passed through the first set of doors, into a small foyer between the courtroom and the hallway. Small rooms were on the sides. He opened the one to his left, reached inside and switched on a light. "I will inform the guard."

Frankie plopped a legal pad on the table in front of her, hung her briefcase on one of the chairs, and sat down facing the door. Through the small windowpane she saw Husam leave with the four men.

When the door opened and the marshal brought Richard into the room, he was shackled. It offended her, even though she felt safer. "Take that stuff off."

"No way, lady. I'm responsible." He stepped into the vestibule and shut the door behind him, smirked at her through the window, then disappeared.

Frankie glared at the door, for Rick's benefit. "If I leave you to complain to the judge, you may not be here when I get back."

"It's all right," he said, sitting down across from her. The chain between his wrists clanked against the table. He hadn't shaved from the day before, and in the closeness of the room she could smell him. "It removes temptation."

"How are they treating you?"

"Like an animal." He grimaced, showing his clean teeth and strong, bony face. "They're zoo keepers, but not bad guys for zoo keepers. They take care of the animals." Frankie liked his toughness. "The only animals they mistreat are those that act up." He wouldn't need someone to feel sorry for him. "Do me a favor."

"What?"

"Stay out of the way."

Frankie smiled at him. If he'd been silhouetted in a picture book for jurors, they might color him in as a hero. Or a jerk. She wasn't sure there was a difference. "Sahar is safe," she told him, watching his head jerk forward and his eyes break open. "You don't need to save her again."

Her comment got his attention. "Where is she?"

"Hiding. Who knows?"

He gulped air, like a drowning man who'd been rescued. "How do you know?"

"Brooking talked to her mother. Her mother is paying for your defense."

He looked like someone whose migraine headache had just quit. The tension went off his face and a peaceful smile replaced it. His eyelids came down. "Hanifah. God love her. Can you get her a message?"

"I can try."

"Tell her thanks."

"Can I also tell her you won't do anything stupid?"

He smiled. "Yeah." He opened his eyes and looked at Frankie.

It felt great, and Frankie lapped it up. She had never had an experience like this as a prosecutor. Her client's dream-filled eyes seemed to surround her, holding her head in place and exploring her mind. Apparently they were satisfied with what they saw—when, with a jolt, Frankie realized he trusted her. She straightened her spine and looked at her notes, a bit frightened. "I spent the morning at the U.S. Attorney's office. Do you want to know how you did it?"

"Hey. I was there."

"I mean, the way they think you did it. And why."

"Sure."

She spread the sketches of the diagrams in front of him and explained the prosecution theory. He didn't interrupt, but when she looked at him, she saw cynical amusement. "They've also done a preliminary match of the blood on the railing to you—or apparently to you. They haven't done DNA, but the matches they have indicate that some of the blood on him came from you, and some of the blood on your clothes came from him. They found some blood on the railing too. It appears to be yours."

"Where's the burglary?" he asked. "According to them, I didn't even go inside!"

"Not necessary. Burglary means an entry with the intent to commit a crime. Case law says being on a balcony is an entry, and they say the crime you intended to do was murder."

"What about all that blood? What does that mean?"

"They can put you on the balcony where Abd al-Hafiz's body was first found." She put her hands on her thighs and pushed, stretching her back. "They can't put the knife in your hand—quite—but the inference is there. You and Hafiz were on the balcony, and that's where you stabbed him."

She was surprised by his expression: anguish. "I didn't want to."

"Rick. The whole thing was in him. Even the handle. Was that an accident?"

He shook his head slowly and looked at his hands. "I didn't even think about killing him. I just wanted to shut him up."

The anguish would play. The rest of it needed a rewrite. "Why the funny face when I told you what you did?" she asked.

"You mean me, standing on the lawn, throwing hooks?" He made a motion with his hands as though he was shooting a basket. "Sure glad I didn't miss and hit a window!"

"Isn't that what you did?"

"No. The grounds would have lit up like the inside of a pinball machine. I came in through the parking garage."

*That* was interesting. "How did you manage that?"

"I'd been a driver and made my own set of keys. I hid in the trunk of the car I used to drive and let them take me in."

"This is going too fast," Frankie said, trying to absorb it. She lit a cigarette, crossed her legs and hovered over her legal pad. "You broke in the embassy to rescue her, right?"

"Yes."

"How did you know her? She was a princess and you were a guard. Since when does royalty associate with the hired help?"

"I was her chauffeur. But I'd known her in Rashidi before the Gulf War."

"Can that be documented? Any witnesses?"

"You mean like diplomats?"

"Anyone who might have seen you with her in Rashidi," Frankie told him.

"I'll make a list. They wouldn't have seen much, though."

"Just get me their names." She thought a moment. "Did you know she was here?"

The love in his eyes would play too. "I knew she was coming. She told me in a letter that the king was sending her to America."

111

Frankie wrote with excitement. "Where is it? The letter?"

"Letters. Five of them. In the top file drawer of my rolltop desk."

The search for evidence had never been as fun. She wrote it down. "So what happened? You were discharged?"

He nodded. "Practically the day after the war. I went right to work for the Rashidis."

"When did you become Sahar's chauffeur?"

"Mid-March. Right after she got here."

"What happened?"

He looked really goofy. "She was supposed to see what America is all about, so we drove around a lot. I was her guide, and she was teaching me Arabic." He smiled. "We fell in love and got married."

"This is getting better," Frankie said, scribbling on her pad. "Where?"

"The Pembarton Oaks Hotel, in Arlington," he said. When she looked at him, he dared her to find it funny.

"When?" she asked.

"The third day of Shawwal, in the Hegirian year 1411."

"What does that mean?"

"April nineteenth, 1991."

"You'd better explain."

He stared at the wall. "The Muslims have a prayer, *istikhara,* for guidance. She got here during Ramadan, their holy month, and couldn't eat, so we never went to restaurants. But after we got to know each other better . . ." He sighed. "She told me about *istikhara.* We asked for guidance. Then we were married."

Frankie tried not to look too skeptical. "Stop me if I'm wrong, but I have the impression there was no preacher, or judge, or marriage certificate?" Just lots and lots of hormones, she thought, trying not to break apart with laughter.

"I know how it looks."

Frankie stared at her pad, long enough to control her face. "Don't the Muslims have certain marriage formalities, which possibly weren't exactly observed?"

"That's why we did the prayer," he said steadily. "If we'd tried to follow the letter of Islamic law, the marriage wouldn't have been allowed. We followed the true spirit, though."

"Did you become a Muslim?"

"No." He opened the palms of his hands to her. "I can't. I mean, I can believe in Allah and Muhammad, but they say that's all you can believe in. I like believing in Buddha too, and Sweet Medicine, and Wovoka, and—"

Frankie raised her hand, shutting off his nonsense. "Do you really believe you were married?"

She saw the obstinance of youth. "We were and are married, and it's eternal. What does the law have to do with it?"

Oh dear, she thought. One of those. "Did anyone know about it, except the two of you?"

"No."

"So then what happened?"

They were at the Pembarton Oaks Hotel, where they always went. Big mistake, he realized now, because he should never have taken her to the same place more than once. He had his coat, tie, and shoes off and his shirt undone. Sahar had stripped to panties, bra, and slip. They were on the bed, staring at the ceiling, holding hands and talking, when four Rashidis blew into the room, using a key. Probably they bought it from the hotel clerk. They beat him, questioned him, beat him, warned him, and let him go.

"You told them you weren't doing anything wrong, right? You were married?"

"No." He looked at the floor. "I was terrified. It didn't even occur to me to tell the truth."

"Oh?" Frankie asked. Surprise. "How did you explain being in bed with her?"

"A bullshit story." He covered his face with his hands, rattling the chains. " 'Not to worry, guys. We're just watching movies.' "

Frankie crossed her arms in front of her, not feeling as much sympathy as she should. "Why didn't you tell them?"

"I panicked." He peeked through his hands. "They'd have killed me—only I don't really know that. It's what I thought."

"What happened to Sahar?"

"They took her to the embassy and accused her of *zina*. They were going to take her back to Rashidi, for justice."

"What do you mean by *zina?*"

"Fornication outside of marriage."

"She couldn't walk away from them? They let *you* go. Why not her?"

"I'm an American. There'd have been an investigation. She's a princess." He sighed. "That makes her just another woman." The chains around his hands rattled. "They were going to take her back to Rashidi and execute her."

"For what? I mean"—Frankie couldn't keep the evil little smirk off her face—"at its worst, you were just—"

His pale green eyes had a computer-generated clarity. "When an Arabic woman dishonors her family, the traditional punishment is stoning. Although a Saudi princess, about ten years ago, got a break. They shot her in the back of the head instead."

Frankie scribbled furiously. "How do you know this?"

"I told you. I was stationed there."

"Did you actually see an execution?"

"I saw a woman get stoned, and a man lose his head."

"Really." Frankie touched the pen with her tongue. "So you broke her out, and she got away, but you were caught?" she asked, confirming the obvious.

"Yes."

"How come she made it and you didn't?"

"A friend of mine on a motorbike was waiting for her at the gate."

"What's his name?"

Rick shook his head. "Sorry. I promised him."

"Don't be a hero, Rick. You're in big trouble." She leaned toward him. "Sahar might not be able to testify, for ex—"

"Sahar doesn't testify. Period. That would be suicide. They'd find her."

Frankie arched her back, trying to stretch the tension out of her spine. "Give me your buddy's name, then."

He thought about it. "Not yet."

At least she knew it was a buddy. "We could have a defense here," she told him cautiously.

"Like, I could walk away from this thing?"

"It's possible." She rubbed her chin with the fingers of her left hand and picked up her notes. "The fence between the legation and the embassy. Are they right about that much? Did you wire the gate?"

"I did that the night before."

"Why?"

"So my buddy could wait there without setting off an alarm."

"Then the next day, you got in the trunk of the car and broke in?"

"Right."

Frankie dropped her cigarette on the floor and crushed it. "In other words, you prepared your escape route before you went in?"

"Yes."

Thoughtfully, she played with a wad of hair. Planning ahead could mean a lot of things, like deliberation, lying in wait, specific intent. "The car. You just happened to see it on the street?"

"A Texaco station near Dupont Circle does lubes on their cars and keeps them shiny. I waited for mine that afternoon—I told you about the key—and when nobody was around, I got in."

"That was better than the other way in?"

He rested his elbows on the table. "Frankie, I'd never have made it if I went in the way they say. They have electronic beams—a grid system—that covers the grounds." He pointed at the diagram Frankie had drawn. "Not there," he said, referring to the legation side of the fence. "Here. The embassy. They turn it on at ten every night, and nothing gets through without setting off the alarm. Not even squirrels."

"But when you came out, isn't that what you did? Set off alarms?"

He nodded vigorously. "The place lit up like a concert stage. That's why Rory waited for us at the gate. I knew we'd be smoking!"

His buddy's name was Rory. Frankie acted as though she hadn't heard. "When you went into the embassy to get Sahar out, you didn't think you'd have to kill anyone, did you?"

"I was ready. But I sure didn't want to."

Frankie tapped her teeth with her pen. For choice of evils, it had to be cleaner than that. "Let me explain something to you. Under our law, murder is as bad as it gets. A person can kill in self-defense, but that isn't murder. It's self-defense. A person can kill accidentally, but that isn't murder either. It's accidental homicide, or manslaughter, or something less than murder. Are you still there?"

He nodded.

"Choice of evils means you can commit a lesser wrong in order to avoid a greater one. Let's assume we can prove Sahar would have been executed if she'd been taken back to Rashidi." It wasn't that simple, but Frankie didn't want to bog down in a treatise. "If we get that far, we should be able to get the judge to rule her execution would have been a greater wrong than for you to break in their embassy. Then it would be okay for you to break in. Do you follow?"

He smiled. "Yes."

"But it wouldn't be okay for you to break in if you knew you were going to have to kill somebody." There were exceptions naturally, which was the nature of the beast. Frankie ignored all the confusing, contradictory complexities. "My question: Did you *know*, when you broke in, you were going to have to kill?"

"No." That wonderful expression of anguish worked its way onto his face. Frankie loved it. "I didn't know that at all. I thought we'd make it without hurting anyone. Just their damned pride."

The door opened and Beacon stuck her head in. The friendly red-faced marshal stood behind her. "Miss Rommel?" Beacon said timidly. "Something quite urgent at the office. Can you finish up quickly?"

"What is it?" Frankie asked, annoyed at the interruption. She looked at her watch: 2:45 P.M.

116

"Someone wants to see you. It's quite important that you be there."

"Who?"

Beacon looked distressed. "A young woman. From a foreign country." She blushed. "I gather a dear friend of Mr. Adamson."

Frankie jumped up, wondering how she could be so stupid. "I'll be right there."

# 9

Beacon led the way. The office was close to the courthouse, and Beacon knew how to negotiate the trip between the two without going out and into the heat, except to cross streets. Still, Frankie could feel perspiration on her forehead and under her arms.

"Is she there now?" Frankie asked, hurrying along.

"No, dear," Beacon said, holding her elbow. Clearly, Frankie had been adopted by the good woman. "She's on her way." She glanced eagerly at Frankie. "She's a princess, isn't she?"

"I think so. It's all very hush-hush."

"How very exciting."

Brooking sat behind his teakwood executive desk, hunched over a legal pad, when Frankie entered his office. He'd changed into a freshly pressed navy-blue suit, a white silk shirt with a bluish tint, and gold cuff links. "You made it. Good." He nodded at Beacon, who shut the door behind her. "The plot thickens, right?"

Frankie glanced around the room. A regal-looking high-backed chair had been placed directly in front of Brooking's desk, like a throne. A smaller chair sat at a corner, close enough to put a pad on the surface. Frankie sat in the small one. "So tell me."

Brooking pushed the pad out of the way. "Rotten timing, I'm due back in District 3:45, Judge Alexander. Alexander the Great." He looked at his watch. "I'm out of court ten minutes ago, hotfoot it over here, but Beacon knows I gotta go back. She says a call I gotta make, ask for Sahar. It's the YWCA lobby, they put this girl on. Sheesh. She says she's leaving the country, her life depends on getting a message to Rick Adamson. No kidding. Ain't young love great? So I suggest a meeting, she's on her way."

"Leaving the country!" Frankie exclaimed. "We don't need that." She tapped her fingers on the desk. "We need a strategy." She pulled her skirt tight and sat up straight.

The hollow sound of an engaged intercom invaded the room. "Mr. Slasstein?" Beacon's voice announced. "Your appointment is here."

He punched a button. "Just a sec." He let go. "How's this. I introduce you, tell her what a great lawyer you are, then leave. You find out what she means, leave the country, where she's going, how long, when she's coming back, you know. I'm in the law library, something comes up."

Frankie felt her mouth get tight and stern, like a fifth grade schoolteacher. She wanted Brooking there. Too much was at stake. "I like you here, Brooking," she said. "You might see something I don't."

"What do you want, a stroke? You can handle it." He punched the button. "We're ready," he said to the speaker.

When the door opened, Brooking jumped to his feet, all charm. "Come in! Thanks, Beacon."

Frankie stood up also. When she saw the princess, she understood Brooking's reaction. The young woman was stunningly beautiful. She moved into the room with a reserve that was perfect, as though the loveliest deer in the world had been dropped into a new forest. Beacon closed the door behind her. "You are Mr. Slasstein?" she asked. Her soft voice had its own vibrant life, carrying into every corner.

"I am, Your Highness." Brooking danced around the desk and stuck out his hand, but a reluctance in the girl's manner stopped him. He covered any embarrassment by pulling the chair with the high back out another foot, bowing toward it, then trotting back to his place behind his desk. "This is Frances Rommel."

"I am please to meet you," she said, nodding at both of them. "I am Sahar bint Rashid."

Frankie fell instantly under the spell of this magnificent creature. Her startling hazel eyes, the classic perfection of her face, the soft brilliance of her long black hair, and the radiance of her complexion were enough to cause a train wreck in Wyoming. She was as tall as Frankie and dressed in a richly tailored brown pleated skirt that covered her knees. A long-sleeved mahogany-tinted blouse fit loosely over her arms and breasts, but did not hide their fullness. She wore no jewelry. She didn't need any.

"Please to sit down," Sahar said. "Mr. Slasstein, forgive me for my manners with you. I am awkward in the presence of a man, especially a Jew."

Brooking had started to sit. He stopped and stared at her with his mouth open. A short laugh pushed out of his face. "Hey. I should apologize?"

"No no no." She smiled and sat with easy grace. "I am very grateful to you, and wish to explain myself. It is difficult for woman of Rashidi to sit with informality with a man. Also in my country, we are taught this prejudice of the Jew. I only wish to explain in the desire not to embarrass you."

There was no hint of guile or malice in her expression. Frankie watched as Brooking melted under her straight-ahead gaze. "You don't embarrass me, Princess. You charm me." When he dropped his face to look at the top of his desk, Frankie realized he was trying to hide the fact that he was blushing.

"Please, Mr. Slasstein," she said, her alert eyes roaming around the room. "I am most comfortable when addressed by name, Sahar. To be called 'Princess'"—she laughed—"often, people laugh."

Brooking looked surprised. "You want I should call you Sahar?"

"That is my wish."

"Okay." He beamed with pleasure. "You call me Brooking, I won't feel so old."

The young woman smiled. "Brooking," she said, as though testing her ability to make the sound. "And your associate?"

"She's my partner this deal, Sahar. Call her Frankie."

The princess appeared confused. "This is a man's name?"

"In our country it works either way."

She burst into laughter. "Oh! That is so funny!" she said, drying the tears that formed in her eyes. Frankie smiled at the girl's delight. Brooking, like a clown, gratefully accepted what could be measured as applause. "What does this mean, that she is 'partner in this deal'?"

"She's a lawyer, same as me, only better," Brooking explained. "She'll work with me on the case."

"I have seen in the newsprint. But a woman? That is allowed?"

Brooking shrugged his shoulders comically. "The judge is a woman too."

Sahar frowned. "Does this not . . ." She stopped, struggling for the right phrase. ". . . create difficulty?"

"Not really," Frankie said. "Should it?"

"Perhaps not," she said, smiling. "But such mixture of women with men is unthinkable in Rashidi."

Brooking got up. "Princess—I'm sorry." He slapped himself on the cheek, as though to punish himself for the mistake. "Sahar. Can I get you coffee?"

"A cup of tea perhaps?"

"Of course. How about you, babe?"

"Coffee. Black."

Sahar watched with amazement as Brooking left the room. He closed the door behind him. "Have you respect for him?"

"He drives me crazy. But he's good. Don't be misled by his nuttiness."

"He does not expect for you to pour the refreshment?"

"He'd better not."

Sahar took a deep breath, then looked toward the ceiling in a gesture that seemed to ask for help. "There is so little time. Please, forgive my conduct." She placed a cool hand on Frankie's arm. "We barely meet. But I must confide in you."

"Hadn't we better wait for Brooking?"

"This is for your ears only." Her voice became heavily dramatic. "My instinct tells me to trust you with this confidence rather than a man who is also a Jew."

"Sahar, Brooking is the lawyer who was hired to do this case." She could hear the reproach in her voice, but would not insist on political correctness. "I'll do a lot of the actual work, but we're on it together." Sahar questioned her with a look. "Whatever you tell me, I'll pass on to him. That's the way it is."

Sahar lowered her head, seeming to look inside herself for an answer. When she lifted her chin, her eyes were steady, clear, and focused. It was like being smiled upon by a person of wisdom and maturity, rather than a seventeen-year-old girl. "Perhaps the man who is a Jew can be trusted. But I give this to you." She smiled her lovely smile. "You will know what to do."

"Whatever you say."

She took Frankie's hands and stared dramatically in her eyes. "I have used Rick. This man I love is not who I live for." Frankie tried to keep her surprise from showing. "I love Rick with my heart, but another commands my soul. I am on a mission for this other being, and pray my Rick is not destroyed by events that I, Sahar bint Rashid, must set into motion because of this task."

"You're on a mission?" She squeezed the girl's hands with encouragement, but felt like a hypocrite.

"Yes. I am the servant of God, and He has tell me what I must do." Sahar let go and sank back in her chair.

Frankie had the awful sensation that this magnificent creature was certifiable. Would this great defense depend on the testimony of a crazy? "Does Rick know?" she asked, forcing a meeting of eyes.

The door opened abruptly. Brooking quickly entered and shut it behind him, leaning against it as though blocking it. "Trouble, ladies, don't panic." He glanced at Frankie. "Your buddy Gleason, out in the main hall, got a paper looks like a warrant. You got to sneak the princess out of here the back way."

Both women rose quickly. "I do not understand," Sahar said. "What does this mean?"

Brooking crossed the room toward the exit all lawyer's offices are equipped with: a door into a back hall. "This way, Sahar. Frankie, get her outta here, explain about a material witness." He held the door open, looking a bit like Napoleon at the height of his powers.

"Where will I take her?"

"Outside, flag a cab, make sure she isn't followed, move it."

"But there is my driver," Sahar said, her eyes wide with excitement. "He will not know what to do. He speaks no English!"

"Where is he?" Brooking asked.

"He is parked on the street."

"Perfect!" Brooking said. "Frankie, go with her, they aren't looking for two ladies, only one. They don't know her car, make sure she gets in, stay long enough to see if she's followed, come back. Hurry now! Gleason's got a warrant, he won't fool around."

What was Brooking up to? Frankie wondered. Cops worked off descriptions of people. Having Frankie along wouldn't change a thing. "Get outta here!" he hissed. Sahar started running down the back hall, and Frankie followed.

"One other thing!" Brooking hollered. They stopped. "Sahar, you still need to talk to my partner here. How about your place? Like, in the morning?"

"No good," Frankie said. "I could lead them right to her."

"Don't worry about it, I'll get you there," Brooking said, then disappeared in his office.

Sahar took Frankie by the hand. "Come! We must hurry!"

They trotted down the back steps, slipped out the rear exit into the alley, and walked as calmly as possible toward the cul-de-sac in front of the building. Sahar whispered her address and gave Frankie her telephone number. They agreed on ten o'clock the next morning. Frankie went through the motions of seeing whether anyone followed them out of the building, then hung back as Sahar walked briskly on. Sahar's driver, in a brown uniform, stood beside a gleaming black Chrysler Imperial. He opened the door for her, and as Frankie went through the charade of watching closely, they sped off.

A few minutes later Frankie found Brooking sprawled casually on the couch in the office lobby, reading the paper. "Has Gleason been and gone?" she asked. "Why didn't I bump into him?"

"Gleason? What're you talking, Gleason?" He continued reading.

"Put the damn paper down!"

He lowered it and glanced over the top. "What's the problem?"

"Brooking, goddamn it, she was parked on the street in a limousine! Why wasn't she picked up?"

"Nobody's after her." He turned the pages inside out. "If the feds wanted her this town, they'd have her by now, she ain't that hard to find."

"Then what was that little game all about?"

"Sahar doesn't want to talk to me, right, I'm a Jew? But she wants to be your buddy. Let her."

"How do you know what Sahar said to me?"

He folded the paper and put it down. "It's wired. Me and Beacon listened in."

"Brooking!"

"Hey, I got a wire in my own office, that against the law?" He sat up and glared at her. "She's the case, right, we gotta have her? So work with her. She wants to take you into her confidence, let her." He started to stand. "Don't tell her you're gonna tell me, what difference? Hey. She tells you something you don't want me to know, you keep it."

"I thought you'd want—"

"Government lawyers, all the same," he said. "Tell her, Beacon." He sauntered toward the door of his office. "Frankie. What I want to do is win."

* * *

Husam did not wish to deal with Abir. He hoped by the time he returned to his office that she would have grown tired of waiting and gone home. But his secretary had let her in, and his wife had the patience of a rock in the desert. As he hung up his coat he could feel her eyes. "What brings you to my office, Abir?" he asked, affecting the posture of a man with grave responsibility and very little time. He sat down behind his desk and picked up a file.

"Our daughter has come home."

He avoided her eyes. "She must leave. She no longer lives in our house." He shouldn't have to explain to his wife this thing. They had not talked of Kawthar since the girl had tried to force him to meet her so-called boss. In fact, they had not talked at all. His house had become a place of silence.

"I have tell her this, but she will not go. She cries."

"She cries!" He opened the file. "She must leave, Abir." Husam could not describe to anyone the way he felt. His daughter had been the cause of his humiliation. He felt like dry ice. If someone were to touch him, their fingers would burn. "She dresses like a whore. Let her become one." He stared with a fury he could barely control at his wife. None of this would have happened if she had given him a son. "I have no sympathy for your daughter, who has taken from me my respect. My grandfather would order me to kill her."

"Husam!" She covered her face with her hands.

He glanced at his watch. "I have work, Abir. Please go."

# 10

## Saturday, August 17, 1991

Sahar opened the door. "It is so nice to see you again!" she said, her radiant face beaming at Frankie. "You are most welcome in my house." She took Frankie's hand and pulled her into the room.

The walls of the large room were a luxuriant cream-brown that held the muted light filtering through a large skylight in the ceiling. There was no furniture other than pillows, thick rugs, and a low table barely a foot above the floor. An ornate silver kettle, matching goblets, and a pot of incense were arranged on its surface.

Frankie had worn a casual blue suit, and at Sahar's request took off her coat and removed her shoes. Sahar was dressed in flowing silken pantalettes, dark purple with floral patterns woven in, and a short-sleeved golden silk shirt. Frankie felt like a guest in an Arabic dream. "Please. Sit here, where there is comfort."

Frankie leaned her back and elbow into a soft cushion near the table and tried to get comfortable. She had no idea what to expect, but was determined not to show surprise. The incense cooked on a hot plate, and occasional wisps of cedar-scented smoke rose from it. "I love the smell of cedar," she said, watching the princess. With slow, deliberate grace that was a pleasure to watch, Sahar—kneeling near it—lifted hair away from her scalp and directed the vapors toward the roots of her hair. "It reminds me of Wyoming." It didn't. Nobody burned cedar in Lander. Only pine and aspen.

"Wyoming?"

"Where I'm from."

Frankie planned to move slowly. Maybe the lunacy of yesterday was a temporary aberration, like the skittishness of a springtime colt. She would ask her list of questions only if the answers didn't come up in their conversation. "I have hear of Wyoming," Sahar said. "The land of cowboys and Indians. We have these too, in Rashidi." Frankie stretched out her legs as though in front of a campfire. "The bedouin of the desert, who are sometimes like cowboys and other times they are the Indians." Frankie smiled, leaning on her palms. "May I ask personal questions?" Sahar asked.

"Sure." The princess sounded imminently sane.

"Are you religious person?"

Frankie didn't want to step off with the wrong foot, but knew she was way too irreverent to get far with a lie to that one. "Not really. I used to go to church, but that was a long time ago."

"A Christian church?" Sahar asked, pouring liquid into the cups. It was tea, and the Lipton labels hanging out of the elegant service seemed out of place.

"Yes."

"Yet, you have married a Jew?"

"Do you mean Brooking?"

Sahar glanced at her with curiosity and nodded, as though to say, Of course.

"We're not married. Why do you think so?" Frankie asked, wondering if it mattered.

"The ease between you! Can there be such freedom between unmarried man and woman?"

"Happens all the time."

"Is not this dangerous?"

"Sometimes. But it's like driving a car. You learn to accept the risks."

Sahar smiled at the answer. "In my country, women do

not drive a car." She handed Frankie a cup of tea. "You are not married?"

"No."

"Then you have no children?" She sat easily, with her legs under her. Leaning on one hand and teacup in the other, she waited expectantly for the answer.

"No."

"What is your reason for life?"

Frankie held the tea with both hands and decided to answer with honesty—at least until she could figure out what Sahar was driving at. "My work. My hobbies. I don't know." With a gesture, she declined the offer of cream and sugar. "Do I need a reason?"

"May I ask, do you prefer the company of women, or of men?" Sahar asked, stirring thick cream into her cup.

"I like both," Frankie said. The cups were exquisite porcelain. Delicate-looking flowers had been painted on the sides and bottom—when it occurred to her that Sahar might have asked about something else. "Do you mean sexually?"

Sahar nodded, her curious eyes wide with fascination.

"I only do men in bed."

A cloud seemed to have blown into the sky. "You are not chaste woman?"

At first Frankie heard it as "chased," and translated it to "pursued." Then she realized the princess was critical of her sexual habits. "I am not a chaste person," she said firmly.

"You have had many lovers?"

Frankie assessed the expression of the princess, which was an odd mix of aversion and interest. "A few," she said.

"Have you a lover now?"

"No." Frankie sat up straight, to show this child she had nothing to be ashamed of. "Unfortunately."

Sahar broke into laughter. With a spontaneous gesture she touched Frankie on the arm. "Yes!" she said, acknowledging that she knew whereof Frankie spoke.

"Is this important?"

Sahar's expression changed. She shrugged. Frankie had the sense she was searching for a way to say what she meant, clearly and honestly. "I am curious. I have many—expectations?" She fluffed her hair. "From childhood in Rashidi, I bring expectations to the conversation. I also feel for you a sympathy."

"You don't need to feel sorry for me."

"No no no." Once again she reached out a hand and touched Frankie. "I mean for you, a rapport. A feeling of trust."

Frankie smiled. "I hope so."

Sahar rested her cup on the table and moved to a sitting position. "As Christian, do you know the story of Joan of Arc?"

Frankie lifted her shoulders. "I saw the movie."

"Oh? I did not know."

"It's a very old film. Please." She tasted the tea, which was as bitter and strong as aspen bark. "I didn't mean to distract you."

Sahar raised her hand slowly and stretched her neck. Like a flower reaching for the sun, she gently ruffled the hair behind her ear with palm exposed. Please God, don't let her be a nut, Frankie thought with a pang. She moved like a goddess, with perfect composure, responding with a sensuous grace and dignity to some inner itch. "In Switzerland, I read the story of Saint Joan, the Maid of Orleans. In the language of *français*. I ask of myself, can this be true? A young girl of thirteen years, who hears the voices of saints?" Her hand slowly descended into her lap. "I study her life with much interest. She hears voices, and they tell her what she must do."

Does the girl hear voices? Frankie asked, as tactfully as she could: "Is some unseen person talking to you?"

Sahar shook her head. "As a girl, the only voice I hear in my ears is my own. As a young child, it talks to me of happy things. But then it changes. From the age of nine, my voice shrieks loudly at me, in torment. My brain becomes a whirl of hate and fear, and my heart a volcano of rage." She stared with sadness at Frankie. "There was no place in my head for voices from saints."

Frankie set her cup down with care. "What happened?"

"I have a nurse, whom I love for her wisdom and gentleness. From a window overlooking the square in Qahtan, I watch as she is stoned by her accusers." The tips of Sahar's fingers touched her forehead. "I hear my nurse cry out in pain. I observe the cloth sack that binds her turn brown with blood. It takes forever for her to die."

Frankie sat transfixed. Sahar shifted her knees in front of her and hooked her arms over them. She tossed her head, allowing her lustrous hair to swarm over her shoulders. "Does a child of nine have an understanding of such things? I will tell you: yes. I had hatred in my heart for all things that could cause such pain. I had hatred for Allah. If He was merciful, why did He allow this to happen? Could He not protect my nurse from such death? Why did He not form her—all women—as men?"

"No wonder you felt like that," Frankie said, leaning toward her. "What an awful thing for a girl to see."

Sahar brushed her hair and smiled easily. "Since that time, Allah has stilled the confusion in my brain and has filled my heart with peace. I believe Allah has a reason to show to me, Sahar bint Rashid, this brutal act." She touched her bosom with the fingers of her hands. "I demand answers of Him! I do not care what He thinks of me! He must ease this torment in my soul." Her voice rose and faded with her emotions. "He hears me and forgives my anger. In His own time, He tells me what I must do." Her head moved gently to one side. "I do not hear voices, as did Joan of Arc. But my heart is filled with His purpose. It brings peace to my soul."

Frankie felt her own heart fall through the floor. She had had ideals too, when she was seventeen. She'd believed the wrongs of the world would be righted by riding through Mississippi on an integrated bus. But the foreboding she felt warned her that Sahar's mission was more involved. "Saint Joan wears the clothing of a man," Sahar continued. Yet her eyes glowed with what looked like love, rather than fanaticism. "I come dressed as a woman."

Frankie shifted her legs and sucked skeptically on her lip. "Do you see yourself as a saint?" she asked.

Sahar lifted her shoulders. "What is that but a label, given by men to those they would deify. I have no interest in being deified. The vision I have of myself is a woman, appointed by God. I believe the story of Joan of Arc is there for my guidance." Her young face shined with eagerness. "There is no doubt of the accomplishment of Joan of Arc. It is a fact, recorded in history, that this girl of seventeen years led an army of soldiers to victory against mightier forces!" Her long fingers moved with expressive grace, like those of a ballet dancer. "This simple peasant girl who cannot even read, follows commands from her voices, and defeats the English!"

Think positively, Frankie told herself. At least she doesn't wear funny hats.

"You think of me as crazy?" Sahar gently asked.

Frankie touched Sahar's arm before answering. "You trust me, don't you?" she asked, wondering if she could successfully lie to this person about anything. "The quality in me that you have sympathy for is my honesty, right?" Sahar nodded. "I have to tell you, Sahar. I don't know what to think. I'm trying to make up my mind."

Sahar clapped her hands in appreciation. "I am right about you! You will know what to do."

There was nothing particularly subtle about her mannerisms, Frankie decided. "Knowing what to do has never been a problem for me." She sat up straight. "I'm not always right, but I'm never in doubt."

"Yes?" Sahar asked uncertainly.

"An expression, Princess. It means I have confidence."

Gravely, Sahar nodded. "There are misunderstandings of expression that may come between us like weeds. We pull them up."

"You bet."

Sahar leaned back, smiling at the ceiling, but Frankie waited for the next misunderstanding. The girl's expression changed slowly into one of sadness. "In three days, I return to Rashidi."

All of Frankie's muscles seemed to tighten at the same moment. "Rashidi! Rick saved you from that!"

"My Rick saves me from the quick and awful anger of my

131

grandfather, the king. Now Allah tells me to return, to fulfill His purpose."

So *that* was what her voices wanted her to do. Frankie shuddered. "Isn't that dangerous? Aren't you afraid they'll—"

"I cannot allow the actions of my life to be controlled by fear." She stroked an ankle with her hand. "I have pray for guidance, and that is what my soul says to my heart."

"Sahar. Shouldn't you listen to your fears too?" Frankie sounded calm and reasonable, which was not what she felt. "They speak to your heart as much as this voice in your soul, don't they?"

"Oh yes. My fears tell me to stay in this country. They wish me to have my baby in America."

"Baby!" Frankie lifted to her knees. "You're going to have a baby?"

"Yes."

"Sahar. You *must* listen to me." Frankie settled back on her heels, forcing the intensity out of her voice. "You are a very intelligent woman. You can't seriously believe that Allah would ask you to do such a thing." She leaned forward, touching Sahar on the wrist. "He might ask you to take a chance with your own life. But do you have the right to risk the life of your child?"

"My life, and that of my child, belong to God. If that is His wish, I have the obligation to obey."

Frankie sat back on her heels and brushed hair away from her face. What should she do? Tell the princess if she really believed that, she needed therapy? "What does Allah want you to do?"

Sahar swung her feet to another position and leaned on the palm of her left hand. "I spread a message of hope to all believers. I release my people from the terrible bondage of the past."

Her tone remained soft and sane instead of disconnected and wild. Frankie scratched her temple. "How dangerous will it be?"

Sahar sighed as she shrugged. "This message can be seen

as blasphemy by the learned men of Rashidi. The punishment for blasphemy is death." She smiled. "But will Allah tell me to go, and not protect me?"

Frankie hated this. She turned away from the girl in utter frustration. "What can possibly be so important to your people that you would consider this?"

"Please try to understand," Sahar said, quietly and with patience. "Allah has tell to me that the Qur'an has been distorted. Many words spoken to the Prophet by the Angel Gabriel have been falsely reported. I have the duty to present the truth."

Frankie hugged her arms to her body, as though to protect herself from a chill. "I don't need to know this," she said. "There are a couple of things *you* need to understand, though."

"My friend," Sahar said, with something like royal impatience, "you must listen to me. For it is you who will know what to do."

"You keep telling me that." Frankie reined in her anger and raised her shoulders.

"Please. Allow me to explain."

Frankie leaned back on her hands. "All right."

"In Islam, Qur'an is regarded—literally—as the written word of God." Sahar's speech patterns were inflected with an odd, almost exotic cadence. "The words were spoken to the Prophet by the Angel Gabriel. But Muhammad could neither read nor write, and so these words were etched on Muhammad's soul." Her hands moved with compelling expressiveness. "Muhammad recite these words of God to others. They burn into hearts with searing, cleansing sharpness, like the calligrapher's torch. As Muhammad speaks, they are instantly written in their hearts too."

She paused, allowing her hands to indicate a point of significance. "This, you must appreciate. The Qur'an is not made into writing by the Prophet. The recording of words on paper was done by men of fallible minds, who arrange them into books and verses, many years after the Prophet's death." Frankie nodded, encouraging the girl to cut to the chase. "My message to my people, and to the Islamic world, is that those who wrote the Qur'an made errors. They did not truly copy the words of God."

Frankie shrank back. She had a horror of religious fanaticism, and from the look of it, this lovely girl was a fanatic. "So Allah has told you what He really meant. Right?"

Sahar nodded. Her eyes continued to shine with love, not craziness. "Allah has tell to me that women are the true equal of men. Therefore, when a man and woman join in marriage—a true marriage—they are one. They become one soul." Her hands opened and lifted with wonder, then dropped back into her lap. "However, men of power, who transcribe Allah's words, cannot accept such truths and distort them. They conform His words to old and traditional ways to think, raising the man above the woman. And so life, to this day, remains brutal to the women in my country. They continue to die by stones."

"If you go back, that's the message?"

"Yes."

Frankie got up. She could no longer sit. All she could think was that this magnificent creature would be sacrificed to dark-age mentality. "Will anyone hear you?" she asked. "Do you really think you'll live long enough to spread it?"

Sahar looked away from Frankie. Her expression showed concern. "It is true, I have many fears."

"Then stay here!" Frankie said, kneeling in front of her and touching her on the shoulder. "Speak from here if you have to. Just don't go back."

"I must." She gazed at Frankie with the trusting look of a child. "I am a princess, with rank, which allows me to speak in my country, even though I am a woman. And I know the Qur'an as well as Joan of Arc knows the Bible. I must confront them with the truth in my country. No one will hear it, from America."

Frankie dropped on her pillow and tried to relax. "Why go so soon?" she asked conversationally. "Your message won't lose anything by delay. It'll get better if you give yourself time to work on it." She straightened her spine, hoping she wasn't too obvious. "Wait until after the trial, after your baby. Then leave the child here, with me"—*that* would be different—"and go face this thing without the guilt of knowing you might be killing the little person too."

Sahar shut her eyes. "I leave on Monday. There are reasons for such haste." With slow, exotic elegance she sifted her hair through her right hand. "My grandfather is king. There are those who say the family of Rashid has lost honor, because of me. For the royal family to lose its honor can bring his rule to an end."

"You're going back for him, is that what you're telling me?" Frankie asked angrily. "To save his precious honor?"

Sahar seemed amused by Frankie's attitude. "My country is not your country, Frankie." She pronounced it "Frawn-key." "If my king has no honor, then there is no platform for me to stand on to give this message."

"But you'll be stoned! Like your nurse!" Frankie said savagely. "It's *zina* or something, right?"

Sahar swung her feet around with supple quickness, facing Frankie directly. "I am not a fornicatress. Rick and I are not animals who act from lust." She glowed. With goofiness, Frankie thought. "We are true lovers. We are married in true marriage. Together, my Rick and I are one soul."

"Is that what you'll tell them?"

"Yes!" Sahar leaned forward, touching Frankie's arm. "I say to them that in the eyes of Allah, Rick and I are married. That is what I plead. And, I receive a trial!"

Frankie squinted at the girl, her head at an angle. A trial meant judges, and judges were appointed by someone. The king? How were trials done in Rashidi? But best case scenario, Frankie still hated it. Where would the defense of choice of evils be if Sahar went back of her own accord? "What Rick did, hauling you out of the embassy. A huge waste of time, right?"

"Oh no." Sahar's expression continued to shine. "For a man to risk his life for a woman in my country is very special." She leaned on her palms. "But for Rick, I would be now in Rashidi, in disgrace, a prisoner. I would not receive a trial. There would be only my execution. Because of Rick, I am in the position to barter with my king. And he has promise me a trial." Gaily, she waved a hand in the air. "I will have an audience. In Rashidi, trial is not theater, as in America. But my story will be told. I will have a platform!" Her eyes flickered shut with a tremor of fear, then opened wide. "You will know what to do."

There it was again: the odd refrain. "I will?"

Sahar took Frankie's wrist in the fingers of her hand. "You can not stand in the courtroom of Rashidi as a mufti. But you have training and experience in how to make arguments, how to act. You can give me advice. . . ." Frankie's face had become a mask of shock. Sahar dropped her hand and moved away. "Please. Forgive me."

"Wait a minute." Frankie grabbed Sahar by the ankle before she could crawl away. "Are you asking me to go to Rashidi *with* you?"

Sahar spoke timidly—especially for a princess. "Yes."

"Why? What good can I possibly be to you?"

"Oh, there is so much!" Her expression shined with hope. "I will trust you. I will tell you what is in my heart. You will not lie to me. You will help me to prepare my statements, my positions. There is love and rapport I feel toward you, and you feel toward me. When we are in the sky, flying toward Rashidi, and I am afraid, you will hold me in your arms."

Frankie felt awful. She knew nothing of Islamic law or culture. How could she do anything except get in the way? The girl believed that she would "know what to do," but Frankie didn't have a clue. What Sahar really wanted was a warm body to huddle next to when she got the "yips"; someone to help her over the hurdles of terror she'd have to face. "It's impossible," she said gently. "I have a case to try here."

"This trial of yours, it does not happen for several months?"

Frankie nodded. The clerk hadn't even set it for trial. With a docket as crowded as the one in the District, it could take a year before they were in court.

"Can you give to me, two months?" Her hazel eyes had

136

the extraordinary power of love. "Our laws move swiftly, compared with yours. My trial in Rashidi will finish long before my Rick's trial in America begins."

What was the point? Still, Frankie let herself think about it. But what if she belched when she shouldn't, or forgot herself and crossed her legs in public, and they put her in jail for a year?

"Frawn-key. I have promise from king of Rashidi that you will have safe passage, and that you will return whenever you wish."

Could this girl read people's minds? "You've talked to the king about me?"

"Yes."

"And he'd give his personal guarantee that I'd be back in Washington—let's say, for the sake of argument—early November?"

"Yes!"

At least her passport was current. She had one case to work on: *U.S.* v. *Adamson.* What kind of lawyer was she if she couldn't take off for two months, and still have it ready in time? "Sahar, something we haven't talked about. Rick needs you as a witness."

"To testify for him?" She smiled with joy. "I will do so gladly! Except . . ." The smile fell away. She remained silent.

"It's very important," Frankie said. "You're his excuse. Your testimony is crucial to his defense." The girl nodded wistfully. "Will the king guarantee your return too?"

Sahar's long, delicate fingers stroked Frankie's knees with shameless affection. "He can make no such promise. But with you to assist my pleading, I will have the chance to return with you."

"Say that again?"

She leaned back on her hands. "What happens with me will happen quickly. If I, as you would say in America, should win my case, then my king will allow me to return with you."

The scene took on an aspect of unreality, as though

137

Frankie had been yanked out of Sahar's apartment and dropped on a magic carpet. She felt out of control. "How good is King Nuri's word?"

Sahar's eyes widened, then dropped away with stiffness. "His word is his life." She frowned, obviously insulted but trying to ignore it. "He does not lie."

Frankie tapped her knuckles against her forehead, trying to make herself think like a lawyer. "What is your travel plan?"

"I fly from Washington to Rome on flight that departs Monday afternoon. From Rome to Cairo the next day. My grandfather will have a plane to carry me from Cairo to Qahtan."

"If I go with you, I'd have to be back in Cairo no later than"—Frankie did a quick calculation—"November first."

Sahar's eyes were wide with hope. "You will do this?"

"Let's do a deal. I'll think about going, if you think about staying."

"Please," Sahar said, her hands in her lap. "You must understand. I go with you or I go alone. But I go."

Frankie didn't understand at all. "I'll talk to Brooking about it."

Sahar breathed deeply, as though there was huge satisfaction to be gained out of the mere act of breathing. "You will know what to do," she said, leaning forward and touching Frankie's cheek with graceful, regal, sexy dignity. Frankie hated it. Sahar seemed to think she could work miracles, and she knew better. "Ah! I almost forget!" Sahar withdrew an envelope from a pocket, hidden in the folds of her shirt. "Please," she said, pushing it toward Frankie. "Give this letter to my Rick."

No you don't. "Give it to him yourself."

"I can do this?"

Frankie nodded. All's fair in love and war, and this was war. Those pale green eyes of Rick might change her mind. "Meet me at the office tomorrow afternoon. We'll go see him." She got up. The texture of the rug made the bottoms

138

of her feet tingle. "Dress like a boy," she said. "It'll make it easier."

Sahar clapped her hands. "Oh, I love you!" she said. "And tomorrow, I will be Joan of Arc!"

Brooking sat behind his desk, hunched over a legal pad. Except for the change of clothes, he looked like he hadn't moved from the day before: a sky-blue long-sleeved silk shirt with cuff links, a tie that looked like a tongue of fire, and every hair in place. He even dressed for clients on weekends. A flicker of annoyance blinked across his face when Frankie walked in on him. "How the fuck do you spell 'stationary'? In the *ary*. An *a* or an *e?*"

"You're a lawyer. Look it up."

"I practice law on the telephone. I got a problem, I ask somebody who knows." He watched her pull up a chair. "Something wrong?" he asked, picking up on a hostile vibration.

The truth was, at that moment she didn't appreciate the way he said "fuck." "Which 'stationary' do you want, Brooking? If the one you want is writing paper, use an *e*. Something that doesn't move, an *a*." She sat down. "I just talked to Sahar."

"How many *r*'s?"

"I don't know."

"Fuck."

"Brooking, wash your mouth out with soap!"

He looked mystified. "Sheesh!" He pushed his chair a foot or so away from his desk, stretched, then rested his elbows on the surface. "So what happened? We got a case or don't we?"

Frankie had made notes on the Metro ride from Sahar's apartment. As she talked she referred to them and made additions. Brooking listened intently. "Rashidi! Whoa," he said when she was done. "Not like government work."

"What should I do?"

He popped out of his chair. "King Nuri gets one look at you, he'll stick you in his harem. Then what?"

139

"Be serious."

"You know what you gotta do, babe, said so yourself. Without Sahar, we got no case."

Frankie brushed hair away from her ear and watched him dance. "All would not be lost, Brooking. An expert witness, someone from the State Department, people from the Rashidi Embassy—and Rick."

Brooking was eye to eye with her, as long as she stayed in her chair. "What do you do when Husam puts on a dozen Rashidis, a couple from American Airlines, they all identify a picture of Sahar as the beautiful young princess flew back to Rashidi August nineteenth, 1991, glowing with happiness, could hardly wait to get there?" He planted his feet firmly on the floor and shoved his open palms in her direction. "Where is choice of evils, they do that? Rick had to kill Abdul what's-his-face to save her from what?"

Frankie didn't need to be told. She knew their case was a loser without Sahar. "What do I do if she doesn't come back?"

"You'll know what happened, right?" He hopped around to his desk and sat down, as though that settled it. "Maybe bring a witness with you saw her get blasted in the back of her head. Then you can argue, see what I mean?"

## Sunday, August 18, 1991

The clock on the wall at the detention center gave the time: 3:30 P.M. The jailer buzzed open the heavy metal door to the attorney conference room, and Sahar and Frankie filed inside the small room with concrete walls.

Rick was already there, seated on the other side of the plexiglass wall, his elbows resting on the counter. Sahar wore Levi's and a denim jacket. Her hair was under a denim railroader's hat with a floppy bill. She kept her head down, but her hazel eyes—which yearned toward the man on the other side of the glass—were unmistakable. Rick got up slowly, his expression registering sheer wonderment. Frankie wished there was some way for her to disappear.

"My Rick. I have missed you so."

His glazed eyes washed over Frankie as though thanking her for this precious gift. Then they fastened on Sahar. "You're okay."

She sat in front of him and he perched on his stool, leaning toward the fingers that reached for his face. "My handsome man." She took off the hat and shook out her hair, which cascaded over her shoulders and chest like splashing water. "You are in my heart."

Frankie smelled the soft, sweet fragrance of cedar and realized that Sahar had prepared herself as though she would spend intimate time with him. There was nowhere to hide. Frankie found a folding chair under the counter, opened it, and sat in the corner, as far from them as she could get.

They leaned forward, touching foreheads—except for the quarter-inch-thick wall between them. They touched hands and talked in low tones and smiled with love. Frankie might just as well have been on another planet. She closed her eyes, wanting to give them as much privacy as she could.

*"No!"* Frankie jerked awake and saw Rick, filling the wall with menace, staring down at Sahar, who huddled below him. *"You can't do that!"* He was screaming, inflamed, out of control. *"Please, Sahar, use your head! Please!"*

"What's going on?"

The door opened and Frankie stood up quickly, charging to the wall and nudging Sahar out of the way. "Rick!" Her voice crackled through the amplifier like an electric shock. "Sit down! Now!"

She saw the wild look in his eye. He seemed to be gauging distances: the guard, the door. Then reason came back. He sat down.

"It's okay, Officer," Frankie said. "Really. He's okay. Right, Rick?"

He tried looking at the guard. His stricken eyes started to fill with tears. "No problem."

"Listen, Adamson, one is all you get. Settle down." The guard shut the door, but Frankie could see his face and

141

watchful expression through the small glass panel on the other side of the steel door.

"He's watching. Are you all right?"

"Yeah." Sahar had fallen to her knees in a corner of the room, her head against the wall. She might have been praying. "Stop her, Frankie."

Sahar stood up. Tear lines streaked her cheeks, but she had regained her composure. "My love. You must not disappoint me. You must know that this is my mission in life." Frankie moved out of the way so Sahar could sit down. "I am called to go. I have no choice. Allah tells me what I must do."

"You *do* have a choice, Sahar. I don't give a fuck about Allah. You'll die."

"And if I die? Will you remember me—"

"I'll hate you."

"—and know that I died, as you have tell me you would do, for all people?"

"Goddamn it, Sahar, don't be stupid! Don't die for the fucking world! It isn't worth it." He put his head on his hands and cried.

Frankie touched Sahar on the shoulder. "We'd better go."

"No." Sahar glanced with majesty at her, then back at Rick. "I do not leave my man like this."

Frankie sat in her chair, distancing herself as much as she could. She heard a crooning sound and realized that Sahar was humming some Arabic lullaby. She closed her eyes and waited.

A few minutes later they talked and whispered in low tones. Frankie couldn't understand what they were saying, and opened her eyes enough to see Rick's face. The two of them appeared to be wrapped inside a large soap bubble.

An old country girl, Frankie knew that some creatures— ducks—mated for life. But it was a mixed blessing. If one of them died, the other one never lived for very long.

# 11

## Monday, August 19, 1991

The flight from Dulles to Rome was scheduled to leave at 1:47 P.M. A car would pick Frankie up at her apartment at eleven in the morning, and Sahar had told her not to bring much clothing. Arabic dress would be provided in Rashidi, and servants would get her anything she needed.

A rain from the night before had turned into a cool, windless drizzle. The clouds were breaking up, and although Frankie could see small patches of blue from the window of her apartment, she did not observe a silver lining. She wore a safari travel suit and tied her hair back. She didn't put anything in her bag she couldn't wash. That morning she called Trigge in Denver, got an earful of his problems, then telephoned Brooking. "We need an investigator. Quick." She told him about the order to check the handgun for fingerprints. "That would be for starters."

"Got you covered," he said. "No real sweat, though. The docket is loaded, have a nice trip, we got a year probably to trial."

At eleven o'clock Frankie stood in the drizzle in front of her apartment. Her briefcase, lightly loaded with notepads, a couple of books, her purse and passport, hung from her shoulder. As she watched the driver load her bag in the trunk of the black Chrysler, she wondered what had happened to Sahar, who was not in the car. The driver opened the rear passenger door for her and she climbed in, his dark eyes probing the world for threats and weaknesses. He banged the door shut as though angry, jumped in the driver's seat and lurched away from the curbing. "Hey!" Frankie yelled. The acceleration jammed her into the cushion, then threw her at the door. "Take it easy!"

He glanced at her through the rearview mirror, shrugged like a person in constant communication with himself, and sped down the road. His darting eyes touched the mirror, the road, and examined oncoming traffic. Frankie buckled her seat belt, glaring at him. When their eyes met in the rearview mirror, his mouth turned into a line with no lips, as though he did not approve of her manner.

Frankie yanked out a cigarette and lit it. The fellow's eyes grew wide, then he shrugged once more and totally ignored her the rest of the trip.

Forty minutes later they pulled into a passenger check-in lane. The rain had intensified, but a roof over the parking area kept everyone dry. The driver jumped out of the car and, without opening her door, trotted to the trunk. Frankie climbed out as he dropped her bag on the curb. "Where is Sahar?" she asked. He stared at her with intensity, as though trying to understand, then shook his head, reached inside his jacket and pulled out an airline ticket. Brusquely, he handed it to Frankie, then jumped in the car and roared off.

The airline check-in agent told Frankie her traveling companion—Sahar bint Rashid—had already checked in. "Where is she?" Frankie blurted. "I mean, if you know."

He appeared shocked, then smiled. "Looked in the ladies' room, have you, miss?"

An hour later, as Frankie stood in line to board, she still hadn't seen Sahar. She took a deep breath and got on.

Sahar was seated in the back of the first-class section. Frankie beamed at the girl with relief. Her long black hair was coiled in a bun, and the dress she wore—silk, full, and purple—obviously had not been chosen for style. In spite of it, she shined like a work of art on the comic page. "I am glad to see you!" she said, exuding excitement and anticipation. She took Frankie's hands and held them against her cheeks. "My heart is at peace."

"Me too!" Frankie peeled the bag off her shoulder, dropped it on the floor, and plopped in the chair next to the girl. The lamb to the slaughter, she thought suddenly. "Sahar. You look wonderful."

"I bloom with child. He is a boy."

"Have you been tested?"

"Test?"

"You know, whatever it is they do. Ultrasound or something, to determine sex."

Sahar laughed. "No." She put her hand in Frankie's. "There is maleness within me. When I feel movement, I feel my man."

Frankie blushed. The intimate revelation took her by surprise. "Who was that jerk who brought me out here?" she blurted. As much as she liked Sahar, two months of Arabic girl talk would be enough.

"Asad?" Sahar asked, extracting her hand. "Was he rude to you?"

"Let's forget it," Frankie said, not wanting to get him in trouble.

"Please, you must tell me."

Shrugging, Frankie described the man's behavior. "He did everything he was supposed to do, but it was like part of the time he was angry at me and the rest of the time I wasn't there."

"Now you know why I choose to marry an American."

Frankie fished around in her briefcase for her purse and a cigarette. Her resolve to quit would never last through the trip, so she'd decided to make a serious effort when she got back. "Do you mind if I smoke?"

"I do not mind."

As Frankie lighted up, she considered the implications of Sahar's statement. Sahar had done the choosing, which came as no surprise. "Why did you choose to marry an American?"

"Asad is more thoughtful of women than most of the men

145

of Rashidi. Yet not even he can see a woman with open eyes."

Frankie didn't think many American men could either—but there was a difference. She had not existed to Asad as a person. He treated her as he would somebody else's dog. "What's their problem?"

Sahar crossed her arms and frowned. "It is not alone the problem for men. It is a problem for women too. Small girls are taught by tradition that men are strong and godlike and that they, as women, are weak and must be cared for." She gripped her elbows in her strong, capable hands, as though that was all they were allowed to do. "So girls pamper and pet men as boys, then become docile as they get older, in the hope they will have the easy life of cows." She smiled at Frankie. "For woman such as you, with obvious strength, my cousin sees an unnatural perversion. He thinks of you as ungodly, perhaps even worthy of his scorn."

Alarms and hackles marched up Frankie's spine. The girl wanted to change the course of Islam. Was that like waving a wand over the Amazon River and ordering it to go the other way? "Sahar, let's get off," Frankie said, jamming her barely smoked cigarette in the ashtray. "Now, while there's still time." She started to stand, prepared to rip down walls if she had to, to get the pregnant girl to safety.

"Come. Sit beside me." Sahar smiled with calmness, seeming to know what was in Frankie's mind. "It is too late for me to turn back. We already have agents of Rashidi for an escort."

Frankie slid back into her chair. "Where?"

"Those men, perhaps." Sahar motioned toward two men seated next to each other, four rows in front. "Or the man in the seventh row. I do not know. But they are here. They will not stop you if you wish to leave, but I am not allowed."

A flight attendant, standing easily in the aisle in front of the portal, began her mannered act. To the accompaniment of a speaker, she pantomimed what to do in the event of disaster. Her movements had the rehearsed, theatrical flamboyance of a clown who appears onstage before the curtain goes up; the tragicomic figure who does the prologue.

Frankie tuned her out, but Sahar listened with rapt attention, as though she had never heard it before. "I think it's time we got serious," Frankie said as the aircraft taxied into position for takeoff. "What's your case all about? What do we need to do to win?"

As a prosecutor, Frankie had never been bothered by demons of doubt. Prosecutors were on the side of righteousness, and Frankie had never tried a case she didn't believe in. Prosecutors were also charged with the responsibility of protecting the legal system. Even when they lost, the system —theoretically—won. But defending Rick had become totally personal, and she was afraid that defending Sahar would be more of the same.

When it's personal, the hell with the system. Frankie didn't care if it was an American courtroom, with its reach backward into the common law, or Islamic law, with its reach into the Qur'an. As a defense lawyer, the system could go hang. All she cared about were her clients.

Listening to Sahar, Frankie tried to appear confident. Sahar didn't need to know how worthless she really felt; like Alice in Wonderland, looking for logic. The fact was, when they got to Rashidi, she wouldn't even know where to sit. Or if the trial would take place in a courtroom, or whether or not there were rules of evidence, or rules of procedure. But Sahar believed in her. The girl thought her lawyer could do her some good. It wouldn't help Sahar to know that the lawyer had no idea where, or how, to start.

There had to be similarities, Frankie decided. Wouldn't there be issues for the Rashidi court to determine? Identify them. Then pick out Sahar's strong points—the evidence and arguments she could present—to prove her side of the case. A piece of cake. Try to anticipate her client's weaknesses too, and suggest evidence and arguments to blunt them.

And she should also keep her chin up, she told herself, patting the skin under her jaw. Both of them.

* * *

There was nothing to see from thirty thousand feet above the ocean, but Frankie found the vast expanse of nothing endlessly fascinating. They flew toward the night and caught up with it. They would fly through it before landing in Rome.

Sahar had grown tired and, with childlike trust, had rested her head on Frankie's shoulder and fallen asleep. Frankie stayed motionless for as long as she could stand it, then eased the princess onto a pillow, covered her with a blanket, and got up.

She climbed the thin spiral staircase to the upper level of the 747, where a stateroom and lounge were located. She found a table where she could review her notes, have a drink, and smoke. She refused to yield to the despair that nibbled at the edges of her mind, choosing instead to actively hate the things she couldn't do anything about. It was always a mistake to accept, without checking, the words of your "client," but in this case she had no choice. The problem in defending Sahar was hugely magnified. Not only must she depend on the girl for the facts, she also had to depend on her for the law.

Yet it seemed to Frankie that—as well as could be expected—Sahar knew the subject. The princess was self-taught, but so was Abe Lincoln. Perhaps Islamic law in Rashidi in the 1990s had not progressed beyond Blackstone of the American frontier. Sahar had soaked herself in all the sources available to her from the day her nurse had been stoned to death in Qahtan. The girl's submergence had been an outlet for her horror, fear, and rage. She was nine years old then; she was seventeen now. The jurists in Rashidi might not recognize her as a scholar, but Frankie believed this Arabian Joan of Arc would be able to stand up to her inquisitors.

For all the good it had done the Maid, who'd been burned at the stake.

With patience, like a second-grade teacher explaining the principles of democracy to a roomful of seven-year-olds, Sahar had worked with Frankie. "Islamic law is called the law of Shari'ah. Rashidi, with its nearness to the holy cities of Mecca and Medina, remains very traditional to Islamic law.

"Shari'ah, for the Muslim, has two paths," she had explained. "First is to reveal what the law of God truly is. Second is to inform the believer how to conduct himself in any given situation, so that his conduct will conform to the law of God."

*That* was a different approach, Frankie thought as she sipped Wild Turkey with a twist, over ice. They assumed the law came from God. Their job was to figure out how to follow it. We assumed there wasn't any law, until "the people" passed it. They said "right" and "wrong" was revealed by God. We said it was determined by statute.

They said God should rule. We said "the majority." Would the difference in approach mean anything, in the life, or death, of Sahar?

"The Shari'ah begins with the Qur'an," Sahar had continued. "These are the words written by Allah on Muhammad's soul, later transcribed by men who hear him speak them as the Messenger of God. Where one's conduct is questioned—as mine will be—the Shari'ah will first look for answer in the Qur'an. But if no answer is found, the learned men who search for the answer will turn to the *hadiths.*

"The *hadiths* are the sayings and actions of Muhammad the man," Sahar had said. "When Muhammad speak as the Messenger of God, he revealed God's words, and God's words are the text of the Qur'an. But the Qur'an instructs the believer to follow the good example of Muhammad the man. And so all that Muhammad said and did in his lifetime—not as God's messenger, but as a human being— was also recorded by the men of that time. And that is the *hadiths.*"

The Qur'an was their Constitution, Frankie decided. The *hadiths,* perhaps, were like their statutes, passed and enacted by one man.

"If still no answer to a particular question of conduct,"

Sahar had continued, "one searches the treatises and opinions of the jurists of the past. These opinions reach back into history for ten centuries."

Their case law, Frankie thought. Would she have to plow her way through ten centuries of the stuff? Had any of it been translated into English? Had it, too, been memorized by the muftis and *qadis*—the "learned men" who spent decades in colleges, studying law? Sahar spoke of them with reverence, and said most of them had memorized the Qur'an.

Frankie was numbed by the thought. She picked up her English translation of the Qur'an and thumbed its pages: more than four hundred. Was there something about the Arabic language that made its memorization easy? She had read chunks of it in English, but wasn't sure she'd understood any of it.

She opened it up, hoping for something like divine intervention, and let her finger come to rest on a passage. Sura 7, "The Heights," verse 189: "He it is who did create you from a single soul, and therefrom did make his mate that he might take rest in her."

When Frankie returned to her seat, Sahar was not there. Even princesses have to go pee-pee, Frankie thought, sitting in the chair next to the aisle.

A pudgy, slightly graying, well-dressed man walked toward her with an air of authority. "Where is Sahar bint Rashid?" he asked harshly.

"I don't know, sir." His dark eyes verged toward black and his skin color was desert-brown. His expression was as heavy as bad weather. Frankie was not intimidated. "May I ask, why do you want to know?"

"That does not concern you. You must tell me where is your companion."

Frankie did not appreciate his tone of voice. "I don't need to tell you anything, sir. Buzz off." She turned away from his glare and opened her briefcase, pulling out her books. The man didn't move. Frankie lowered the tray, rested her elbows on its surface, and opened the Koran. Why was it spelled Qur'an by some translators and Koran by others? Was one English spelling more politically correct than the other?

"I do not leave this place until you answer my question," the cancerous growth declared.

"Suit yourself."

"I know who you are, Miss Frances Rommel." He spoke in the same harsh, flat voice. The decibel level had neither risen nor lowered since his initial demand, and the pitch and tone stayed constant. "You will make matters most difficult for Princess Sahar and yourself if you do not answer my question."

Frankie closed her book and considered her options. Doing what he demanded was not an option. She could ring for the flight attendant, yell for help, or smack him in the balls. Or ignore him. Or tell him to go away. "Go away."

"Ah." He straightened up and cast his eye down the aisle. Sahar appeared. With a frown of disapproval he watched her approach. Frankie made room for the princess by swinging her knees out of the way, but the man barely moved, forcing Sahar to brush against him as she squeezed into her seat. He addressed Sahar in Arabic, a smutty, judgmental sneer on his face and a lascivious gleam in his eye.

Sahar seemed to shrink. Angrily, Frankie started to stand, but was restrained by Sahar's hand on her arm.

"I am Prince Muhammad abu Ibrahim ibn al-Rashid, Miss Rommel. You will please to answer all questions of mine when next we meet." He marched quickly away, his posture and bearing sending an unmistakable message of righteousness for all to see.

Sahar's hands had become tiny fists. They touched her temples. Frankie reached for the girl with both arms. She was as rigid and cold as an ice statue. "Come here," Frankie said, pulling Sahar's head onto her chest. "Who is your friend?"

"Muhammad is the brother of my king." Sahar huddled

into Frankie, who could feel her shake. "He is a very pious man, a respected mufti. He has tell my mother to prepare herself for my death."

## Tuesday, August 20, 1991

They had flown through the night. Beneath them the island of Corsica radiated different shades of green. Frankie sat by the window, at times enthralled by the scene, at times wanting to stand up and scream, at times dragged by her mind into her books. "Sahar. Where does it say a woman will be executed if she commits *zina?*" The question brought a quick look of shock, and Frankie wanted to take it back. "I'm in the Book of Light. Isn't that the right place? It says the punishment is one hundred lashes."

"Correct place is Surah Four, the Book of Women, verse fifteen. It instructs that fornication is proved against a woman when four witnesses testify against her. 'Confine them to their houses until death take them,' the passage recites, 'or until Allah finds for them another way.'" Her breathing changed into shallow little puffs and she frowned at her hands which lay in her lap. "The word 'way' is key to this passage. It has been interpreted as sentence of death."

Frankie flipped through the book until she found the passage Sahar was talking about. "Then they need the testimony of four witnesses, right?"

Sahar shrugged. "Four men have seen us together, in the closeness of a hotel room. I will confess to intimacy. I am pregnant. Do I claim immaculate conception? Why do you ask such question?"

"It's called looking for loopholes," Frankie said. "It doesn't always work. There's a difference, isn't there, in the Shari'ah, between adultery and fornication?"

"Yes." Sahar spoke softly, still staring at her hands. "As with Christian and Jew. Adultery is misconduct of married person. Fornication is misconduct of unmarried person."

"That would be you, right? I mean, what they will claim?"

"Yes."

"Is the punishment the same?"

"The traditional interpretation under the Shari'ah, it is not the same. For those who commit fornication, one hundred lashes—except for slave girls, who receive fifty lashes. But for adultery, the punishment is death."

Frankie took a deep breath. "Then all you're risking is one hundred lashes?"

"Some say, when properly administered, that is a death sentence, and the tradition of stoning is the equal of one hundred lashes." Sahar's voice remained calm, but her chest heaved like the surf.

"Would that be your sentence?"

"No." She shut her eyes for a moment, then opened them wide, as though knowing she had to confront the situation totally. "If I die, it will not be because Shari'ah prescribes the punishment. If the *qadi* decide I am married in accordance with the law of Shari'ah, then there will be no dishonor to the family of Rashid, and I will live."

"And that's what your trial is about?" Frankie asked. "It's to determine whether or not you are married?"

"Yes. But if the *qadi* decide I am not married, then in the eyes of the law, I am a fornicatress. I will have brought grave dishonor to everyone in my family. The stain of the dishonor can only be removed by my death." Her face folded in on itself and Frankie put her arm over her. "I am sorry for tears."

"Don't be absurd," Frankie said, holding her tight with her left arm and stroking her hair with a hand. "You are the toughest little pony I've ever met." She blinked some of her own. "Does the king have the right to do that? He can just order it done?"

"Of course. Not only as the ruler of Rashidi, but as the head of his family. Everyone in the family and all of his subjects will suffer the shame of dishonor if I, a fornicatress, am allowed to live."

"Do all fathers, all heads of families, have that right?"

"Yes."

"That's awful! It's legitimized murder."

Sahar lifted her head and looked at Frankie. "To murder

is to take life, without right. But what if they have the right?"
She put her head back on Frankie's bosom, allowing herself
to be cuddled. "I am torn in two pieces. One piece agrees
with you, but the other tells me it is just. The family is a gift
from Allah. In the family are deep bonds of love, from
which spring eternal peace and security to all its members.
How can that be maintained unless the father has the right
to purge the family of dishonor? How can the family
provide strength and comfort to all its children, without
discipline?"

"Let's not get into a big debate," Frankie said, stroking
Sahar's back. "See if I've got this figured out. There are two
systems of law. The Shari'ah is the law of Islam, and if you
win your trial in that one—if they decide you're married—
you're home free. But if you lose, this other law kicks in. Is
that it?"

Sahar smiled. "That is the explanation of a lawyer. But
this 'other law' is not a system, as is Shari'ah. It is merely the
operation of the family." She tucked her head back into
Frankie's bosom. "For those with need to give it a name, it is
called tribal law."

"Is that what you call it?"

"No. The name is for those who try to understand, not for
Arabs. To the Arab, this 'other law' is their blood. It is part
of me and needs no name."

The blue waters of the Mediterranean were still beneath
them, but the 747 had turned from an easterly course to a
southerly one. Frankie could feel it. She had the sense of
direction that country girls acquire, a built-in compass that
appears to be instinctive. They were aimed at the African
continent, and in four short hours would land in Cairo.

Frankie sat next to the window. Sahar—leaning back in
her seat, her eyes half closed—talked, possibly to keep her
mind busy. Frankie didn't know how she could stay so calm.

"In Qahtan is a large square in the old town, the *medina*.
On the west side of the square is the mosque, with minarets
that reach upward like outstretched arms, for God. On the
north side is the original palace for the house of Rashid. It

stands like a fort." She stirred in her chair. "From palace window, looking down on small courtyard between the mosque and the palace, I watch my nurse die."

What a brutal memory. "Where are the courtrooms?"

"On the south side of the square is the law court, with library for students and others, offices for mufti, and the courtroom."

Frankie turned toward her. "Have you ever sat through a trial?"

"Yes." A smile worked across Sahar's face. "With as much frequency as I am allowed. I am fascinated by the dignity of the *qadi* and the mufti. They move slowly, as though walking through water." She sat up, mimicking their slowness.

"Then there won't be a problem in my going to watch?"

Sahar shrugged. "There is no prohibition. But spectators —especially women—are discouraged and can be excluded. The law of the law court is private, as between persons. It is not a public spectacle, as in America. When I sense hesitation at my presence, I leave."

"The *qadi* are the judges, but you told me before the mufti aren't exactly lawyers. What are they? Clerks?"

Sahar tilted her head. "They are advisers to the *qadi*. There is much interchange of roles between mufti and *qadi*. Often, a mufti will be *qadi* and a *qadi* may take the part of mufti." She looked with amusement at Frankie. "I have witnessed one of your trials. Our trials are not like yours."

"How are they different?"

"Your lawyers strut in front of a jury, like peacocks." She imitated a lawyer on the prowl. "Your judges will often make faces, of boredom, or disgust." Her eyes rolled and her mouth opened wide. "Tell me, Frankie. Do you prance about, and shout, when you are before a judge?"

"Not me."

"In Rashidi, the mufti and *qadi* wear the same kind of clothing, and identical expressions." She put her hands in front of her, pressing the tips of her fingers together, and looked like an angel. "They never lift their voice. With each other, they are very courteous."

"Are any of them women?"

"Not in Rashidi, or in Saudi Arabia. I have heard, in Cairo—even Baghdad—there are women. But they are rarely asked to serve."

"Will you have a mufti?"

Sahar nodded. "The *qadi* has already appointed a mufti to advise him as to my assertion. That is the role of the mufti. This man will have no interest in *me*"—she touched her chest—"and will not represent me." She touched Frankie's arm. "I will fool them. I will have a lawyer from America to represent me."

Good luck, Frankie thought. "I don't get it. If you have a mufti, who will he represent? Whose side is he on?"

"The side of God. In the Shari'ah court, everyone seeks to find the law of Allah."

Frankie stared at the girl, then looked out the window. She didn't like this at all. "Do you know who your mufti is?"

"A man from Jeddah, but I do not know his name."

"What about the *qadi?*"

"My uncle. Prince Muhammad."

# 12

## Tuesday, August 20, 1991
## Cairo, Egypt

Frankie didn't know where the men came from. She and Sahar had barely stepped onto the tarmac at Cairo International Airport when a cordon of male bodies formed around them, building an oval of protection from the crowd. They floated through the surging, gurgling torrent of people like a bottle in the Wind River during spring runoff. Frankie gripped Sahar by the arm, aware of the fact that it shook, in spite of the heat.

One of the men had peeled Frankie's briefcase out of her hand and hooked it over his shoulder. Frankie watched it swing back and forth in front of her. They couldn't have been off the plane more than ten minutes when they were bundled into a stretch limousine with rows of seats, like a jitney. Sweltering masses of people boiled around them, but from inside the air-conditioned comfort of the Lincoln limousine, the sounds of the people could barely be heard.

Frankie and Sahar had been guided into the center row of seats. In silence, six men climbed in behind them and six more arranged themselves in front. Through the tinted windows the world they passed through looked shadowy and dark. An eerie sensation grew in Frankie. It might have been only the fulfilling of an expectation, but in the closeness of the car, it felt like she, as a woman in the Arab world,

157

was literally a separate species of animal from the men. "Do these guys speak English?" she whispered to Sahar.

"They prefer the richness of Arabic."

As though to prove Sahar's words, low conversations began around them. The language may have been rich to the rest of them, but to Frankie it sounded guttural and harsh. At some point Sahar let go of Frankie's hand and her posture stiffened.

"What are they talking about?"

"They make foolish jokes."

The slow-moving car eventually broke through the crowd and onto a highway. Frankie's sense of direction told her they were driving south. She recalled what she could of Cairo. The airport was east of the Nile, which flowed from south to north along the valley floor. They climbed into the low mountains that provided the huge building blocks for the pyramids. She tried to remember which side of the river the pyramids were on, but couldn't. Twenty minutes later they stopped. Men jumped out and opened doors on both sides of the car. Frankie ignored the man standing by her door, and slid across the seat. She chose to follow Sahar, not wanting the car or anything else to come between them.

"Where are we?" she asked, standing next to Sahar and shading her eyes. Sahar still wore her purple dress and continued to look like a work of art. The late afternoon sun burned at an angle on her back, blaring at them from a desert-blue sky in the west. Frankie knew her instincts regarding the direction they had driven was right.

"Muqattam." Sahar spoke in a low voice. "It is here we take the airplane of my grandfather to Qahtan. You see?" She pointed to a sleek twin-engine jet aircraft being wheeled out of a hangar. The men surrounded them again, even though there were no crowds of people to protect them from. Like a small herd they walked toward a low sandstone building that grew out of the barren landscape near the hangar. Sahar breathed deeply, as though luxuriating in the taste of the air.

The atmosphere inside the building was more to Frankie's liking. The air-conditioning washed over her like a cool shower. There were folding chairs along the walls of the large, barren room and a counter near one wall, toward the back. A young Arab male dressed in white robes stood behind it. His mouth dropped open when he saw the women, but he quickly—fearfully—averted his gaze.

Frankie's eyes had to adjust to the relative darkness. She saw Prince Muhammad standing near a large bay window that faced the landing strip. His hands were thrust behind his back and his feet were wide apart and planted firmly, in a classic Napoleonic stance. He waited until they were aware of his presence, then strode over to them as the men busied themselves with chairs, unfolding them and facing them toward the window. "Sahar. Miss Rommel. You will wait in the women's section. A servant will attend to your needs."

"Yes, my uncle," Sahar said. "Come, Frankie."

"I need my briefcase," Frankie said, searching for the man who had it.

"It is quite safe, Miss Rommel."

"My purse is in it, sir," Frankie said. "My lipstick." The bastards weren't going to rip off her passport either.

"Mazin!" Muhammad shouted, then spit out what sound like invective. The sharp-eyed young man with Frankie's briefcase over his shoulder materialized and handed it to her.

Sahar led them to a thin hallway that extended along a side wall at the rear of the room. When they rounded the corner, there weren't any furtive eyes following them. Frankie could let go of the tension. It had built in her like the time years before, when she'd been in a prison during a lockdown. Sahar had felt it too. She smiled at Frankie with girlish foolishness, as though they were conspirators who had gotten away with some prank.

At the end of the hall, on the left side, a metal door opened into a large, black cavity. Sahar flipped on the light switch, and overhead flourescent tubes flooded the space with light. One of them flickered, like an uneven pulse. Sahar held her mouth, then let go of it and started to laugh.

"What's funny?"

She put one hand on Frankie's hip and the other on her

159

shoulder, like a dancing partner. She took a step forward, then waltzed to the side. "It is just the way I feel. Safe in this room with you, where my righteous uncle cannot see!"

"It *is* a relief." Frankie disengaged herself and glanced around the room. It looked like the inside of a hangar, except there weren't any windows and the only door was the one they'd come through. "Speaking of which, Princess, I need to pee. Big-time." She dropped her briefcase on the concrete floor.

Sahar laughed. "I am so glad for your company!" she said. "You are like a cool breeze."

"Are you going to tell me where it is, or do I piddle all over the floor?"

"Over there," Sahar said, pointing at a curtain along one of the walls. "You will become aware of it as you approach it."

Frankie wasn't quite sure what Sahar meant, but understood when she pulled back the curtain. The chemical toilet, in the middle of a small closet, stank. Hurriedly she relieved herself and pushed through the curtain, walking briskly to put distance between herself and the odor.

A small dried-up woman with gray hair, dressed in black, with clothing over one arm and a tray with ice-filled glasses and Cokes in the other, scuttled into the room. Her dark eyes bounced around like a bird forced to land on the back of a crocodile. Bowing to Sahar, she addressed her in Arabic. Sahar replied in a soft, kind voice, taking the clothing from the woman and gesturing toward the floor for the tray. Her kindness actually seemed to terrify the woman, who almost dropped the tray on the floor in her hurry to leave. Like an exposed mouse in the living room, she ran for the door.

Sahar watched her go, then turned toward Frankie. "My uncle request that we dress in traditional fashion. Will you wear the *abaya* with me, and the veil?"

"Am I allowed to refuse?"

"Yes, of course." Sahar's expression suggested that Frankie should not think of her people as savages. "There are women of the west in Qahtan. But they are subjected to gaze, and at times admonishment of the *muhaddin.*"

"Who are they?"

"The holy police. They compel obedience to Islam."

"You are my guide, Sahar." Frankie touched the black clothes in Sahar's hands. The cloth was fine, soft silk and they smelled clean and fresh. "Will it make things easier?"

Sahar smiled. "My uncle will not frown with such fierceness."

She handed one of the garments to Frankie, then opened hers and inspected it for length, holding it against her shoulders. "This is most sexy," she said. "See how much ankle? My cousin when he sees me will have an orgasm!"

Then she dropped her garment on the floor, shrugged out of her dress, and let it fall to the floor in a circle around her. She stepped away from it. With extraordinary grace, and with wonderfully slow, rhythmic movement, Frankie watched Sahar move around the room. It was as though her hands, arms, back, and shoulders had independent wills of their own, but each thrilled to the same heavenly music.

"Ah," Sahar said as her eyes closed and her mouth opened wide, in a smile. "It is so nice to dance." Her slightly swollen belly made slow circles, as though reaching for warmth. "I think of my love." Her vibrant body, clothed only in a bra, panties, and a short slip, was erotic and beautiful. With a pang Frankie compared it to her own: not bad for an old broad, although the flesh under her arms had started to sag, and veins would appear for no good reason, like bruises, on her legs.

It was different inside an *abaya,* Frankie decided, listening to the solid hum of jet engines as they flew at a low elevation over the Red Sea. It was peaceful and serene. As travelers, they were required to wear full veils, covering even the eyes, and she couldn't see as well as she'd like. There was also a musty taste in her mouth from breathing air filtered through the black lace. She suspected she was inhaling invisible bits of lint, which probably wasn't much worse than what she usually breathed, so she didn't worry about it. She felt the way she imagined nuns did: with no concern for appearance, and no need to compete. It gave her an odd sense of freedom and security. Like an invisible person, she could see everything and had nothing to fear.

Frankie and Sahar sat next to each other, at a round table with four swivel chairs on thick posts bolted to the floor. The low-ceilinged aircraft had a wide, spacious interior with three other table-and-chair groupings in the rear section. Rich red-velvet curtains divided the room into compartments. Frankie could hear the sound track of a movie in the forward section.

"May I join you?"

Frankie looked up and found the dark eyes of Prince Muhammad searching for hers, through the veil. It was a question, not a command. Sahar sat up straight, but the request was aimed at Frankie. "We would be delighted and honored," Frankie said, wondering if she should stand, then deciding the hell with it.

"I hope you are comfortable," he stated, sitting down. Sahar tucked her ankles under her chair, as though to remove them from his vision.

"Quite comfortable," Frankie told him. She sat up straight also and leaned her arms on the chair rests. "The lamb and rice pilaf was delicious."

He smiled cordially. "Will you join me in a drink to settle the stomach?"

"I'd love one!" Frankie exclaimed. "Is it allowed?"

"For a Western woman, I will make an exception." He turned toward Sahar. "What of you, Sahar?" His voice hardened.

"No thank you, my uncle."

"You appear to be at ease in Western clothing. I thought perhaps you were at ease with other customs of the West as well."

"The Qur'an forbids alcohol, my uncle. It does not forbid Western clothing."

He smiled at her, then turned toward the steward who had

opened the curtain behind them. "Miss Rommel, may I suggest Courvoisier?"

"That sounds wonderful."

The steward—a small, thin man wearing an all-white uniform—disappeared, and the prince turned toward the women, placing his hands on his knees. He was at a disadvantage, with nothing to hide behind. His facial expression and body language hung out like signs. "You are a brave woman, Miss Rommel. To come into an unknown, savage country such as Rashidi, on such short notice, and with no protection from your government." His voice didn't give away much, however. "You must have heard stories of our barbaric ways, especially with women."

"Am I in danger?"

The steward appeared with an ornate silver tray. He set it on the table and poured the amber liquid from the dark green smoke-colored bottle into two crystal snifters, each in a holder over a candle. He set the bottle on the table and stood respectfully, waiting for orders. "A dessert perhaps?" Prince Muhammad asked.

"Not for me, thanks," Frankie said. Sahar shook her head, and Frankie watched the thick-bodied man in an impeccable European suit wave the steward away.

"You ask of danger," he said. "You will find the streets of Qahtan quite safe, at any time of the day or night. You will have no need to lock your door. And no one will touch your valuables and possessions without your permission— except, of course, to return to you that which you may have misplaced."

"Not like the District," Frankie said.

He nodded with satisfaction. "Or any large city in your country."

Frankie decided to treat him like a judge who wanted to get chummy. "Pardon the change of subject, but I'm delighted to get a drink! We hear stories all the time of liquor being found in someone's bag, and people going to jail." She waited for a reply.

"So." He turned the crystal cups over the flame, watching

for movement in the liquid. "You are surprised that a person of the royal family, in authority, will join you to drink?"

"Isn't it against the law?"

In the manner of one quite used to the finer things, he lifted the snifter closest to Frankie and handed it to her. Then he picked up his own. With a ceremonial gesture, he touched her glass. "You ask this question as a lawyer, seeking advantage for a client?"

Frankie was glad for the veil. "I hadn't thought of it." Awkwardly, she lifted the veil from her face and held the snifter to her lips.

"Please, Miss Rommel. You may remove the veil." He turned to Sahar. "May she not do this? Am I not of your family?"

Frankie watched Sahar's meek nod as the princess lifted her veil and spread it over the hood covering her hair. Frankie put her drink down and did the same.

"Abroad, as a member of the royal family, I have many responsibilities." He sipped from his glass. "In that capacity, I make an exception to the rule of the Qur'an prohibiting the use of alcohol." He replaced his glass on the candle holder, watching the heat lines move through it. "Do you not agree that those in power, of necessity, are above the law?"

He stared at her as an equal in the discussion. "I'd have to think about it," Frankie said.

"Come," he scoffed. "Your president has a National Security Council, responsive to no one. Your police must speed through a city with reckless abandon, with pistol blazing, in order to catch an offender. It is the same principle I employ to justify an occasional drink." He smiled, lifting it back toward his lips. "Which, I readily admit, I also enjoy."

Frankie picked up her glass and let the scent from the brandy fill her nose. "I understand from Sahar that you are a mufti."

"I am indeed." He beamed with grave pleasure. "Sahar

has also told you I am the *qadi* who decides the question of her status?"

"Yes sir." Frankie suspected she was on thin ice, but thought she could get away with a plea of ignorance if she fell through. "In the U.S., for a judge to decide a case involving a relative would"—she searched for the right tone—"be most unusual. As Sahar's uncle, you'd be disqualified." She sipped from her glass, watching him.

"In your country there is a presumption, is there not, that the mufti are biased by such things?"

"Yes."

"There is no such presumption under Islamic law. I have studied law in universities for twenty years. The Prophet Muhammad, may the blessings of peace be upon him, has said: 'When God wishes to favor one of his creatures, he sets him to learn the law, and word by word makes of him a jurist.'" He smiled with either serenity or smugness. "As *qadi*, my search will be for the revealed law of God. There is recognition in Islam that jurists are beyond such influence."

"What about the people?" Frankie asked.

"I am not certain I understand." He tossed the liquid back and refilled his glass, putting it on the candle holder.

"You are the king's brother, aren't you, sir? Will the people in Rashidi be satisfied in the correctness of your decision?"

"I have been chosen precisely for that reason. For that, I give Nuri credit." He watched his glass over the candle, eagerly, it seemed to Frankie. "I am Nuri's older brother and have a large following in the kingdom. I am known by all to be beyond his influence. Let me assure you. Insofar as it is humanly possible, my decision will be correct. The people of Rashidi know this is true."

Frankie thought she had a sense of him: a man who wanted to create the appearance of integrity. It wouldn't hurt to plant a seed or two in his mind. "Another question, if I may," she said, facing him with the directness she used in American courtrooms. "It's my understanding you've already expressed an opinion on the case. Doesn't your law ask you to keep an open mind?"

The question didn't faze him in the slightest. "I have an opinion," he said, smiling courteously. "I have told Sahar's mother to prepare for the worst." Sahar might just as well have been on another airplane. "But who can say what Allah will direct me to do?"

Frankie tried not to scream as he turned to Sahar. "My niece," he said to her. He spoke with affection. "Before menses, as a young girl, you had the ability to make us laugh with your gaiety and observations of life. I detected a note of disdain when Miss Rommel and I discussed the use of alcohol by those in authority. May I ask for your feelings about such things?"

Frankie saw a flash of annoyance in Sahar's expression. "I am not surprised at what you do, my uncle. I have heard of it."

"But you do not approve of it in your heart?"

"My uncle. I do not approve of it in my head, where my thoughts are. It has little to do with my heart."

His expression took on a touch of malice. "As a woman, you reject the wisdom that your role in life is to feel, rather than to think?"

"I feel deeply, my uncle. But I know also that I think."

The prince wore an air of superiority. "Very well, then, I shall ask for your thoughts on a matter of principle. Do you agree with the principle that for the ruler there are exceptions to strict adherence to the law?"

Sahar's shoulders squared at him like a running back charging the line. "I do not."

Muhammad sat back in his chair, smiling like a cat having fun with a mouse. "You are not as clever as you were as a child, Sahar. If the principle applies to me, might it not also apply to you?"

If anything, Sahar sat straighter. "As a matter of principle, my uncle, it should apply to no one."

"So." By his eyelids, it looked to Frankie as though he were about to deliver the coup de gras. "You do not believe that the ruler—even the Prophet Muhammad, peace be upon him—was above the law?"

166

Sahar dropped her eyes, as though she knew she was being led down the garden path. "No."

"Yet it is a fact of history that he had more than four wives, which is all the Qur'an allows to any man. Does not his action establish the precedent that the ruler is above the law?"

"My uncle, I truly do not believe any Muslim is above the law of God." Her eyes begged with him to understand. "That would include the Prophet. Was he not only a man, as Ali proclaimed? Rulers should not have special exemptions from the law. They have the special responsibility to be examples."

Prince Muhammad sat up sternly. "My child. Do you seriously maintain that Muhammad, peace be upon him, could do wrong?"

Sahar looked down. Her voice was soft, but loud enough to be heard. "Only Allah is incapable of sin."

With controlled anger the prince put his goblet down. "You accuse Muhammad of sin? This, when it is obvious to all the world that you carry a child?"

"I have broken no law. I have acted on—"

Frankie's glass dropped out of her hand. "Oh, my goodness!" she exclaimed, jumping to her feet. "I'm sorry!"

"Saddam!" the Prince commanded, moving his feet out of the way. He gave some directions in Arabic.

"It just slipped out of my hand," Frankie said. "I don't know what happened." Sahar lowered her veil before the steward could get there, but Frankie didn't bother with it. She took the damp cloth the steward offered her and blotted moisture off her robe and chair as he mopped up the table. When he had gone, she sat down.

Prince Muhammad's head tilted with speculation. He refilled Frankie's glass, placed it over the candle and watched it heat up. "Most opportune," he said, lifting his cup and gently swirling the contents under his nose.

Frankie acted as though she hadn't heard. "Your English is wonderful," she said, adjusting her posture so as to block Sahar out of the conversation. "Is everyone in Rashidi bilingual? There aren't many Americans who speak Arabic, and I sure wish I was one of them!"

He smiled. "English is now taught in our schools. But for my generation, even the generation of my sons, only those with need have learned it."

"Does the king—"

"Nuri is fluent in your language, as is Umar, the ambassador to the United States. However, Prince Khalid and Prince Faisal have no facility for such intellectual pursuits. Their abilities as hunters and horsemen are legend in Rashidi, but I shudder to think what will happen if one of them becomes king."

"Could that happen?" Frankie asked, picking her glass off the holder. "I hope you will forgive my impertinence." She could not believe how nice she was being. "But how is succession to the throne handled in Rashidi? Will it go to King Nuri's descendants?"

"We are not European," Muhammad said. "Royal lines of succession do not pass from father to son in Arabic kingdoms. We are of the desert. Our mentality, if you will, is formed by the vastness and harshness of the desert." Sahar had lifted her veil. Her face shined with pride at her uncle's words. They were on the same side of this one, Frankie thought.

"It is the constant struggle for life on the ceaseless sand of Arabia that has formed the patterns of our mind," Muhammad continued, with oratorical relish. "As on the waves of an ocean, there are no lines of political order to be seen. There are no roads or pathways to follow. Even footprints, in the sand, disappear." His hands seemed to smooth out the sand. "One is aware of the beauty of the night, and the clean purity of the air. But to survive, one must learn a simple, but supreme, lesson: for the individual, the family, the clan, and the tribe, there is only power."

Sahar leaned toward her uncle and smiled at him with affection. Frankie realized how much her smile was like his. "My uncle has not forgotten your question. This is perhaps the answer of an Arab." She looked at Frankie. "It is most thorough."

Muhammad chuckled, accepting the gentle teasing with grace. "Sahar has always had a clear understanding of the operations of the mind. Do not think I have forgotten your question."

"The thought never entered my head."

He sipped his drink. "To understand succession in Rashidi, one must have appreciation of life on the desert. To the bedouin—and our fathers and grandfathers were these romantic nomads who wandered the Arabian desert—attack and warfare was the way of life. Survival depended on what could be taken from a neighboring tribe by force. But to allow that which is yours to be taken away by another eliminates your own ability to survive." His hands made appropriate gestures. "Therefore, any attack must be repelled by greater aggression."

Frankie wondered where all this was headed. "The weak have no chance on the desert," Muhammad declared, resting his cup on his knee. "To survive, those without power must come under the protection of a tribe *with* power. Our lines of succession thus follow the lines of power, and experience."

Frankie frowned. "I'm sorry. I was with you until then."

He leaned forward. "It is usually the case that the oldest living man has the experience to maintain the strength of a clan." Frankie thought she had a glimmer. "My father had thirteen sons, but no brothers. Thus when my father died, his oldest son—my older brother—became king. But he was killed in a struggle with Yemen over a boundary of land. He had many sons, but to elevate any of them to the position of king would be unthinkable. Therefore I—as my father's second son, and as the oldest man in the family of Rashid—could have been king. But my interests are of more spiritual and scholarly matters. I declined in favor of Nuri, who has a unique gift in the exercise of political power."

"You gave it up voluntarily?" Frankie asked.

He smiled. "That surprises you. You see, the family is the first consideration of the Arab." He picked up his glass. "The clan, the tribe, are extensions of family. There is in all

169

Arabs an intense loyalty to family, which is rooted in the necessity to survive, imposed by the desert."

Sahar continued to show signs of pride, and nodded in agreement. "That which enhances the family will grow," Muhammad proclaimed. "That which weakens it must be weeded out." Her smile faded, but her look of approval remained. "The men of a family are its greatest resource. All men must be used to their greatest advantage. I could be king, but such is my family loyalty that I yield to my brother."

"Is that common?" Frankie asked.

He shrugged. "It is the ancient way of the desert, of nomadic people. There were tribes of Indians in your country—stamped out, unfortunately—with such traditions." He wasn't all bad, Frankie decided, as long as you let him keep the floor. "However, when such traditions come into conflict with the lineal system imposed by monarchs of Europe, the so-called divine right of kings, results can become grotesque."

"What happens then?"

"In Persia, centuries past, many sultanas were from Europe. These Christian 'queens' "—he gave sneering emphasis to the word—"believed kings were descendants of God and that only the lineal descendant of the king— namely, their children—had the right to rule." He grinned at the idiocy. "These sultana-queens exercised their charms over Persian kings, to secure the throne for their sons." He laughed. "Kings thus found it necessary to kill their brothers, and the sons of their brothers! They destroyed this precious resource, down to the age of an infant son, so that the oldest, most experienced male of the family would be the queen's son!"

Frankie tasted her Courvoisier. "Radical," she said. "But logical."

The prince roared with laughter. When he dried his eyes, he smiled at Frankie with real appreciation. "The idiocy changed the course of history by weakening the Islamic tide that otherwise would have swept through Europe." He smiled at Frankie. "What a pity. Would you not agree?"

"Do I have to?"

He continued to smile with pleasure. "In any event, such idiocy will not occur in Rashidi, or any country with experience in desert survival." He settled back into his chair. "In Rashidi, there is the recognition that *all* of the men, used to the highest potential, are the resource."

"What of the women, my uncle?"

Frankie glanced with apprehension at Sahar. Muhammad changed his posture. "The Qur'an instructs that women are most valuable as the comfort for men," he explained in a reasonable voice. "This follows the laws of nature. It is men who by their nature are aggressive, and can secure a place of safety. Women provide the family with the niceties of life, and provide nurturance for the children." He sounded like a nice, decent parent, outlining the proper boundaries of life. "Women are uniquely gifted to raise girls into women and boys into men. That is the nature of women."

"Allah wrote, 'God created you from dust, then from a little germ. Into two sexes he divided you,'" Sahar said. Her soft voice still sounded like a call to arms. "What does this mean, my uncle?"

"Perhaps," Muhammad said, "you will explain the meaning to me."

She didn't hesitate. "That a man, and a woman, together, are one."

"And as one, isn't it obvious that the man provides for the woman, and the woman provides for the man?" Muhammad turned toward her with a no-nonsense attitude. "Each in the way that is most natural?"

"But what was natural on the Arabian desert in the time of Muhammad, fourteen hundred years ago, is not natural for all time. Is it natural for a woman of today, who lives in the modern city, to do nothing with her hands except prepare food for the man and take care of infants? Is it natural for the modern woman to do nothing with her mind except to think of pleasing things to say to her man?"

Muhammad's face had gotten as dark as his eyes. "You would have woman as warriors, as in America? You chafe under the restrictions imposed on members of your sex by the law of Islam?"

"I question them, my uncle." Sahar's head dropped with humility, but her back remained straight. "Did not the Prophet Muhammad encourage questions?"

"Enough!" He leaped up, somehow missing the table. "You, a woman of less than twenty years, who refused a marriage arranged for her with the son of my son!" He glowered over her. "Who now pretends to an unlawful marriage with an infidel in order to justify obvious fornication!" His hands were fists. "You presume to instruct me, a mufti of distinction with years of study at the universities in Bokhara and Cairo, regarding the law?"

He glared at Frankie, who didn't move, waiting for the storm to play out. Then his large head swung back to Sahar. "I am sorry for you, my child," he said, deadly serious. "I am sorry for Nuri." He bowed toward Frankie. "Miss Rommel, I hope your stay in my country is pleasant. I thank you sincerely for this conversation. You are as intelligent as you are handsome." Abruptly, he left.

Frankie's stomach turned to ice. She felt the chill in her hands and feet. Sahar covered her face with her hands. "Honey, you need lessons in how to handle judges," Frankie said. "You never take them on in public."

"Did I act badly?"

"Actually, I admired the way you acted. But it's a mistake. Don't attack him, Sahar. Don't let him draw you into debates about women."

"But that is my command from Allah!"

"Your command is to change things. You won't change anything from the bottom of a pool." Sahar jerked her hands away from her face and stared with terror at Frankie. "Can you believe that Allah sent me along to help you stay alive?" Frankie asked, willing to try anything.

"Yes. I believe that."

"Then I hope you'll listen to me." Frankie picked up her snifter. Her hand trembled, but she was able to knock it back. "You have the guts, lady. It's your technique we need to tinker with."

# 13

The mountains below gleamed with pale greenness in the bright clarity of the moon. There were no gleams of light on their surface; nothing to show the touch of mankind. The scene had a changeless quality, the look of the landscape for millions of years before time—when suddenly they were over desert sands.

The smooth-sailing jet was so low that Frankie could see its shadow, enclosed in a halo of blue moonlight, pushing ahead of them like a porpoise leading a ship. The plane droned on. Frankie slept with her head against the window, but woke to a shift of speed and attitude as they slowed down.

Off in the distance a row of rock-studded hills reached for them. The jet was only a couple of hundred feet over the ground. Dry desert shrubbery grew sparsely between rocks when a grassy meadow opened beneath them like an unexpected yawn.

Frankie saw a scattering of yellow lights. A few appeared like splashes of fire on the hillside east of a wide valley floor. "Qahtan," Sahar said, her eyes bright with anticipation.

"Are you sure it isn't Bethlehem?" Frankie asked, enthralled with the view. "It looks like a nativity scene."

173

The airport in Lander, Wyoming, was bigger than the one in Qahtan. A blond-headed, blue-eyed man guided the pilot to a location painted on the tarmac. They stopped near a low, brightly lighted building made of sand-colored brick. "What about luggage?" Frankie asked.

Sahar sat with her head bowed, staring at her hands. "Someone will bring our baggage." Lifting her face she smiled at Frankie with fear, and anticipation. "From this point, all our wants are provided." She pulled her veil over her face.

The charm of wearing a veil had worn off, and reluctantly Frankie got hers in place. The damn thing was a nuisance that turned walking at night into an adventure. She carefully made her way down the ramp to the pavement, then moved through wonderfully clean, cool air into the small terminal building. It gleamed bright, like an all-night diner. Prince Muhammad nodded with severity at them as they entered, then strode away. "We are expected to wait in the women's area," Sahar said.

The women's area suffered from blight. One door, no windows, and the smell of a chemical toilet filled its emptiness. Frankie touched the money belt on her hip, but—even though it held her passport, five one-hundred-dollar bills in U.S. currency and an equivalent value in dinars—there was no particular comfort gained from knowing she had it on. She lifted her veil, dragged out a compact and stared at herself. "Four o'clock in the morning and all's well." She glared at the lines on her forehead. "How are you doing?"

Sahar smiled. "To borrow an expression, I am on hold."

Ten minutes later they climbed into the rear seat of a luxurious Chrysler Imperial. Sahar had adjusted their veils to cover only half the face, leaving their eyes free to see. The eastern sky glowed at the rim with turquoise-green, and the full moon—hanging over the low hills to the west—floated like a huge balloon. It could have been Lander, Frankie thought, before the cowtown filled with garish lights, motels, and roads. She felt instant affection for the sagebrush and boulders scattered through the desert.

Sahar opened her window in spite of the frowns aimed at her by the driver. Frankie did the same. The cool clean air had a sensuous quality, like a lover's breath. "It has rained," Sahar said. "See how the tamarisk stretches with happiness?"

It was true. The car kicked up only small amounts of dust, and Frankie could see occasional blossoms in the desert brush, like muted candles. They rounded a corner and dropped into a pasture enclosed in a shallow valley. "Look!"

Ahead of them a shepherd tried to keep his flock of goats from scattering. As the car flew by they heard his angry screams, inflamed beyond endurance. The driver glanced quickly into the rearview mirror, a look of malicious joy on his face.

"Where does the water for the pasture come from?" Frankie asked.

"In ancient times, Qahtan was an oasis on the edge of the Rub al-Khali, which is the name for the large empty space of the Arabian desert." As Sahar spoke she stared dreamily out the window. "Scientists of today know the water bubbles up from an underground river that flows from the mountains of Asir to the Arabian Gulf." Her hands rippled softly like a river. "With money from oil, my grandfather brings water into this valley from the river below, giving it life."

The car slowed and the ride softened as the surface of the road changed to pavement. They turned to the left, driving toward a spacious-looking complex of modern stone-colored buildings. On Frankie's side a pool and fountain appeared, surrounded by grass and carefully tended shrubs. It was lovely, but out of place, like an industrial park on the moon.

Sahar seemed to shrink. "I am home."

A huge stone castle with open balconies, thick columns, and high rounded arches loomed into view. It would easily cover a city block. They drove around a corner and an older building emerged, with a gleaming white face and balconies that reached four floors over the ground. Elaborately carved wooden screens, at least ten feet high, stood on the balconies, covering the doors and windows.

The driver stopped near the wide steps at the entrance and opened Sahar's door. Frankie slid out behind her. Sahar trotted quickly up the steps, as though in a hurry to get it over with. Frankie had to run to keep up.

A high, pointed arch vaulted over the entrance. The huge wooden door, with stiff, stylized carving, was tucked under it. Slowly the door opened inward, as though being dragged by a mouse on a leash. Sahar stepped inside and Frankie followed.

Tapestries hung from walls off in the distance, fields away. A high ceiling hung over the marble floor. Electric lights, covered with ornate golden shades, burned like torches from the top of dark wooden poles. The door closed behind them.

A small, sharp-eyed older woman stared at Sahar. She wore an *abaya,* with no veil and no cover over her short, white hair. Sahar quickly unhooked the veil on one side, letting it hang down from one ear. It looked stylish, somehow. "Umm Majd!" she exclaimed, leaning toward the woman. But as though to keep herself from contamination, the old lady jumped back.

Another woman, as tall as Frankie but heavier, wearing a nightgown and lavender robe, stood quietly to one side of the old woman Sahar had called Umm Majd. Her luxuriant black hair was grained with threads of silver, and her face radiated with remarkable beauty. Her resemblance to Sahar was extraordinary. She stared at Sahar without expression. "Bushra?" Sahar asked, taking the same hesitant step in her direction.

The woman nodded, but cut off any approach by stepping up to Frankie and holding out her hand. "Miss Rommel, I am the Princess Bushra, the wife of Prince Muhammad abu Ibrahim ibn al-Rashid." She spoke in a low, melodic voice. "You are most welcome."

Frankie did as Sahar had done with her veil, then smiled at the woman and took her hand. "Thank you." She turned toward Sahar. "We made it," she said cheerfully, trying to include her in the welcome.

"Will you follow me please?" Princess Bushra asked.

"You are no doubt exhausted by your travels. Allow me to show you your room."

Frankie hesitated. She couldn't walk away from Sahar, who stood like a statue, her face turned away from the violent glare of Umm Majd. "Tell me what to do, Sahar."

"You must go with my aunt."

"Will you be all right?" she asked foolishly, as though somehow she could make it all better.

"Of course."

Frankie touched the girl's shoulder. It felt like an iron spike. She pulled Sahar into her and hugged her. "Chin up."

Sahar smiled. "Okay."

"This way, please," Bushra said, touching Frankie's elbow.

When they turned a corner and were out of sight, Frankie felt the weight of Princess Bushra's eyes. "Thank you for showing me to my room," Frankie said in an effort to break the ice.

"We are not animals without education or feeling, Miss Rommel," Bushra said, with an odd mixture of warmth and reserve. "But surely you have heard the proverb: As ye sow, so shall ye reap."

She was direct enough. "I've heard it," Frankie said, aware that she wasn't in a position to get critical. "But Sahar's been looking forward to coming home. And she's so young."

Bushra angled her head. "Perhaps, after your stay in our country, you will understand." A light, clean fragrance—not like any perfume Frankie had ever smelled—misted out of Bushra's hair. It fit the aura she projected: an assurance that bordered on arrogance. She walked like a queen, not a princess. "I have love in my heart for Sahar, but there is also loathing. As for Umm Majd, it will be easier for her to wash and bathe a leper than to stay in the same room with her granddaughter."

Frankie bit her lip. "I'm sorry."

Bushra took Frankie by the arm. Sahar had shown the same easy familiarity, woman to woman. "For her sake, of

177

course, I am glad you are here. She will need a friend." But where Sahar's touch felt like a pat on the back, Bushra's grip controlled like a trucker's hand on the wheel. "There is much to do and see in Qahtan, and I trust you will take advantage during your stay in our city. However, you should know that certain conduct is prohibited. I will be pleased to assist you in any way, and answer for you questions you may have." She steered them up a wide staircase.

"Thank you," Frankie said, not wishing to tread on any toes. "Everyone I've met so far speaks perfect English," she said, searching for common ground.

"The women learn at the University for Women in Qahtan. The instruction is most thorough and extensive."

"*That's* a surprise," Frankie said. "I'd have sworn you learned in England."

"I am complimented." She let go of Frankie's arm.

"Have you traveled much?" Frankie asked, doing her best to smile.

"There is no need inside of me to travel. Beyond the borders of my county, I have been to Mecca, Riyadh, and Jiddah." She sounded proud of her provincialism.

"You've not been to Europe?"

The princess frowned, as though she found the question stupid. "Like most of the women of my country, I have not even been to Cairo. The shallow surface image one acquires through travel cannot compare with the rich intricacy of one's own land."

They reached a landing at the top of the stairs. A long balcony, guarded by an elaborate wrought-iron rail, wrapped around a large, open courtyard. With measured steps Bushra lead them to a platform that looked over the ground below. A fountain gurgled beneath them, ringed with tropical plants and a colorful garden. It generated a coolness that lifted up like a mountain cloud. "This is beautiful," Frankie said. The rug underfoot was worn, but bright with color. Overhead, there was no roof over the patio. Through the large opening she saw the final gleam of a planet in a radiant sky that was no longer dark.

"You are in the Royal Palace of Rashid, for Women. It is

quite typical of traditional Arabic architecture for centuries." Bushra sounded bored, like a tour guide who had been on the job too long. Resting a hand on the rail, she looked at the garden below. "The architecture, with thick walls of bricks made of the sands of the desert, and many floors that surround a courtyard, is centuries old."

Frankie admired the huge wooden doors she had seen, and the wood exposed between the rug and the wall. The luxuriant strips looked like layers of chocolate. "All this wood. It's mahogany, isn't it?"

The princess nodded. "It was brought to us from Africa, by camel caravan, forty years ago." Her expression flickered momentarily with the anguish of someone more comfortable with the past. "Today, the caravans are trains. The drivers are not bedouin of the desert. Each week, these trains bring more riches to Qahtan than could be carried on the backs of camels in a month."

"How old is the palace?"

"It was built in Hijri year 1375, which corresponds to Christian Era year 1955." The princess's eyes, also hazel, flashed occasionally with arrogance. "To the Christian, time begins with the birth of the Prophet Jesus. However, to the Muslim, it starts with the birth of Islam." She looked like a statue of Sahar, carved out of ice. "Islam was born when the Prophet Muhammad began his long, arduous journey for Allah, in the Christian Era of 622."

Frankie knew that much already, from her English translation of the Qur'an. "Is there also a palace for the men?"

Bushra gazed up through the aperture at the clean sky. "No. The man of power has his own palace." She looked steadily ahead. "This building in which we stand was the palace for King Najib, the first of the sons of King al-Rashid. However, Allah took him away before he could live here. Nuri, the third son who is now the king, preferred a palace of his own. You observed it as you drove in from the airport?"

Frankie smiled. "An immense building. I didn't think we'd be able to drive around it."

Bushra's smile was thin, but could still be characterized as a smile. "The palace for women is not as modern as the king's fortress, but is far more comfortable. The old way is best. Our walls are thick"—she showed with her hands a wide distance—"of mud brick. We are cool during the day, yet warm at night. The cool air is natural, from the garden. It is not artificially refrigerated, which pulls in dust and grit."

"Who lives here?"

Bushra answered with civility, if without pleasure. "It is for the women of the royal family without husbands or fathers for protection. The sultana, Umm Majd, is the head of this house. She is the divorced wife of King Nuri."

"Does Sahar's mother live here?"

"My poor sister." Bushra examined the long fingers of her hands. "Yes. She has remained here since the death of her husband, Sahar's father, Prince Majd. However, Hanifah enjoys to see glimpses of the outside world, and has traveled much with Sahar. One can observe the result. King Nuri has wisely ordered her to stay in Switzerland until after . . ."

Frankie didn't pursue the unfinished comment. "Do you live here, Princess Bushra?"

"I do not." She sounded angry. "I have a husband, who provides for me a palace. It is in the mountains above Qahtan. I remain here during your visit, to assist Umm Majd. It is my husband's wish."

Frankie let her hand feel the texture of the iron rail. She'd have loved a nightcap before toddling off to bed. There were a flock of questions she wanted to ask, but Bushra turned away from the rail and started to walk along the balcony path. Frankie followed. "What time will Sahar get up?" she asked, cheerfully. "I'd like to see the *souqs.*"

"My niece will not wish to leave the palace, Miss Rommel," Bushra said without glancing at Frankie. "There are the emotions of the people for her to fear. It is only within these walls that she is safe." The princess stopped in front of a door with an ornate brass handle. Geometric designs had been carved into its borders and Arabic calligraphy had been burned into its wood surface. She pushed the lever down, opening the door. "Your room, Miss Rommel," she said, clicking on a light switch.

The light switch activated three wall lamps, like torches on top of thick vines, seven feet off the floor. There were no windows in the large room. A carpet with borders of gold lace, filled with elaborate, colorful floral designs on a deep purple background, covered the floor. A rope braided with threads of gold hung from the ceiling two feet from one of the walls. Vivid seascape photographs were on two of the walls and a photographic mural depicting a mountain valley and blue sky hung from the third. In one corner a silk comforter and pillows spread over a thick queen-size mattress, and a curtain covered a doorwell in the other.

The toilet. Frankie's bag and briefcase were stacked in the middle of the room. "This is nice," she said heartily, wondering where she was supposed to hang her clothes and what she was supposed to sit on.

The voice of a man suddenly vibrated through the room with vivid clarity. *"Allahu Akbar! Allahu Akbar!"* Frankie jumped. She had heard it before, in Cairo, but it still startled her. *"Ashhadu Alla Ilaha Illa Allah! Falah! Allahu Akbar!"*

When Frankie jumped, Bushra smiled, then calmly walked over to the curtain and pulled it back. "Here is the water closet," she said. "If you need the help of a servant, pull the rope. But do not expect a quick response." She moved to the door. "Most are quite lazy. I will leave you now. That recording is the call to prayer, played throughout the palace. I go now to pray with Umm Majd." She nodded with civility. "I hope you rest well. Please let me know if there is anything for me to do for you."

"I will."

Bowing slightly, Bushra backed out the door and pulled it shut.

## Wednesday, August 21, 1991
## Chicago, Illinois

Husam al-Din frowned at his watch. Not even a minute had gone by since the last time he peeked at it. He glanced at other lawyers in the law library of the Midwest Securities and Exchange Building and sighed. All of them seemed absorbed in their tasks, but he couldn't concentrate on his: a reply brief in a sexual assault case.

Money should not be wasted on such offal, he thought. The man who does such things was not entitled to protection from law! For a fifty-seven-year-old doctor to fondle the genitalia of a six-year-old girl was abominable. Such men should be castrated, or killed.

His eyes closed as a dreamlike expression bloomed on his face. To fondle the genitalia of a dancer with red hair was another matter. The prospect excited him. He imagined the softness, the warmth of Emily Scot—only a promise—but why else would she ferret out his telephone number from their casual meeting of weeks ago, and send him a ticket to see her performance? He felt his face moving slowly down her firm, muscular stomach, as he had witnessed the technique of lovers in the movies. His hands would stroke with tenderness her ankles, her naked blushing breasts, her mouth, her ears. . . .

"Sir, we close in ten minutes," a thin well-dressed young man said. "Can I help you with these?" He referred to the pile of books in front of Husam, half of which he had not had the time to open.

"May I leave them out?" Husam asked. "I will finish with them in the morning."

The librarian hesitated. "Sure. Leave a note with them, okay?"

"Of course."

He had a small steak at the restaurant in his hotel: the Robert Browning. Afterward he rode the quaint old elevator, operated by a bellman, to the seventeenth floor. He was confident that Emily would love their rooms. In the bedroom a huge king-size bed thrust away from the wall like a peninsula pushing into a warm, soft ocean. In the small sitting room that was down a step, large windows rose above quaint steam radiators. He opened them and the breeze pushed into the sheer lace curtains, billowing them out like sails.

He peeled down to the waist and splashed water in his armpits, then shaved, brushed his teeth, gargled, and slapped after-shave lotion on his cheeks. Rarely did he take such care of his appearance. He put on a clean shirt and stared at himself in the mirror, tying his tie. Of late it seemed that his eyes were pushed deeper in his head, and new lines etched his face. He didn't want to think about it.

Shutting the window in the sitting room to a mere crack, he turned on the floor lamp and peeled the lead-coated seal off a bottle of Grand Marnier, loosening the cork. He placed the liqueur on the antique table in front of the couch, with two rose-colored glasses on fine stems on either side. If they met a second time—and he was certain they would—he would bring candles.

At the theater, Husam took his seat in the eighth row, very close to the center. He read the program given him by the woman who showed him where to sit. A musical play. He had heard of such things but had never seen one.

The lights dimmed, the conversations faded out, the curtain went up. Husam wasn't sure if Emily could see him. The lights shined brightly in the faces of the performers and none of them seemed aware of the audience. They lived in a world of fantasy behind an invisible wall, and Husam quickly became engrossed in the story. He laughed and applauded mightily. When Emily was on stage, he delighted in the enthusiasm with which she would kick and was amazed at the athleticism of her twirls and leaps. He heard himself growling, and knew it was with lust.

After the performance, he waited for her under the marquee as they had agreed. The crowd in front of the theater dissipated, although traffic on the streets continued to blare and curse its way through the night. All manner of people hurried and wandered along the sidewalk. When Emily appeared, the sight of her stopped his breath. She wore black satin tights, red shoes with low heels, and a colorful cape over her shoulders. She was gorgeous to his eyes! Her red hair had been brushed but not tamed.

Why had he been such a fool, he thought, rushing toward her. He had no flowers. "Emily!"

"Hi, Husam," she said, waving. "You made it."

"I would not miss this for the world." He wanted to take her in his arms and crush her, but all she would allow was a quick hug. "You are so beautiful tonight, like a rare jewel!" he exclaimed lavishly. "How I love to watch you dance. You were wonderful!"

"What do you know about dancing, Husam?" she asked, flushing with delight and hooking her hand through his arm. She guided him down the steps. "How would you know if I was wonderful?"

"I am an Arab." He felt free as an animal in the wild, untroubled by thoughts that line the face and deepen the eyes, with nothing on his mind but the satisfaction of instinctive drives. "We know everything of life, and never lie." Except to our wives. "I have reserved for us rooms at the Robert Browning." His voice rumbled with lust.

She stopped and pulled away from him. "You've done what?"

"Come." He reached for her with confidence, but when he tried to pull her toward him, it was like dragging a tree out of its roots. "Is something wrong?" he asked. "Have I misjudged?"

"Well. I don't know. We don't really know each other, do we?"

Husam felt foolish. He wished for experience in these matters. He had many acquaintances. Why hadn't he talked to one of them? "You are embarrassed by me," he declared, seeing it in her face.

"No I'm not," she said. "I'm starved! Let's go eat."

"Yes! With pleasure!"

He hailed a cab, loaded Emily inside, and ordered the

driver to take them to the finest restaurant in town. "Wait," Emily said. "Husam. Do you know what I really love?"

"What?"

"Mexican."

They rode six blocks to Las Margaritas. Once there, they sat in a long, narrow bar filled with screaming drunks. Blazing overhead white neon lights glared on them, as over a Ping-Pong table. The clothes the patrons wore, and the language! Obscenities were traded back and forth with hilarity, among men and women with no respect! Was this the prelude to sex?

Emily ordered a margarita as they waited for a table in the dining room. When Husam found out what was in it— tequila with a worm in the bottom of the glass—he ordered a beer.

"Al Din. Aladin?" the maître d' called. "Table for two!"

The dining room was another world, with soft candlelight, red tones, and bullfight scenes on velvet murals. The waiters were dressed like matadors. When the door to the bar opened and shut, sound blasted through like arctic air. "I hope you like it here," Emily said, taking hold of his hand as they were led to a far recess. "It's quiet—anything would be, after that!—and the food is great." She looked at him with worry, as though realizing it had been a mistake to bring him here.

Husam squeezed her hand, trying to recapture the wild and free feeling that had exhilarated him earlier, in front of the theater. But when they were seated, he could not help but observe that her appearance had changed. Across the table from him in a romantic booth for two, there was fragility in her expression, and he thought he saw the expectation of pain. Where was the animal on the stage, with the high kicks? Or the provocative passenger on the airline, who talked to him of ships that pass in the night? "How is your case?" she asked.

She asked for love. Husam had none to give. He looked only for escape. "It cries for justice," he said.

"Really. Tell me."

185

He had never understood the savagery of this Rick Adamson, but in talking of it to Emily, in this Mexican restaurant in America, it became clear to him. Americans have no control over their impulses. The brutal wound inflicted on Abd al-Hafiz was completely predictable, given the influences of life in America! Consider the barroom they had just been in. A public establishment where bestial behavior was encouraged! Or the television which he avoided, or the contamination from the movies, available for anyone to see.

He felt her hand on his. "Now I've made you sad."

"No. You have made me see."

Husam did not tell her of his disgust for the food. The rice and beans were covered with sauces made of pork fat and cheese. The peppers did nothing but burn holes in one's mouth. He picked at the offerings on his plate and encouraged her to talk to him of her feelings and her existence. Everything she said about her family life and undisciplined early years confirmed the thoughts that rippled in his brain. Women want love. And in America they believe the freedom to flaunt their sexuality will bring it to them.

They know nothing of Islam, submission to the will of God. They do not understand the simple truth: love and happiness is possible only through control, and discipline.

"Will you marry me?" he asked, with no understanding of why he would ask such a thing.

She smiled, as though the question was perfectly reasonable. "You already have a wife. Besides, Husam, we don't need to get married." She twisted her body in a provocative stretch that arched her breasts, and pressed her leg against his.

He felt sadness for her. For them to come together with lust would be a perversion, but he knew he could not explain that to her. She was a fragile vase; a woman who needed a man to guide her growth, and for protection. He could never bring himself to smash the fragile vase. "It was a foolish question," he said, thinking of Abir and her silence. There was no longer a link between them. "If my wife had given me a son, I would not be here."

"That's a real turn-on."

He reached for her hand across the table. She allowed him to cover it, but could not keep the tears from her eyes. He sighed deeply, knowing it was too late for Emily—then was suddenly jolted by thoughts of his daughter. Was it too late for Kawthar? She too had been infected with the wild desire for freedom, like an animal with no God to guide its movements; only instinct. Where was Kawthar? Had she found a shelter? He hoped that Allah had guided her toward men who would pity her youth rather than exploit it. He wanted to cry. "I will take you to your home."

In the taxicab he felt a rightness about himself that approached piety. Emily sat next to him, her arms crossed, staring out the window. "It's been unreal," she said.

"Yes. I thank you for the ticket. You were marvelous on the stage. I will not forget."

She laughed. "What a waste." He didn't respond. Why should he cause more pain? "What do you know about genetics, Husam?"

He shrugged. "It is the science of genes. I have never studied it. Do you have an interest?"

"Your wife can't give you a son, Husam. She isn't responsible."

Husam frowned. "What is it you are saying?"

"It's the male sperm that determines the sex of the baby." She looked at him with triumph. "We learn that in high school. Your wife can give you babies, but the male of the species is responsible for its sex."

# 14

Sahar had been sitting on a pillow on a thick rug, reading a book, when the tiny, dried-up-looking servant woman unlocked the door and let Frankie in. They were in a large room, as barren of furniture as all of the rooms Frankie had seen. When Sahar saw who it was, she slammed the book shut and jumped up. "Frankie! I have been so worried for you!" she exclaimed, rushing over.

The servant scuttled out the door, pulling it shut behind her. They hugged one another, long and hard. "I'm okay," Frankie said, comforting the girl.

She wasn't. She'd been awakened by the noonday call to prayer and it had been uphill ever since. The same male voice that had blared through a speaker at the crack of dawn had boosted her out of bed. After getting up and washing her face, she'd tried the door. It was locked. It had taken ten minutes of incessant chain-pulling before someone let her out. And then she realized she had nowhere to go. Finally Bushra appeared on the scene. Reluctantly she issued the order for Frankie to be taken to Sahar's apartment.

"How are you doing, girl?" She heard the key turn and realized the little servant woman had locked the two of them in. "Let's hope there isn't a fire."

Sahar wore magnificent red silk pantaloons, a white silk

blouse with a soft collar and no sleeves, and shimmering purple slippers. "I am treated as a prisoner by my family. It is humiliating beyond words!" She pushed away from Frankie and stalked the floor in anger. "No one will speak to me. My cousins and aunts hide from me, like a person with contagious diseases!"

"Not very friendly, is it?" Frankie said, doing her best. She wore the same *abaya* she'd been in for two days, without the veil. It had started to smell. There was nothing to put her briefcase on so she dropped it on the floor. "Adversity must make for beauty," she said, wondering if she'd started talking in proverbs. "In spite of what they're doing to you, you look great!" Frankie made herself shine, wanting to inspire confidence.

Sahar nodded vacantly. "I have lived in these rooms since age thirteen. It was my gift, with appearance of menses, when first I became a woman." She grabbed Frankie by the hand and led her to the window. "I am on the highest floor of the palace. Perhaps they wish me to jump."

"Don't even think about it."

"Do you see?" she asked, pushing drapes out of the way and pointing to the north. "The minarets of the Mosque al-Rashid. I open my window at night in time to hear the muezzin sing the call to prayer, and I hear him again as the sun breaks into the sky. Now his song is a recording, piped through the palace like orders on a ship at sea. His voice sounds of metal, like a steel robot, rather than a man who would bring you to Allah." Angrily, she turned away. "What does it matter to me? I am used to praying with Umm Majd, in the servant's quarters, with women to whom prayer is fulfillment." She clawed at her face with her hands, gritting her teeth, then tossed her head proudly. "Now, I pray alone. It is enough."

Frankie wanted to touch her, but Sahar's attitude wouldn't allow it. "You will beat them," she said, reaching for encouragement.

Sahar whirled on her. "Beat? I wish to beat no one."

"I mean you're tougher than they are."

The large room radiated with light, from a string of windows along the north wall and an opaque white bubble in the roof. There were three doors in the walls, obviously to other rooms. "We are locked in this apartment. But I do not need my Rick for escape," she declared. "Come. I will show you."

She led Frankie through a heavily curtained, double-paneled sliding glass door, to an outside balcony. The sudden blast of heat smashed into Frankie like a wave of hot water. Sahar quickly shut the door behind her. "There is an entrance between apartments." She marched along the balcony to a doorway and pushed through a heavy wooden door into a hallway inside the building. "Come." As she led the way back to her front door, Frankie could feel her rage. "Yet my door is locked! You see?" She twisted the doorknob and rattled it, proving it was locked.

"What's the point?" Frankie asked as Sahar spun around and marched back down the hall and onto the balcony. Frankie trailed along behind.

"A symbol. A statement to my cousins that I am to be shunned, as one with a virus!" She reentered the room, banging the door shut behind her.

"Well, I'm immune from whatever it is you might infect me with," Frankie said cheerfully. "I'll move in. We'll talk constantly. Day and night."

Suddenly, like a madwoman, Sahar dropped on a cushion and began hammering it with her fists. "I am not humbled by them! I am a woman, as Allah intended me to be, not as they are, bent and shriveled by lies! When I go to my death, I will march proudly into the square and shake my fists!"

Frankie watched with horror. She knelt down next to Sahar and put her hand on the girl's shoulder. "You are not going to your death," she said firmly. "Sahar. I am so glad I am here."

Sahar stopped. She turned her face toward Frankie, her eyes red and her nose dripping. "Why? You have never had an opportunity to witness the actions of a crazy woman?"

"Honey, *I'm* nuttier than you are. You are so tough! I have more admiration for you than anyone I've ever known."

Sahar smiled at her. But then she bounded to her feet with frantic energy. "The mufti my king has appointed for me is a mule!"

"A common client complaint," Frankie said. "Have you seen him? What's he like?"

"We speak this day on the telephone. I know nothing of his appearance. But I suspect he is covered with hair, like the ass of a horse! To my questions he has but one answer: 'That is of no importance.'"

Frankie looked for a cushion to sit on. "Can he speak English?"

"He will speak with you," Sahar said, anticipating Frankie. "He will expect to see you soon." Soft greens and yellows, in expanding sworls like the nebula of faraway galaxies, covered the rug. Frankie was about to drop on a cushion when Sahar bounded toward a door. "I will fix you a cup of tea."

Frankie grabbed her briefcase and followed. They entered a smaller room furnished with a beautifully carved table and matching chairs. Heavy drapes covered the windows. A compact kitchen arrangement was behind a counter, with sink, electric stove, and modern refrigerator. Frankie headed for one of the chairs at the table and sat down. She had not realized what a luxury a chair—any kind of chair—could be. "Where do I find this mufti of yours?"

"Have your driver take you to the law court in Old Town," Sahar said. "Unless you too are confined to this jail." She filled a teakettle and placed it on the stove, then stomped angrily into the dining area and paced the floor. "You must be veiled, otherwise the *muhaddin* will attack with their evil eyes and thoughts. You must keep your head down like this"—she mimicked a humble servant—"and walk hurriedly from place to place, like a crab who cannot stand the light of the sun. Go in the morning when it is cool, before the noonday call to prayer. He will have a small office in the courtyard. His name is Wadi abu Tamir ibn Ahmad."

Frankie dragged out a pad and pen and made Sahar spell his name as she wrote it down. "What can you tell me about him?"

She shrugged. "He is of the Ghamid clan in the Asir. They have the reputation of enjoyment of life, but he has been to the *madrasah*—Al Azhar University in Cairo—perhaps since it began, a thousand years ago. He sounds to me very old, and without humor." She poured tea into elegant white china cups. "His first document is ready. He has reviewed it with a jurist from Cairo and believes it is perfect." She sat down, picked up her tea and glared at Frankie. "I do not think the statement will be perfect. But we shall see."

The call to prayer, Frankie learned, was determined by the sun. The first call was at the crack of dawn. The second came at noonday, at the precise moment when there was the least amount of shadow. The third occurred in the afternoon, when the shadow and the stick that caused it were the same length. The fourth filled the city with its resonance as the sun was setting, and the final call came four hours later.

Frankie concluded that Arabs generally were small and ascetic-looking because they didn't get enough sleep. Only the dead could remain unconscious through the call. She couldn't account for the exceptions to her rule, the men and women whose growth hadn't been stunted.

She was determined to stay with Sahar until someone threw her out. She hoped it wouldn't be Sahar, who might tire of her phony optimism. That evening, after the muezzin's fourth call, a servant woman brought them chunks of lamb on a silver platter, surrounded by a deliciously scented rice. They wrapped it in large leaves of lettuce and ate with their fingers. Both of them were reading when there was a knock on the door.

Angrily, Sahar jumped to her feet. "Does not the fool know I cannot open my own door?"

"Sahar," a woman's voice urgently whispered through the door, followed by words in Arabic.

The effect on Sahar was electric. She blushed all over with happiness and rushed to the door. "Jamilah!" She pressed her face into the door and words gushed out. Frankie listened to them jabber in Arabic, when Sahar—the desperate loneliness in her face replaced with joy—flew past her, to the sliding panel that opened onto the balcony. "My cousin Jamilah! She doesn't care what anyone thinks. She wishes to see me!"

Moments later, with their arms draped over each other like old pals, they gaily jumped through the balcony door. Jamilah had the elegant thin face and beautiful complexion of a Navaho Indian. She was dressed entirely in black silk, loose-fitting pantaloons, and flowing shirt. Frankie smiled with pleasure as they were introduced. After a hug and a kiss they were old friends.

Frankie left as soon as she could, but not until Jamilah gave her some advice. "The driver will insist to take you all the way to the law court, which is terrible mistake." Her English was not as good as Sahar's. "Have him leave you at the wall, and walk to the law court. Because of so many people, it is quicker to walk through the marketplace than to drive through it." Jamilah skipped with youthful exuberance as she talked. "There is also the excitement of the *souqs* you will wish to experience," she continued. "Be not afraid. Ours are not a tangle of vines like Marrakesh, or others you may have seen in Egypt. Our Old Town is not an anthill. Rashidis are devout Muslims, obedient to the law. We do not lie, cheat, or steal."

Jamilah stopped, her sharp eyes punching at Frankie with good humor. "As for your driver, order him to leave you at the wall and wait for you, rather than park importantly by the law court. It will piss him off."

Frankie hoped the door to her room would not be locked. She was ready for bed. It opened and she staggered inside. A clean *abaya*, freshly scented underwear, and a filmy silk nightgown was stacked neatly on her bed.

She didn't hear the final call to prayer.

193

# 15

## Yawm al-Khamis, 11 Safar, A.H. 1412 (Thursday, August 22, 1991)

In the darkness of the palace rooms without windows, the only way to know which call to prayer was blaring at you was to turn on the light and look at your watch. Allahu Akbar, God is great, so what? Frankie thought, wishing she had something to throw at the speaker. She turned on a light and looked at her watch: 6:23 A.M.

She felt drugged. The last thing she wanted to do was get up, go to the water closet, and look at her face in the mirror. It would be puffy and lined. She'd a lot rather stay in bed the rest of her life and dream. There were so many nice things to dream about: beaches, mountains, romance, money, power. She sighed, thought how wonderful a toasted bagel and a cup of coffee would taste, and got out of bed.

The water closet had a red porcelain tub, spigots, and a fan in the ceiling. There was a wall cabinet with several jars, filled with what appeared to be lotions, creams, and soaps. A huge Turkish towel hung on a hook, near the light switch. She shrugged out of her nightgown and drew a bath. She scooped up some of the jars that looked interesting, spread them on the floor within reach, and climbed in the tub. It was wonderful, luxuriating in all the heady scents and soap bubbles. Later she scrubbed herself dry with the towel, loving the feeling of its texture on her skin.

She experimented with one of the lotions, rubbing its coolness in her face and hands, then slid into her clean *abaya,* letting the hood and veil hang off her back. She fixed her face with a clear lipstick and a trace of eye shadow, checked her briefcase—the money belt and passport were there, along with a legal pad, some ballpoint pens, and the Qur'an—and tried the door.

Locked.

"God damn."

She alternated between yanking on the cord and glaring at her watch, allowing fifteen seconds between yanks. Two minutes later she heard footsteps hurrying down the balcony to her door. The key turned and it opened. "Good morning," Princess Bushra said, smiling and frowning at the same time. "Did you have a nice rest?"

Frankie spent the next hour with Bushra, trying to line up her expectations with the reality of her situation. She asked that her door be left unlocked, explaining that she had been assured by Prince Muhammad of the absolute safety of her person and possessions, and wasn't in the least afraid. Bushra promised to take the matter up with Umm Majd. She met the servants who had been assigned to her: the dried-up weasel-eyed woman who had locked her into Sahar's apartment, and a young Filipino girl with a pretty smile. Neither of them spoke English, but with Bushra negotiating, they agreed on some signs. Then Tasha, the Filipino, brought them breakfast, which they ate in the garden. Biscuits called cakes, figs, bananas, and tea.

Frankie didn't know whether to ask for permission to go see Sahar's mufti or simply announce that she had an appointment to see him. "I have business to conduct at the law court this morning," she said. "Will that pose a problem?"

"You are quite free to leave the palace at any time you wish, Miss Rommel," Bushra told her. "I will accompany you, if you wish—although you will be quite safe, alone. You will of course wear the veil. It is lawful, in Qahtan, for a woman to wear the veil of the bedouin rather than the full cover required for the traveler."

Frankie hadn't looked at her veil that morning. She tried to find it with her hand, pulling it in front of her. "How is it different?"

"The costume of the bedouin is more practical. The veil covers only the nose, mouth, and neck of the woman. A band is stretched across the forehead, but there is no shield over the eyes." She bent her head slightly, indicating disapproval. "With some women, unfortunately, it is most provocative."

The figs were delicious, but the cakes were an acquired taste. The tea was as thick and black as coffee.

"Your driver is Talal. There is a telephone in our library from which he can be called, and he speaks quite good English."

The resemblance of Bushra to Sahar continued to amaze Frankie. It went beyond looks. They teased their hair with identical gestures, and when they raised their eyebrows or opened their mouths, their faces reflected the same elegance. "You and Sahar could be sisters," Frankie said, in as inoffensive a voice as she could muster. "You look so much alike. I can't get over it."

Bushra actually smiled. "My sister Hanifah is the mother of Sahar. Hanifah and I were born of the same mother, Umm Amal, at the same time. What is the word?"

"Twins." Frankie wondered if she should have guessed. "And you are married to the king's brother, Prince Muhammad, while Hanifah was married to the king's son?"

"You are surprised at this?" Bushra asked sharply.

"No," Frankie said. "I'm just trying to get it straight."

"I was divorced by my first husband, who is the son of Prince Umar, the ambassador to your country. This was because of my inability to have sons and daughters." She frowned, but obviously expected no sympathy. "My uncle, the prince, gives me his protection. In return, I give him my love."

"Are we at the *souq?*" Frankie asked her driver, Talal. She sat in air-conditioned comfort, in the backseat of a Chrysler

CHOICE OF EVILS

Imperial. The slowly winding road, through a neighborhood that could best be described as eclectic—farms, desert, hovels, and estates—seemed to end at a throng of colorfully dressed men in *ghotras* and *thobes,* with a few drab *abayas* mixed in. The bunched-up mass were all trying to crowd through the same archway in the high mud wall that surrounded the *medina.* Stretching away from the archway, under shelters from the sun that hung out from the wall like awnings, tethered camels chewed and watched with eyes that never blinked, along with a few horses.

Talal—a thin young man with a tight, trim beard—bore a scar that slashed across his face. It started above his left eye and rearranged his brow like a fault line, ending below his cheek. "The market?" he asked, driving relentlessly forward. "Which market do you wish?" He glanced at her in the mirror, then averted his gaze.

"They're all together, aren't they? On the other side of the wall?"

"Yes. But you do not wish to mingle with bedouin of the desert or the unwashed common people of the *medina,* or the traders. All is chaos in the markets." He spoke with assurance, honking at a mule loaded with produce and the man who guided it.

"Actually, I do," Frankie said. "Let me out here."

"But we are not at the law court. You will get lost."

"Stop!"

With surprise, he looked at her again, slowing down. "You wish me to stop?"

"Yes."

He slammed on the brakes, throwing her forward. "I have stopped for you," he said with satisfaction.

Frankie opened the door, slung her briefcase over her shoulder and got out, ignoring Talal's impudence. She wanted relief from the oppression she'd felt in the palace, and the dry heat of the day felt good to her. She adjusted her veil, grateful it was the bedouin variety rather than the drape over her face she'd had to contend with as a traveler. She couldn't breathe, but at least she could see. Talal

197

watched with curiosity, then opened his door and jumped out. "I will go with you," he said. "You must have the protection of a man."

"Talal. Take the day off."

"But you cannot find the way to the law court."

"It's in front of the mosque," Frankie said, staring at the spires that pointed at the sky. He frowned. "How can I get lost?" She started toward the archway.

Passersby glanced at them furtively, then ducked past them. "How do you return to the palace?" Talal asked. "Do you wish for me to wait for you?"

They were only two miles from the palace, which—on another day—might have been a pleasant walk. But Frankie suspected this one would be a scorcher and that it couldn't be done without packing along at least a gallon of water. "Are there telephones at the law court?"

"Of course."

"Then I'll call you from there, and you can pick me up here."

Sahar and Jamilah had told her that a mud wall, twenty feet high, circled the perimeter of Old Town. There were cuts to accommodate roads, but it remained intact. If she walked through the *souqs* toward the mosque, she would reach the law courts. If she wasn't inside the wall, she'd gone too far and was out of town.

The women she saw walked in the way Sahar had described, like groundhogs wary about the hawk that circled overhead. Frankie knew she couldn't walk that way if her life depended on it. She was aware that her posture and stride attracted attention, even within the shield of an *abaya.* In spite of it, she did not feel threatened, and the farther she was from the car, the less she seemed to be an object of interest. The men walked proudly, most of them wearing *ghotras* and *thobes,* but some were in suits and a few of them wore nothing but rags. Urchins darted in and out—boys, she assumed—who were also literally dressed in rags: pieces of cloth that had been sewn together into shirts and short pants.

Once through the archway, the scene changed. Mud brick

structures leaned into the wall, which formed the back of houses and shops. Most had sections and panels of tinted glass, inviting passersby to peer in at cool displays of rich merchandise. Wide areas between streets were filled with rows of stalls made of poles ten feet high and roofed over with chicken wire and leaves, or canvas, or silk. The stalls established the margins for thin paths. She could have been in Taos, New Mexico, or the flea market in Denver, except for the smells, sounds, and heat. Conversations would erupt into screaming matches, the combatants with their faces two inches apart. They never touched, but appeared to heap fearful abuse on one another. Possibly they were discussing the weather, although the sounds and inflections would ruffle the fur on a cat.

Insistent commands and imploring tones were aimed at her as she walked past tables filled with cloth, gold pieces, lamps, headsets, cassette tapes, dolls, sandals, produce, meats, spices, books, rugs, hand-carved statuary of animals, more spices, candles, pillows, lamps. The odors ranged from dead meat to perfume to spice to sweat to cedar; from the intoxicating to the disgusting. Frankie loved it. No one touched her except in the accidental jostling of the crowd, and no one threatened or tried to corral her, with anything other than words.

The ground was surfaced with the excrement of millions of animals, packed into the earth by bare feet, sandals, and hooves, then baked by the sun. There was very little dust, but lots of foot traffic meandering through the labyrinth of stalls. A narrow thoroughfare winding in the general direction of the mosque flowed with two opposite currents: one going in, the other coming out. The currents bubbled with people, some leading goats and burros loaded with goods, and an occasional car.

The sky was as big as Montana and as clean and blue as it gets. It was like standing on top of a peak in Colorado. Possibly it was her mood, but she wasn't destroyed by the heat, as she expected. It seemed to clean rather than cook. Side streets wound into the nameless main drag like mountain streams, following invisible contours. They were lined with mud buildings that crowded in like forest along a stream. Electrical lines and wires, organized like a huge hair net, hung overhead and faded off into the town. The minarets of the mosque approached too quickly; she didn't want to get there.

The women with escorts were worse off than those without them. The men acted with the bluster and crudity of someone on constant guard for insult. In their zeal to protect, they abused the women, shoving them around like objects. The women who weren't afflicted with an escort scrupulously avoided looking at the men, although the men would glance furtively at—what? Eyes above the veil, an ankle, the soft bumps of female breasts? Frankie thought of Sahar. "There should be intimacy between man and woman, but it is denied to my people. It is not allowed, except in the bedroom, often with clothes still on, and with no conversation. My people are burdened with false beliefs! That is what Allah wishes me to change."

Thinking of Sahar, Frankie quickened her pace toward the towering minarets of the mosque—when suddenly she felt a weightlessness on her left shoulder, and realized her briefcase was headed south. She grabbed for it, but it was gone. "Hey!"

A boy in rags, with red hair, disappeared around the corner of a stall. He weaved and ducked as he ran, darting between people without touching.

"You little bastard!" Frankie shouted, running after him.

The boy almost collided with a shopkeeper. When the man saw Frankie running toward him, an instant understanding of the situation registered in his face. He started a clamor, which quickly covered the market like a cloud. Without that, the boy would have escaped. Because of it, he didn't have a chance. Panting, Frankie stood by the man, who brusquely stopped her and shouted at her in Arabic.

"I'm sorry," Frankie said. "I don't speak the language."

His eyes lifted with astonishment. "Onglese?"

"Yes."

He nodded imperiously, then let her know with his motions that she should stay exactly where she was. He frowned and growled at her, his face turning into a storm. Frankie tried to leave, but he shook his head and motioned with his hands. "No, no, no!"

A foam of people surged toward them. They surrounded the boy, dragged along by a large man in a brown uniform. The uniform had her briefcase over his shoulder. He tried to hand it to the shopkeeper, who refused to take it. After a loud exchange, during which Frankie heard the word "Onglese," the policeman approached Frankie.

His dark eyes, wide apart, gazed at her with curiosity and neutral courtesy. "I speak no Onglese," he said, obviously uncertain as to what to do.

A small woman insinuated herself next to Frankie. Her *abaya* was of the finest material, and there was something stylish about her veil. The elastic band below her eyes was embroidered and the filmy material over her face tantalized, like a nightgown. "Perhaps I can help," she said in a low voice to Frankie. Staring at the policeman's feet, she spoke to him in Arabic. He replied respectfully, his gaze averted. They exchanged words with great civility. "He wishes for you to describe to him what happened."

"That little thief yanked my bag off my shoulder and ran off with it! If it hadn't been for this man"—Frankie made a gesture toward the shopkeeper, who glowered at her angrily —"it would've been gone."

After translating, the policeman said "Ah," handed the briefcase to Frankie, and spoke softly to the woman. "He wishes you to look inside to see if all the contents are there."

Frankie opened it and looked. Passport, money belt, pad, pencils, Qur'an—"Yes. I am very grateful to him and this man."

The woman nodded. "He would like your name and to know who you are with in Qahtan. He does not wish to offend, but must see your passport."

Frankie dug it out and handed it to him. He glanced at the photograph and handed it back. She gave her name, and said she was staying at the palace for women as the guest of Sahar bint Rashid.

The small woman looked at her with surprise. When she

translated the information, a murmur started, which spread through the small crowd like a wave, dissipating quickly. Those around them drifted away, glancing at Frankie then dropping their eyes. "He wishes you well, and asks me to tell you the matter will be taken care of."

The redheaded boy—he couldn't have been more than twelve years old—gazed up at Frankie with startling blue eyes. Suddenly he fell in front of her and touched the hem of her *abaya*. His long, thin arms clutched at her like branches of a tree, in a dark forest, at night. He jabbered at her in a high voice until the policeman scooped him off the ground and dragged him away.

Frankie felt oddly like a rock poking up in a stream. All the water coursed around her and the small woman. "I am Nur, of the clan of Dayyin," the woman said, her voice low and her head down. "Please tell to Sahar that many hearts are with her." She faded away.

When Frankie approached the shopkeeper, he turned away as though he couldn't see her. The table in his stall was covered with small, beautifully carved wooden boxes with exquisite lids. Frankie found one made of mahogany, large enough to hold three-by-five cards and small enough to fit easily into her briefcase. "How much?" she asked, picking it up. He said a few words. Frankie dug in her money belt and pulled out a note for one hundred dinars. According to the rate of exchange, it was worth $243. She handed it to him.

He sucked in his breath and took it from her hand carefully. In sudden torment, he closed his eyes, reopened them, and stared at the sky. He gave the note back. "Please," Frankie said.

"No no." He made motions with his hands, shooing her away.

"Well, here, then." She tried to give him back the box.

"No no. Onglese." He scowled at her, then a generous smile opened his face up with warmth. He opened his palms. "Da. Da." He nodded his head vigorously, smiling broadly, in obvious enjoyment.

He wanted her to keep the box, and might even have been

insulted by her crude attempt to pay him. Frankie was touched by the gesture. "Thank you very much."

"Da. Da."

Walking away, she saw the minarets of the mosque reaching into the sky. Oddly, the sight gave her a feeling of peace. They didn't thrust up like spears. They looked up, like eyes. Small chips of white and pale blue tile, in elaborate patterns, covered the surface, winding up to an open balcony on a platform a hundred feet over the ground.

Beyond the final row of stalls she walked out of the crowd and into a large open area surfaced with sandstone slabs. The original palace—the one Sahar had lived in as a girl—lined the northeast side. The huge fortress, four floors high and as long as a city block, was made of red mud with slits for windows. One set of huge double doors, closest to the far end but near the center, opened like the mouth of a whale, and men in desert costumes milled near it, passing in and out. Three or four cars were lost along its wall.

Ahead of her, across the courtyard—in the general direction of Mecca—stood the colonnades in front of the Mosque al-Rashid. Beyond them were steps rising to another vast courtyard. She could see an umbrella of water, like the top of a geyser, and beyond it the soft brown wall of the mosque. The twin minarets reached up like outstretched arms.

The southeast side of the courtyard was the law court. A colonnade marched in front of it. Behind the columns steps lifted into a courtyard lined with quiet buildings that looked like modern museums: wide, low steps, high ceilings, glass walls bordered with stone. A few men in low turbans and business suits walked slowly, almost prayerfully, with their hands laced together and their heads bent forward, as though in deep thought. Frankie was caught in the majesty of the place: the marbled floor with its beautiful mosaic patterns of white, blue, green, yellow, turquoise; the colonnades behind her, and the space! She found an entrance to a building and walked through glass doors into an air-conditioned hall.

She was in a library. Walls of books stood on both sides of a wide, carpeted aisle. Chairs, tables, and comfortable sofas were scattered throughout the immense open room. Natural lighting from skylights, in the ceiling twenty feet above the floor, filled the room with daylight. The men she saw, seated at tables or in small groups, worked diligently with scrolls on rollers, or pads of paper. She wandered through the stalls, trying to understand how it was organized, paying little attention to their strange glances.

She pulled down a thin volume and opened it, touched the page covered with Arabic calligraphy, and put it back. How could they read that stuff? she wondered, wandering deeper into the hall. Some patterns emerged. Maps of the Mideast were plastered to the ends of bookcases, with a particular country outlined in red. An Arabic word, followed by another word—often in a different alphabet—was beneath the map. The books in those shelves clearly referred to the map: Persian or Iranian, or Pakistani, or Egyptian.

It didn't occur to her that there were no women to be seen—when all at once there was tension in the air. No one had touched or spoken to her, but as one who has been in the sun too long suddenly feels sunburn, she could feel anger. She knew she didn't belong, and felt like a bear that had been airlifted into some other bear's territory. She looked for the exit.

Near the entrance—the doorway she'd come in—two uniformed men hurried toward her. Their expressions were easy to read: outrage. In quick steps a man was on either side, fingers gripping her arms like iron traps. They dragged her outside, whispering angrily at her in Arabic.

Frankie tried to help, but they hurt her arms, and she tensed the muscles in them. The taller of the two glared at her with surprise, which became a suspicion. In the courtyard he stuck his face in Frankie's and snarled at her. "I don't understand!" she said, looking around for help.

The few men in the area averted their eyes. The suit styles were European rather than American, with no shoulder pads in the coats, and cravats rather than ties. All of them wore headdresses: turbans, scarves, low black hats with wide brims. All of them walked alike too. Their steps were deliberate and measured, as though even the act of walking required concentration; as though it too was a matter of grave importance.

She took a deep breath and smiled, but no one saw it. "You're hurting my arms. Look, I'm sorry." It didn't matter what she said. "I didn't know I was in the men's toilet, okay? Let go?" She moved her arms.

The short, heavy one released her and peered at her. "Anglash?"

"American."

He continued to glare at her, but with some understanding. The taller one released her too. Pointing at the door they had just dragged her out of, he shook his head no and waved his hands, clearly advising it was off limits. She nodded her understanding, but they still gave her the impression that she was under arrest. She felt surrounded, like a spider in an anthill.

The men spoke to each other in Arabic. One of them circled behind her, examining her ankles. "Wadi abu Tamir ibn Ahmad?" she asked uncomfortably, feeling sweat trickle down her back.

The tall man approached her from the front. As though not wishing to create a scene, but willing to suffer through one if necessary, he pointed a finger at her left breast, then touched it. Frankie was too surprised to react. He nodded at the other man as though satisfied about something. Together, they marched away.

"Madam Rommel?"

A small man, shorter than Frankie and wearing a double-breasted business suit of ancient vintage, stood quietly in the shadow cast by the colonnade. A soiled turban, not much larger than a sock hat, sat on his head, exposing a thinning hairline. He had obviously watched the episode. Frankie glared at him over her veil. "Are you Wadi abu Tamir ibn Ahmad?"

"I am. I have waited for you, but did not see you." He lowered his eyes, but a light smile mischievously played with his lips. *"L'école?"* he asked. "The college? Women are not

205

allowed. This is not America." Frankie nodded at him, smothering her feelings. She could feel herself blushing. "As for the business of . . ." He blushed also and looked down, but continued to smile.

"You saw that too?" Frankie asked. The little wimp might have done something about it.

"That was unfortunate. Most unfortunate. You see, the *muhaddin* thought perhaps you were a man masquerading as a woman, which would have been a most serious offense."

Was she supposed to be grateful that she'd passed the creep's examination? "I hope he wasn't disappointed by the experience." She adjusted the loop over her shoulder.

"Follow me, please?"

He hurried off in front of her at a pace that made everyone else appear to be walking in slow motion. His attitude suggested he didn't want anyone to think they were together. They aimed toward the structures on the far side of the courtyard. As they approached one of several doors in the middle of a long wall of glass, he held it for her and ushered her inside.

They were in an air-conditioned hallway. The courtyard looked cool through the blue-tinted glass. A wall of stone bricks lined the other side of the hall. It was interspersed at regular intervals with doorways, but no doors.

He turned into one of them and Frankie followed. The ceiling was ten feet from the floor, and pillars of light, from long vertical window wells along the back wall, opened the large room up to the day. Wooden benches stretched along the outer walls, two heavy wooden chairs stood around a wooden table in the center of the room, and a tall, thin bookcase with seven or eight shelves leaned against the wall near the doorway. The shelves were cluttered with books, documents, scrolls, and papers. A modest carpet dominated by a pale green pattern covered most of the wooden floor. An old-fashioned dial telephone, its cord thrust under a rug, stood on the desk. A briefcase—government issue, 1970s, American—sat on the floor, leaning against one leg of the desk.

In the privacy of the cell, Wadi abu Tamir ibn Ahmad

turned on the charm. "Ms. Rommel, I am delighted. Very delighted." He faced her and graciously extended his hand. "So. Now you see the law office of the Arab. Please." He held a chair for her.

"There isn't anything pretentious about it, is there?" Frankie remarked, sitting down. No secretary or receptionist, no magazines or coffee tables, no diplomas, paintings, or pictures on the walls. The room had all the flair of a monastery.

He pointed around the room proudly. "You see, this is a most complete arrangement. Very complete. There are benches enough for a clan of bedouin from the desert, and a chair for the spokesman." He gestured at the furnishings. "A table upon which to spread documents, and a telephone to make inquiries."

"And that's all you need?"

"Of course." He walked briskly to the bookcase, searched through one of the shelves, and brought back a scroll on two rollers. "I have seen the law office in America, and was amazed. Amazing! Such expense! Who pays for such extravagance?" He sat down, placing the scroll carefully on the surface. "The client, in America, is encouraged to fight. Do you not call it the system for adversaries? But it is the lawyer, like the prizefighter, who collects the purse."

Frankie laughed. "You've got *that* right."

He reached below him, in the briefcase, and pulled out a pair of bifocals. He seemed unaware of Frankie's laughter and comment. "Under our system, we do not encourage litigation or dispute." He put them on, tucking the plastic stems under his turban and over his ears. "The lawyer—the mufti—has the obligation to tell the client the truth. Our disputes are not trials between champions. The mufti joins the *qadi* in the search for the correct answer. He does not advocate, with vigor, the position of his client."

"Shouldn't someone?" Frankie asked. "I mean, isn't it a bit dangerous, having everyone on the same side?"

He looked astonished. "Miss Rommel. Isn't there but one law?"

"Not in America." She picked at the band and veil over her nose. "Do you mind if I take this thing off?"

His eyes opened wide and he swallowed, as if she had said something suggestive. "It is prohibited," he said sternly, as though determined not to succumb to any attempt at sexual manipulation. "But you are from the West, and I will not call the *muhaddin.*"

Frankie dropped her hands to her lap. "It's not that important," she said, her mind churning angrily, but determined to get along. Still, whose law was it that made it wrong for a woman to breathe? "It will keep me from talking too much."

When he nodded in total agreement, Frankie could have killed without blinking. "I have a document which Princess Sahar bint Rashid has requested me to discuss with you." He began to unroll the scroll. "It is in Arabic. It is the Statement of Claim. I am prepared on this day to present it to our *qadi,* Prince Muhammad abu Ibrahim ibn al-Rashid, and to mufti Ghassar abu Diya al Din."

Frankie dragged her notepad out, and a ballpoint pen. "May I have a copy?"

"No no no," he said impatiently. "We do not prepare extra copies of documents for all to see and criticize."

"But . . ." Frankie wanted to unload, but forced her face into a smile. He couldn't see it, which was probably a good thing. He'd have had nightmares. "You'll have to tell me what's in it."

"First, allow for me the explanation. I have study the operation of law in America, and there are similarities." From his smug expression, there was no doubt as to which system was superior. "The Statement of Claim is similar to your complaint. The *qadi* will no doubt allow mufti Ghassar abu Diya al Din—who will represent the position of the Kingdom, similar to the manner in which your Solicitor General acts for the United States—five days to answer the Statement of Claim. I do not anticipate the need for an order to make proof, in that all factual matters are known with certainty."

"What is the order to make proof?"

He made a judicious steeple with the tips of his fingers. "If there is a contested issue of fact, it must be resolved before the proceedings begin. The procedure is termed 'order to make proof.'"

"That's the trial, isn't it?"

"No no no. It is quite simple. It does not, as in America, require juries to deliberate on the obvious."

Frankie hoped it wasn't *too* simple. "Is that when Princess Sahar will testify?"

He smiled with superiority. "We do not require that witnesses testify, as you do in your courtrooms. Their statements are recorded by the lawyers, and presented to the *qadi* in writing."

"Then how will Sahar give her side of the case?"

"I have done this. I have presented the statement of Sahar bint Rashid in the Statement of Claim. There is no need for time-consuming manipulations and posturings under our law."

"But—what have you said? Doesn't she have the right to approve it before you file it?"

"Miss Rommel. I am a mufti. I studied law at prestigious colleges in Baghdad and Cairo for thirteen years. One does not graduate until one demonstrates an impeccable, unswervable, and absolute devotion to two things: objective truth, and the Word of God." His voice throbbed with sincerity and his eyes burned with the same impervious look of righteousness Frankie had seen—in Sahar! "You must understand that it is quite impossible for me to misrepresent, in any way, the position of Sahar bint Rashid. Therefore, there is no reason for her to approve it. Such a step is contrary to our procedure. As her mufti, I have the God-given obligation to report her position correctly. To ask of her approval beforehand will only fuel the temptation to distort."

There was obviously nothing to argue about. It was so simple. "Can you tell me what's in there, then?"

He looked at his watch. "There is a matter on the other side of the square, where the king administers his justice, which I must witness. It will occur this morning, before the call to prayer. I must ask you to return this afternoon." He pulled off his glasses, dropped them in his briefcase, and allowed the scroll to wind itself shut.

She would love to go with him. "Wadi abu Tamir ibn Ahmad," she said in her nicest, cleanest, sexiest voice. "I am an attorney from the United States. I have great curiosity about your legal system. Would it be possible for me to accompany you?"

His expression took on the neutral aspect of a Ping-Pong ball. "There are difficulties."

"I promise to do exactly as you wish, even if it means walking behind you and to one side. I beg of you."

He swallowed. "Very well. Follow me, please."

# 16

All else being equal, walking behind and to one side of a mufti in a turban was not a preferred way to travel. At least no one took her picture. They proceeded out of the law court and across the bricked courtyard, toward the wide doors that opened into the original palace of al-Rashid.

Earlier there had been two or three cars parked near the long, massive building. Now there were several. Chauffeurs squatted in the shade and smoked. A small crowd milled around outside before funneling through the doors; mostly men in *ghotras* and *thobes*, but a few women in *abayas* with the bedouin veil. The men greeted one another with enthusiasm and displays of friendship, while the women silently stayed out of the way. Frankie formed the impression that, for the Rashidis, watching their king mete out his justice was a spectator sport.

Once through the doors, she found herself in a mammoth hall, as large as an indoor field house. Knots of people in a loose line approached a platform at the far end of the hall. Wadi abu Tamir ibn Ahmad took Frankie by the elbow and roughly propelled her forward toward tiered benches constructed along the sides of the hall, not far from the raised platform. "We must hurry if we are to find a seat." Like an adept supermarket shopper searching for the shortest check-out line, he wormed them through the throng standing in the main part of the hall, crossed to the other side, and found seats seven or eight rows up in a section that gave them a great view of the platform. "I will explain what I can," he said when they were seated.

"I am very grateful," Frankie said, leaning close enough to hear him, but careful to maintain some space. She didn't want to scare the little fellow.

"We call this the divan because in days gone by, it was conducted in the chambers of the king. You of course see him?"

Frankie looked toward the platform, as long as the stage of a small theater, but no more than ten feet wide. It stood five feet off the ground. The king of Rashidi sat on a huge mahogany chair, ornately carved and cushioned with leather. The edges appeared to have been embroidered in gold. The armrests were wide apart, and King Nuri had to reach his elbows out to rest his arms. The back of the throne thrust up and out, like a peacock's tail, but rather than bands of color, the beautifully grained wood held elaborate carvings of words, in Arabic script.

He wore a shimmering white *ghotra* over his torso. A gold band, studded with jewels, held his *thobe* in place. His brown eyes were alive with power. Broad-shouldered, thin-waisted, clean-shaven and youthful-looking, he had the thin face and healthy complexion of a trained athlete. Yet he had to be at least sixty. His high, prominent cheekbones gave prominence to a wonderfully Arabic nose and a wide mouth with thin lips. A hint of ruthlessness complemented the loneliness in his eyes. He looked like a king.

Four men in *ghotras* of differing colors and styles stood on the platform, two on each side of King Nuri. Each had a rifle—one in a sling over his shoulder, one casually in the crook of his arm—pointed at the floor, and two with the butts resting between their feet, holding the barrels. Though not at attention, they were attentive to the crowd. "May I ask questions?"

"I will be pleased to find answers."

"Those men on the dais with the King. His personal guard?"

"They are tribesmen from various tribes. They are picked by their chieftains and assigned to the divan to keep order."

"Have we missed anything?"

"No. As you say in the West, the show will soon begin. You see the people, lined up like waves approaching the beach." He tossed his hand at the long line that stretched back to the end of the hall. "They have complaints. They wish for justice."

"There are hundreds of them!"

The mufti smiled. "It will go swiftly. King Nuri gives his justice four days a week, often for six hours. He will hear anyone of his people with a grievance."

Suddenly it grew quiet, as though the curtain had gone up. Two clumps of men approached the dais. Some in each group looked as though they could barely restrain themselves from leaping on those in the other group. They were dressed very differently. The men on the left wore red-and-white-striped *ghotras;* seven of them; led by a thin man, stooped with age, whose brown, lined face had obviously been burned by a lifetime in the sun. Those on the right—five in number—were physically thicker, softer-looking, and dressed in clothes that had the glossy look of wealth. Frankie had seen men like them through the windows of the indoor shops. Two wore suits, and two wore conservative, rich-looking *ghotras* of black. They stood like bodyguards around the young man in the middle.

The adolescent-aged youngster had black hair, no head-dress, and an expression that switched back and forth between defiance and smothered fear. A gold satin shirt bagged away from his narrow shoulders, and black trousers accentuated his thinness.

Nuri nodded at the old man on the left, who stepped forward boldly. In a loud voice filled with outrage, he spoke explosively for two or three minutes, after which he bowed his head, gestured with his right hand, and stepped back with much dignity. Nuri acknowledged the gesture, then nodded at the spokesman for the other group.

Wadi Ahmad whispered, loud enough for Frankie to hear. "Those men," he said, inclining his head toward the group on the left, "are bedouin, of the Khalid clan, in the mountains near the coast. These others are a merchant family in Qahtan. Their son ran into the Khalid tent, while swerving to avoid a camel." Wadi Ahmad had to suppress his amusement. "The automobile, with cloth from the tent obstructing vision, then ran into a rock and suffered much damage. It was expensive American car. The Khalids wish to be compensated for their tent. The merchant family asks who should pay for the car? They assert the accident would not have happened if the camel—belonging to the Khalids —had been properly tethered."

"Is much money involved?" Frankie asked, hunching forward as she saw some of the other women doing.

"Indeed, if values can be assigned to such things. Inside the tent were vases, more than a thousand years old. The tradition of the Khalids is that they were used by Fatima, a revered descendant of the Prophet Muhammad."

The king asked questions and made statements in a quiet, authoritative voice. The answers invariably caused eruptions on the other side, quickly controlled by the king, who had only to raise his hand to instill quiet. Wadi Ahmad provided a sportscaster's account of the action. "Nuri talks to the merchant, Rahman. The boy was driving too fast, right, my friend? If he had been driving carefully, he would have avoided both the camel and the tent.

"He turns to Kahlid. Allah values the life of a camel more than a vase, even such a vase as this one, will you agree, my father? And so perhaps the boy did his best. Nuri faces the merchants. Yet I do not believe, entirely, that the young warrior wished to spare the life of the camel, eh, Rahman? I believe he may have wished to avoid the camel because there would be less damage to his car. He chose the tent, which billowed out like a soft cushion. When it blinded him, he did not see the rocks."

Frankie watched Nuri touch his mouth with the fingers of his right hand. Then he spoke, followed by the whispered translation. "This young man is at fault. He should not hang

214

in a cage for this offense, however. Let him serve for six months in the house of Khalid." Excited talk from both sides, stilled by a wave of Nuri's hand. "He needs the discipline of the desert, the understanding of the true value of a simple vase. He shall do as he is commanded, in the service of Khalid, but there shall be no cruelty. Neither shall there be corporal punishment, without application to me. None. He shall eat at the same table as the men of your clan, and wear the same *ghotra*, I hope—in time—with as much dignity. This he shall do, to compensate for the broken vase."

Murmurings were stilled with a wave of the king's hand. "I am not done. Rahman, your young man shall pay for this privilege. The question is, how much?" With a gesture, Nuri invited discussion, which came at him like a storm. He listened attentively for a moment, then cut it off. "Two hundred dinars a month." The Khalids appeared satisfied, the merchants stunned. "In addition, there shall be payment for damages to the tent and its contents." They repeated the process, with an opposite result. The merchants nodded comfortably, but the bedouins did not. "My young friend," Nuri said, addressing the boy. "It is your time. Walk away from your family. You are now, for six months, under the protection of the house of Khalid."

Frankie imagined she heard him swallow. He hesitated and stared at one of the men in his group, who reluctantly motioned the boy toward the other circle. The old man glowered at the ground. "Khalid," the king said to him. "The vase is not as important as the soul of this young man. Use him for your profit, of course. But attend to that which matters, eh? Let him be your son." Lifting his head, Khalid nodded.

Frankie glanced at Wadi Ahmad, who averted his eyes. They were wet with feeling. "So. Do you now see what is meant by the personal justice of the king?"

"I'm impressed," Frankie whispered, watching the merchant family stalk out. *"They* aren't."

Wadi Ahmad shrugged his shoulders. "The merchants will talk to each other, of course. They will agree with the

215

judgment. The young man needs the desert, they will say. When he returns, he will wear his *ghotra* with pride, and an alliance between families will have been formed."

A stirring of activity rippled toward the dais from the tall doors to the left of the hall. "These are the prisoners," Wadi Ahmad whispered. Two men, surrounded by brown-suited guards, were led in. Frankie could only see the man in front.

A burst of sound started from somewhere in the middle of the hall, and the four men on the dais behind the king instantly held their rifles at a ready position. Nuri stood up. He shouted something in Arabic, raised his hand, and the noise quickly abated. Then he waved, in a gesture Frankie understood. You, come forward, it said.

"What's happening?" she asked.

"The prisoner is a murderer. Nuri has commanded the men of the clan affected by the murder to come forward."

As they made their way to the front, Frankie stared at the prisoner as though she had seen him before. Except for the color of his eyes, which were brown instead of blue, he was a replica of one of the trial lawyers for NASP: Davey Reddman. Part of his upper body was covered by a soiled robe, and there was nothing on his head but wavy blue-black hair, as intensely brilliant as the night sky in Wyoming. It spilled around his shoulders like rapids around rocks. As he approached the dais, a few short steps from the roiling knot of men in garishly colored *ghotras,* he shrugged away the guards who held him and hobbled proudly before the king. His facial features, his bearing, his arrogant self-confidence were exactly those of Davey.

The turbulent little boil of men surged toward him, and one of them spit. A shot rang out and dust kicked up in front of the closest man's feet. They were jolted to a stop. Nuri spoke sharply and they moved back.

Nuri sat down, resting his arms on the armrests, and nodded at the prisoner. The young man spoke proudly in a firm, clear voice. Frankie had no idea what he said, but thrilled to the sound. Nuri asked a question of one of the men in the knot, and received a low, surly reply. When another started to talk, Nuri lifted his hand. He asked another question and received a barely audible reply. Nuri slid down in his throne, then spoke with a resonance that reached at least halfway into the hall. He was interrupted by the men in the knot, who boiled angrily. Nuri jumped up and his guards leveled their rifles at them.

Order in the courtroom, Frankie thought.

Nuri sat down and finished his comment. Turning toward the young man, he made a gesture of respect, then jerked his head toward the doors. Two of the guards led him away.

Wadi Ahmad had been transfixed by the drama. As he watched them march off, he spoke to Frankie. "He is indeed a king," he said in a normal voice. He didn't have to whisper. The room buzzed with conversations, like the intermission between acts.

"What happened?"

"The prisoner is of the Ghamal clan, whose father suffered insult from Qudamah, of the house of Adham. The prisoner's father refused to take offense. The prisoner brooded over the insult, then rode into the camp of his enemies and shot Qudamah through the heart. He was captured by the police yesterday and will be executed Friday."

"My God," Frankie said, realizing she'd just witnessed a murder trial. "What was the disturbance about? Weren't the men from the house of Adham satisfied with the sentence?"

"No," Wadi Ahmad told her. "They wanted more in the way of vengeance, than the death of the murderer. They demanded the right to perform the execution themselves, but Nuri will not allow it."

"I don't get it."

"The Adham would strike him with the axe, perhaps five or six times, before killing him. They would disfigure him and make him suffer. Nuri ordered the execution performed by the public executioner, out of respect for the young man and his family."

The hall quieted down. Frankie could see the other prisoner in front of the dais: not a man, but a boy whose bare feet had been hobbled with a rope and whose wrists were tied. Suddenly she recognized him. The little thief who had run off with her briefcase! His reddish-blond hair swirled thickly around his head like a torch, and his blue eyes shone with the innocence of an angel.

"This is Ahmed," Wadi Ahmad said contemptuously, his voice lowering as the crowd noise dropped. "He has been before the divan more than once."

"I know him!" Frankie whispered. "He tried to steal my briefcase!"

"Ah. Most annoying. However, you will soon understand why there are so few thieves in Rashidi."

Ahmed looked wildly around him, then sat down. Quickly he rolled to his knees and prostrated himself before the king. Nuri spoke sharply. The youngster tried to stand but could not. He had to be lifted to his feet by the men on either side of him.

Nuri nodded at the policemen who'd come to Frankie's rescue. As he spoke, Nuri slumped in his chair and the line of his mouth tightened with disdain. Brusquely, Nuri said a few words and jerked his head toward the tall doors the prisoners had come through. As the policemen dragged him off, the boy sobbed his heart out. "What happened?"

"On Friday, his right hand will be struck off. Praise be to Allah."

Frankie stood up. "Excuse me!"

Nuri—everyone in the hall—stared at her. "It was my bag he took. May I come forward?" She recognized the voice she heard speaking: it was hers. But who ordered the script?

King Nuri's eyes closed to slits. He said something in Arabic, then motioned her forward. Frankie glanced at her companion, who no longer knew her. Magically, a way down the steps appeared, and she walked toward the dais. The guards with the boy stopped.

Frankie didn't know what she would say, but Prince Muhammad had told her the king spoke English, and she had to do something. "Your Majesty, may I be heard?" she heard herself say.

Nuri raised his hand, commanding attention. He said some words in Arabic to the crowd, then looked down at her. "I translate for my people your words to me, so that they may follow the progress of this conversation. You have a question?"

"Will his hand be cut off?"

Nuri spoke to the crowd. There was a buzz, some tittering, then quiet. "That is my judgment. Twice before, I have released him. But he refuses to learn, and you see the result."

"But must you cut off his hand?" Frankie stood up straight. "I will feel responsible for that," she said. "I will hate myself forever. I ask you to give him another chance."

"Are you a Christian?"

Frankie made a small gesture of uncertainty. "The last time I was in a church, it was a Christian church."

Nuri looked over her head and spoke at some length in Arabic. His statement seemed to end with a question, which was followed by some laughter and a few shouts. Then it grew quiet. Nuri motioned the guards to bring the boy back. He spoke to the young man with intensity. His eyes burned like rays of the sun focused by a magnifying glass.

One of the guards produced a knife, cutting the rope between Ahmed's ankles. The boy stood for a moment, not knowing what to do. The king spoke again, and Ahmed raised his two hands and looked at them. Then he ran. Without looking at Frankie, he ran like someone being chased by a lion.

Sounds of laughter, scorn, and derision followed him out of the hall. "I do this for you, Miss Rommel," Nuri said, in a low voice that barely reached her. "Perhaps, at the right time, you will do as much for me."

When Frankie turned to go back to her stadium seat, she realized that Wadi Ahmad was gone and other men were sitting in their seats. She looked around helplessly for a moment, then walked to the back of the hall, where most of the women were gathered. They seemed to know who she was, but made no effort to include her. She decided to leave.

As she crossed the courtyard she heard the blaring recording of the call to prayer. *"Allahu Akbar! Allahu Akbar! Ashhadu Alla Ilaha Illa Allah! Ashhadu anna Muhammadan*

219

*Rasula Allah! Hayy Ala Saalah! Hayy ala-al-Falah! Allahu Akbar!"* God is great! the voice proclaimed. God is great! I testify there is no God but Allah! I testify Muhammad is the messenger of Allah! Come to prayer, come to success, for God is great! The courtyard quickly filled with men, who streamed toward the Mosque al-Rashid.

Frankie walked as quickly as she could, against the traffic, to Wadi Ahmad's office. He was not there. In the coolness of his room she peeled off her veil and sat on a bench, leaning her back into the mud brick wall. She must have slept. The next thing she knew, she heard footsteps in the hall. She was hooking the veil over her nose when Wadi Ahmad, walking prayerfully, entered the chamber.

When he saw her, he stopped. "Hello," Frankie said, standing up. "I hope I didn't embarrass you with my performance in the divan."

"No no no," he said, but his expression was one of annoyance. "Please. Sit down." He motioned to a chair by the desk and waited for her to sit. "You have more questions?" he asked politely, also sitting, but glancing at his watch.

"You were going to tell me what's in the Statement of Claim."

"Ah." He put his glasses on and picked the scroll off the table, unrolling it. "The princess asserts she is married to Richard Adamson, an American." He squinted at the words as he read them. "She requests a ruling from the *qadi,* recognizing the marriage. She admits Adamson is not Muslim, although presumably he is Christian, and therefore of the Book. Unfortunately, her petition is quite groundless." He glanced at her apologetically. "The fact he is not a Muslim, in and of itself, defeats it. There are many opinions—I have cited the leading ones—that make it quite clear that although a Muslim man may marry a non-Muslim woman, as long as she is of the Book, the opposite situation is forbidden."

Frankie watched the wrinkles in his forehead lift when he glanced up at her. She hadn't eaten since breakfast and could hear her stomach growl. But she wasn't hungry.

"The princess seeks to justify her status by asserting that the fundamental requirement of marriage was observed: the mutual agreement of the parties. However, she admits the formalities of marriage were not followed. In addition to the fundamental requirement of mutual agreement, all the schools insist on the following conditions to marriage: that a male guardian be appointed to advise the woman, that a dowry be paid to her, and that the ceremony of marriage be attended by two male witnesses. None of these conditions were observed."

He clucked his tongue and shook his head as though that too ended the matter. "She seeks to avoid the consequence of such failure in two ways. Firstly, by the bald declaration that the formalities imposed by the law are for the protection of helpless women. They are not needed in her case, she would ask the *qadi* to believe, because of her wealth and status. Unfortunately, all of the authority on the subject is to the contrary. It is an obvious fact of nature that a woman, in matters of importance, needs the guiding hand of a man. It has been said that the wealthiest and most powerful of women need the protections of men even more than the lowly, because they attract the reckless adventurer.

"Secondly, she testifies to the performance of *istikhara*, in which she sought the guidance of Allah. The assertion cannot stand. *Istikhara* is not available to those who would use it to break the law. Opinions on that subject also date back in time for many centuries, and I have cited many of them."

Frankie could feel sweat trickling down her spine. How do you argue with stone? She watched him look up, and when he did, she tried to smile with her eyes. "The formalities of law you refer to are based on the opinions of scholars and jurists, aren't they?" Frankie asked. "Sahar tells me there is nothing in the Qur'an that prohibits the declaration of marriage between two people who would unite into one cell." She felt foolish, like a liberal of the sixties advocating free love.

"Her position is romantic nonsense, Miss Rommel. As a lawyer, surely you have encountered examples of wishful thinking." He sighed. "There is also the specific prohibition against the secret marriage."

"But again, it isn't in the Qur'an, is it?"

Thoughtfully, he touched the edge of his nose with his fingers. "No. However, opinions from scholars in all four of the major schools—well-reasoned statements elucidating with force and clarity the obvious intent of Allah—have declared the secret marriage to be *haram*. Forbidden." He pressed his palms together and extended his fingers in an attitude of reverence.

The sweat along Frankie's back turned to ice. "Can you give me a procedural timetable?"

He nodded agreeably. "The mufti for the kingdom will have five days to respond to the Statement of Claim. The *qadi* may order additional proofs of some of the claims, although that is not likely. I will have the opportunity to respond to the brief filed for the kingdom, but do not expect there will be anything more to be said." He raised a shoulder. "The *qadi* will then set a time for the deliverance of his opinion. He may adopt mine, or that of Ghassar abu Diya al Din, or write one of his own. It will be delivered—I should say—within thirty days."

Frankie sat rigidly forward. "Will Sahar and I be allowed to attend any of these proceedings?"

Wadi Ahmad sighed. "I will do what I can do." He regarded her with a mixture of sympathy and contempt.

"If Sahar's request for the recognition of her marriage is turned down, what then?"

"The princess will have obviously engaged in fornication," he said. "There will be stigma to the honor of the house of Rashid."

"Will she be hauled before the king in the divan?"

"Of course." The lines of his forehead lifted thoughtfully. "Perhaps not, however. Because of her rank, her hearing before the king, and her execution, might be conducted in private. But credible witnesses would attend. The people would know."

Frankie stared at him with horror. "Will he really order it?"

The small man with the soiled turban obviously did not have a problem. "Miss Rommel, you have seen this king with his people, have you not?" He waited for her to nod. "You have even stated that you were impressed with his personal justice. It is quick, certain, and popular. His people have trust in his judgment and respect for him."

"But she is his granddaughter!"

"The Prophet Muhammad himself, peace be to his memory, said that if his daughter Fatima were a thief, he would order her hand to be struck from her body. What kind of personal justice will permit of favoritism in such matters?" He glanced at his watch. "If Nuri does not remove the stain to his honor, his people will not follow his justice. They will seek another king." He regarded Frankie with patience. "It is a simple truth, after all. To be a king, one must first be a man."

223

# 17

## Yawm ath-Thalatha, 15 Safar, A.H. 1412
## (Tuesday, August 27, 1991)

Frankie dragged back to the Palace for Women before noon, sticking to the *abaya* she'd been wearing. One of Princess Bushra's servants waited for her at the front door. "Come please?" the small woman asked. She could have been anywhere from thirty to sixty. Teeth were missing, but she smiled as though she had a full set.

At least once a day Bushra made like a hostess. Frankie endured the encounters, partly because they gave her glimpses of Rashidi life she wouldn't otherwise see. One endless night had been spent at a gathering of royal women with Frankie on display. Twice they'd visited the University for Women, and once Bushra had taken her to the *hareem* in Prince Muhammad's palace, above Qahtan. They had also toured the countryside in the air-conditioned luxury of Bushra's limousine. Frankie nodded without joy and followed the servant.

They proceeded to Bushra's apartment at the northeast corner of the palace, on the third floor. Bushra waited outside the door. In spite of the hand held out in greeting, Frankie could feel her contempt. "Have you shopped at the *souq* today?"

"No, Princess. I wanted to watch a trial, but couldn't get in."

Frankie hadn't been in Bushra's apartment. The high ceilings were hidden behind billowing red silken sheets that drifted down like clouds. The pale blue walls were clean enough to walk through, like desert sky. A luxuriant earth-colored rug seemed made for bare feet. Once inside, both women took off their shoes. Frankie could hear gurgling water, and wondered if there was a fountain in another room. "This is lovely," she said, removing her headdress and shaking her head. She hated hats and enjoyed the physical pleasure of loose hair.

"Thank you," Bushra said. "Come. Sit with me." Frankie sat on a wildly colored cushion as Bushra gracefully lowered herself onto a fiercely red one. She wore attractive loose-fitting pale green silk pantaloons and a gold-colored long-sleeve blouse. Her bare feet were beautifully manicured. A jeweled cigarette holder blazed in the large, decorative ashtray on the rug in front of them. "You have become the subject of conversation, my dear Frances." With a gesture, she offered Frankie a cigarette from the ornate jar in the ashtray, and stuffed one in her holder. Frankie took one and accepted the light from the gold lighter.

"Oh dear," Frankie said, exhaling. "What did I do?"

"Your boldness in the king's divan. Your manner in the *souqs.*" Frankie picked up a hint of annoyance. "My husband has asked me to speak to you."

Frankie didn't take criticism well, and on top of that, she was hot. She felt her chin get hard. "I couldn't let them cut off the boy's hand."

Bushra laughed. "Do you believe *you* prevented this?" she asked, resting her cigarette holder in the ashtray and primping her hair.

"No. Of course not."

"It is true," Bushra continued, "that you have the ability to draw the eyes of men. Even my husband, a man of law, smiles with pleasure when he speaks of you. But you will stop nothing."

So that was the problem. Frankie smiled at Bushra. "Your husband is a very attractive man."

Like boiling water, Bushra lifted to her feet. "I know you, Frances!" she proclaimed loudly. "I have seen you in Jeddah, and Riyadh! I have seen you flaunt your body at men with flagrant license, only to complain bitterly when you are raped!" Frankie stared in amazement. She hadn't intended to start a war.

Bushra suddenly appeared stricken, as though she'd been shot. A distraught hand cupped her face and her expression became flamboyantly apologetic. "I am so sorry!" She dropped to her knees and tried to take Frankie's hands in hers. "I have spoken in anger and you are my guest. Can you forgive me?"

"Princess, I need this." Somehow Frankie managed to get her cigarette in the ashtray, then took Bushra's hand. "Really."

"But why?"

"I want to know you. I want to understand. How can I help Sahar if I bumble along like an idiot?"

"You can do nothing for Sahar." Bushra slumped dramatically, like a wilted flower, but clung to Frankie's hands as though wanting to maintain a bridge between them.

"Tell me anyway. We're from different sides of the planet, but it's the same planet. Why am I so repulsive to you?"

Bushra rocked back on her heels and released Frankie's hands. She didn't deny Frankie's assessment. "Do you wish the truth?" She sounded as though she was dying to tell it.

"Yes!"

"You are without God." She picked up her cigarette and held it like a wand. "Women of the West do not understand that life is submission to the will of God. They—you—believe you have the right to freedom, but freedoms are false." She took a quick hit, like a snakebite. "Such freedoms permit tasteless, obscene display of your bodies to men. Such freedoms transform love and tenderness into ugly lust. They lead you falsely to surrender the true subtleties of womanhood, bestowed by God."

Frankie blinked, then picked up her cigarette. "May I speak with as much honesty?"

Bushra crossed her arms. "I insist."

"You allow stonings, you cut off heads, and speak to me of God. What am I missing? How can you justify the killing of someone as exquisite as Sahar? Or her baby?"

"Oh!" Bushra covered her face with her hands.

Frankie waited for some huge black eunuch to toss her into a pit of crocodiles. She didn't care. She could no longer stand it.

It came in torrents, a swollen river forced to travel through a narrow canyon. Later it meandered meditatively through a wide valley. When the words slowed, Frankie would open another spillway with a question.

Tears streamed down their faces as they talked. Before Frankie left, the women hugged. In her room, she wrote down as much of the exchange as she could remember.

"Are human beings no more than fish in an ocean, with the freedom to swim in any direction? Does that make them free?

"Freedom is a lie. Discipline is the truth! You do not see this, because you have never experienced the fruits of discipline, in your wild reach for this false freedom.

"I look into your eyes, and see your heart. I see the loneliness and fear of a woman without a family, a bird without a flock. You laugh and make jokes, to create a belief in yourself that you have happiness. But 'happiness' is an illusion, like freedom. It is a scab with which to cover the wound of loneliness and fear. You have not the stability of the family, the protection of the clan. All there is for you is illusion.

"The fish in the oceans are not free. They are prey to the sharks. They spend their short lives running in fear, darting to avoid death, gulping food without enjoyment.

"It is true we have stonings in Rashidi. But notice that our children do not carry pistols and knives. Statistics from your newspapers, which I read with interest, reveal: one million children in your country that have no home. Hundreds of thousands of women in jails! A child born in America has a greater opportunity of *any* child, from any country in the world, to be shot to death, or raped! Yet you criticize Rashidi, because it compels submission to the law of God!

"Five times each day we face Mecca and pray. Our laws are simple, but strictly enforced. If one steals, and steals again, and steals again, one loses his hand. You will notice there is hardly any theft in my country. It is the same with murder. But in the West, people are driven by a mad, insane quest for freedom from the will of God. Constantly you deny the reality of the One God.

"Look at the consequence before you criticize! Your novels, your movies, your popular music, appeal to the most base instincts in humans. Freedom! You are free to teach, to preach, and to believe that you are evil. See the results!

"In what other country is murder so manifest? Or so creative? During your Easter season, when Christians celebrate the death and resurection of the Prophet Jesus, I read of a wife whose husband was confined to a wheelchair, soon to die of cancer. In her absence, he ate her chocolate Easter bunny. She must act quickly, before he is released from her affections by death. She covered him with gasoline, struck a match, and turned him into a living torch.

"A statement perhaps? Should she be allowed to make such statements, because of your constitution?

"When Allah revealed himself to the Prophet Muhammad, the divine revelation was as blinding as lightning, as deafening as thunder. The revelation aroused terror in Muhammad's heart. The fear thus generated is meant to soften one's heart to Allah; to enable the believer to submit. For a child to witness an execution can arouse a similar terror in the child's small heart. I personally have witnessed this, and know of what I speak. There is power in the experience! Islam means submission to the will of Allah— but Sahar refuses to submit.

"Her mind has been invaded by apostasy. Her body has been defiled with the seed of an infidel. I have pity for her, perhaps, as a woman, and would not have the strength to throw a stone. I am grateful to Allah that such decision is not mine to make.

"Did you know there was a time in the history of my country when fathers would bury their infant daughters in the sands of the desert, rather than use the resources of the clan to nourish and feed them? Such practice was not cruel. It was essential. In the days before Islam, the bedouin tribes depended for their survival on the men. There were never enough, because always their lives were forfeited in the constant struggle. To carry and nourish an unneeded daughter could threaten the existence of the entire clan.

"Such decisions of life and death have been made by our men for centuries, which is only natural. There is recognition of the ability of men to decide such things. Men are the heads of families and of clans because they can make such terrible decisions. How can a woman be charged with that awful responsibility, when her body cries out with the need to hold the infant?

"Allah made man, and woman. But it is right and natural that men control and rule, and that women do not.

"A family is like a tree. The head of the family is charged with the duty to give the tree strength, and keep it strong. Bad seeds take root, and flourish, and strangle, and destroy. Do humans become weeds? That is what we see happening in the West. And more and more, such weakness invades Rashidi. The winds have carried thistles to our gardens."

# Yawm al-Arbi'a, 23 Safar, A.H. 1412 (Wednesday, September 4, 1991)

It took Frankie a moment to realize someone had a hand on her shoulder and was shaking it. She sat up, trying to see in the darkness.

The door to her room was open, and the thin light that stars sprinkle over the desert filtered in her room. She saw the small, huddled figure of a woman bending over her. "Come . . . with . . . me . . . please." Each word was enunciated carefully, but without understanding, as though the sounds had been memorized and practiced by a person with no hearing.

Frankie reached for the small floor lamp beside her bed and switched it on. "Umm Majd!" she exclaimed when she recognized the old woman. "What's going on?"

Umm Majd scurried over to the door and shut it, as though afraid that the light might be seen. "Come . . . with . . . me . . . please." This time the words were supported with gestures. As small as a gnome, and dressed as always in a formal-looking *abaya*, she pantomimed the act of getting up. Then she pointed at the door and rolled her hands around each other, suggesting that the two of them go out.

"Yes. Of course." Frankie jumped out of bed and trotted toward the bathroom. She pushed through the drapes, splashed water on her face, and looked at her watch. It wasn't even three o'clock in the morning. Back in her room, Umm Majd had Frankie's *abaya* in her hands. She reached up with it like a dressmaker who would like to pin it on a customer. "I'm supposed to wear this?"

The old woman smiled. "Da. Da."

Frankie slid into it and stuck her feet in her black slippers. When Umm Majd hooked the veil over her face, Frankie did the same. Then the old lady held her index finger over her mouth, signaling for silence. She opened the door. The light from the bed lamp cast an eerie shadow on the balcony, which was quickly extinguished when the door was shut. Through the large square opening above the courtyard, Frankie could see the brilliance of the stars, embedded in a sky lightened by a full moon.

Umm Majd looked up at Frankie with the innocence of a child and held out her hand. Frankie took it and the old lady led them down the balcony to the stairwell, like spies sneaking through the camp of the enemy.

They circled around the garden in the courtyard of the palace, staying in shadow. When Umm Majd opened a door near the kitchen, they slipped inside. She pressed her finger to her lips and they slid by the kitchen, where a yellow beam of light leaked through an open door. Women were at work, talking and cackling. She opened another door and suddenly they were outside. She shut it behind them.

Frankie looked up. A full moon at two o'clock, as bright as polished ivory, glistened with light. It was an absolutely dry moon, with no rings of moisture to provide a halo, lighting the sky and landscape with pale blueness and casting shadows of black. Only the brightest stars survived. Toward the horizons the void of eternity in a bottomless, shimmering blackness met the line of the land.

The fierceness of the Arabic belief in God no longer surprised Frankie. Anyone with a grain of feeling in their soul would tremble at the magnificence of the scene. Umm Majd stopped, forgetting everything else. Her shining eyes smiled at the sky, as though in gratitude. Then she grabbed Frankie's hand and started down a path Frankie couldn't see.

Frankie realized they walked toward Nuri's palace. The immense area between palaces had been landscaped with lawns and gardens of flowers, interspersed with trees and fountains. They approached the fortress from the north and quickly got in shadows cast by moonlight. No guards; no dogs; they walked on grass. When they reached the expansive wall, it reminded Frankie of the sheer sandstone slabs at Canyon de Chelly. Somewhere along the way, Umm Majd stopped. She smelled the air, as though that would help her find what she was looking for. Then she let go of Frankie, scuttled over to a door that seemed to materialize out of stone, and tapped on it lightly.

When the door opened—barely a foot—yellow light pushed through like the escaping spirits in Pandora's box. A tall, skin-headed black man wearing sandals, loose trousers, and a robe opened the door, ushered them in, and shut it behind them.

The difference between the palaces went far beyond the composition of the walls. The palace for women was like a well-maintained but older hotel; but Nuri's palace surpassed the modern elegance of anything Frankie had seen, even in magazines. The walls of the hallway they walked were twenty feet high and layered with a rich wall covering that looked more like golden silk than paper. The carpet—a deep red that ran to lavender—was like wading through a sunset. Frankie couldn't figure out where the lighting came from.

They were herded in an elevator paneled with tinted mirrors and whisked upward. When the doors opened, the black man nodded at them and with his hands made a gesture to move out. They stepped into high-ceilinged, expansive, luxuriantly carpeted splendor; a room large enough to require pillars, which were made of glass. Twenty feet away, impeccably dressed in tailored light blue slacks belted with a black cummerbund and a solid-red blazer with the crest of the Kingdom of Rashidi emblazoned in gold over the pockets, stood the king.

He fit the room perfectly, just as Geronimo fit the New Mexican landscape, and as Zeus fit in his niche above the clouds over Greece. Umm Majd was beside herself. She radiated energy, like a hummingbird whose wings move so fast they can't be seen. Nuri glanced at her with amusement, smiled, and said something to her in Arabic.

She chittered like a busy squirrel and removed her veil, then reached up and removed Frankie's. "This one was my first wife," he said to Frankie. "She has since become my mother."

The old woman moved between them, churning busily and protectively, like a swarm of bees. With easy grace Nuri allowed her to lead them away from the elevator to a sitting arrangement near tinted-glass panel doors that opened onto a balcony. Through them, shimmering like the blue flame of a jet of burning gas, could be seen the minarets of the mosque.

Like a nervous hostess, Umm Majd prepared a comfortable high-backed chair for Frankie to sit in. Frankie all but disappeared in the elaborate cushions and armrests. Across from it was a wide matching couch. "Would you like something to drink, Miss Rommel?" Nuri asked, sitting at one end of the couch. "Coffee, or tea?"

"You wouldn't have something like Wild Turkey?"

He laughed. "No." Umm Majd hovered over them like a waitress. "The mother of my son would be pleased to bring you something else, however."

"Coffee."

Nuri said some words in Arabic, and the woman scurried away. He turned toward Frankie. "So. Are you comfortable in Qahtan?"

"Very comfortable, Your Highness." Frankie didn't know how to address him. From this distance, he wasn't anything more than a nice-looking man, with silver hair, dark eyes, and a prominent nose. He puts his pants on one leg at a time, Frankie reminded herself. "How should I address you, sir?"

"What you call me does not change who or what I am, eh?" he asked sardonically. "Call me King. Will that offend you? I would ask you to call me Nuri, but she will hear, and will think it too familiar." He stared at Frankie for a moment in a decidedly sexual manner, appraising her face, the silhouette of her breasts, what he could see of her ankles and figure. When he looked at her, he smiled with appreciation. "You are an unusual woman, Miss Rommel. With much bravery in your personality, for it took the bravery of a soldier to stand in the divan."

"I'm complimented."

"In America, you are a lawyer?"

"Yes."

"What does a lawyer in your country do?"

"He, or she—many of our lawyers are women—represent people. Or entities. We protect their legal rights and go to court for them. We are champions—advocates—for our clients."

"Then you are like fighters in the ring? It is as my brother, Prince Muhammad, has told me?"

Umm Majd—as unobtrusive as a well-trained waitress—appeared. She carried a silver tray that held a large silver pitcher on top of a glowing brick, and three matching cups. She set it on the floor, careful not to step between them, and prepared a greenish liquid. Nuri got the first cup, Frankie the second, and she kept the third. Then she sat on the couch near Nuri, beaming with joy.

"We fight for our clients, of course, when it's necessary."

"But it is not always necessary to fight, is it? Lawyers in your country seek also to negotiate, to reach compromise?"

"Yes." Frankie did as they did with the coffee. She held it in both hands with the tips of her fingers, sipped slowly, and rested it on the armrest.

"Are you as to Sahar, her lawyer? Is she as to you, a client?"

Frankie could smell the aroma from the coffee. "I'm trying to help her, but there are problems. Your system doesn't work that way."

"No." He leaned back. "Our lawyers do not battle each other in a ring. Our mufti present petitions before a *qadi*, and together they pray for Allah's guidance in their search for truth."

Umm Majd breathed fully and blissfully. She watched her master with the loving eyes of a devoted dog, and Nuri accepted her devotion with the tolerant affection of a kindly animal trainer. Frankie was touched by the display, but offended by the implications and wondered at their history. He leaned forward, speaking conversationally, but with sudden intensity. "Do you wish for my granddaughter to live?"

"Very much!" She watched him pick a tiny silver spoon with a long, thin handle off the serving tray and stir his coffee. The line of his mouth—in the divan, it had looked like a wire—softened into skin.

"As her lawyer, will it be possible for you to persuade her to negotiate?"

Frankie stared at him with rapt attention. Umm Majd saw another purpose, but didn't move. "I can try. But what does Sahar have to negotiate with? Is there anything she can offer you?"

The intensity in Nuri's voice spread to his expression. "Ask her to withdraw her petition in the law court, for recognition of this spurious marriage. For her to demand a

234

trial on this issue is an embarrassment! Ask her to admit her sin, and come to me for justice. I am not then forced to bring her before me as an evil woman. After all is said and done, this is a matter for the family. If she will come to me now and ask for mercy, rather than add to my disgrace by this foolish trial, I can spare her her life."

"Will you release her? As you did that boy?"

"No. But I can confine her in my house until death take her." He leaned forward and his voice became electric. "The Qur'an allows the head of a house such an option. It is rarely interpreted literally, but there are instances. If Sahar will do this for me, then I will sentence her to a life of luxury." Pain flashed through his expression and he dropped his gaze. "I have no heart to order her death. But she must deserve mercy from me, before I can extend it." His anguished eyes lifted and locked on Frankie. "I have love for Sahar. I have no wish to extinguish the dawn."

## Yawm al-Khamis, 24 Safar, A.H. 1412 (Thursday, September 5, 1991)

Frankie started a journal, entering the dates according to the Islamic as well as the Christian calendar, trying to make herself think like an Arab.

A moon watcher, Frankie liked their calendar, because it tracked the stages of the moon. On the fifteenth day of the month, the moon was full. The first day of the month began with the thin crescent of a new one. But although the twelve months of the Islamic year came close to a solar year, it was eleven days short. Part of its charm, Frankie thought that morning, debating whether to go to Sahar's apartment and wake her up. Ramadan, their holy month, regressed its way through the seasons of the year, drifting from winter to fall to summer to spring and back to winter in thirty-four lunar years, or thirty-three solar ones.

She found Sahar sitting on the patch of lawn by the fountain in the courtyard, leaning on her hands, her eyes closed and an expression of contentment on her face. The night before, Frankie had heard the younger women dancing and talking and watching *Gone With the Wind* on Jamilah's VCR. She assumed Sahar had been with them. "Don't you ever go to bed?"

Like the shift of a bud to a blossom, Sahar's body changed from a belly dancer to a pregnant woman. Her face radiated with a heightened awareness of life, her coloring deepened, her mood swings were often out of control. She made forays into the kitchen, pestering the servants with strange requests for food. Then she began to satisfy her hunger for the companionship of her royal cousins. With no regard for the lock on her door, she would visit in their apartments as a guest, receiving their ingrained Arab hospitality and breaking down the barriers of formality. She even broke in on Bushra, pretending that her mother's twin was her mother. Bushra had not been charmed.

Umm Majd tried to put her back in jail. Sahar gently teased the old woman, who reacted first with anger, but finally tossed her hands in the air and laughed. The game was over.

Tears occasionally clogged Frankie's vision as she watched Sahar operate. The princess was enough to make her believe in miracles, and Frankie knew they needed a couple of fast ones. "I will sleep when I am old," Sahar said, lifting an arm and glancing at her watch. "It is nine o'clock! I was up with the call to prayer."

She wore pantaloons with an expandable waist, and her legs were curled beneath her. She looked to Frankie, who had never had a child, like an egg. "How do you feel?"

"Wonderful!" Sahar leaned forward. "My senses are alive with wonder. Everything is so exquisite! Except, of course, when I throw up." She breathed deeply, lifting her head and closing her eyes. "The sound of the fountain, the shining light of the moon, the coolness and smell of blossoming things. And to eat the figs from the gardens of Najd is a sensual experience!"

Frankie sat on the bench near the fountain, close enough

236

to feel its spray. She wore comfortable brown shorts from Banana Republic. "Have you been to the doctor?"

"I am crazy, is that what you mean?" she suggested happily.

"Absolutely out of your mind. I meant for your baby."

Sahar beamed, patting her stomach. "He does not need advice from a doctor on how to live. But Bushra has also asked. My new mother has arranged for me a visit to the clinic." Her expression changed. "I must sneak in for treatment like a person with an awful disease no one must know about. But . . ." She shrugged. "It shall be done."

The small Filipino servant, whose name Frankie could never get right, walked toward them carrying a tray. Her eyes were empty, but she wore a nice smile. Sahar spoke to her pleasantly, and she set the tray on the bench beside Frankie. The smell of coffee pulled Frankie's head around. "I hope there's more than one cup!"

"You may have my coffee. But I *must* have your figs," Sahar said, standing slowly then arching her back. The servant girl walked away and Sahar sat down on the bench.

"Ugh. On an empty stomach?" Frankie asked, pouring coffee. She watched Sahar eagerly explore the tray of fruit with her fingers, pick up a banana and peel it. "I saw your grandfather."

"Yes. At the divan. I hear of your exploit."

"Since then," Frankie said. "Two nights ago, at his palace. I was with Umm Majd."

"Is this true?" Sahar asked, astonished. "You must tell me."

As Frankie talked, Sahar listened with wide-eyed attention, devouring all the food in sight. But her expression closed at the end of Frankie's recital and she got up. "So. You bring me from the king an offer, as in the United States, for settlement of this dispute?"

"That's about the size of it."

"No!" She turned angrily toward Frankie, her hands wrapped into fists. *"No!"* She swung at the silver coffee pitcher, striking it and sending it sailing.

Frankie jumped up. Coffee squirted out of the twirling pitcher, but didn't hit either one of them. "Hey, don't kill the messenger!"

"My anger is not toward you." Sahar stood rigidly, her hands at her sides. "He knows my enjoyment of life. He dangles this treasure before me, like the temptation of Satan."

Frankie tried to keep a cool head. She touched Sahar's shoulder. It felt like concrete. "Sahar, he's a good man. He doesn't know what to do with you."

"He knows too well."

"Shouldn't we at least talk about it? Like, if he wants to negotiate, can't we make a counteroffer?"

Sahar glared at Frankie. "What does he say of my child? Will my husband's son live, or will he be buried in the sand, as were the daughters of Arabia before the Prophet?"

"You're right." Frankie tried touching her again, with the same result. It was like dragging one's fingers along hot sandstone. "That's something that needs to be clarified."

"I will not live in this place for the rest of my life! Even if he allows me to travel, he will never allow me to be a woman!" She buried her face in her hands. "I cannot submit to him! Please! Do not tempt me with his talk of settlement of a dispute!"

"Sahar—"

She spun away. "He is so cruel!" she sobbed, running away. "He is so cruel!"

## Yawm al-Jum'ah, 25 Safar, A.H. 1412 (Friday, September 6, 1991)

Frankie could feel the humidity as she walked through the *souqs* toward the law court. She looked up, half expecting to see a thunderhead. All she could find was the intense blue of an afternoon sky. But it seemed to shimmer, more like the radiance over Jackson Hole and the Tetons than the dry blue she associated with the desert.

The marketplace wasn't as crowded with people as it should have been. Rather than jostling her way through a beehive, Frankie walked easily toward the minarets of the Mosque al-Rashid. The men averted their gaze and many of the women appeared to be scurrying away from the market, as though there'd been a report of a bomb.

She felt a peculiar tension, like a magnetic force that both pulls and pushes. She wore an *abaya* with a veil over her nose and mouth, but everyone seemed to recognize her anyway. Brief nods of recognition and the word "Onglese" rippled away from her. Her briefcase and carriage gave her away. She looped a thumb through the strap as she would a backpack, as though to ease the load.

Gradually she heard the sounds of voices coming from somewhere. The closer she got to the law court, the louder the buzz, like the expectant sounds generated by a stadium full of fans. It sounded like Friday night high school football in Lander, before the game.

When she entered the square, she saw a crowd of men milling noisily in the far corner, some pushing forward, as though searching for better seats. They were in the small courtyard between the mosque and the old palace, some of them chanting and warbling with their tongues. The men in back began standing on their tiptoes, trying to see over the heads of those in front. Some held the hands of boys, others had lifted them on their shoulders. A few women and well-dressed men, some wearing turbans, stood on the wide steps that led to the mosque. Like a hillside—although farther from the action—it afforded a better view. The expressions Frankie read on the faces of the men were avid with interest, to the point of lust.

Intrigued, she walked toward the steps of the mosque and climbed them, craning her neck, trying to see. All she saw was the throng of men who faced a mud wall at the end of the courtyard.

A couple of men turned toward her and she heard a chattering of interest. It created a wave of its own that spread through the crowd. Many of the men in the courtyard, pinched between the high walls of the mosque and the old palace, turned to look at her. Then a hand gripped her arm.

At first she thought someone wanted her attention—only to realize she was being pulled, gently but firmly, into the crowd. Freezing, she tried to stick her feet down like poles. But the movement behind her wouldn't let her get them planted, and the packed mass in front kept opening for her to move through it. Some of the men smiled at her, as though to reassure her. "Onglese! Be not afraid! For you to see!" someone called in English. She saw the friendly face of the shopkeeper who had given her the carved mahogany box. He smiled and made a motion forward, like an usher. Frankie tried to relax. She didn't feel physically threatened, even though she could smell their sweat. But she didn't like it.

Suddenly she was funneled into an opening in the corner of the courtyard, thirty or forty feet from the wall of the old palace and slightly more than that from the shimmering white mud wall between the buildings. No one touched her; the men—many of whom were shorter—opened their hands and pointed with their faces at a small group of uniformed men in front. They wore light khaki shirts and pants, short white capes over their shoulders, and blue headdresses. They were the *muhaddin:* the religious police. She saw the two men who had escorted her out of the law library. All at once, as on a military command, they marched toward a door in the wall of the palace.

A hush spread through the courtyard. The door opened and a tall man in a white *ghotra* strode out, a long black-handled scimitar in his hand. He raised it over his head, and Frankie and everyone else shrank away from him, like a huge collective intake of breath. One of the *muhaddin* pulled out a wide leather strap, which he waved at the crowd. The watching mass had formed into a large animal, which responded with anticipation.

Two of the policemen yanked the redheaded thief, who had snatched Frankie's briefcase, into the bubble. With a jarring shock, Frankie realized what they wanted her to see: justice. The boy had blown the chance she'd given him, and stolen again. She gasped, feeling her stomach twist into a cavity. She huddled over herself, when her legs let go. A hand gripped her arm, holding her up.

Frankie turned toward the man who kept her from falling: short, swarthy, dressed in a red and white *ghotra*. All the others had lost interest in her, but she read his expression: concern. She nodded her thanks and he nodded back.

They dragged the boy into the arena, like a burro up a trail. Frankie's eyes tried to snap shut, but wouldn't close. She could feel the tips of her fingers on her forehead, and once again her knees sagged toward the ground. The man's hand tried to hold her up, but she had to sit down. A couple of men moved out of the way, scooping a small patch of ground for her, and the short man stood behind her as though guarding her from touch. Huddled on her knees and unaware of the sounds of her voice, Frankie tried not to see.

The man with the belt wrapped it tightly around the boy's right arm. The boy stared wildly at the crowd, like a calf about to be branded. His high-pitched bleating voice prick-led through Frankie like an electric pulse. Two *muhaddin* held him around the waist and another grabbed his hand, pulling it toward him, exposing a long, thin, freckled forearm.

Please God let it be quick, Frankie begged. But the knife wielder—like a butcher in the market, searching for the correct place to cut—sliced around the wrist, exposing white bone. The crowd-animal went wild at the boy's screams. Many of the men lifted their hands heavenward, chanting and yelling, in the throes of emotion. Even the man protecting Frankie vibrated, unaware of his sandal-covered ankles knocking rhythmically against her back.

Frankie could hear the grating and cracking of bone over the noise of the crowd. She saw red blood spill out of the boy's arm. A sudden final thrust with the blade, and the soldier holding the boy's hand pulled it off. He held it up for the crowd to see, then dropped it on the ground.

Frankie could no longer feel. She stared at the hand and watched it open, as though relaxing after having been closed in a fist. It was the color of gray paper except for a thin line of blood along the ragged edge. As in a dream, she watched another uniformed man hurry forward. He carried a bucket by the handle. Steamy heat fumes rose away from it and she smelled the odor of hot oil. With a quick, violent surge, the *muhaddin* leaped on the whimpering boy, thrusting the stub of his arm in the bucket. He went wild with pain. It took all of them to hold him. The pupils of his eyes twirled out of sight, leaving only the red-veined whites, like marbles, and his voice trailed off in a strangled sob—when his shaking body went limp.

It was over. Frankie heard a siren, and the man behind her helped her to her feet. "Da?" he asked. She smiled at him vacantly, which didn't matter, because of her veil. "Onglese. O-kay?"

"Yes, thank you," she heard herself say. He grunted, touched the top of his forehead and backed away from her. She thought he'd been very nice.

The boy still breathed, and she watched them haul him off on a stretcher, through the door into the old palace. She was alone; the courtyard had cleared. She seemed to float toward the steps at the other end, which led to the mosque.

Still feeling nothing, she stared up at the palace wall. A few windows had been carved out of the dark mud-red surface. She wondered which one Sahar had been behind, watching, when her nurse had been stoned.

242

# 18

## Yawm al-Ithnaya, 7 Rabbi al Awwal,
A.H. 1412
(Monday, September 16, 1991)

Frankie crushed another cigarette into the overflowing ashtray, then tried to relax on the stone bench. She was jumpy as a cat in a dog kennel, had been chain-smoking for more than a week, and hadn't slept. Everytime she closed her eyes, she saw the redheaded boy's gray hand in the dirt.

Sahar, wearing an *abaya* with a full veil, sat next to her. Frankie could hear the girl's rapid breathing, like someone forced to walk along the edge of a high building. She found Sahar's hand, tugged it over to her lap and held it in both of hers. "When does the shouting start?" she asked, trying to sound cheerful.

They waited in the anteroom of the Great Court al-Rashid of Qahtan. Earlier that morning, in the main courtyard, a mob of women—standing around like a flock of crows, in their black *abayas* and with unblinking eyes—watched as the two of them climbed out of their limousine and mounted the steps into the male sanctuary of the law court. Mufti Wadi abu Tamir ibn Ahmad, dressed in a green turban, odd little yellow slippers with pointed toes, and a cream-colored robe, met them and provided escort.

Someone had thrown a rock. It clattered harmlessly behind them, and was followed by the high, piercing trilling

243

sound of the women. It sounded to Frankie like the mindless expression of rage and frustration she'd heard in the sixties, in Alabama. The display didn't bother Wadi Ahmad, who didn't alter his pace, manner, or expression. But it shook Sahar, and scared the hell out of Frankie.

The court anteroom was a huge, thick arc of space, wrapped around the courtroom like the glass cover that encases a jewel on display. Tall pillars, spaced twenty feet apart, gave the chambers an aura of vastness. No one moved quickly, as in an American courtroom. Everyone Frankie saw walked with the slow, deliberate precision of men whose minds were occupied with matters not of this earth. Mufti Wadi Ahmad found them a bench to sit on, then disappeared into the courtroom. It was a hundred feet from their bench, across a beautifully tiled floor done in shades of yellows and greens, and behind an enormous archway.

They waited long enough for Frankie to sneak two cigarettes through her veil, when a tall man marched slowly toward them from the courtroom. He wore a soft, beautifully folded turban of green, a long white robe of felt over a light green vest, and gold-colored slippers that curled over his toes, like the blades of ice skates. His dark eyes poked holes through thorny eyebrows. The palms of Frankie's hands suddenly dampened as she watched him approach. His fingers were laced together in an attitude of prayer, projecting sincerity and spirituality. He spoke to Sahar in Arabic. Prayerfully, she repeated his words. "Come with me please," he said in English.

They followed along behind him, forced to walk at his pace. It seemed to take forever to pass under the high arch and enter the sacred bubble of the courtroom. The ceiling domed over them like an old-fashioned electric light bulb with a point at the top.

Tiled walls in the courtroom, white with shades of green, radiated light that seemed to be sucked in through tall, thin windows. The walls curved majestically around a low platform that projected out into the courtroom. The platform, forty feet from the archway and clearly the focus of attention, was covered with green and yellow cushions.

The *qadi*, Prince Muhammad abu Ibrahim ibn al-Rashid, sat cross-legged on one of the cushions in the center of the platform. He wore a plain burlap-colored robe of coarse cloth. A small, undistinguished green turban covered his head and glasses gripped the end of his nose. He too wore yellow slippers that curled at the tips; an Arabic affectation, Frankie decided, like the wigs worn by the Brits and judicial robes by Americans. His feet were smaller than Frankie would have guessed. He continued to read from a scroll fed to him by mufti Wadi Ahmad. They took no notice of the women.

Stone benches with no backs faced the *qadi*'s platform, enough to accommodate forty or fifty people. Fifteen men —some in robes, some wearing turbans, others in business suits—sat in reverent attitudes on the benches. The man who led them in motioned at the rearmost bench, and Frankie and Sahar sat down. He proceeded slowly up to the head of the room and took his place, kneeling then sitting on a cushion on the other side of *qadi* Muhammad.

Mufti Ghassar abu Diya al Din, Frankie realized. For the Kingdom.

Occasionally someone moved. Other than that, the only sound was from the parchmentlike paper as it accumulated on the floor beneath the dais. *Qadi* Muhammad asked a question in Arabic, and mufti Wadi Ahmad replied. Muhammad nodded. "What was that about?" Frankie asked in a whisper.

Sahar put her mouth next to Frankie's ear. "The *qadi* asked if there were additions of fact to the Statement of Claim. My mufti replied there were no additional facts in his knowledge."

Muhammad continued to read and stillness settled again over the courtroom. His expression was one of resignation. He looked again toward Ahmad and addressed him at length in Arabic. Frankie stuck her ear near Sahar's chin. "He reads, for all to hear, the Reply of Mufti Ghassar al-Din, to the Statement of Claim." Sahar grew rigid. Frankie could barely hear her. "My Rick. What did he say to those men?"

245

"What are you talking about?"

"When questioned by the imam in America, Rick told an unbelievable story to explain his presence, unclothed, with me in the hotel room in America. He did not tell him of our marriage." Her hands covered her face. "Such circumstances weigh heavily against the Statement of Claim."

Frankie felt like she'd been blindsided. Mufti Wadi Ahmad hadn't told her anything about the Reply! *Qadi* Muhammad continued speaking to Mufti Ahmad. "Sahar. What is he saying?"

"He asks of my mufti if such facts, alleged by Mufti Ghassar, are admitted."

"And?"

Sahar relaxed and smiled vacantly at Frankie, like Ophelia wandering, alone, on the balcony. "My mufti has said the facts are neither admitted nor denied."

Frankie shut her eyes. She watched the hand of the redheaded thief slowly open. In the background of her mind she also saw the tormented cloth that covered the body of Sahar's nurse. Her eyes popped open and she stood up. "I ask the indulgence of the Court," she said loudly, directing all her energy at the prince. "There may be facts in my knowledge that this Court should be aware of."

Muhammad stared at her with utter astonishment, as did all the men in the room. "In the name of God, the Merciful, the Compassionate," he said in Arabic. Frankie had heard the intonation enough to know it. Then in English: "Miss Rommel, for you to speak without being addressed is a serious breach of decorum in our proceeding." He was no longer the worldly figure who had heated Frankie's Courvoisier. As a *qadi,* his expression had become gentle and serene. "Let me remind you that your attendance here is a courtesy rarely extended. Please do not abuse the privilege."

The hell with privilege, Frankie thought, turning toward Sahar. She needed help. The girl seemed to battle with madness, but drifted to her feet. Her eyes radiated a peculiar light that reflected back on her face, illuminating her expression. "In the name of God, the Merciful, the Compassionate," she said in Arabic, standing beside Frankie. Then

246

in English: "Most learned *qadi,* this woman is a lawyer from another land. She does not scream or make a spectacle. Nor will I, Sahar bint Rashid. But I ask you in the name of God, truly to give answer: Is the decorum of the courtroom to be valued more than the truth?"

All of the men turned toward Sahar and frowned. Many of them muttered under their breath. Mufti Ahmad looked totally scandalized, to the point of tears. He addressed the *qadi* in Arabic, obviously prepared to jump to his feet and bodily throw the women out. *Qadi* Muhammad settled him down with a gesture of his hand. "I will allow Miss Rommel to speak, in the name of Allah," he said in English. He looked troubled, like a priest at a confession who has learned something he'd rather not know. "But I warn you, Sahar bint Rashid, of that which you obviously know. Our proceedings do not tolerate blasphemy."

Frankie could feel the strength of the woman standing beside her. She felt plugged in to something she didn't understand. Sahar nodded at her, and Frankie faced the *qadi.* "In the United States, I am the lawyer for Richard Adamson Junior, who is the husband of Sahar bint Rashid," she said, perhaps too loudly. But if saying it could make it so, her voice proclaimed, then it was so. Her assertion obviously irritated all the spectators. "I have talked to him about his marriage. It is true that he said nothing about it to the Rashidi authorities. He was afraid, and lied to them. But he regrets the lie and would never lie about it again. He told me that his marriage and his wife are the most important things in his life. He believes that he and Sahar Bint Rashid are truly one soul."

Muhammad frowned, then nodded, first at Sahar, then at Frankie. "Praise be to the one God," he continued in English. "And may the blessings of Allah fall upon you, Miss Rommel. Unfortunately perhaps, under Shari'ah, your statement is of small value. It is merely the unsubstantiated assertion of a woman. On the other hand, mufti Ghassar abu Diya al Din has presented a statement from imam Ismail Yusuf al-Faruqi, a member of the Rashidi Embassy in Washington, D.C., who questioned Mr. Adamson the very day he was found in bed, in an obvious tryst, with the Princess Sahar. That fornication occurred is additionally proven by the fact that—as is set forth, and not denied— she is pregnant." He frostily glared at the princess, but her soft and steady gaze somehow peeled away at his intensity.

"Mr. Adamson's recollection on that day, all will agree, was fresh in his mind," Muhammad continued. "His words were carefully reported by the imam. What he may have imagined later, in preparation for a trial in your country to salvage his freedom, has small influence or bearing here." He turned toward mufti Wadi Ahmad.

*"Qadi* Muhammad, my uncle, forgive me," Sahar said quietly. "Is it not the obligation and duty of this Court to determine the true facts of a case before it makes a ruling based on the law of God?"

"Praise be to God!" Muhammad declared. "What can be more clear? The true facts have been satisfactorily and unmistakably established!"

"But are you, as the *qadi* in this proceeding, completely satisfied as to their truth? I hear impatience in your voice, and determination to finish with this proceeding. Do I also hear uncertainty?"

"Please, sir," Frankie said. "Might I be allowed to testify on this point? Isn't the life of this woman worth—"

Four or five of the quiet, peaceful men in the courtroom exploded in Arabic. The two mufti also were on their feet, shouting. Frankie glanced nervously at Sahar, wondering what she'd said that triggered such a reaction and wishing she'd kept her mouth shut. Sahar's arm reached around her for comfort.

*Qadi* Muhammad sat for a moment, then dominated all the voices with the compelling power of his own. The bedlam instantly stopped. He showed surprising physical strength in standing, which he did by leaning forward on his knees, then lifting to his feet by straightening his legs. He said something in Arabic, and all the men, their heads bowed, sat down. "Miss Rommel, this Court is instructed to find the law of God," he said softly. "Your tasteless appeal for pity is an insult to the integrity of all Muslims."

Frankie started to apologize, but Sahar interrupted. "May I be heard, my uncle?"

Muhammad's face momentarily gorged with blood, but he nodded, then folded his hands and lowered his head. "You may speak, Sahar bint Rashid."

Sahar lowered her eyes. "Before you rule on this petition, I ask you—as a man who truly seeks the law of God—to consider the possibility that Allah wishes to work His will through me."

Two of the men stood involuntarily. They threw their heads back and stretched their arms to the ceiling, as though to catch it if it should fall on them. "Silence!" Muhammad thundered. He stared at Sahar with fury, and horror. "Do you deliberately add blasphemy to your crimes?"

Sahar appeared serene and untouchable, like Crazy Horse when his magic worked, supremely confident that none of the soldiers' bullets would hit her. "No, my uncle." Her voice throbbed, but not with self-pity. The concern seemed to include and touch every person in the room. "Please, do not judge only by words. I ask you to open your heart, as well as your mind. I ask you to open your soul, so that it too may receive other meaning."

Muhammad glared at her, then abruptly sat down. Sahar turned toward Frankie, smiled, and also sat down, motioning for Frankie to do the same. She took Frankie's hand, which felt warm and dry. "What's happening?" Frankie asked.

*He is making up his mind.*

Five minutes dragged by. The *qadi* raised his head and spoke in Arabic to mufti Wadi Ahmad. Frankie pushed her ear toward Sahar, to get the news. "He asks if there is any known authority that will allow the unsubstantiated testimony of a woman. He is told, none. He asks if the opinions refer to Muslim women only. He is told they include Christian."

Another five minutes passed. The *qadi* addressed questions to mufti Ghassar al Din. "He wishes to know if the affidavit of the imam described all the circumstances of the interview with my lover." Frankie got burned by the heat from Sahar's face. "He wishes, in particular, to know if threats were employed, or torture, or undue influences that could challenge the truthfulness of my lover's statements." Her eyes sparked through her veil. "He is told that the mufti is aware of no fact that would suggest anything of that nature. He is told that the imam is a man of great reputation for honesty and devotion to God, with experience in the conduct of such investigations."

More time went by. The *qadi* asked questions of the status of Adamson, and was told he was in an American jail, awaiting trial for the murder of the Rashidi, Abd al-Hafiz. He was told that Adamson, in all likelihood, would remain in prison for the rest of his life.

*Qadi* Muhammad squared his shoulders, sat up straight, and glowered ahead—then frowned and lapsed into thought. Later, he glared at one of the men in the audience, then took a deep breath and resumed his thoughtful posture.

Another ten minutes of silence. Finally, *qadi* Muhammad sighed heavily, opened the palms of his hands and looked up. "All praise to the one God," he said, in English. "In the name of Allah the Just, the Mighty, and the Wise, I now proclaim *fatwa*—the ruling of the Great Court of al-Rashid—on the petition of Sahar bint Rashid." Frankie felt the palms of her hands break into a sweat, which they always did when the jury came in with a verdict. "To give *fatwa* in a language other than the language of God, though unusual, is permitted in extraordinary situations. It is imperative that these words be understood by Frances Rommel, who does not understand Arabic. I therefore speak in English."

Sahar's hand slipped into Frankie's, and hung on. Muhammad glanced briefly at the two mufti on either side of him. "My beloved brethren, whose piety and devotion to the truth is known to all, please closely attend to my words, so that you may transcribe them into writing." Both men folded their hands over their chests in prayerful attitudes and nodded in obedience.

The *qadi*'s expression became still and meditative, as though he were concentrating on something unseen. "Sahar

250

bint Rashid requests this Court to declare that, under the law of God, she is a married woman." With a barely perceptible motion, his head registered *no*. "This, he said, "I am unable to do." Sahar's hand turned to ice and tightened, and Frankie couldn't breathe. "However, for reasons which I will now develop, neither am I able to declare that she is not."

Frankie stared toward the man. What does *that* mean? she wondered, aware that others in the room appeared mystified.

"There are few rules of behavior which Shari'ah, through the centuries, has so consistently given guidance to Muslims than those that involve marriage. Such matters have been decided time and again, by all the schools. With respect to them, the door of *ijtihad* has closed." His eyes closed as though to emphasize his words, and he lapsed into silence.

When his eyes and face opened, he continued. "It is the law that a Muslim woman may not marry outside the faith. It is the law that the formalities of marriage must be observed. Such formalities include the appointment of a guardian for the woman, the payment of a dowry to the woman, and a formal declaration of marriage, evidencing the mutual agreement of the parties, attended by two male witnesses. Such formalities do not allow for the observance of secret marriages, which for centuries have been declared *haram*: forbidden; not allowed."

He bent his head over hands held prayerfully near his chest. "For all these reasons, it would appear of little consequence whether Sahar bint Rashid"—he looked at her—"and the American, Adamson, in the privacy of their hotel room, believed themselves to be married, or not." His lips came together and his eyes closed momentarily, evidencing pain. "In truth, it approaches blasphemy to suggest anything other than the obvious: that the claim of marriage is no more than an excuse, so that lustful passions might be satisfied.

"And yet, I am troubled. There is nothing in the Qur'an that forbids such marriages. The laws of marriage that have evolved over the centuries have been designed to protect the

251

weak, from the strong. Surely, such interpretation is Allah's will! Is it not self-evident that, were Allah to speak to us now, as he did through the Prophet Muhammad—peace to his name!"—he looked with reverence toward the ceiling—"He would have us protect the weak and vulnerable woman from the aggressive, overreaching conduct of the man? Yet, I am troubled."

He took a deep breath, then plunged ahead, as though he knew there was no other way. "One must always remain open to the possibility of miracle: *mujahid.*" Frankie could hear the sounds of surprise. Sahar squeezed Frankie's hand and let go of it, sitting straighter. "It is possible," Muhammad continued, "that Sahar bint Rashid is the instrument of new vision. As was the prophet, she may be *mujtahid.*"

Frankie heard a difference between *mujahid*—miracle—and *mujtahid*—the person who did them. Muhammad paused, as if to give the others the opportunity to catch up.

Mufti Ghassar al Din stared first at mufti Wadi Ahmad, then at *qadi* Muhammad. "Praises to Allah," he said fearfully, his head bowed. He appeared afraid to speak, but more afraid not to. "My most exalted brother, on whom Allah has bestowed wisdom and devotion, I too am troubled. May I express to you my concern?" Muhammad nodded, and the tall mufti for the Kingdom took a chance and looked up. "To be *mujtahid* requires perfection. The claim of such purity, possessed only by the prophets, is—in the opinion of all jurists—heresy and blasphemy! The consequences are most severe. I ask you to consider what you say, before such words are included in your *fatwa.*"

"Praise be to the one God, my brother. I am grateful to you for your concern." Muhammad spoke with force. "My opinion will make this quite clear. Any heresy to be found will rest on the head of the person who asserts such perfection in herself: Sahar bint Rashid."

Frankie glanced at Sahar. The princess sat with pride. No one could measure the full extent of her expression behind her veil, but no one needed to.

*Qadi* Muhammad craned his head around, searching for Frankie. "Miss Rommel. Please stand, so that I may address

252

you." Frankie did, and he hooked his eyes on hers. "Praise be to God. It is of vital importance that you have a full understanding of my *fatwa*." He paused thoughtfully. "Our law—Shari'ah—begins with the Qur'an. It is supplemented by the *hadiths*—the sayings of the Prophet Muhammad, may peace and blessings forever attend his name—and has continued to reach for truth with opinions from jurists for more than thirteen centuries.

"At the beginning of the development of our law, most of the situations considered by the jurists had not been ruled upon. Your law is the same. New situations, for which there is no precedent, present themselves in your jurisprudence also, do they not?"

Frankie nodded, with respect. "Yes sir."

"In Shari'ah, there is a name for this situation: *ijtihad.* We have also developed the expression 'the door of *ijtihad* is closed.'" He stared at her with his soft, gentle face—not at all the one Frankie remembered—wishing to make certain she understood his words. "By that expression, we mean that the rules of conduct that govern a particular fact situation have been decided. They are no longer open for discussion or interpretation. They are fixed, immutable, beyond challenge. Do you understand me?"

"Yes sir. We have—"

His hand went up. "Praise be to God. This is not a classroom, Miss Rommel, with an exchange between student and instructor. I wish only to be certain of your understanding."

Frankie nodded.

"To continue. Even though the door to *ijtihad* has closed, there is always the possibility of *mujahid:* the revelation of new doctrine. But *mujahid*—which has been compared to a revolution—is rarely invoked, for most sensible reasons. It requires the overthrow of established doctrine!" The intensity level in his voice rose a notch. "New rules of conduct, based on revisionist doctrine, are its consequence. The comparison to revolution is most apt. On those rare occasions when *mujahid* has been allowed, the new doctrine imposed on previous dogma resulted in turmoil, confusion, and blood. The departure from that which is established is never accomplished with ease."

He folded his hands over his stomach and gazed with quiet wonder at the floor. "For centuries, all of the jurists, and all of the schools, agree that a Muslim woman cannot marry outside the faith, and that the formalities of marriage must be observed. Yet Sahar bint Rashid would challenge Shari'ah on these points. She asserts that her so-called marriage—though performed in secret, and not attended with the formalities prescribed by Shari'ah—is valid, because the parties contracted between themselves to enter that blessed state, and Allah gave his blessing. Such assertion, initially, appears a flimsy and transparent attempt on the part of a woman to justify her conduct. But on examination, one realizes that the assertion is blasphemous."

There was quiet shock in his voice as he spoke. "Perhaps out of deference to her rank, the mufti who has represented her petition has avoided the heretical nature of her claim. However, it has now been raised in such a manner that it cannot be ignored."

Frankie had the awful sinking feeling that she and her big mouth had made matters worse. *"Qadi* Muhammad—"

"Praise be to God, Miss Rommel, I beg for your silence."

Know when to fold them, Frankie thought. She laced her hands in front of her and stared meekly at the floor.

"Khalif Omar," Muhammad quietly continued, "in advising the jurists of his reign, more than one thousand years ago, said to them: 'If today thou seest fit to judge differently from yesterday, do not hesitate to follow the truth as thou seest it; for truth is eternal, and it is better to return to the true than to persist in the false.'"

A sardonic gleam briefly pulsed through Muhammad's eyes. "In spite of the nobility of the sentiment, it is rarely followed. One sees that there would be a tremendous loss of stability—especially as it relates to marriage—if one were to follow the dictate.

"Yet, truth *is* eternal. And in spite of the difficulty of change, it truly *is* better to change established doctrine than to persist in the false." There was low murmuring, and Muhammad raised his hand, shutting it off. "It therefore follows that this *fatwa* must be framed in the open-ended, easily modified manner of the jurists during the reign of Khalif Omar. This must be done in order to give to Sahar bint Rashid the opportunity to prove she is what she claims: *mujtahid*."

A soft but electrifying menace entered his voice. "Is she a heretic, or has Allah—praise to his name!—truly blessed this woman with the grace and vision of the prophets? If she is *mujtahid*, her place in Heaven, and her memory on Earth, will be forever assured. If she is a heretic, she will burn forever in the fires of Hell."

Frankie held her breath. It sounded as though Muhammad was arranging a test of some kind, a gantlet. What would they do if Sahar didn't get all the way to the end? Burn her at the stake?

*Qadi* Muhammad adopted his most reverent expression. The tips of his fingers came together, and he regarded them as though each cuticle was a miracle. "In this most difficult opinion, I strive to allow for the true manifestation of the will of God. My intention is to allow Sahar bint Rashid the opportunity to prove her claim."

When he looked up, his face had closed with a hint of malice. "The man she claims as her husband has said nothing of marriage. However, Francis Rommel, a Christian woman, reports he did not mean it when he spoke words of denial to the imam. There is thus the possibility that Adamson truly believes himself to be married. If that is so—and if Sahar bint Rashid is what she claims to be: *mujtahid*"—he allowed an ominous silence to build—"then it is possible that this secret arrangement, outside the law, should be recognized as a true marriage. How will it be possible to know?"

He folded his arms over his stomach. "For good, sufficient, and unassailable reasons, Shari'ah does not accept the testimony of one woman. However, it accepts the testimony of a man, even though he is Christian. Therefore, if the

American, Adamson, will appear before this Court, and submit himself to an examination, it is my opinion that this claim of marriage may yet be proved."

In the silence that followed, the expressions of the two mufti went through subtle changes, from perplexity to some form of understanding. "My brothers," Muhammad said. "Have you any questions?" He appeared to have forgotten Frankie, who had plenty of them.

"The American is in an American jail?" Wadi Ahmad asked.

"He is."

"How then will he submit himself to our examination?"

"If Sahar bint Rashid is *mujtahid,* then Allah will find a way."

The mufti slowly nodded. Their expressions, and those of most of the men in the room, opened with understanding. But Frankie couldn't control the shock in her eyes, and Muhammad looked at her. "Miss Rommel, do you understand this *fatwa?*"

Frankie lowered her head before answering. He might have thought her head was bent in prayer. Bullshit. She needed time to think. "I have some questions, sir," she said reverently. "May I ask them?"

"You may."

"Must this examination of Mr. Adamson take place in Rashidi? Arrangements could be made for him to be questioned, at any time, where he is."

The *qadi* thought a moment before answering. "He must be here. This is not a trivial matter. He must be willing to pay with his life for his answers."

Frankie's mind absorbed this information before her knees did, which began to tremble. "But if he is unable to come to Rashidi through no fault of his own, what then?"

"Praise be to God. You will not be blamed, Miss Rommel. His failure to attend will be regarded as the expression of Allah's will."

Frankie's ribs held her lungs in a vice. "But Sahar? Wouldn't some allowances be made—"

He raised his hand, cutting off further comment. "If

Sahar bint Rashid is not *mutjahid,* but is a heretic who blasphemes our law, then I will order her execution." He laced his hands prayerfully over his chest.

Frankie couldn't breathe. Her voice sounded hollow. "May I assume then that this Court will wait until after my client has been tried—and I hope, acquitted?" she asked, wondering how long she could delay the trial.

Muhammad's expression changed slightly. He allowed himself a full minute before giving answer. "Praise be to God. Miss Rommel, what this Court declares can never depend on the action of an American court. But you have raised a question: How much time can this Court allow the American to submit?" Another minute went by in silence. Then he nodded to himself and glanced with serenity at the mufti. "Sahar bint Rashid is pregnant. In the event she is found to be a blasphemer, would Allah, Who abhors cruelty, desire the taking of two lives, or one?"

He opened his palms for answer. "The American must give answers to his examiners before Sahar bint Rashid gives birth to her child."

# 19

## Thursday, September 19, 1991
## Washington, D.C.

Frankie's flight took her to New York, where she caught a commuter jet to Washington National. Her tan safari travel suit had been freshly cleaned when she boarded at Cairo, but thirteen hours of sitting pressed in a few wrinkles. She could smell herself, and thought about swinging by her apartment, but her energy level was high, it was mid-afternoon in the District, and there were a thousand things to do. She ducked into the ladies', washed up, sprayed her arms and neck with cologne, and put on a clean blouse. Then she slung her bags over her shoulders, hopped the Metro to the Judiciary Square station, and half an hour later pushed through the door into Brooking Slasstein's office.

A beehive somehow had located in her stomach after the ruling of the Great Court of al-Rashid. With bees swarming around inside her, she wondered if booze would quiet the little bastards. She decided it wouldn't hurt to experiment.

When Beacon looked up at her, the woman actually smiled. "Miss Rommel!" she exclaimed. "How nice to see you!"

"Hi, Beacon," Frankie said, dropping her bags. "Nice to be back." She would have liked a hug, but Beacon wasn't the type, and besides, the good woman had something on her

258

lap. It would have been too complicated. "You got the note I faxed from Rome?"

"Yes." Beacon continued to beam and even held out a hand, which Frankie took. "It was wonderful, dear. For the first time in a week, Brooking actually smiled."

Beacon blushed. Someday, Frankie thought, she would tell Beacon it was okay to call Brooking by his first name. "Things been a little crazy around here?"

"Worse than you can imagine," Beacon said, picking up the telephone. "I want to hear everything about your trip, but first you'll have to talk to the boss." She blushed again, as though knowing she was being naughty. "I'll get him for you." She punched in a number.

"Take it in my office?"

"Please."

"Frankie!" Brooking whispered loudly to her a minute or two later. "We're in deep doo-doo, babe."

"Where are you?" Frankie asked, glancing at the clock: 3:07 P.M. "Why are you whispering?"

"In court. Judge don't like phone calls." His voice seemed to lower, and Frankie had an image of him turning his back on the bench. "Thinks he's God, what's new? District Court judge, what should I expect? Listen. Adamson set for trial—"

"Mr. Slasstein, what are you doing?" boomed a voice that sounded exactly like God.

"—October twenty-second. This year, oy vey. See you half hour, okay?"

It took Brooking longer than half an hour. At four-thirty that afternoon he exploded into her office and gave her a hug, which included a pat on the ass. "Sorry." Then he started to talk.

Frankie would have preferred him to sit rather than bounce around like a hyperactive child. "Take it easy," she told him, watching him from behind her desk. As a matter of fact, the bees in her stomach had received the news of the trial date with grace. They'd stopped biting. "It's okay. Those things happen."

259

In a torrent of verbiage Brooking complained that Husam had changed. He'd found out Frankie was gone and taken advantage of the opportunity to turn up the heat. He knew the defense would put the case on hold until Frankie got back. "I didn't even have an investigator this case you left, what's the hurry? Then State jumps in. The government will crumble, we don't show the Mideast we mete out Justice with a capital J, they want a conviction! Presidential reelection hotshots behind the scenes, want it behind them, could be a factor in the election. Justice. Sheesh!" He plopped in a chair. "What if the trial pumps up the price of oil a month before the election? Judge Clardy's on the same track, like she could parlay her cooperation into Court of Appeals, who knows?"

He peeked up at Frankie to see how she was taking it. "So that's what happened in the land of the free, you were in Rashidi. We make a good record, we can get another trial, *this* mother goes in a month, we haven't even had a month to investigate! Who'd have thought so quick? We got a case? Where's Sahar?"

Frankie told him. She watched the expression on his face change from petulance to wonder. "No shit. When is she due?"

"The middle of December. She thinks it's a boy."

"So trial setting in October, perfect, right? A fucking sign from Heaven?"

"Careful. You'll get hit by lightning."

He leaned with his elbows on Frankie's desk. "I ever tell you about the golf match between Jesus Christ and God?"

Frankie laughed. It felt wonderful just to laugh.

The prisoners at the detention center had dinner between four-thirty and six. At six-thirty Frankie waited in the lawyer conference room for Rick. When he appeared on the other side of the clear plastic wall, she smiled like an old friend paying a surprise visit.

"Frankie!" His electrified voice pulsed through the voice amplifier like hard rock. He bounded over like a Saint Bernard greeting a long-lost master. His head waggled back and forth and he even pretended to lick the plexiglass between them. "You got all your parts?" The sockets of his eyes had deepened and he'd lost weight, which made him more interesting-looking. Frankie thought of a holy man on a hunger strike. "You look great!"

Frankie didn't feel great. She still hadn't been to her apartment, and felt grimy. But the impact of jet lag hadn't flattened her. She felt energized, like the batteries that won't quit.

She liked the goofy sheer happiness he showed in greeting her too. It dampened her eyes. "Hi," she said. "You don't. You look like you haven't eaten for weeks."

"Try the food around here. They can't even get the maggots to eat it."

"Sahar says hello," she said lightly. The tension in his expression dissolved, allowing it to glow. "She's been writing to you. Are they coming through?"

"No! I've written to her, like every day, then send her a book a week. Is she getting them?"

"No." Frankie had suspected as much. She didn't know who was intercepting their mail, but would do all she could to find out. "The big thing is, you know she's trying."

Rick sagged, but it wasn't despair. It was as though the rigidity that had held his body from collapsing had melted down. "Didn't she say more than just hello? She can do better than that."

"You're right." Frankie squirmed in her seat. "She loves you. That's the first thing. She wanted me to tell you that over and over, so you'd know it's true."

"Oh, man." He snuffled.

Why did emotions have to produce so many fluids, Frankie wondered, watching his nose drip through her own moisture-laden eyes. The serologists loved it. It gave them something to work with. "I'd give you a tissue, but there's this plastic wall between us."

He laughed, and cried. "Yeah." He snuffled some more, then shrugged his shoulders and wiped his nose off on a forearm.

261

"She's fine, by the way," Frankie said, glowing too. "She's seeing doctors—"

"What for?"

Frankie realized no one had told him. "She's pregnant."

His eyes tightened, then closed. "God!" When he moaned, Frankie couldn't tell if it was with happiness or in agony. "She might as well be dead."

"Rick. You will see her again."

"Yeah. In the garden."

"No. In this life. Believe me." What was she doing? She knew better than to promise.

But what would he do if she didn't deliver? Sue for malpractice? The important thing was to keep him alive. "You mean it, don't you?" he asked.

"I know it."

His chest continued to heave, but he seemed to push more air out of his body than he took in. "Okay. What happened?"

She told him. She'd already told Beacon and Brooking and knew how to get through it quickly. But she left out the part about the Davey Reddman lookalike and the hand. She told him of the trial in the Great Court of al-Rashid, and how moved she'd been when Sahar stood up and spoke, and what the *qadi*—Prince Muhammad—decided.

"What's happening, Frankie?" he asked when she finished.

"What do you mean?"

"Like, it's written, right? Now the trial's been set in October. Do I have a chance?"

Whatever it takes, Frankie thought, watching him. Her stomach turned into a small, frostbitten ball bearing. "I keep telling you, kid," she said, smiling with confidence. "A piece of cake."

Jet lag from west to east was like the twenty-four-hour flu. Frankie always recovered in twenty-four hours. But east to west was more dramatic. She functioned normally, until leveled by a speeding train. Then she went to the hospital; but after the operation, she was okay.

Frankie was reading a report in her office at eight-thirty, waiting for Brooking. She'd expected him to be there when she got back from the detention center, but found a note instead, asking her to wait. The words on the page started to blur. She got up in a daze, feeling like she'd just been bucked off a horse.

The door broke open and Brooking bustled in, looking as always like the best-dressed dwarf in the world. She pushed the heavy tiredness as far from her as she could. "I'm back," he announced, unnecessarily. "Frankie, Arnold Daven."

A large man, wearing brown slacks and a short-sleeved open-collared Hawaiian shirt, filled the doorway. "Hi, Frankie," he said, coming toward her and sticking out his hand. He wore thick glasses, stood six-four, was flat-stomached, and rolled like a sailor when he walked. "Heard a lot about you, all of it good."

"That's a comfort. Nice to meet you." She took his hand, then realized she'd been reading his report. "Oh. The investigator?"

"That's right." He had a nice handshake and the grace to know when to let go.

"Arnie's been busting his balls, he got this thing not even a month, guess what he found," Brooking said, pulling up a chair and plopping in it. "Cassettes!"

Frankie sagged back into her desk chair, wondering what on earth he could be talking about. Daven leaned against a wall, then pulled a pipe from his shirt pocket and started scraping the bowl out with a pocketknife. "Is that good?" she asked.

"Video cameras, babe, covert surveillance, the Rashidi Embassy, Arnie's got the goods!" Brooking enthusiastically opened his hands and leaned forward. "The whole scene, it'll show Rick sneaking in like *we* say he did! It'll show Abd al-Hafiz chasing after him, want a bet? In black and white!"

Daven drew the blue flame from a lighter into the bowl, filling the room with the sweet scent of pipe tobacco. "Actually, we don't know what, if anything, was recorded," he said between puffs. "All we know is, they have the

263

equipment. If it was operational on July twenty-sixth, it'll show what happened."

Her tiredness vanished and her spine straightened instantly. "Do that again?"

"Covert surveillance cameras were installed in the Rashidi Embassy in May of this year," the large man calmly replied. He held the bowl of the pipe in his right hand, and his right elbow in the cup of his left hand. "They cover the parking garage, the main floor, and the hallways and administrative offices on the second floor. Nothing on the third, fourth, or fifth floors."

"Balconies?" Frankie asked.

He shook his head. "Interior only. Nothing on the

"How do you know?"

"I located the company who sold them the equipment."

Frankie propped her arms on the desktop and leaned her face into the palms of her hands. "Why didn't we think of it, Brooking? Banks, department stores, stop-and-robs, those—"

"'Stop and rob,' what's that?"

"What cops in Denver call convenience stores. Those cameras are everywhere. It didn't even occur to me."

"Hey, beat yourself up you want, leave me out." He hopped off his perch and ricocheted around the room like a cue ball bouncing off cushions on a pool table. "Husam, the son of a bitch, the straight arrow, a piece of shit! Sure, defense lawyer supposed to ask, *Brady,* but the Arab didn't give us a clue!" With the suddenness of an eight ball being smacked with authority into a corner pocket, he dropped back on his chair. "Raises some questions, right? If they got a tape shows Rick sneaking in, where'd that other scenario come from? Him climbing the balcony, all that garbage, what's going on?"

Frankie struggled to keep her focus. "Maybe they don't have a tape. Husam may not know anything about cameras."

"Fat chance." But Brooking rubbed his hand in his hair with uncertainty, probably coating it with oil. "He'd find out, right? If you were prosecuting, first thing you'd do is find out, right?"

"It's also possible that Husam has seen the cassettes and they don't show anything." She didn't know why she was on Husam's side. It must have been habit. "What if Rick's lying?"

Daven found a high-backed chair, turned it around and sat down, leaning his elbows on the top of the back, the smoking pipe still in his hand. She'd seen a thousand cops sit the same way. "He went in the way he said he did. No question."

"How can you be so sure?"

"They have an alarm system on the embassy lawn, which he knew about. I've talked to him, and to them. It's no big secret. But he doesn't know a damn thing about an internal surveillance system. None of the American guards that work there do either. I asked them about it, they all agree the Rashidis wouldn't permit anything like that, like it's against their religion. Rick also admits the homicide. Where's the profit in making up a story about how he got in?"

Frankie brushed hair off her forehead. "I still don't like it. He was on the security staff. He'd know." She wasn't sure, but Arnold Daven may have grown another head. Two mouths were drawing on two pipes.

"Brooking, this woman is about to crash," Daven said. "Let's do this tomorrow."

"No," Frankie said, realizing the problem. Her spine had turned to mush. She tightened all the muscles in her back, which forced her to sit up straight. "We've got some decisions to make, and no time," she said, pounding herself on the head, smiling at them. "There."

"Sheesh," Brooking said.

Daven came together into one unit. "Arnie," Frankie said. "Why wouldn't they do it?"

"Rick told me the Rashidis would never have internal surveillance," Daven said. "It's totally contrary to the way they think. Arabs don't spy on each other."

"What changed their mind, then?"

"I don't know. I'll ask them."

"Not yet," Frankie said. "Let's think about it." She pounded her head again. "Does Rick know now?"

Daven shook his head. "I just found out myself."

Frankie squirmed in her chair, then stood up and paced the floor. She didn't think she would fall asleep as long as she stayed upright. "Do the feds know you've been snooping around?"

Daven stared at his pipe. "I don't think so. But I can't put a muzzle on Jamie Roon. He's the guy I talked to."

"Have the cops talked to Roon, or anyone in his company?"

"He says no."

Frankie leaned against the edge of her desk. "What do we do, Brooking? A *Brady* motion?" She registered the question in Arnold Daven's eyes. "Discovery," she explained. "We can get a court order to force the feds to disclose evidence favorable to our side. But they don't have to give it to us unless we ask for it."

"We don't bring nothin', babe," Brooking said, peering up at her. "We stay in the weeds, you know, the things lawyers lay around in. Let the bastards prove all that bullshit about mountaineering, a grappling hook, right? How Rick snuck around the outside of the building, then wham!" He slammed a fist into his hand. "We show the jury the tapes!" His eyes and nostrils flared like a rutting buffalo.

"The trouble with that scenario is: Where are they?"

"The pricks," Brooking said. "Bet your sweet ass they've had 'em from the beginning, know the whole story!"

"Then why the other scenario?" She watched Brooking rub the back of his neck, a fierce frown closing his mouth. "You'd think they'd love to have pictures of him sneaking in."

"That bastard Gleason," Brooking said, with an obvious need to pin the blame on someone. "Up to no good."

"But what is he up to?" Frankie leaned on her hands. "Arnie. If the Government doesn't have the cassettes, the Rashidis would still have them, right?"

Thoughtfully, he squirted more flame into the bowl of his pipe. "Probably. But a lot could happen." He sucked on the stick in his mouth. "Storage problems, for example. That many cameras could generate a shelf load of cassettes in a hurry." He snapped the lighter off, but continued working the pipe. "All the agencies are different. Some save them, some don't. Some automatically reuse the tapes, wiping off what was on. But to my way of thinking, if they showed something, they'd keep them. For a while anyway."

"Can you find out, without letting them know what you're doing?"

"I can try."

Frankie felt the muscles in her back relax. She couldn't seem to make them hold her up. "Damn," she said, slumping—then arched her spine. "Could copies have been made? Backup?"

"Not likely." He watched her patiently, as though waiting for her to fall over.

"If the Rashidis have them, or if they aren't gone already, they could be gone by trial time," she said, trying not to slur her words. "Brooking, we've got to do something."

"Yeah." He watched her too, as though expecting her to collapse.

"What?" She blinked at both of them. Her voice sounded hollow, as though filtering into the room through a thin wire.

"Discovery motion, all I can think of, if nothing else works we make them produce." He grimaced with dissatisfaction. "The trouble, then we tip them off what's in them, if they don't already know, the bastards. They adjust the theory of their case to fit a new set of facts, maybe Rick doesn't go down on the felony murder pop, but we don't walk him." He took a wrinkle out of his pants. "You know what that means."

Frankie didn't know if he meant they would forfeit their bonus pay, or Sahar would lose her head. "Wouldn't it be great if we found a copy?" she said again, looking at Daven. The outlines around him blurred, and she struggled to her feet. "I've got to go."

\* \* \*

Daven drove her home in his pickup truck. She opened the window wide, leaned her head against the cushion and aimed her face at the rushing air, letting it blow against her skin.

She could listen but couldn't talk. He'd been a D.A. investigator in Humboldt County, California, for twenty-five years, he said. Two years ago he'd moved to the District to retire so he and his wife could be near the Smithsonian. "I'll take a client like Brooking, but I turn away more than I take." Wire-brush hair surrounded male-pattern baldness, and Frankie hated the way he dressed. But she recognized his honesty, and knew she would need his thoughtful, thorough professionalism.

Daven had to help her out of his truck. He got her up the stairs of her apartment, pushed her inside, told her to take off her shoes before she sat down, then left.

She must have listened. Later, when she staggered off the couch to go to bed, she wondered, as she undressed, where her shoes were.

# 20

## Tuesday, October 22, 1991

The bees that buzzed around in Frankie's stomach pissed her off. Why hadn't they died of starvation? She couldn't eat. She'd also tried suffocating them in smoke, which may have taken out some of the weaker ones. The rest of them thrived on bad air.

"You're ready," Brooking said, standing on the balls of his feet in his office. He smiled at her with approval, like a dress designer admiring clothes he'd styled on his favorite model. She wore a pale blue suit, with lots of shoulders, which snugged around the waist and hips. It made the most of her bones. The rinse she'd used on her hair brought out the red, and the pearl and turquoise combs buried in the cloud of hair generated some nice fluffs and ruffles, leaving interesting wisps she could blow out of the way, or brush back with her hands.

That meant her hands would be exposed, and they were not objects of beauty. She put rings on her fingers and carefully manicured her nails, hoping to turn them into something people could see without throwing up. With heels, she stood close to six feet, and the muscles in her legs, above her thin ankles, moved nicely under the silk of her stockings.

"Not that it matters to a woman," Brooking continued in

269

his voice that allowed no interruption. "I mean, what's up here is what matters, right?" He tapped his forehead, but gave Daven a wink so big it opened his mouth. "You look terrific."

"Will it work?" she asked him.

"Can't lose." Then his head rocked back and forth and his hand wobbled like the wings of a glider. "I mean, you know. But I'll tell you, babe." He strutted toward her and took her hand, raised it ceremoniously to his lips and kissed it. "It's the only game we got. *I* couldn't do it, too slow, I gotta stand on tables, tap dance. Abe's right, anybody can, you can."

As she walked toward the Superior Court she told herself she would never, ever, do a defense again.

"What's this plan of yours?" Daven asked, shuffling along next to her, carrying the briefcase she'd packed with the file.

She and Brooking had spent days working it out, but they'd hardly seen Daven. He'd been too busy, scrambling all over the country, locating Rory Bern and other witnesses. "It's complicated," she said. "I'll explain as we go along."

"Am I part of it?"

"Are you kidding? You're at the heart of it." He wore a top-of-the-line, mail-order, solid brown suit, with bell bottoms and a red tie. His shoes had a dress-Marine polish. What a klutz, she thought with affection. "That tape you found is our case. If this works, you will definitely share in the spoils."

He shook his head, as though to say, Lawyers and their games. "I don't see the good in it," he said. "It proves *their* case. Not ours."

Frankie took a deep breath. "Cross your fingers."

As they marched up the low steps into the Municipal Courthouse, a black man, standing on the grass on the north side of D Street, praised Allah. He wore a red and purple *ghotra*. Whose side would he be on if he got picked to serve on the jury? Even with bees in her stomach, she loved the street scenes in the District. The low serious-looking buildings, the wide stately streets, all the little parks with statues of great men, including a few women. They formed perfect backgrounds for the dramas endlessly staged all over town.

She wondered how she'd feel about them after the trial. With Daven leading, they pushed through the security portal, into the courthouse.

They marched down the aisle of Courtroom 145 like they owned it. The prospective jurors were in the first five rows, but who were all those people behind them? She sorted out some of them: media types, spectators, a dozen or so from the Rashidi Embassy, and Rick's sister Tami, who waved at Frankie.

The dark-haired girl had a feminized version of Rick's bony face, with dark, bright eyes. She was squeezed against the wall. Good, Frankie thought. Make it hard for people to find her. They'd remember her better. Husam turned toward Frankie and nodded as they pushed past the bar into the pit, but didn't get up. Lamar Gleason, acting out the part of the world's most perfect gentleman, stood and made a show of holding the gate open. "Miss Rommel. Mr. Daven." He sounded like the maître d', fawning over a couple of big spenders.

The courtroom hadn't changed. It was still shaped like a large circle that had been cored, then quartered. Dark wood paneling, twelve feet high and interrupted by doors, plastered the walls, and Frankie counted the rows of auditoriumlike seats that ringed the pit.

Twelve of them, in arcs that got smaller as they approached the bar; the low wall that separated the spectators from the participants. The bench, faced with polished cork-colored wooden slats, stood well above the floor of the pit, looking like the big rock, dropped in the lake, that caused the waves of seat rows to radiate away from it. The witness box, between the jury and the bench, was grafted on to the bench platform like a smaller bubble.

The jury box stretched along a side wall, from a point near the witness box to the bar, and the lectern, counsel tables, and bailiff's desk were like cannons that could be aimed at the action.

The door marked COURTROOM PERSONNEL ONLY, near Clardy's throne, opened and Richard Adamson, Jr., between two men, was escorted in. He wore dark blue slacks, a gray sport coat, and a solid blue tie. Except for the guards on each side and the way they gripped his arms, he looked like a professional tennis player on the town. When he saw Frankie, he smiled, then searched the audience for a friendly face. What he saw froze him momentarily. "Mom?"

Frankie turned to look. A small woman dressed in a soft lavender suit sat next to Tami. The family resemblance was unmistakable. "Hi, Rick," she said, waving at her son and daubing her eyes. "Go get 'em!"

Frankie jumped up to go meet the woman, but Judge Barbara Clardy bustled through the door. She looked more like a model displaying judicial robes than the judge. Her silk-black hair, neatly coiffed in a nicely tossed wave, complemented the richness of her skin and the elegance of her facial features. She mounted the throne with style, regarding all her subjects with her usual benevolence. "All rise!" the bailiff, a heavyset woman in a brown uniform, intoned from a desk near the back of the pit. She didn't need to. Practically everyone was already on their feet. Clardy sat down and nodded at the woman. "Be seated!" the bailiff ordered.

"Good morning, ladies and gentlemen," Clardy said, smiling about. "Counsel. And Mr. Adamson." She nodded at everyone. "Mr. al-Din, will you announce the case?"

The court reporter sat with her back against the bench, under the witness box. She was positioned so she could see the mouths of the questioners and hear the replies of the witnesses. She glanced up at Husam, who stood behind the lectern, then nodded at him. "Your Honor," Husam said, "this is the United States versus Richard Adamson Junior, who is present and represented . . ."

Soon they were engaged in the first duel: voir dire. Frankie relaxed when she could as they relentlessly marched through the motions. She was introduced to the prospective jurors and given a chance to address them, starting off by asking Rick to stand. Later she introduced his mother and sister, under the guise of making sure none of the jurors were acquainted with either of them. "Actually, my name is no longer Adamson," Rick's mother said. "I've remarried and taken my husband's name." She smiled at Rick, who couldn't seem to look at his mother enough. "It's Doolittle."

"Mom. Doolittle?" Rick asked.

Frankie glanced apologetically at Clardy and put her hand on Rick's shoulder, as though to keep him under control. She was good at voir dire and watched Husam glare at her performance. With western hospitality, she questioned the jurors from a list that had been approved by the judge.

Voir dire in Clardy's courtroom was a controlled rite. The judge wouldn't allow the lawyers the freedom to wander all over the carpet. Neither could they describe the case ahead of the evidence, or ask loaded questions designed to search out and strike the jurors who didn't agree with the verdicts they posed. It suited Frankie, but Brooking had told her it didn't work for him. He reacted to the restrictions like a two-year-old in a playpen who wants out so he can jam a plug in the wall. "Woman frustrates me," he had said.

It suited the Government also. Husam's tactic was as neutral as Frankie's, as though he didn't want to give away any more than she did. Did he know they'd seen the cassette tape? Frankie wondered as they stalked each other through the exercise. A shift in theory?

She picked through a salad for lunch, as Daven devoured a monster beef sandwich on French bread. He managed to get his mouth around it by mashing the bread, which he easily did with his large hands. Frankie would have had to sit on it.

By four-fifteen that afternoon they had a jury: twelve jurors and two alternates. Other than Rick's family, the spectators and media had gone. Opening day had not been the action-packed slugfest the media had hoped for. They were primed for the antics of Brooking Slasstein, but—along with most of the audience—had trickled away because they were bored.

Clardy did not swear in the jury, which struck Frankie as odd. The judge instructed the chosen ones not to talk about

273

the case, to stay away from media accounts, and ordered them to return in the morning at nine o'clock. "You will be sworn in at that time," she informed them, excusing them for the day. "Mr. al-Din, Ms. Rommel, may we confer a moment in chambers before you leave?"

Frankie had no idea what the judge wanted. She shrugged at her team: Daven and Rick. "Of course," the lawyers agreed.

Judge Clardy's chambers—the quartered core of the huge circle that was the courtroom—were shaped like a large piece of pie. The lines of furniture were arcs and circles, as though attitudes might soften if the hard angles they bounced off of were taken away. Clardy stepped out of her robe and hung it up, revealing some nice bones of her own. She wore a light tan cotton skirt topped with a tight satin gold blouse, molding her upper body to advantage.

Her desk fanned out in front like a peacock's tail. Rick and his ever-present guards sat at the end, Frankie and Daven on Clardy's left, Husam and Gleason on her right. The court reporter set up her stand at the end, near a corner, where there was room to spread documents if needed.

"Voir dire was peaceful," Clardy said, opening the file in front of her. "After that rather stormy session when we picked the trial date, I can't really say I miss Brooking." She stood a moment, found the lever on her desk chair, raised it, and sat back down. "Well. You probably wonder what this is all about."

Frankie certainly did. Husam stared with violence at the surface of the desk.

"Ms. Rommel, this must seem to you like a biblical rush to judgment," Clardy said softly. But she didn't look at Frankie. Her eyes rested on Rick. "I find a hole in my calendar. A date has opened in March, which will be easy enough to fill, but it's available now. Would you like some additional time to prepare?"

The request struck Frankie as a genuinely nice gesture, from a judge with second thoughts. She smiled, but shook her head. "We're ready now, Judge."

Clardy turned toward Frankie, the question still on her

face. "Perhaps I was too firm, earlier, when this case was set for trial. Mr. Slasstein was quite vociferous then and complained loudly." She smiled, as though to say, You shoulda heard him! She also ignored the sound of Husam al-Din's throat as he tried to interject. "What concerns me is this. No defense motions have been filed. No *Brady,* no *Jencks,* no motions to suppress. Nothing. I'm bothered by the thought that perhaps you've determined it wouldn't do any good."

She'll find out soon enough that a lot has happened, Frankie thought, trying not to let her face show anything.

"If it please the Court," Husam said in a voice that couldn't be contained. "I have many subpoenas out. The Government would object to a continuance at this time."

"I am aware of that, Mr. al-Din. I am quite willing to risk your displeasure." She turned back to Frankie. "Ms. Rommel, I'm offering you a continuance."

Frankie glanced at Rick. Slowly but emphatically he shook his head no. Frankie moved a wisp of hair that had gotten in her eyes out of the way. Her hand felt heavy; all those damned rings. "Your Honor, my client and I have discussed the possibility of a continuance and he doesn't want one. He wants to go ahead now."

Clardy shrugged, as though to say she'd done what she could, in the interest of fairness. "Are you certain he's aware of the risks?"

Frankie watched the nonverbal exchange between them and realized she liked him. At least she had that much going for her. "I'm satisfied he is."

Clardy allowed her elegant hands to caress the surface of the executive desk. "I'm going to suggest, Ms. Rommel, that you discuss this matter carefully with Mr. Slasstein." She smiled at Frankie, who found herself blushing. "I'm also going to give you until tomorrow, before the jury is sworn in, to change your mind. I—I hope you aren't offended, but—"

"Not at all," Frankie said, blushing with embarrassment. "I appreciate your concern for my client." The words snapped out of her mouth.

Clardy did not appear totally satisfied with Frankie's reply. Husam al-Din did, however. Frankie noted the malevolent look on his face: pure, unadulterated joy.

Brooking jumped up when Frankie and Daven walked into his office. "Hold calls," he said to Beacon after rushing around his desk and going to the door. Shutting it, he rubbed his hands and pulled up a chair. "So?" he demanded, motioning for everyone to sit down.

"Guess who showed up," Frankie said. "Rick's mother!"

"No shit." He scratched the back of his neck. "The jury get a look at her?"

Frankie nodded. She was too pumped up to sit, and prowled the room, smoking. "A tiny thing, but she looks just like him. Her name's Doolittle now. No wonder Arnie couldn't find her."

He made a face. "Sheesh. From Adamson to Doolittle. Fuckin' goys."

"She's Jewish, Brooking."

He made a rumbling sound in his throat. "Don't tell the Rashidis. So where is she? I'd like to meet her."

"She's with Rick."

"Sit, okay?" Brooking asked. "Get ashes on my floor, use an ashtray, makes me nervous, you too, right Arnie?"

Daven leaned against the wall near the door. He kept his mouth shut.

"We have a jury," Frankie said, ignoring his request. She felt like an electric lightbulb at its brightest and hottest, just before going out. "They look"—she grimaced—"okay. What do you think, Arnie?"

"Hell, I don't know. Four degrees out of twelve, two others with some college. I like that. Seven women, all black. Five men, three of them white. I'd like to see some kids." He frowned judiciously. "What I don't like is the prosecution. They like them too."

"Felony murder, you get a jury, one day, amazing." He bounded out of his chair and started pacing the floor on the other side of the room. Frankie sat down. "All those black mothers, could be a problem, you can't tell. But the jury won't hang up, can't afford that." He growled. "Why the hell couldn't Rick be black?"

Watching him bound around, Frankie knew how badly he wanted to be there. "They like him," she said. "Clardy does too."

"How do you know?"

When she started to tell him about the in-chambers exercise, he sat down. His feet didn't reach the floor, and his polished shoes—bright enough to send signals—swung back and forth like pendulums. "She wanted to give us a continuance."

"Bullshit," Brooking said. "She's covering her ass. But it won't work."

"What do you mean?"

"She's right, rush to judgment, Appeals Court'd give us a new trial, she took that away. But we'll get a new trial on appeal anyway, we have to, won't do Sahar a lot of good." His teeth gritted and he pulled an ear. "Now we got you, turning down her offer to continue, perfect." He nodded glumly. "Incompetence of counsel."

## Wednesday, October 22, 1991

Frankie felt a stillness that was spiritual, watching Husam al-Din approach the lectern. The jurors were in their box and Clardy had sworn them in. The court reporter, her fingers poised over the little box, was ready to roll. Reporters from several news agencies had taken one row of seats, a contingent of Arabs sat in a clump toward the back, and Tami and Mrs. Doolittle had been positioned where the jury could see them. Several spectators filled in the gaps.

Frankie hated it, but loved it, knowing she had to walk the edge. The slightest delay—a mistrial, or a continuance—was as fatal to Sahar, and her baby, as a first degree murder conviction. She needed a flat-out, hands-down win: an acquittal. Daven had dug up some great stuff, but Frankie

277

could have used more time to polish her act. No such luck.
She'd be winging chunks of this one, flying by the seat of her
pants. But that day, the bees left her alone. Decent of the
critters, she thought. That, or they were curious to see if she
could pull it off, and couldn't buzz and watch at the same
time.

Blue shades were the color of friendliness, according to
the jury selection experts. Those tones should dominate the
clothing of the defense. Because most people associate
shades of brown with sincerity, the experts recommended
them for prosecutors. Frankie wanted the jurors to like her,
but they should know she meant it too. She wore a pale
green jacket over a soft yellow dress. Her hair, gathered in a
bun, was out of the way. Arnold Daven, sitting next to her,
wore the same suit and tie he'd had on the day before. She
hoped he'd changed his socks. Rick—on the other side of
Arnold—wore the same coat, but dark gray slacks. They
seemed more in line with his somber attitude. He'd tightened up overnight.

"Thank you, Judge Clardy," she heard Husam gravely
state as he arranged his legal pad on the angled surface of the
lectern. The charcoal-gray suit he wore looked severe and
righteous, matching the electric intensity of his voice. He
might have been an angel of death in a disguise. "My
distinguished adversary," he continued, acknowledging
Frankie. But he turned his back on the defendant, suggesting
to all his feelings: contempt. "This is opening statement,"
he told the jury, who appeared to be hanging on every word
he said. "It is the chance for the Government to outline to
you what we expect the evidence will show: the simple,
uncomplicated, unbelievably brutal murder of a man of
Arabic extraction."

Frankie found herself critiquing Husam's performance, as
one prosecutor might do for another. She approved of his
intensity, and admired the immediacy of his appeal. Opening statement was not argument, the jury had already been
told. But every trial lawyer in the land knew better. A good
opening statement planted a hook in the jurors from the

get-go, persuading them of the rightness of that side of the case. All the studies on the subject showed it was when jurors made up their minds.

Husam knew how to plant the hook. As an Arab, he would have no trouble in personalizing the victim. Frankie expected him to flinch for them when he described the dagger piercing the victim's back.

"Our evidence will show that the man who died in this case was young, twenty-seven years of age, not yet a father. From the Kingdom of Rashidi, this young man's name was Abd al-Hafiz. In Arabic, this name has spiritual significance to all who understand it. It means 'Servant of the one God, when He manifests Himself as the Protector.'" Husam paused long enough to take a sip of water. Frankie watched him grind his jaws with helpless anger. "For simplicity here, I will refer to him as Mr. Hafiz. There is so much about this young man I should like to tell you, but—"

"Mr. al-Din," Clardy said. "Counsel. Please approach the bench."

Husam glanced inquiringly toward the judge, which Frankie recognized as an act. She stared at him sardonically as she got up, hoping some of the jurors would understand what prompted her expression. The lawyers gathered in front of the judge and the court reporter wedged her way into the huddle. Clardy activated the sound screen. A buzz of static interference radiated away from the small circle. The high-tech device grated like fingernails on a glass pane on the nerves and ears of the jury and the public, but it kept the conversation between the lawyers and the judge private.

Frankie wanted the jurors to see Clardy's face. Anger was written all over it, which the judge quickly controlled, turning her expression to stone. "Mr. al-Din, that last statement of yours. You told the jury there was much you would like to say about the victim." Her eyes were sharp enough to peel skin. "A blatant reference, sir, to inadmissible evidence. A totally improper appeal for sympathy for the victim. I will not tolerate that kind of conduct."

Husam knew enough to keep his head down. "If it please

279

the Court, I said nothing at all about the young man. I stopped."

"The implication was quite clear, sir. You will stay within the bounds in my courtroom. Consider yourself warned."

"Of course." He looked at her and smiled, but Clardy's expression remained rock-hard. "Will there be anything else?" he asked.

"That will be all."

As Frankie returned to her chair, she wished she could tell the jury who the judge was pissed off at. Otherwise, they wouldn't know. She felt better anyway. She always enjoyed it when a judge chewed on her opponent.

Husam took his time before continuing, as though needing to work himself up to the right pitch. When his ears generated some color, he started in again. "Mr. Hafiz, as I was explaining, was the head of the security forces for the Rashidi Embassy, which is on New Hampshire Avenue, here, in the District of Columbia."

A nice transition, the critic in Frankie decided. Husam made it sound as though whatever had caused the interruption hadn't been his fault. "Our evidence will also show that the defendant, Mr. Adamson"—he waved at Rick—"was an American employee of those same security forces. He obviously became acquainted with the security systems used at the embassy."

"Obviously"? Frankie thought, mouthing the word. She chose not to object, but scribbled the statement down, word for word. Did they have facts? Or did they only have inference? "Mr. Adamson also became acquainted with certain nightly routines, conducted by Mr. Hafiz, known generally as 'making the rounds.'"

Frankie glanced toward Rick. His expression wasn't right and she made a mental note to talk to him. He should show surprise by looking astonished. You don't show surprise with a sarcastic smile.

"Our evidence will show that the defendant was discharged, fired, terminated of his employment with the Rashidi Embassy. This"—Husam paused for effect—

"insult was delivered to him on July twenty-first of this year." He took another drink, then walked over to his table and found the so-called CIA letter opener, encased in a clear plastic envelope.

"You will discover that the defendant was not pleased to be fired." He held the dagger over his head for all to see. "On July twenty-sixth, in the darkness of the early morning hours, the defendant hid on a balcony at the Rashidi Embassy, waiting for the man who had fired him to appear. Then he buried this instrument, fashioned of plastic—a specially designed blade, with the hardness of steel— entirely in the back of Mr. Hafiz." He sucked in his stomach and winced involuntarily, as though in pain. Then he pointed at Rick. "The evidence will show it was done by that nicely dressed man, sitting near that nicely dressed woman, who defends him here today."

He went on to describe how the Government would prove its case. First, an officer of the Capitol Police Department— the agency with the jurisdiction to investigate the case— would testify. Through him, diagrams would be introduced that would show exactly how the defendant had committed the crime. First he wired a gate between the grounds of the legation and the grounds of the embassy, so he could slip through without setting off an alarm. Then he worked his way across the embassy lawns to the second-floor balcony off the office of the deputy ambassador. The defendant climbed the balcony with the aid of mountaineering equipment, Husam told the jury, where he waited for his unsuspecting victim.

"These are not bald assertions. We have evidence to prove to you these facts."

He glanced at his notes. "On a surface of the gate were found his fingerprints." He nodded quietly, as though to himself. "In bushes on the lawn, he left a grappling hook and nylon line. On the balcony were traces of blood from human beings. An expert will explain to you that, in her scientific opinion, the blood came from two sources: the defendant, and Abd al-Hafiz, Servant of the Protector."

281

Frankie felt the excitement of a chess player who watches an opponent move into a trap. Husam had hooked his case to a scenario that was totally wrong. But could she take enough advantage to wrap the Government's case in checkmate? Rick had killed the man. Could she keep the jury from deciding, "What difference does it make? He killed him, didn't he?"

Husam described in detail what the expert who examined the blood would tell them. She was a forensic serologist. "A serologist is one who, among other matters of scientific inquiry, studies and identifies the fluids of human beings."

The serologist had received, in hermetically sealed containers, blood drawn from the person of the defendant and the body of the victim, Husam explained. She analyzed those samples and compared them with the traces found on the balcony, the victim, and the defendant. "She will tell you that the blood on the balcony comes from two persons: Mr. Hafiz, and the defendant." He flung an arm in Rick's direction. "She will also tell you that blood from Mr. Hafiz was found in the clothing of the defendant, and blood from the defendant was found on the body and in the clothing of Mr. Hafiz."

He returned to the dagger. "You will also meet a forensic pathologist, the doctor who conducted the autopsy in the case. He will tell you of the cause of death of Abd al-Hafiz." Frankie detected a hitch in Husam's throat. "He will tell you of the prominent role played by this so-called letter opener." He showed it to them again, then let it fall on the top of the lectern. "This office equipment, you will learn, is not available for purchase in stores that sell chairs for the office, or stationery. Rather, one must go to an establishment that specializes in cutlery. Knives for the kitchen, and with which to hunt. You will meet a man from the Knaked Edge. This man you will meet sold this"—he held it up—"to the defendant."

The black plastic blade, through the clear plastic bag, was easy to see. "Called a CIA letter opener, it is not intended to open letters. It measures slightly less than seven inches, from its tip to the back of the handle." Setting it down, he helped himself to a sip of water. "All of this instrument—all seven inches of hard plastic—were buried in the back of Abd al-Hafiz."

As though in passing, he made reference to the other charges: possession of a firearm, based on the weapon found in Adamson's shirt pocket when he was arrested, and the burglary count. "To summarize, ladies and gentlemen. You will be presented with a motive for murder—although who can know what impels one man to take the life of another? You will also have, for your consideration, a mountain of evidence offered to prove the accomplishment of the evil design. At the conclusion of this case, you will be asked to return the only responsible verdict: guilty, as charged."

Frankie waited for Husam to sit down before glancing toward the judge. He hadn't used all his ammunition, also good trial technique. Better to save some surprises for the jury. Nothing had been said about Rick, covered with charcoal and dressed in black, when the police arrested him. Pictures showing him looking like an assassin would make for a compelling introduction. Frankie gave Husam an eight. "Ms. Rommel?" Clardy asked. "Do you wish to make your opening statement now, or at a later time?"

Frankie got up. "If it please the Court, now."

"Very well. You may proceed."

She had worked for two hours on a statement that would take less than two minutes. She would have preferred not giving one at all, but couldn't let the jurors make up their minds on the basis of what Husam had told them. Her statement, like her case, had to walk the top of a high, thin wall. It had to sound like a factual summary, without disclosing any facts. It had to pry the jurors' minds open with a crowbar, then wedge it in tight to keep their minds from snapping shut until she could put on her case. It needed to create skepticism for the Government's claims and leave the jurors with a sense of intrigue and expectation, all without letting Husam or Gleason know what she really intended to prove.

Easy.

She walked to the lectern without any notes and rested her hands on its surface. "Good morning," she said to them cheerfully. Some of them smiled and nodded. "Thank you, Mr. al-Din." She smiled at Husam, as one performer might at another. He didn't smile back. "Members of the jury, after hearing Mr. al-Din, you probably can't wait to get in the jury room and convict my client."

"Ms. Rommel," Clardy said, leaning forward and frowning. "Please."

Frankie nodded at her pleasantly. With the side of her facing the judge, she tried to say, It won't happen again. With the side that faced the jury, the message was: I wonder what that was all about? "If it please the Court, may I continue?" she asked.

"Yes."

She turned toward the jury and waited while number seven—Mr. Markson, a forty-seven-year-old bookstore manager—picked up whatever it was he'd dropped on the floor. She smiled at him too. "From Mr. al-Din you've heard one side of a very complicated situation," she said to all of them. Hearing no objection, she continued. "To hear *him* tell it, however, it sounds simple." Her throat dried out and she washed it with water. "Please understand. What you've heard so far is only one side of the story. Members of the jury, there *is* another side."

Frankie no longer smiled. She put the water cup down and made eye contact with as many of them as she could, radiating sincerity. "The first thing our evidence will show is that the Government plainly and simply does not have a clue. Either they don't know what happened at the Rashidi Embassy during the early morning hours of July twenty-sixth, or they are deliberately trying to mislead you."

She was grateful for District practice which confined her to the safety of the lectern. In other courts, lawyers were allowed to wander around and hammer on things, but the federal system was more formal. Her legs had decided to tremble, but none of the jurors could see them. "Our evidence will show you that this alleged crime did not happen the way Mr. al-Din has claimed at all!"

She had their interest. "For example, he has told you of an alleged motive for murder. Our evidence will clearly demonstrate that there was *no* motive or desire in the mind or heart of Mr. Adamson to kill anyone." She hoped that statement sounded better to the jury than it did to her. Whoever analyzed it would see it as an admission that Rick had killed the man. "Another example. Mr. al-Din has told you of this invasion into the embassy grounds. Our evidence will show you—not only that it didn't happen—but it couldn't have!"

She stopped again for water, realizing that theatrics was not her forte. Most jurors were neutral in their expression, but two were openly skeptical. She couldn't decide whether to challenge the skeptics or ignore them.

"Our evidence will show you that the Government has also misled you as to what this case is all about." She spoke softly, but with the same aura of intensity. "We will show you that Mr. Adamson—a former Marine, who risked his life for us during the Gulf War and who had been stationed in Rashidi—had no choice in his actions."

She didn't have a clue, either, as to how those impassive faces were receiving her words. Were they hearing all the things she couldn't say? "For reasons which our evidence will disclose to you, you will learn he *had* to do what he did. Our evidence will prove to you that Mr. Adamson, my client, did not—I repeat, did not—commit *any crimes at all,* in those early morning hours of July twenty-sixth."

She'd heard a hundred opening statements like it, from the mouths of lawyers with no defense. "In summary, ladies and gentlemen, please understand—in spite of what Mr. Al-Din has told you—that there *is* another side. Our evidence will show you what *really* happened. It won't be the narrow little focus the Government wishes you to see. It will be the true picture." She let go of the lectern.

"And when you know what really happened, I am confident you will do your duty and acquit Mr. Adamson of all charges."

As she sat down, she wondered how Husam would have graded her. Not high marks, judging from the look of satisfaction on his face.

# 21

Corporal Warren Bronson, the Government's first witness, wore the expression of a man who didn't expect people to like him. His jawline seemed to say, So what? Being liked was not as important as the job. The crew-cut tow-headed thirty-six-year-old officer impressed Frankie as the kind of cop the thin blue line needed more of. He was the perfect choice to kick off the case for the Government.

"Will you describe your duties?" Husam al-Din asked. The tall, haunted-looking prosecutor stood behind the lectern like a bird of prey. He'd changed in the month Frankie had been in Rashidi, but so had she. Whatever his problem was, it hadn't mellowed him out.

Bronson's blue eyes flickered over the jury then landed squarely on Husam. He spoke in the style of a guest on *Meet the Press* who talked with the moderator but was aware of the reality that the show was for the benefit of the audience. "Essentially, it's guard duty," he said. He went on to explain that the mission of the Capitol Police Department was to guard the perimeter—the boundary—of the foreign embassies in the District.

When asked, Guard them from what? he replied that you never know. Anything from invasion to vandalism. As agents of the federal government, they didn't wear uniforms

287

because they wanted to be as inconspicuous as possible. Mostly they patrolled in cars. And the embassies appreciated them too, after they understood.

"Directing your attention to the early morning hours of July twenty-sixth of this year. Were you on duty at that time?"

He was, in a patrol car, with Sergeant Timothy Gore. When asked if anything unusual happened, he replied that it had.

"Please tell the jury of this unusual occurrence."

"I was driving, Sergeant Gore riding shotgun, on patrol near the entrance to the legation of the Rashidi Embassy."

Then the lawyer and witness went off on a tangent, chasing after the meaning of words. Bronson explained that the Rashidi legation was not the embassy, even though they were attached. They were on separate properties that butted up against each other, taking up close to a large city block. The embassy was the official headquarters of a foreign nation, where the diplomats and ambassadors lived: those with diplomatic immunity. The legation was kind of the servant's quarters where support personnel were housed. It was still quite comfortable, Bronson said. "You might say posh."

Husam frowned. "As you patrolled near the entrance to the legation, what happened?"

"At about two o'clock that morning, the lights turned on, lawn lights, floodlights"—his hands went up—"blam. A real blaze." His hands dropped out of sight. They immediately got in radio contact with Corporal Warren Johnson, who was in a rover unit, at that time on New Hampshire— and lawyer and witness chased off after another term. Rover units were unattached cars that traveled between embassies, able to respond quickly to emergencies.

Back to the big screen. Bronson described a scene of sudden, galvanized action, all of it headed one way. Men from the legation funneled through the gate that separated it from the embassy, spilling into the embassy grounds.

Other rover units were contacted and the perimeter

around the Rashidi properties surrounded. Bronson opined about the natural tendency on the part of people, in emergency situations, to run toward the scene of the disaster. "When a fire starts, you want to stomp on it to put it out." Frankie could have objected, but didn't. She even allowed him to explain that that was what the Rashidis were doing. However, good law enforcement technique at such times is to block off the exits, which was why the Capitol Police surrounded the place. "When something bad happens, the perpetrator will often be seized with a compelling urge to depart."

Their training paid off. Four or five minutes later a figure was observed proceeding in a stealthy manner, from bush to bush and tree to tree, toward the ungated driveway in front of the legation. Once he crossed the sidewalk, he straightened up and began walking rapidly across the street. Gore turned on the lights of his unit and Johnson did the same, catching the individual "in a cross fire of light."

His clothes were black, Bronson said: bicycle shirt, running tights, even black canvas beach shoes. His arms and face were smeared with charcoal. There was also a reddish-brown substance on his clothing, which Bronson recognized as possibly blood, and the heels and palms of his hands appeared to have been scraped. He had no identification on his person, but said his name was Rick Adamson. Bronson recognized him as the individual sitting at the defense table and identified him for the record.

Adamson didn't have anything in his hands, but a 9mm Heckler & Koch pistol with a thirteen-round clip was observed in the middle pouch pocket of his black cyclist shirt. The helpful Gleason found a white paper sack in the box under their table and handed it to Husam, who pulled out a pistol. A blue evidence tag hung from the trigger guard. Ceremoniously, Husam inspected the weapon, the barrel at all times aimed at the ceiling. He ejected the clip, then worked the slide mechanism to clear it of any cartridge in the chamber. Gingerly, as though handling a live hand grenade, he passed it to the witness, asking him if he could identify it. Bronson compared the serial number stamped on the barrel housing with the number he had recorded that night. "This is it."

Husam ran the drill on admitting it in evidence, then placed it on a tray table near the court reporter. "Was this pistol loaded or unloaded when you took it from the defendant?"

"Loaded. Ten rounds in the clip and one in the chamber."

As the lawyer continued to examine the witness about the gun, Frankie tried to watch it like a movie. The clip and exterior portions of the weapon were examined for fingerprints on August 20 by Arnold Daven, a private investigator, the man sitting next to the defendant, Bronson said. In the movie in Frankie's head, she saw them at the Capitol P.D., scratching each other on the ass. Bronson wouldn't let Daven dismantle the weapon until after it had been testfired by the FBI, he testified. "Hey, dumbshit, you know better than that," Bronson said in the script Frankie heard. The next day, Bronson hand-delivered the pistol to Davis Strawley, a technician at the FBI laboratory.

"When first detained at the legation entrance, was the defendant questioned regarding Exhibit Seven, this weapon which was seized from his person?" al-Din asked. His heavy-handed use of buzz words like "defendant," "weapon," and "seized" struck Frankie as less than subtle. They painted Rick in as a crook.

"He said he'd stepped inside the driveway of the legation to relieve himself. While engaged in that activity, he noticed a pistol nearby and picked it up. However, the officers were skeptical, and they placed Adamson under arrest. From their car they telephoned the Rashidi Embassy and gave the name and general description of the suspect to the deputy ambassador: Faris abu abd al-Rahman. "Mr. Rahman told my partner that Mr. Adamson was a former employee at the embassy. He said he'd just killed Mr. Hafiz."

At some point the defendant was photographed, and the pictures were introduced as exhibits and shown to the jury. They showed a tall, broad-shouldered, desperate-looking man standing in front of an unmarked police car. He looked like a captured commando. The whites of his eyes lent them the piercing quality of a cornered animal, and his lips curled away from his teeth.

The suffering prosecutor gravely reviewed his notes, nodding to himself as he made check marks on his legal pad. Then he stepped to the exhibit board and folded back a cover, revealing a large diagram of the general area. The embassy building along New Hampshire Avenue was outlined at the top and the grounds behind it were drawn in, including the gardens and shrubs. The walled fence between the embassy and the grounds of the legation was a thick line that curved gently toward the intersection of Twentieth and N. The gate between the legation and embassy was clearly indicated, and the grounds and buildings on the legation side of the fence were shown toward the bottom.

Frankie, like a nice Girl Scout, offered to stipulate as to the foundational elements, allowing the chart into evidence for demonstrative purposes. Husam grudgingly accepted. Bronson climbed out of the box and stood in front of the diagram with a red marking pencil. He told the story again, putting checks, circles, and initials, showing where the action had taken place. The tactic annoyed hell out of Frankie, even though she'd have done the same thing. It forced her to listen as the witness hammered all that good stuff into the juror's mind one more time.

"Your witness," Husam said. With icy courtesy he waited until she stood behind the lectern before sitting down.

Bronson smiled at her before she could smile at him, like a friendly rival. "Hello, Corporal Bronson," she said.

"Hello, Miss Rommel."

"Must have been an exciting night," she said, glancing at her watch: almost eleven.

He could have gotten cute and asked her if that was a question, but he nodded with agreement. "Yes. It was." She liked him for that, and had no doubt the jury did too.

"A couple of items I'd like you to clear up for me," she said. "At the moment when the lights went on—'blam,' I think you said, when the excitement started"—she tried to bring the jurors along with her, as though they were asking

291

the questions—"at that moment, you and Sergeant Gore were parked near the legation driveway?"

"No ma'am, we weren't parked." He peered at her with the same disinterested honesty he'd given Husam. "We were rolling, but slow. I remember the window was down and the breeze on my face felt pretty good. It was hot."

"Then the window was open?"

"Yes ma'am."

"Did you hear or see anything on the street, near the legation driveway?" Her hands—collective instruments, belonging to the whole panel—moved as though to extract his answer.

"I don't remember anything." He seemed to struggle as he scratched an ear. "A lot of yelling. Is that what you mean?"

"Did you hear a motor, the sound of a motorcycle?"

He shook his head. "All I remember is commotion, you know. A lot going on."

"Then there could have been a motorcycle, but you aren't sure?"

He shrugged. "How about, there could have been the sound of a motorcycle. But I don't remember hearing one."

Frankie smiled with good nature. "Then you acknowledge that a motorcycle could have left the legation grounds, either during the commotion or possibly ahead of it, without your hearing it?"

"Objection."

"Sustained."

Frankie smiled in apparent appreciation at the judge. "Corporal, you testified that the embassies come to appreciate the Capitol P.D., once they understand what you're all about. Right?"

"That's right."

"Then you get to know the people who work there, and they get to know you?"

He shrugged. "It varies."

Husam al-Din loomed upward. "I will object and move to strike."

"Basis?" Judge Clardy asked.

"Relevance, if it please the Court. Also, beyond the scope of the direct examination, which I intentionally confined to the arrest of the defendant and the introduction of a diagram of the scene of the crime." His voice heaped scorn on the word "defendant," and venom all over "crime."

"I don't think so, Mr. al-Din," Clardy said. "The door was opened by the witness. As to relevance, it's too soon to tell. Proceed, Ms. Rommel."

"Thank you." Frankie ventured from behind the lectern, anchoring to it with one hand. She felt as though she'd balanced herself on the end of a flagpole that stuck out at a right angle from the top of a tall building. "The victim in this case, Mr. Abd al-Hafiz." She pronounced the name carefully. "Had you known him?"

"Yes."

Frankie saw the look of satisfaction that grew on Husam's face. She fully expected to find out, on redirect examination, what a wonderful fellow Abd al-Hafiz had been. "He was the head of the security force at the Rashidi Embassy, right?"

"He was."

"Did you ever discuss the alarm systems, or surveillance systems, in place at the embassy with him?"

"Not that I remember," the witness said helpfully. "But I knew about them."

Ah. She started tiptoeing back along the bobbly flagpole toward the lip of the building. Don't ask him how he knows, she cautioned herself, which would call for hearsay. Just ask him what he knows and hope Husam doesn't object. "Describe their outdoor alarm system for us, please." She smiled confidently, like a good prosecutor, even using the prosecutorial "us."

"It's an electronic grid, I understand," Bronson said.

"Your honor," Husam al-Din said severely. "Object." He grew before the bench like a black cloud.

"Basis?" Clardy asked.

"From the answer of the witness, it is obvious he does not have personal knowledge."

Frankie had seen enough of Clardy's court to know that

293

even though it was formal in some respects, it was a free-for-all in others. The judge had no tolerance for boredom, and liked to keep things lively. She enjoyed the give and take of speaking objections. If it got too showy, she'd make the lawyers battle it out on the other side of the sound screen, but up to that line, she allowed them to perform. "Your Honor, this is Mr. al-Din's witness," Frankie said. "I'm satisfied he is quite trustworthy." She smiled with innocence at Husam. *"I'm not worried."*

"Your reasoning is hardly legal, Miss Rommel," Clardy said. "Sustained."

Frankie moved to the other side of the lectern, anchoring herself with the other hand as the scowling prosecutor sat down. "Corporal, when the lights first went on—when you said 'blam' and the place lit up—those lights were entirely inside the embassy grounds, weren't they?"

"Yes."

"No lights came on in the legation grounds, I take it?"

"Well, they did later. It took a minute or two, then they started coming on."

"But the embassy grounds were suddenly flooded with light? As though an electronic grid alarm system had been activated?"

"Object!"

Frankie smiled at everyone. "I'll withdraw the question if it causes so much trouble," she said. Careful, girl, she warned herself. "Nothing further." She sat down.

Two of the jurors stroked their chins. Probably they didn't get it, but they would when she argued it. Obviously an electronic alarm system guarded the embassy grounds, she would say. If Rick Adamson "invaded" the embassy grounds as the Government claimed, why didn't it light up when he first went in?

"Redirect, Mr. al-Din?"

"Yes, if it please the Court." Husam marched slowly for the lectern like an avenging angel. Frankie tried to decide if his humorless severity was tactical. Did he want to convey to the jury how he, a man of Arabic descent, felt about the killing of an Arab? Not a bad ploy, when pitched at a jury of nine blacks. "I believe you testified you were acquainted with the victim, Mr. Abd al-Hafiz?"

"Yes I was."

"Perhaps you will tell this jury what you know of him?" He kept his back to Frankie, ready to be astonished when she objected.

Frankie chose to let it in. She expected his answer to be consistent with her defense: that the death of the victim was a tragedy. To that extent, Husam was proving her case. "I liked him," Bronson said. "He wanted to have a good outfit. He was very interested in upgrading the quality of his department."

"He was a generous man?" Husam suggested, obviously pushing for all he was worth.

"I don't know about that. He was a very pleasant man, very friendly to our department. I felt bad about what happened to him."

Frankie looked slowly toward Rick, hoping the jurors would follow her eyes. His expression became one of solemn sorrow as he nodded with downcast eyes, agreeing with the witness.

"And the defendant," al-Din said, gesturing with contempt toward Rick. "After his arrest for this"—he paused, as though to cool his blood—"incident"—the word stuck in his throat—"can you tell us what you saw of him that night?"

Bronson frowned. "I'm not sure I understand, sir."

"He was handcuffed, was he not?" Husam asked impatiently.

"Yes."

"What happened with him?"

"He was placed in the back of our car. We took him over to the embassy entrance."

"And then?"

"Sergeant Gore telephoned, and had a conversation with Mr. Rahman. . . ."

"Yes yes. And then?"

"We took pictures of him."

"You have told us of them. And then?"

A light came on in Bronson's eyes. "I took him to another car. Milton Zwicker and Aaron Melrose. I told Officer Zwicker to take him to the Federal Detention Center."

"Very good." Husam smiled ironically. "I have no further questions," he announced, marching to his chair and sitting down.

"Ms. Rommel?"

"Nothing further," Frankie said, standing high enough to lean on the table.

"Mr. al-Din, I assume your next witness is either Milton Zwicker or Aaron Melrose?" Clardy pronounced "either" as "eye-ther."

"Yes, if it please the Court," Husam said, returning to the lectern. "The Government will call Officer Milton Zwicker."

Clardy glanced at the clock above the door across the courtroom. "After lunch, Mr. al-Din. It's five minutes before twelve." She turned toward the jurors. "Members of the jury, we'll adjourn for lunch in just a moment. First, we go through a very important little ceremony called admonishing the jury. . . ."

# 22

Trials were like stage plays, according to some trial technicians. It made the action easier to follow if the lawyer/director would link the witnesses/characters up. Husam al-Din's lead-in to Milton Zwicker may have been clumsy, but he'd bridged the gap.

Frankie watched Officer Zwicker—thin, stiff-legged, late forties, Adam's apple like a yo-yo sliding up and down a pencil-thin neck—crawl with apprehension into the witness box. He looked the way she felt. Two bites into a Cajun chicken salad during the noon recess and her appetite dried up like wet leather over a hot stove. She'd closed her eyes to rest them, and seen that awful hand. What if their game plan didn't work?

Brooking would have screamed, postured, objected, wept, pontificated, interrupted, and allowed himself to be jailed for contempt. He'd have made the scenes in Husam's play hard to follow, with ad-libs and unexpected interruptions. But Frankie had adopted the role of a helpful stagehand, with a few suggestions to clear up ambiguities for the audience. In the process, she intended to stick in a few lines of her own.

Zwicker gingerly settled into the box, as though he expected it to be infested with scorpions. In a high-pitched hesitant voice he testified to the "transport of the defendant" from the Rashidi Embassy to the detention center. With Husam leading him like a horse with blinders, he told the jury he was present during the strip-search of the defendant, then stared—seemingly without recognition—at the clothing Husam handed him.

All the articles were visible in transparent plastic bags. Log sheets clipped to the top, which Zwicker had initialed, were on each bag. He had trouble recognizing his own initials. But Frankie offered no objection, and they were admitted in evidence.

On cross-examination she asked only if he'd heard or seen any motorcycles near the Rashidi Embassy that morning. He told her no. As a rover unit on Massachussetts Avenue, he hadn't arrived on the scene until 2:23 that A.M. She let him go.

Frankie was adding lines to the Government's play in the time-honored manner of the crafty defense lawyer. She hated them all for the tactic, even though doing it was fun. Her proof of a motorcycle in the vicinity was thinner than restaurant soup. It consisted of questions answered in the negative.

Husam didn't try to lead into his next witness: Faris abu abd al-Rahman. He brought the deputy ambassador of the Kingdom of Rashidi into the Government drama like a new scene. Rahman wore the formal apparel of an ambassador prepared for an audience with the pope. His perfectly tailored dark blue Italian suit turned defects into assets. A protruding stomach evidenced the girth of a person of power, rather than a fat man.

His mannerisms added to the overall impression of a man of importance. Measured hand gestures punctuated every statement with emphasis. Large, clear brown eyes embedded in a handsome, hawklike face gleamed with intelligence. They reflected the emotions of a decent man of courage. There was no place in those eyes for lust, cowardice, arrogance, or hypocrisy, as though such feelings had been lost to discipline, or never felt.

The rapport between witness and examiner was like that

between brothers, separated at childhood but together at last. Frankie had to concede that Husam al-Din was a better choice to prosecute the case than she'd have been. With one foot in Arabia and the other in America, he was perfect: a living link between the victim and the jury.

"Your name has meaning in Arabic?" Husam asked.

"It does. May I explain?"

"Of course." Husam had grown used to getting away with whatever he wanted.

"'Faris' is horseman," Rahman said, then raised and wobbled his right hand, suggesting something lost in translation. "Or perhaps, knight on horseback. 'Abd al-Rahman' speaks to a relationship with Allah, as the Merciful, the Gracious."

Husam al-Din thoughtfully stroked his chin. "This is common in Arabic?" he asked. "For one's name to express a relationship with Allah, or God?"

"Most common." The eyes of the witness seemed to open to true meaning. "To acknowledge the existence of the one God is all-important to the Arab. Allah is our life. Our language, and our law, pays to Him constant tribute."

The tall prosecutor might have been conducting a friendly interview. "You are more than merely the deputy ambassador for the Kingdom of Rashidi, are you not, sir?"

Al-Rahman nodded graciously at his brother. "I have love for the sound and expressiveness of language, as do all who call themselves Arab." His eyes smiled. "I am also a poet."

Husam continued to lead the witness like a dog on a leash, and Frankie sat like a fireplug, affording the dog a place to relieve himself. Without interruption, Rahman testified to his duties and responsibilities, likening himself to the CEO of a corporation. The embassy employed over a hundred people, twenty of whom had diplomatic status. He oversaw the office of information, the heads of security, protocol, personnel, policy formulation, departmental organization. He was the liaison officer between the United States Department of State, other federal agencies, other governments. He was as the prime minister, and the ambassador was the king.

With soft intensity and glaring disregard for the rules of evidence, Husam took Rahman through his relationship with Abd al-Hafiz. Biologically they were uncle and nephew, but emotionally they were father and son. The young man of only twenty-seven years had been trained in security in the best schools of Europe and America, including courses at the FBI Training Academy at Quantico, Virginia. Serious-minded and deeply religious, he had been encouraged by his father to take a wife. He chose not to, out of a desire to wait until he could devote the time to truly cultivate the pleasures and blessings of female companionship and family in the way Allah intended.

When Frankie couldn't stand it, she wrote messages to herself. "Husam is an idiot who thinks because I let him get away with all the crap, I'm an idiot too. I am building my character by listening to all this bullshit. I will be a better person. Husam. I won't take this personally, as long as you tell my story too. But it's embarrassing, Husam. I am embarrassed because I have to sit here like a mule. If any lawyers are watching, they will think I'm a complete ninny. I am *not,* Husam. When this ordeal is over, I will kill you."

It got worse when Husam asked Rahman about the duties of the security staff, and of Abd al-Hafiz. The questions—leading, calling for opinion rather than fact, irrelevant—brought tears, they were so bad. The answers were worse. But the story the witness told would help her case too, so Frankie doodled on her pad and stayed in her chair. Clardy glowered at Frankie, inviting her to object, but Frankie avoided looking at the judge and hoped she would stay out of it. She did.

Eighteen Rashidi nationals guarded the embassy, Rahman said. They were the interior force, posted at the entrances and at sensitive locations inside the building. Exterior guards at the front and rear gates were American. The defendant had started as an exterior guard. The drivers of the kingdom's limousines also came from the security staff: three Rashidi, two American. The Americans were assigned to nonsensitive missions "for their own protection and to avoid the appearance of incident, if anything of ugliness should occur."

The defendant became the driver for the Princess Sahar bint Rashid. Particular trust had been placed in him because of his background, which included service as a soldier in Rashidi, Rahman informed the jury. He was well-liked by the Rashidi nationals because of his rudimentary understanding of Arabic, and his bearing. They admired the way he walked. Rahman glanced at Adamson, long enough to identify him. Then he looked at his fingernails, as though he would rather examine the dirt caught underneath them than the defendant.

The witness painted the duties of the victim with the same broad, freely moving brush. Abd al-Hafiz trained and disciplined his men, purchased and disbursed equipment including firearms, made and enforced schedules, interacted with the Capitol Police, stayed current with the latest advances in technology, hired Americans to supplement his staff and fired them on those rare occasions when it was necessary. He also made nightly rounds of the embassy. Rahman, on two occasions, had personally followed Hafiz on his tour. Like night watchmen, they inspected the offices and hallways on the first and second floors. When asked whether Hafiz checked balconies, Rahman firmly replied that he had.

But when Husam invited Rahman to tell the jury of the firing of the defendant, Frankie got up. The play needed some changes in the script before the audience saw it. She asked for permission to approach the bench, and on the other side of the sound screen raised hell. She got what she wanted. As an exception to the hearsay rule, an incident report in the personnel file of Rick Adamson was allowed into evidence, but Frankie restricted the testimony to the incident report. Rahman read the translation to the jury:

"'On Sunday, July twenty-first, 1991, Private Abdullah ibn abd al-Wahid, imam Ismail Yusuf al-Faruqi, Private Ibrahim ibn Nabhan, and Sergeant Tarif al-Jafari, witnessed Private Richard Adamson, one of the Americans detailed to service as a driver, known as Rick, make sexual advances of a most serious nature toward the Princess Sahar bint Rashid. Reprimand is not sufficient and Adamson is dismissed from service for the Kingdom of Rashidi. This is done with sadness. Adamson had formed a place in the hearts of those who know him, which is uprooted by this betrayal of trust. The soil torn by his conduct will not heal soon.'

"Signed Abd al-Hafiz, dated July twenty-second, 1991."

Rahman was then asked to give his account of the early morning hours of July 26. The previous night, he'd gone to bed at ten o'clock, he told the jurors, shortly after the final call to prayer. As a Muslim, he derived peace and strength in the observance of the daily rituals. He briefly described his apartment, on the third floor of the embassy, which he shared with his wife and two of his daughters. His only wife, he added ironically. A telephone call from one of the guards woke him up, summoning him with urgency to his office on the second floor of the embassy. Dressing hurriedly, he arrived within minutes.

He quickly learned that an outdoor alarm had jarred the security forces into action. But Abd al-Hafiz had disappeared, and they were leaderless. Following standard procedures taught to them by their revered commander Abd al-Hafiz, and thinking perhaps that this was an exercise designed by him, they quickly searched the first and second floors—only to find his lifeless body on the balcony outside the office of Faris Rahman. Immediately, the duty corporal telephoned him.

When Rahman arrived, his beloved nephew had already been lifted with care and tenderness from the deck of the balcony and laid on the sofa in his office. The fine young man's arms had been crossed over his chest and his eyes had been closed. The absence of spirit removed all expression from his thin face. Dry-eyed, Rahman identified photographs of the nicely dressed corpse, stretched out on the couch. After shoving them distastefully out of the way, they were introduced in evidence and shown to the jury.

Rahman had no time for the luxury of grief. He was

expected to take charge. Assuming the worst—that the embassy was under attack—he ordered a general alarm, requiring all the able-bodied men from the legation and embassy to assemble. They were being armed when the telephone call from a Sergeant Gore of the Capitol Police was received. Gore told Rahman of the arrest of a man leaving the legation grounds. The fellow was dressed in black, his arms and face were black with charcoal, he was carrying a pistol, and he'd been bloodied, as though in a fight. The name he'd given to Gore was Rick Adamson.

Rahman was familiar with the incident report in the defendant's file. He had an immediate understanding of the situation. He stared for a moment at Rick, and Frankie stood up, deflecting his gaze and signaling a readiness to object.

Husam moved carefully into the next line of questions. "After receiving this information from Sergeant Gore, what did you say to him? Please use exact words, if possible."

Rahman leaned back, remembering. "I said to this voice that Adamson is an American, on the staff for the Rashidi Embassy. I am certain this coward has just murdered a man, and has run away."

Frankie sat down. That wasn't so bad, the playwright in her decided. The drama she wanted the jury to see was still being staged.

Husam al-Din gazed impassively toward Rick, who had turned his hands palms up and was staring at them. Many of the jurors followed Husam's gaze. "Thank you sir for your testimony," Husam said after a deliberate pause. "I have no more questions at this time." Like a slow-moving hearse, he picked up his legal pad and returned to his chair.

"Ms. Rommel?"

With businesslike cheerfulness, Frankie approached the lectern. The bees in her stomach buzzed with excitement. The next gambit was Brooking's idea: she was too straight to have thought of it. If it worked, the tale would develop a nice twist. "Good afternoon, Mr. Rahman," she announced, putting her pad on the lectern. "I certainly admire your language skills. To be fluent in Arabic and English is an accomplishment." She placed her hands on the edges of the lectern and peered at him with friendliness, inviting response.

"Thank you."

"Do you mind if I try an Arabic greeting?" He looked surprised and said nothing. *"Is-salaam 'alaykum,"* Frankie said.

His eyebrows shot up. "Ah. That is very good. Something you practice?"

"Yes."

He smiled with grave good nature. *"Wa-'alaykum is-salaam."*

Judge Clardy wearily raised her left hand, as though to hold back the annoyance of the court reporter. "Ms. Rommel, do you anticipate further exchanges in Arabic?"

"No, Your Honor."

"Very well. Proceed."

Frankie took her time. "You testified you are an Arab, and a poet." He acknowledged her statement with a smile. "May we also assume you are a man of honor?"

Husam cleared his throat and Clardy glared with impatience. But they didn't interrupt. "Of course," Rahman said.

"In fact, you are here because you are a man of honor."

He shrugged. "I have been provided a subpoena."

"But you could have ignored it if you'd wanted to, right? You have diplomatic immunity?"

"Yes." He regarded her warily.

Frankie didn't want him afraid of her. She held on to the lectern with one hand and moved around it, exposing her body to him, as though to say, "Look at me. I'm defenseless. You have nothing to fear." "And if I were to give you a subpoena, you could ignore it too. Isn't that also correct?"

"Object, Your Honor," Husam rumbled. "This line of questions is not relevant, is far beyond the scope of the direct examination, and calls for legal conclusions. It serves no purpose whatever."

Clardy tipped her head. "I'm not so sure, Mr. al-Din. Ms. Rommel?"

"Judge, I have a problem." She looked with candor at the judge. "I'd like Mr. Rahman to testify for me, during my case. But because he has diplomatic immunity, there isn't any way I can make him. That's why I'm asking him now, as a man of honor, if he will—"

"I protest this indignity!" Husam said. "This is outrageous, to take advantage of this situation in such fashion!"

"I hardly think it's outrageous." Clardy appeared to consider ducking behind the sound screen. "Your dilemma, Ms. Rommel, is that you have no way to enforce his appearance later, when you put on your case," she said, as though explaining the situation to herself. "Why not call him now, as your witness, out of order?"

Frankie looked like she was thinking it over. But she and Brooking had anticipated the suggestion and worked out an argument to get around it. "That won't do it, Judge," she said. "My questions may be different later, depending on what other government witnesses testify to." The beehive in her gut was attacked. By a bear.

Clardy shrugged her shoulders. "I don't see the harm," she decided. "You may ask."

Frankie tried not to let her relief show. "Mr. Rahman, you understand my problem, don't you, sir?"

He nodded.

"I'm sorry, sir, you have to indicate verbally," Frankie said. "For the court reporter."

"Yes," he said loudly. "I understand your problem."

"I'm going to ask you, as a man of honor, to remain available for the rest of the trial, and to testify for my side if I need you as a witness." She sounded as reasonable as anyone could whose stomach was a battleground between a beehive and a bear.

He folded his arms and glowered at Rick. "This means to be witness for Adamson?"

"It means to be a witness for the truth," Frankie countered. "You will not be asked to lie. Only to tell the truth, as you have done for Mr. al-Din."

Rahman looked inquiringly at Husam al-Din, who jumped to his feet. "Again, I protest," Husam said. "Such indignity! Does Ms. Rommel wish this man of important duties to wait in the hall, with witnesses who have been sequestered, and allow his diplomatic responsibilities to take care of themselves?" He was talking to Rahman, providing him with reasons to say no. "It is preposterous!"

"Mr. Rahman can wait wherever he wants, as far as I'm concerned," Frankie said. "He can wait here in the courtroom"—she pointed at the floor—"and listen to everything that goes on. I don't care. Or he can wait at the embassy until I'm ready." Quickly she faced the witness and kept talking. "What about it, Mr. Rahman?" she asked, trying to get to him before he picked up on the prosecutor's cues. "Will you continue to be a witness to the truth?"

"Of course," he said graciously. "You have my word."

"Thank you, sir." Frankie picked up her pad. "I know something—not nearly enough—of your culture. The word of an Arab is far more binding than a piece of paper." *That* ought to bring him back, she thought. "No further questions."

The buzz in Frankie's stomach turned into applause at her brilliance with Rahman. With wrenching suddenness, it demanded food. She couldn't think of all the chicken she'd wasted, and pay attention to Sergeant Timothy Gore—the government's next witness—at the same time. She got her focus back after he'd been on about five minutes, hoping she hadn't missed anything.

Gore's face had been marked by smallpox. Frankie recognized the pits and scars because she'd seen them before, on the faces of Shoshone Indians in Lander. His gray hair, abundant and closely trimmed, had the texture of buffalo grass.

He and his officers experienced difficulty in gaining entrance into the embassy, she heard him say when she came back on-line. He had the wordy style of a person who wanted others to think he had a brain in his head. But it wasn't until two-thirty that particular morning, perhaps thirty or forty minutes after arresting the defendant, that he and Corporal Bronson were invited inside. They were escorted to the office of the deputy ambassador, Faris abu abd al-Rahman.

They viewed the body of Abd al-Hafiz—Gore's Arabic pronunciations had a French accent—then learned the man's remains had been discovered on the balcony. At that point the doors to the balcony were closed, to prevent any further contamination of the scene.

Gore encountered many problems in persuading the Rashidis to allow outside agencies to handle the investigation. It wasn't until 3:18 that Faris abu abd al-Rahman permitted him to go to work. The FBI had a crime scene unit waiting in the street, and they went to work immediately. Gore worked with them.

Gleason popped up, marched to the exhibit board and folded sheets of paper out of the way. He stopped at the diagram of the balcony. Husam managed to bore the jury to death as he made everything clear to the point of confusion. Frankie had put a few juries to sleep also, but that had been fifteen years ago. It would be fun to take advantage, but she couldn't. She wanted the jury to see his picture. With luck, he would annoy the jury in the process.

Blood smears on the deck and railing had been photographed. The pictures were introduced and meticulously keyed to the diagram. Scrapes, indentations, and nicks in the paint of the railing were noted—blah blah blah. Rick kept his head down, Daven took notes, and Gleason looked apologetically toward Frankie as nails were driven in the coffin of the defendant. Frankie smiled at Rick.

Two long, tedious hours later, the government established what Frankie would have stipulated to: the location of the blood smears on the deck, the position of the body when first seen, outlined in chalk, the pool of blood inside the chalk marks, the location of the black stripe of rubberlike substance "with the appearance of a scuff mark," the blood smears on the rail and the location of the nicks, dents, and chips in the paint, the collection of samples of all that gore, and who Gore gave the samples to. Whew.

"In seven minutes it will be five o'clock," Clardy said, when Husam paused for water. "How much longer do you expect to take with this witness?"

"A few more questions, and the introduction of one exhibit," Husam said.

Frankie stood up. "Is the exhibit the grappling hook and nylon rope?" She could see them in the box near Gleason's feet.

"It is."

Husam would do better to lighten up. If she were Brooking, she would mimic his lofty righteousness. "I'll stipulate Sergeant Gore found it, collected it, and gave it to whoever you say he did at the FBI lab. Probably along with all those other things." She waved her hand at the pile of plastic bags on the clerk's table.

Husam did his best to find fault. "Much time might have been saved if you had made this offer earlier."

Those who watched the play should understand that al-Din was the obstructionist. Not Frankie. "Mr. al-Din," she said. "You didn't ask."

The gavel in Clardy's hand was ready to bounce off the marble plate, stopping the exchange. "Will you accept, Mr. al-Din?"

Husam stretched the situation out, to include where the hook was found—under a cedar bush near the balcony—and when: the same morning. After quick consultation with Gleason, he made it even longer, adding two further exhibits: a vial of blood drawn from the victim that night, and one taken from the defendant a week later.

"So stipulate," Frankie said, facing the bench. "My cross examination won't take long, Judge. If we finish with Sergeant Gore, he won't have to come back tomorrow."

Clardy glanced at the clock on the wall. "It's five o'clock, Ms. Rommel. Will you need more than fifteen minutes?"

"More than enough time," Frankie said, walking confidently to the exhibit table and picking up the gun. For the first time suspicions drifted across the expression of Husam al-Din. "Hello, Sergeant Gore," she said in the style of a defense lawyer who wants the witness to think she's a nice person.

"Hello, Ms. Rommel." His tight-lipped manner sent the message that he wasn't fooled.

"During your search of the balcony, were any nine-millimeter Heckler and Koch pistols found, like the one in my hand? I refer to Exhibit Seven."

"No."

"These guns are used by the Rashidi security forces, aren't they?"

He paused like a chess player, making sure there weren't any hidden traps before making his move. "Yes."

She put the weapon down and walked to the lectern. "Did you or anyone in your presence do a pat-down of the body of the victim to see if he was carrying one?"

Frankie picked up a glint in his eyes, that sudden flash of brilliance that witnesses display when they think they have the drift. "That was done by Corporal Bronson in my presence."

"The victim wore a shoulder holster, designed for pistols like Exhibit Seven, correct?"

"True."

"But the holster was empty. Correct?"

"Also true. May I explain?"

On cross-examination, never let the witness take charge. "Please do," Frankie said, inviting the worst.

"You perhaps are wondering what happened to the pistol carried by Mr. Abd al-Hafiz, and you might even be suggesting that the weapon carried by the defendant actually belonged to Mr. Abd al-Hafiz?"

Frankie did her best to appear annoyed. "Sir, I'll ask the questions," she said in the manner of one keeping her cool. Then, as though to say, what difference can it make?, she added: "Go ahead."

Husam al-Din snickered at her ineptitude and Clardy stared at the legal pad in front of her. "The pistol on the person of Mr. Adamson was stolen from the weapons locker in the Rashidi Embassy. The—"

"Wait! Object!" Frankie said angrily. "How do you know it was stolen?" She sounded desperate.

"It was missing from the weapons locker and found on the person of Mr. Adamson."

"Your Honor, objection! The answer is not responsive and calls for facts not in evidence!" she demanded shrilly.

Clardy signaled to Husam with a raised hand that she didn't need help. "I believe it *is* responsive, Miss Rommel. Furthermore, the answer itself puts the fact—that the weapon was missing from the weapons locker—in evidence. Overruled."

Frankie seemed to have lost her composure. She stared helplessly at Daven and her client.

Gore took advantage of the silence. "The weapon on the person of Mr. Abd al-Hafiz was removed from his person, I have reason to believe, by Mr. Abraham, or Ibrahim is the way they say it, bin Nabhan," he said, "of the Rashidi security unit."

Angrily, Frankie searched through her list of witnesses endorsed by the Government. "Your Honor, this is rank hearsay! The man mentioned by Sergeant Gore hasn't even been endorsed as a witness!"

Husam al-Din stood, looking like a buzzard on a telephone pole. "If it please the Court, he has been recalled to Rashidi."

"Then I move to strike the obvious hearsay testimony of this witness!" Frankie said furiously.

"Your motion is granted." Clardy avoided looking at Frankie. She instructed the jury to disregard the answer of the witness, as it related to the removal of a weapon from the person of the victim. "Do you have any further questions, Ms. Rommel?"

"No, Your Honor."

"Redirect, Mr. al-Din?"

The prosecutor appeared completely satisfied with the turn of events. "No redirect, Your Honor."

Wearily, Clardy gave the standard admonishment to the jurors before adjourning for the night. She told them not to discuss the case with anyone and to refrain from watching, listening to, or reading media accounts. Then she tapped her gavel on the marble block. "We're adjourned."

When Frankie opened the door to the office, she could hear Brooking. It sounded like he'd jumped out of his chair, over his desk, and all the way to his door in one mighty leap. She looked down at him, staring up at her. "How'd it go?" he asked.

"I'm starved," Frankie informed him. "If I don't get some food, I'll die."

"You can eat again, right? Don't move, wait a sec!" She heard the sound of a bull in a china closet as Brooking disappeared in his office and reappeared two seconds later, his coat on and his boutonniere in place. "On me, Queens Bench, we hurry we beat all them lushes just there for toofers, you can tell me!" He grabbed her arm and whirled her out the door.

# 23

## Thursday, October 24, 1991

"The timing is bad, our problem," Brooking said, strutting around the law library and waving a mug of morning coffee. He wore blue jeans and a worn, paint-smeared work shirt. It was the first time Frankie had seen him in rags. She'd dressed in a blue suit with wide lapels and a silver-and-turquoise conch belt. She'd been tempted to put on her high-heeled, tooled-leather white boots which reached her ankles, but that would have been too much. Still, she felt like the queen of the rodeo, and wanted to send the message: Howdy y'all. Wait for the calf-roping contest, hear? "We need to finish our case noon tomorrow, the latest," Brooking continued. "Any sooner they'll have the weekend, get ready for rebuttal, they'll think of something."

Frankie tapped her teeth with a fingernail and stared out the window. In Denver the leaves on the trees would have changed colors and fallen onto lawns, cluttering gutters and clogging sewers in the unlikely event of rain. In Washington the leaves were in the process of turning gold and red. "I could drag their case out," she said. "We wouldn't start ours until Monday. They'd still have the weekend to think, but they wouldn't have anything to rebut." She looked at her watch: 8:37 A.M.

"You think you could drag theirs out, two days?" he asked. "Who they got left?"

"A firearms expert, a physical evidence person, a serologist. The nice, wonderful, lovable pathologist who did the body. A salesman at the Knaked Edge, where Rick bought the knife."

"You couldn't stretch that into two days, babe, no offense, you don't have the mouth. *I* could, takes the touch of an outlaw, you got too much respect. Can you make sure theirs don't leak into tomorrow? That's your best shot." He slowed down to a walk and looked at her.

"I don't know."

"Gleason? You gonna get that chance to bust him up?"

There was a difference between testosterone and estrogen. Taking care of Gleason had lost its importance. The life of Sahar bint Rashid and the future of Rick Adamson was all that mattered. She shrugged indifferently.

Brooking plopped in his chair. "This is killing me, why I look like a bum, keep me in the office no one can see me. Worse than when the wife had her first, my son, the dipshit." He rubbed his hands through his hair. "I wanna do it myself, make sure it gets done right, but I couldn't do this one a million years. I snuck in yesterday, watched what I could stand, you're doing great."

Frankie took one long, last, deep drag of her cigarette and butted it. Her briefcase was already packed. She got up. "I'd better go."

"Break a leg."

As she sat at counsel table, waiting for the morning feast to begin, she tried to think of some way to make them hurry. She should be able to put her case on in half a day, but it had to be the final scene. If Husam and Gleason were given time to line up rebuttal, the ending of the play could take any number of twists: mistrial, conviction of a lesser-included, request for continuance. If they had the weekend to put themselves back together, she knew they'd use it.

She had to manage the trial so the Government would finish that day. Otherwise, she'd have to drag theirs out so she wouldn't start her case until Monday. But Husam had started to get suspicious, and if he had the weekend, he might use it to dig. He wouldn't have to get down very far to find out. "Don't look too good, does it?" Daven asked in a low voice, sitting down next to her.

He wore an atrocious green double-breasted suit with bell-bottom trousers and a red tie. He looked like a carnival barker. "It could be worse," Frankie said. Daven donned a studious expression, pulled out his legal pad and readied himself to take notes.

Two U.S. marshals, in blue uniforms that could be mistaken for cheap business suits, marched Rick into the pit. He grinned when he saw his mother and sister. How could anyone so young look so old, she wondered, wishing she could spend more time with him. The marshals stuffed him in his chair, removed the cuffs, and commandeered a couple of seats in the front spectator row, directly behind him.

The jury hadn't come in and neither had the judge or court reporter, but the spectator area had filled with people. Turning around, Rick talked to Tami and his mom about nothing: how they were doing, telling them to go to the Smithsonian, ordering them to take advantage of the town. They could stare at him and glare at Husam al-Din, but couldn't seem to look at Frankie.

An idea popped into Frankie's mind. She got up quickly and walked over to the prosecutor, who sat sternly next to the Creep. "Miss Rommel," Gleason said, smiling at her. As though to demonstrate he was a today kind of guy, he added: "I like your hair."

"Husam, can we talk a minute?"

He wore a charcoal-brown suit of synthetic wool. It complemented everything about him: black hair, dark eyes, Mediterranean complexion. "Of course."

"We'll need a day to argue instructions. Let's do it tomorrow."

He turned his pad over, as though to protect it from Frankie's vision. "Judge Clardy does not ask for argument. If you submit instructions to her, she will give, refuse, or modify. But she hasn't the patience for argument—unless, of course, there is a real question of law. Do you have such an instruction?"

Frankie managed a blush. "I could." She leaned on his table, as though to tell him there was more to it than that. "I'm in a bit of a crack," she confessed. "I have a witness for Monday, but we could be finished by then. It's gone so fast!"

"Who is this witness?"

She hesitated. "I can't say."

"You wish help from me, but refuse to tell me the name of this witness?" He looked at her with obstinance.

She stiffened up. "Forget it." Angrily, she stalked back to her table.

Clardy and the court reporter bustled in. The jurors filed into their seats immediately afterward. "Your next witness, Mr. al-Din," Clardy said, as though anxious to make up for lost time.

Husam marched briskly to the lectern. "Call Davis Strawley," he said.

A no-nonsense quality characterized the prosecutor's approach to the witness. From the FBI crime laboratory, Husam swiftly trotted him through his qualifications and offered him as an expert witness in the field of firearms identification and operation. A large man with gray hair and spectacles that looked like magnifying glasses, he hunched in the witness box as though preparing for a ride on a roller-coaster.

Husam picked the HK pistol off the exhibit table and zipped through the clearing ritual. "I hand you Exhibit Seven," he announced, presenting it to the witness grip first. "According to the evidence, this weapon was seized from the person of the defendant on July twenty-sixth, 1991. Apart from brief exterior examination on August twentieth, it was not touched until surrendered to you by Corporal Bronson of the Capitol Police on August twenty-first. Can you identify Exhibit Seven?"

The witness examined the serial number. "I can indeed." He held it easily in his mammoth hands.

"Did you conduct tests with this weapon to determine

whether or not it was operable?" Husam asked, glancing at his watch.

Frankie loved it. Her treachery had worked.

"I did indeed." On August 23 he test-fired it at the laboratory firing range. Using the clip in the pistol, he fired five rounds at a target from ten yards. All projectiles entered the target area within a tight grouping, somewhat left of and below the point aimed at.

"Based on such test, and based on the evidence I have stated, have you an opinion as to whether this weapon was in operable condition on July twenty-sixth, when seized from the defendant?"

"I do indeed." He tossed the pistol casually back and forth in his hands like Magic Johnson toying with a basketball. "No question about it. It was in operable condition on that day."

"Were any other tests performed on Exhibit Seven, by you or in your presence?"

He smiled at Arnold Daven. "I had been instructed to allow Mr. Daven, a private investigator hired by the defendant, to examine for fingerprints. This was done by him in my presence on August twenty-second, right after I test-fired." Daven had dismantled the weapon and searched all interior surfaces for prints. To the witness's knowledge, he hadn't found any.

"Thank you, sir. Nothing further." Husam folded his legal pad and marched quickly away from the lectern.

Frankie requested a moment to consult with Arnold Daven, then wandered to the lectern. She asked her questions slowly and repeated the answers. With impatience, Husam al-Din drummed his fingers on counsel table. She had the witness demonstrate some of the unique aspects of the weapon. Holding it away from him and toward the jurors, he explained the safety: a finger-grooved lever at the front of the grip, under the trigger guard. "Before this weapon will fire, the shooter must squeeze the grip." He showed them what he meant. "Once the grip is released, the safety is on. She won't shoot."

"Doesn't that make it difficult to use?"

"No indeed," he said. "In fact, that feature makes her quite attractive to many police agencies."

"Will you explain?" Frankie asked, as though trying to keep him on the stand.

"It prevents accidents, accidental shootings."

Frankie glanced apprehensively at Husam. "Then if the weapon were dropped on the floor, it wouldn't go off?"

The witness shrugged. "If she hit the floor at exactly the right angle, she might. But not likely. I'd have to test."

After a slow march to consult a final time with Daven, Frankie smiled uncertainly at Strawley and let him go. He was on and off in thirteen minutes.

With the determination of a climber who must reach the peak before the afternoon clouds roll in, Husam forged ahead with his next expert. Also from the FBI crime lab, he showed with photographs how the negative impressions of a tool had been printed on the metal railing around the balcony. They matched the shape and configuration of the fingers of the grappling hook, which the jury had already seen. He couldn't be specific as to when, but could state with a reasonable degree of certainty that it had been affixed to the balcony railing.

Next came a small woman with a girlish voice and an assertive manner. A physical evidence identification expert, she gave the jury a quick course on spectrographs and spectrophotometers. Alien traces of paint on the grappling hook were consistent with the paint on the balcony railing, and vice versa, leading her to conclude that they may have come into contact. She had also analyzed trace evidence from the scuff marks on the balcony deck with scrapings from the soles of the shoes worn by the defendant. There was consistency in seven points of comparison, and no inconsistency. She therefore proclaimed, with a reasonable degree of scientific probability, that the marks on the deck were from the shoes worn by the defendant.

Frankie asked her if she had examined the nylon rope attached to the grappling hook. She had. "Were you looking for anything in particular, such as blood smears, or flecks of skin that might have come from a person's hands?" That was precisely what she had looked for. Frankie didn't like her smile, but jumped in anyway. "I take it you found nothing, or you'd have told us?"

The smile might have been a bluff. "Correct."

After a short recess, Frankie hurried back to her seat at counsel table. She was two minutes late. Husam al-Din stood at the lectern and a forensic serologist smiled at her from the witness stand. "I apologize," Frankie said, deciding to leave it at that, rather than explain she'd had to wait for a booth in the ladies'.

The witness identified the blood samples provided him, matching them with diagrams and exhibits. Sufficient quantities of blood had been found on the defendant's clothing, the balcony railing, the deck, and the clothing of the victim, for positive identifications. "It takes very little, with modern techniques." But the traces of blood in the hair of the victim weren't enough for positive identification. He concluded that the blood on the railing was the defendant's, the pool of blood on the deck had been the victim's, identifiable traces on the victim's shirt had come from the defendant, and identifiable traces on the defendant's running tights had come from the victim.

Frankie asked him if he'd examined the nylon rope, attached to the grappling hook, for blood. "No ma'am, I didn't."

"If the palms of a person's hands were bleeding, and that person used the rope, would you expect to find traces of blood on the rope?"

"Objection," al-Din said. "The question is speculative."

"Yes. Sustained."

"This man is an expert, Judge," Frankie said combatively. "Can I ask him if he has an opinion?"

"No."

"Thank you." Frankie smiled at the jury and sat down.

Eleven twenty-two. Her ploy may have worked *too* well. She might have to start her own case that afternoon. Gleason brought in another witness, who was sworn and seated in the witness box.

The tall, thin young man wore the distant expression of a

holy man or a psychopath. He was a salesperson at the Knaked Edge, a cutlery store near the Eastern Market. He remembered the defendant, which you do when a person asks for a CIA letter opener. He remembered the transaction too, partly because he was reminded of it only ten days later. But he could not identify the exhibit itself. "I won't go that far." However, he could state that the name stamped on the handle was a brand carried by the Knaked Edge.

He gave Frankie the creeps. She could feel him like a cold cloud. "No questions."

They broke for lunch at eleven-thirty.

Frankie had finished a plate of fruit and was relaxing with a cigarette when Daven slid into the booth across from her. He looked worried. "Your saddle is slipping," Frankie told him. "If you aren't careful, you'll fall off your horse."

"Rory Bern wiped out on that bike we bribed him with."

"Bad?"

Daven nodded, assuming a protective attitude. "He's in intensive care. Got as far as West Virginia, where he hit a deer."

Frankie took a long, thoughtful hit. This was a disaster. Apart from Rick, Bern was her only proof that Rick had rescued Sahar. "Goodness," she said. All that time and work, getting him to testify, down the drain. Arnie had spent a week in Corpus Christi with the man. The Marine Corps corporal had been less than helpful, for good reason. It might have ended, for him, in a court-martial.

Frankie snubbed out her cigarette and reached in her purse for a credit card. The afternoon session would begin in twenty-four minutes. "Did he do it on purpose?"

Frankie guessed that Dr. Myrick Tannenbaum, the next witness for the Government, would be their last one. Brooking had told her Tannenbaum was "killer," although —in the parlance of the medical profession—his first impression was not remarkable. Slightly built, soft eyes, middle-aged, he came across as the kind who'd give up his seat to an elderly person on a crowded train.

A forensic pathologist, he had performed the autopsy on the victim. He identified two photographs showing the undressed body of Abd al-Hafiz, on his stomach, facedown, on a gurney. The round smoothness of the top of the handle of the plastic knife stuck up like a periscope, half an inch out of his back.

After a short argument behind the sound screen, Gleason wheeled in a life-size skeleton. It was mounted on a platform and hung from a crossbar, between two poles. The witness would be allowed to use it for demonstrative purposes, Clardy ruled. It was needed to prove, among other things, the force applied by the knife. The proposed demonstration would be far less prejudicial than the gruesome photographs the Government might have used.

With the CIA letter opener in the palm of his right hand, Tannenbaum approached the skeleton. "This is a male human facsimile," he said. "He belongs to a chiropractor friend of mine." The doctor was quite comfortable on his feet. If he traded his soft southern accent for a Belgian one, he'd have made a perfect Hercule Poirot. A thin chain had been screwed into the top of the skeleton's skull and hooked to the crossbar. Chains also stretched from the poles to the tips of the shoulders, affording some stability, but not much.

"The thrust was at an upward angle," Tannenbaum drawled, standing next to the skeleton and facing the jury. "Rather slight, from right to left." He demonstrated. "Of course, those directions are relative. If Mr. Hafiz's torso had been leaning, which is most likely"—he bent the skeleton, causing it to rattle a bit, like a breeze fluttering aspen leaves—"then the thrust, in relation to the ground, might have been at a greater angle, or none at all."

He rested the tip of the blade at a specific location on one of the ribs. "This is the approximate area of the insertion. The intercostal space, between the ninth and tenth ribs." His soft voice contrasted nicely with his subject, which had taken on a sense of horror. "It was perhaps two inches from the right edge of the spinal column." He examined the spot closely, making sure. "These ribs are termed false ribs, incidentally, because they are not directly connected to the sternum." He reached around and touched the breastbone at the front. "This is the sternum." He stopped, as though reluctant to go on. "My friend calls him Ajax," he said absently. "I must say I've never known anyone by that name."

"Please go forward with your demonstration, Doctor," Husam said, with respect, but with much seriousness.

Tannenbaum let the handle of the knife balance in the heel of his hand. "This instrument is slightly less than seven inches in length." He drew it out and showed it to them. "Six inches, from its tip to this point here"—he touched a place on the top of the handle—"was buried in the abdominal and thoracic cavities of Mr. Hafiz." He put the tip back where it had been, held a shoulder of the skeleton with his left hand, and again let the end of the handle balance against the heel of his right hand. "Like this." He pushed the blade forward with the heel of his hand, letting it fall through the skeleton and onto the platform.

The sound hung in the stillness as he bent down to pick it up. "Of course, Ajax is a skeleton. Mr. Hafiz was a human being. The abdominal cavity"—he indicated a position—"is filled with organs needed to sustain life. It houses, among others, the stomach and the liver." He inserted the weapon three inches into Ajax's back. "The thoracic cavity holds the heart—behind and a little to the left of the sternum—and the lungs." He stuck it in further, not allowing it to fall, demonstrating the direction. "This instrument had to push through the layers of muscles in the back, through portions of the stomach—perhaps not too difficult—through the liver, which is quite dense, the heart even more so, and into the left lung."

His mouth had hardened and his eyes, closed slightly with pain, searched through the panel of jurors. "One may conclude that great force was applied."

Husam let the moment expand. The witness gave a slight shrug of his shoulders and dropped his eyes. "Please return to your seat, Doctor."

In the short walk from the skeleton to the witness box, Tannenbaum aged. The eyes that flicked across Frankie's grew old and tired. The force applied might be compared to pushing a sharp, pointed object through several inches of meat, he said. A seven-inch pin would go in quite easily, perhaps, but the blade used in this case had an increasing thickness, and the handle even more. It needed to displace the densities of the muscles and organs it penetrated.

When asked to describe the medical cause of death, he spoke in the flat tone of a person who tries not to feel. The impression was of ineffable sadness. As the blade passed through the various organs, it inflicted irreparable trauma. The heart survived long enough to fill the lungs with blood, so that perhaps the correct diagnosis was asphyxiation, brought about by drowning in his own blood.

But of course there was also the failure of the heart, achieved by the insult of the blade. "It would be quite impossible to assign any particular cause. The respiratory and circulatory systems—as well as the digestive system—could no longer function."

Husam turned slowly toward the defendant, who sat quietly next to Daven, his hands folded and resting on the table. There was no question who was responsible for this atrocity, his accusing look said. "Thank you, Doctor. I have no further questions."

The man had lived up to his billing. "Doctor, did you know Mr. Hafiz?" Frankie asked, leaning on the lectern.

He looked near her but not at her. "That depends on what you mean by 'know.'"

"Were you acquainted with him?"

"No."

"I ask, because you seem to have such sympathy for him. Do you have sympathy for him?"

"Yes," he said, meeting her eyes.

Frankie nodded. "In your opinion, great force was applied. Correct?"

"I would say, close to superhuman force."

"Maniacal?"

He shrugged. "Perhaps."

"Driven by fear?"

"That too is a possibility."

"You aren't prepared to give an opinion as to what motivated this force, are you?"

"Not at all."

The words "adrenaline rush" stared at her from her notepad, but she crossed them off. "Your sympathy for Mr. Hafiz. Is it something you feel for everyone?"

He looked at her with interest. "No. Not everyone."

"Would you care to elaborate?"

He leaned slightly toward the jury, but his manner included more than the people in the box. It seemed to include all of humanity. "This man was like millions of young people—men and women—and I know them all, in the sense that I know how their bodies function. And I am thrilled by it."

Frankie glanced toward the judge, who frowned at the witness. "Thrilled?" she asked.

"There is such magnificence to life. The"—he searched for the words—"wondrous interplay of the organs of the human body. It was the same for Mr. Hafiz as it is for you, or me, or Mr. Adamson." He acknowledged the defendant with a nod. "Their unbelievable complexity, the virtual miracles that occur in something as simple as eating an apple or taking a breath of air. To have all of that stopped"—he picked up the CIA letter opener—"by this." He set it down. "I am saddened."

At least three of the jurors slouched in their bucket seats. Frankie struggled to inject what she could use in argument: a sense of universality. "You are saddened, not just by Mr. Hafiz, but when this kind of thing happens to young people?"

"Or old, or middle-aged, or infants. There is such awful disregard for the miracle of existence. Why?"

Frankie backed away from the lectern, and the question. She thought it a good place to stop. "Thank you, sir."

"Mr. al-Din?" Clardy asked, staring with severity at Husam. Frankie suspected the look was intended for her.

"No further questions."

"You are excused, Doctor." As Tannenbaum climbed down, Clardy looked at Husam. "Your next witness?"

323

"The Government rests its case," he said.

"Very well." Clardy directed the malevolence she apparently felt squarely at Frankie. "Ms. Rommel, I assume you have a motion to make?" She tried to sound nice about it, but her words were like the chops of an axe. "It's two o'clock. We'll excuse the jury for the afternoon and hear it."

Frankie turned around, searching through the spectator area for Faris abu abd al-Rahman. She found him sitting near the aisle. "Actually, I don't intend to make one at this time, Your Honor," she said, making up her mind as she stood up. Clardy glared at her with impatience, then looked away. No one but an incompetent fool would throw away the chance to make a motion for judgment of acquittal, her gesture said. "Mr. Rahman is in the courtroom. I'd like to call him now, as my first witness."

# 24

"You are still under oath, Mr. Rahman," Clardy said. "Proceed, Ms. Rommel."

Frankie smiled at him from behind the lectern. "Hello, Mr. Rahman. You are indeed a man of honor. I appreciate it very much." He nodded sharply, as though to say, Your flattery doesn't fool me. "This is painful for you, I suspect, in view of your closeness to Mr. Hafiz?"

He shrugged. "I only wish to see justice done."

He hadn't forgotten whose side he was on. "Mr. Hafiz and Mr. Adamson were close friends, weren't they?" she asked.

"I do not know this," Rahman said.

Frankie looked confused by an unexpected answer. "But didn't Mr. Hafiz call Mr. Adamson by his nickname, Rick, in his report?" She found her notes. "He also said, 'Adamson has a place in the hearts of all those who know him' and something about 'betrayal of trust.' " She looked at the witness. "They were buddies, weren't they? Do you know the term?"

"I am familiar with your slang expression." He lifted his shoulders. "They were of different religious faith. There is allowed friendship, but not closeness."

She had rehearsed the line of questions with Brooking. Work your way through the forest like a commando on a raid, he'd said. When you get there, make it look like an accident. "What about you, sir? Were you friendly with Mr. Adamson?"

He glanced harshly at Rick. "I would speak to him with courtesy." He looked away.

"In Arabic?"

He smiled. "Mr. Adamson did not indulge me in such fashion."

"He expressed an interest in Arabic culture, didn't he?"

Husam stood up. "If it please the Court, object. There is no relevance."

"Yes, Ms. Rommel. What is the relevance, if any?"

"Your Honor, I'll connect it up."

The judge did her best to maintain a neutral expression. "Mr. al-Din, if appropriate, I'll hear your motion to strike later."

Rahman followed the exchange with the sardonic amusement of one who finds the antics of American lawyers amusing. "Do I answer or do I say nothing?"

"You may answer, sir," Frankie told him.

"He appeared to have an interest in our ways."

Frankie moved a strand of hair out of the way. "You testified that you would go around the embassy at night to make sure everything was secure?"

"Yes. On several occasions."

His memory had improved. Earlier, it had been once or twice. "Did you note down the dates?"

Husam again rose to his feet. "Your Honor, these questions should have been covered in cross-examination. I would not object, but this seems quite senseless."

Clardy didn't appear to be enjoying it either. But her clenched jaw said, In spite of the klutz he has for a lawyer, I'd like him to have a fair trial. "I'm going to allow it."

Rahman glared at the judge. "Do I answer the question? Or do I not?"

"Please answer, sir."

"I made no record of the dates. But I remember quite clearly, walking with him through the offices of the building."

"About when was the last time, sir?"

He shrugged, annoyed. "In the springtime of this year."

"That's what puzzles me," Frankie said. "My investigator—" She interrupted herself and looked at the judge, as though for assistance. "Your Honor, I could interrupt the testimony here and put Mr. Daven on, but . . ." From Clardy's expression, it was clear Clardy would not tell her what to do. Frankie looked at the witness. "My investigator has been in the building. He says there are cameras—"

Husam al-Din shot up. "She is testifying, Your Honor! Move to strike!"

"Ms. Rommel, please!" Clardy looked at the jury. "You are instructed that questions of counsel are not testimony. You are not to regard that last comment by Ms. Rommel as evidence." Frowning at Frankie with displeasure, she nodded at her. "Proceed."

Frankie appeared quite horrified at herself. Apologetically, she looked at Faris Rahman. "Are there cameras, surveillance equipment, in the embassy?"

Rahman glanced worriedly at his fellow Arabs. Then, jerking his head in the affirmative, he answered. "Yes."

"These are cameras inside the building that take pictures?" she asked with curiosity.

He responded with a chagrined nod, keeping his eyes away from the shocked expressions of the other Rashidis in the room.

"You'll have to answer verbally, sir," Frankie said, as though not wanting to embarrass. "The court reporter."

"There are such cameras."

"Then—I don't understand." She appeared to have a real problem. "Why did you walk the halls with your nephew? I mean, Mr. Hafiz? Weren't the cameras enough?"

"I will explain. These cameras"—he blushed noticeably, his desert-colored face darkening with embarrassment— "were placed in operation by my nephew, at his request. But it did not occur until this summer."

Frankie still appeared to be sorting it out. "Then when you walked with your nephew, that was before the cameras were put in?"

327

"That is correct."

"When were they installed?"

"Perhaps four or five months ago."

"Before your nephew was killed?"

"Yes."

Frankie nodded, as though now she understood. "Then they were in operation on July twenty-sixth of this year?"

"Yes."

She stared at the prosecutor. Gleason was whispering in Husam's ear. "Did you tell anyone about them?"

"I did not think of it. However, Lieutenant Gleason—these cameras I could not see in the hallways. But the lieutenant seemed to know they were there, and asked me about it."

"Lamar Gleason?" Frankie asked. "The man sitting next to the lawyer for the government?"

"Yes."

Frankie appeared to need some time to collect herself. "May I confer a moment with Mr. Daven?"

"You may."

She huddled with Daven. "Jamie Roon," she whispered. "Can you keep him under wraps tonight?" Daven nodded. "How does this look?"

"Like you stumbled onto something."

She went back to the lectern. "Mr. Rahman, a man by the name of Abdur Yusuf Rahim was the information officer at the Rashidi Embassy at one time, wasn't he?"

Rahman reacted as though he'd rather not remember. "Yes."

"When was he there, sir?"

"He departed our service months ago. In your wintertime."

Husam got up to object. "Nothing further," Frankie said quickly. "Thank you again, Mr. Rahman."

"Mr. al-Din?" Clardy asked.

The prosecutor shrugged. "No questions." He started to sit down.

Clardy was far from satisfied. "Will counsel approach?"

328

When the lawyers were on the other side of the sound screen, she stared between them, but talked to Frankie. "Ms. Rommel, I won't presume to tell you how to try your case, but there are many questions raised by this development. The jury will want answers. If you don't pursue this matter, it would be my responsibility, and I will."

"I intend to pursue it, Judge," Frankie said. God damn it, woman, stay out of it, she thought. "He said he told Lamar Gleason about it, and I'd like to call him as my next witness."

That didn't satisfy the judge. "I would like to know why this matter was not explored ahead of trial."

"The simple answer, Judge, is there was no request." Husam straightened his back but kept his head down. "It is obvious from counsel's questions that she knew of these cameras, or suspected them. But the Government has not been asked to produce them."

Clardy regarded the backs of her hands with helpless fury. "Ms. Rommel, I'm having serious misgivings here. Do you want to proceed, or do you want a continuance, long enough to explore this matter?"

The well-meaning judge could blow everything. "Your Honor, I've been a trial lawyer for fifteen years," Frankie blurted angrily. "I resent what you are suggesting here. This isn't the first time you've implied I wasn't prepared." Maybe she could buy her a drink after the trial and explain. "I am offended by your attitude in front of my client, who has started to doubt me! I would like the opportunity to present this case in my own way, without interference from the Court!"

Clardy stared at her. Frankie glared at the wood paneling in front of the bench. The judge's mouth closed slowly, along with the rest of her face. "You may proceed, Ms. Rommel," she said evenly. "You may be certain of no further help, or concern, from me."

Husam had the pious, satisfied expression that Frankie's grandfather would have described as a skunk eating shit. Frankie slid behind the lectern. "Mr. Rahman, you are

329

excused," she heard Clardy say. "Your next witness, Ms. Rommel?"

"If it please the Court, I'll call Lamar Gleason."

Gleason stood up quickly, as though anxious to set any questions to rest. He smiled at Husam and the jury as he marched to the witness box.

"Your Honor, I'll ask for permission to lead the witness," Frankie said, staring at Gleason's fat face.

"Granted."

"Officer Gleason, suppose you start off by telling the jury who you are and why you've been sitting there all this time with Mr. al-Din."

Gleason was happy to do just that. He gave his rank, the number of years he'd been with the Capitol Police Department, and summarized his background before moving to the District. He alluded to his experience in Bridger City, Wyoming, recalled watching Frankie try a case and how impressed he was with her performance.

"It's *your* credentials we're concerned with here, not mine," Frankie told him. "Suppose you tell the jury what your connection is with *this* case."

He did. He was the lieutenant in charge of the investigation, and sat with Mr. al-Din as his advisory witness. "I am to Mr. al-Din as Mr. Daven, Arnold Daven, is to you." He smiled affably, as though that made them all one big happy family.

"You've been with this case from the beginning?"

"Since the very first day, Ms. Rommel. July twenty-sixth, 1991. Lived it, breathed it, smelled it."

"Then what Mr. Rahman testified to, surveillance cameras and so forth inside the embassy, came as no surprise. Correct?"

"Not at all. I've reviewed the tape, and there's nothing on it."

Clardy went so far as to clear her throat. She clearly expected an objection, or a motion to strike the answer, or a motion for mistrial. The tape itself was the best evidence, and for a Government witness to blurt out what was on it, in front of a jury, was improper to the point of being reprehensible. Frankie blocked the judge's face from her vision. "Do you mean it's blank?"

"That isn't what I mean at all," he said. "It doesn't show anything is what I mean."

Frankie sucked in her breath as though very, very worried. "Let's back up. You've been inside the embassy on several occasions in the course of this investigation?"

"Yes ma'am. I was there on a daily basis for a week." He leaned back in his chair.

"That's when you noticed these cameras in the hallways and other places?"

"Correct."

"Where are they?"

He turned toward the jury, as though more anxious to explain to them than her. "The hallways, first and second floor. The staircases. Certain offices." He smiled at them. "They have a basement too, a parking garage. Down there also."

"Mr. Rahman's office?" Frankie asked.

"That's right. His, but not the ambassador's. Don't ask me why."

"The balcony outside Mr. Rahman's office?"

He smirked. "No ma'am. That we could have used."

Frankie poured herself some water and took a sip, thinking. "How did you see the cameras? Aren't they always hidden or something?"

"Actually, most aren't." He seemed to take pleasure in contradicting her. "In department stores, liquor stores, they put cameras out in plain sight, reminders to the general public how they're being watched."

"But these weren't like that, were they?"

"No." He smiled at the jury, as though to say, *you* folks might be able to understand, but I doubt *she* can. "These are covert surveillance. Hidden sure, but you can spot them if you know what to look for."

"What do you look for?"

"There'll always be something, a little aperture or bubble,

for a lens." He shifted his weight. "These were little opaque bubbles, looked like jewels, stuck in the ceiling like a ceiling design."

"And you, a trained observer, knew what they were immediately?"

"I had an idea."

"You asked Mr. Rahman about it, and he told you you were right. Correct?"

"Yes."

"And he gave you the tapes or cassettes or whatever it was they were loaded with?"

"Not exactly. He said he'd have to ask a few questions before giving me the tapes. I read between the lines."

"Go ahead. Tell us what you read between the lines."

"He wanted to check things out, see if anything was on the tapes, that sort of thing, before letting me have them. He's a diplomat. Everything to him is very sensitive."

Frankie nodded. "In any event, he gave you the tapes?"

"What he gave me was one cassette. It looks like a regular TV cassette, but you can't play it on just anything. It takes specialized equipment."

Frankie gave a couple of tentative clicks to her ballpoint pen. "You said sixteen cameras. Did all that fit on one cassette?"

When he smiled, his fat cheeks lifted like gas bags. "That's why the specialized equipment."

Frankie shrugged, indicating less than complete understanding. "In any case, you viewed the cassette?"

"Yes I did." He smiled like a toad, luring a fly to within flicking distance of his tongue.

"Where was that done?"

"At the embassy. They have everything all set up in a room in the basement."

"Was anyone with you?"

Gleason thought back. "Mr. Rahman, but he couldn't stay. A Rashidi guard, but he waited outside at Mr. Rahman's orders. When I finished, the guard escorted me out of the building."

"But you took the tape with you?"

"I did."

Frankie moved slowly, as though stepping on rocks that protruded above quicksand. "Have you showed the tape to anyone else?"

"No."

"Were copies made?"

He shrugged. "No reason."

"No reason?" Frankie asked, as though repeating the question would give her time. "That's because there was nothing on the tape?"

"Correct." His toadlike eyes opened wide enough to see the fly. "Nothing."

"Weren't you surprised by that, Officer Gleason?"

He glanced at Husam, then back to Frankie. "No. I didn't expect to see anything."

Frankie appeared perplexed again. "According to your evidence, Mr. Adamson climbed on the balcony with the grappling hook. Right?"

"That's correct." Gleason seemed to sense something was miss.

"But the victim, Mr. Hafiz. How did he get on the balcony? Did he also climb up from the outside?"

"Oh. Yeah." He raised his left arm, propping it informally over the top of his chair. "When I say nothing, I mean nothing of importance. There was only the kind of movement depicted inside the embassy you would expect."

"Then you saw Mr. Hafiz on tape, inside the building, before he went out on the balcony?" Frankie asked helpfully.

"That's right."

"But you didn't think that was important?"

"Hey." He showed her his palms. "He just went outside. He was in Mr. Rahman's office and went outside is all. The last anyone seen him alive."

"What was he doing in Mr. Rahman's office?"

"Nothing!" Gleason sounded angry over an unnecessary challenge to his action. He glanced at the prosecutor and appeared to collect himself. "Nothing."

333

"Then you don't know why he was in Mr. Rahman's office?"

"Lady. Ms. Rommel. He was there because he was making the rounds."

Frankie tried to look embarrassed for him. "Lieutenant, didn't you hear Mr. Rahman testify, just ahead of you?"

"Yes I did, Ms. Rommel."

"Mr. Rahman said he quit making rounds after the surveillance equipment was installed. Didn't he say that?"

Gleason's lips curled with contempt at the lawyer. "That isn't what he said. Mr. Rahman said *he* no longer made the rounds with his nephew. He didn't say Mr. Hafiz quit making them."

Frankie seemed to back away from his assertiveness. "Then your testimony is that the cameras picked up Mr. Hafiz, making the rounds inside the embassy that morning?"

"That's right."

"In spite of the fact there wasn't any need for him to do that?"

Gleason glared at his antagonist. "There is always the need, Ms. Rommel. Mr. Hafiz, as a good security unit commander, understood you have to check things out, equipment can fail, that sort of thing."

"That sort of thing," Frankie repeated. Cool it, girl, she told herself. Don't give it away. "The tape shows the inside of Mr. Rahman's office, I believe you said?"

"Yes."

"Then when Mr. Hafiz was carried from the balcony inside, that was recorded, correct?"

"Yes."

"But you didn't think that was important?"

He looked with exasperation at the jury. "That isn't where the crime took place. The crime occurred on the balcony. Everything that happened that was significant to this crime happened on the balcony, not in Mr. Rahman's office."

"Did you tell Mr. al-Din about the cassette?"

He tossed his hands in irritation. "Not until just now.

Like I said, it wasn't . . ." He chose not to finish his statement.

"Important?"

"Not in my judgment. And I happen to think I'm a very good judge of what is or is not important in a criminal investigation."

"I'm sure you do," Frankie said. "Where is the cassette now?"

"At the Capitol Police Department," Gleason said.

"I'd like to see it." Frankie waved a hand at the jury. "So would this jury. Will you bring it tomorrow?"

"Certainly!" he said emphatically.

"Can you also bring the special equipment needed to show it?"

"It will be my pleasure, Miss Rommel."

"Thank you." Frankie looked toward the judge, who avoided her eyes. "Nothing further, Your Honor."

"Mr. al-Din?"

"No redirect, if it please the Court," Husam said without standing up.

"Call your next witness, Ms. Rommel."

She turned to Daven. "Is Morley here?" Daven nodded, got up and went out in the hall. "The defense calls Morley Phillips."

A skinny thin-haired man in a tweed sport coat and horn-rimmed glasses was sworn, and moved into the witness box. He spoke with a cultivated British accent. Frankie tried to hurry him along. He identified himself as an experienced mountain climber who had participated and led several expeditions into the Himalayas, the Peruvian Andes, and the Alps. "My friends call me Spider," he informed the jurors. "I have an affinity for the creatures, you see, who can progress along quite easily on the underside of a rock."

Frankie grimaced along with the jurors. Phillips supported his "addiction" as the owner and manufacturer of a quality line of climbing equipment. The Paragon name was a fine one, indeed, and he had brought a catalog with him, in case of interest. He lifted it out of his lap and held it up to the jury before Frankie could stop him. "I don't think we need that, Mr. Phillips," she said, finding the mountaineering equipment. "Can you identify this exhibit, Number Five?"

"Yes, of course." He held the hook in his strong fingers with admiration, as though displaying the color of a fine wine in a goblet. "It's one of mine."

"How do you know?"

He enumerated its excellent points: lightness, strength, grip, release, finally identifying the serial number, stamped in the handle.

"Do you keep records, showing the names of buyers?"

"Yes," he said, then explained the procedure at length. Warranty cards accompanied all his products, for everyone's protection and because of the deep responsibility he himself felt toward anyone who might use them. The purchaser had but to date the card and fill in name and address. The card did the rest. It contained the name of the product, the serial number, and the warranty. In most cases they were filled in and left at the sporting goods store, then forwarded on to his manufacturing establishment in Pennsylvania.

"Was such a card filled out for the grappling hook you have in your hand?"

"Indeed it was, and I have it with me." Carefully placing the hook on the banister in front of him, he extracted a postcard-sized card from the catalog.

Two or three minutes were consumed in comparing the serial numbers, marking the card as an exhibit, and showing it to the prosecution team. Neither al-Din nor Gleason appeared impressed, but Gleason's smile had tightened and he caught himself, pulling at his collar. The card was admitted in evidence.

The hook had been purchased, according to the date on the card, on September 21, 1990. The buyer's name was Abdur Yusuf Rahim, who listed his address as the Rashidi Embassy, Washington, D.C.

There was no cross-examination. Frankie hadn't expected any and remained standing. "Your next witness?" Clardy asked. She seemed more interested in Frankie's case.

It was four o'clock. "I've run out for the day, Judge," Frankie said.

"Well. Then all we can do is adjourn."

"Would it be possible to start early tomorrow, Your Honor? If we can, I think we can finish."

Clardy's attitude toward Frankie had softened. "Let's see what the jurors think." She turned toward the panel. "Ladies and gentlemen, we're going to adjourn early today. How would you feel about starting early tomorrow?"

The jurors liked the idea, especially if it meant finishing the case. A couple of reporters in the second row groaned, however.

In the commotion after court was adjourned, Frankie watched Gleason and Husam muscle their way past the reporters and disappear. "Arnie," she said to the hulk. "You couldn't put a wire on those guys, could you?"

"Are you kidding?" he asked, watching the door shut behind them as he loaded the file.

"I think so." The marshal had handcuffed Rick, then let him talk to his mother and sister. "But I'm not sure." She smiled vacantly at a reporter who waited for her on the other side of the bar.

"It's illegal, Frankie."

"True. But wouldn't it be nice to hear what they're talking about?" She picked up her briefcase and put her hand on Rick's shoulder. "See you tomorrow, sport."

He turned his head toward her and smiled. "Do or die day, right?"

She nodded, hoping her breath didn't smell as bad as her stomach felt. She squeezed his arm. "Arnie," she said, looking at all the people out there who wanted a piece of her. "Let's go out the back way."

# 25

"How does this happen?" Husam al-Din asked, glaring at Lamar Gleason as he snapped on the light. They had sprinted past the reporters, avoided the Rashidis, and found privacy in the small conference room of a courtroom on the second floor. "Do you not see how this may appear to the jury?"

"No big deal." Gleason started toward a chair, but Husam stood in his way. "I didn't think about it."

Husam did not believe him. "I must view this cassette at once. As you testify, I ask myself. Do we have another embarrassment, caused by my astute investigator? Will the fiasco of the Motion to Disqualify repeat?"

Gleason flushed. "We all make mistakes, Husam." His voice seemed to contain secrets.

If the man wished to speak of some matter, he should speak directly. Husam did not care for any man who must beat around the bushes. "Is there hidden meaning in what you say, Lieutenant?"

Gleason smiled, a cruel expression on his face. "How's your daughter?" he asked.

The blood drained from Husam's arms, legs, and face. It felt as though his heart had stopped, forcing the blood to run backward to fill the void. "What do you know of her?"

"Sixteen, working the streets. My sources tell me a very playful trick with a real future."

Husam reached back with a fist and started to swing. But with the trained reactions of a street cop, Gleason grabbed his wrist and twisted his arm behind his back. His briefcase dropped to the floor.

"Thought you had more cool, Husam," Gleason said, breathing heavily.

The harder he tried to extricate himself, the tighter the armlock. Husam quit trying. "Where is she, Lieutenant?"

"Ask your wife," Gleason said, gasping for air.

Husam yanked his arm free. He whirled around and faced Gleason. The red-faced man was shaking with exertion, and backing away. "What does my wife know?"

Gleason's hands were up and his coat was open, revealing a shoulder holster and pistol. "Kawthar, right? Back home. Check the basement."

Husam had the urge to hammer the man's ugly face to a pulp. Instead he turned on his heel, picked up his briefcase and pushed into the hall. He trembled with rage brought on by this humiliation. He would find his daughter, and . . .

No. He must not lose control. He would not allow his emotions to destroy him.

At six-thirty that night, Husam telephoned Abir from his office. He told her he must wait for an important telephone call from Lamar Gleason and would be late. But she knew him too well, he feared. She could read his thoughts by the brusqueness of his tone of voice.

Yet, there was no immediate indication. "Does the trial go well?" she asked, speaking to him in a lightly accented English.

Abir rarely asked such questions. A man's business was his own. "There are always surprises," Husam replied, masking his complicated emotions. "Why do you ask?"

"There is talk among the women."

Husam shut his eyes impatiently, then opened them with an odd feeling. It occurred to him that his impatience was an attitude. "What do they talk about?" he asked, monitoring the tone of his voice. It became *too* patient, as though he were speaking with a child.

"They say there is love between the American and Sahar bint Rashid. They believe—"

"Love!" Husam exploded angrily. "Perhaps it is 'love' that has destroyed Kawthar. I learned today that our daughter has become a woman of the street. A whore, a prostitute. Did you know of this, Abir?" There was no reply. "Abir. Did you hear my question?"

She answered in Arabic. "Kawthar is headstrong, like a boy, my husband. But she is not a whore."

Husam could barely keep all that he felt inside of him. He must change the subject, or give away what he knew. "What is this gossip from the streets?"

"There are those who believe the American saved the Rashidi princess from death. They say her life once more is threatened with violence, and that he will save her again."

"What nonsense!"

"I only repeat, so you will know of it."

"Do people believe such foolishness?" But of course in America, where wild ideas were not only allowed but encouraged, even Arabs lost their footing. They come to believe anything. "Abir. I have talked to the ambassador himself. He assures me there is no truth to the whisperings of servants, who must create some excitement in their lives. Sahar bint Rashid lives comfortably in Qahtan, in the Palace for Women."

"I only tell you what they say," Abir said meekly.

"Who knows what this man Adamson will say when he testifies, with nothing to lose?" Husam continued angrily. "You and your women have heard the stories of a flight from the embassy with this hero carrying the poor princess away in his arms?"

Her voice shrank. "Yes."

"It is my hope that Adamson will tell such a story from the witness stand. He will find I am ready to expose his lies." Husam stopped before telling her more. He knew nothing of

340

the intricate web of communication that weaved the women of the world together, but suspected much.

"How will you do this?"

"I cannot say." Frankie Rommel would learn from him, at the last possible moment. She would not hear of it through the vast spiderweb. "But ask this question of your women, Abir. Would Sahar return to her homeland of her own will, if she had escaped from Rashidi prison?"

There was no immediate reply, which did not surprise him. What was there to say? "I love you, my husband."

Usually that signaled the end of the conversation. And usually the words were spoken perfunctorily, in Arabic. But Abir cloaked them with emotion, and Husam suspected the reason: the wiles of the woman, who had hidden their daughter from him. "Yes. And I love you."

As he hung up, there were tears in his eyes. He yearned for his mother, who alone could be trusted. His daughter had become a whore, and his wife a vessel of deceit.


"Look at it this way," Gleason's voice over the telephone mocked. " 'Raindrops keep falling on my head.' We're like Butch Cassidy and the Sundance Kid."

"This is totally beyond the comprehension of all people."

"Hey. Shit happens."

Husam had just been told that the cassette tape had been used to record an official function at the Laotian Embassy. The record of the Rashidi Embassy had been wiped off in the process. "This will require extensive explanation to the jury, Lieutenant." He glanced at the government clock on the wall of his office: 8:43. "You must bring the tape to court, and the person who committed this blunder."

"Sure. Easy. Husam," he said, sounding quite friendly. "We got nothing to worry about. Listen to me."

"I will listen."

"One. You got nine blacks on the jury and a white defendant. They're gonna want to hang his ass, and for sure they aren't gonna buy a bullshit story. Two. You got that plastic knife in his back. All the way in!"

341

"Lieutenant. Are you certain of my daughter?"

"Hey pal, I know that's hard. Don't worry. Your secret stays with me."

There it was again. The veiled threat. "But how do you know of such things?"

"It's like this. I heard about it. If she was my daughter, I'd want to know what was going on. So I checked it out for you."

Husam could feel the blood in his head. "Does someone follow her?"

"Trade secrets, my friend," Gleason said. "See, I like to get a little background on the people I deal with, know what I mean?"

"What do you mean?"

"Take Emily Scot, for example. I like to know about possible problems before they develop. Not that anything did."

"Lieutenant," Husam said with feeling. "You make me sick in the stomach."

Abir slept like a stone. Husam stared at her shoulder as he crawled into bed next to her. So. His stained, dishonored daughter, who also slept like death, was in the basement of his house. He had been tempted to see for himself, but it must wait.

Gleason made him sick in the stomach. His wife made him sick in the heart.

# 26

**Friday, October 25, 1991**

The packed courtroom was quiet with expectation. "Is the defense ready to continue, Ms. Rommel?"

"We are." Frankie stood at the lectern, wearing a tailored charcoal-gray dress suit that softened her complexion and deepened the color of her hair.

"Well and good." The judge had the bright-eyed, bushy-tailed look of a cowgirl who'd just been in a fight and was ready for more excitement. "Call your first witness."

Frankie glanced toward the plaintiff's table. "Lieutenant Gleason?" She found that by pretending he was her grade school principal, whom she had hated but had been forced to deal with, she could smile at him.

Gleason climbed into the witness box, carrying with him a normal-looking VCR cassette tape. "You've been previously sworn, sir," Clardy told him. "You are still under oath." He nodded at the judge, sat down and faced Frankie.

When their eyes met, Frankie assessed his expression. Perfect, she thought. He's going to lie. "Yesterday, Lieutenant, we learned from you that there is surveillance equipment in the embassy." She held up her hand, letting him know she hadn't finished setting the scene. "We further learned that a videotape of some kind was taken, showing everything that happened inside the embassy immediately before, and immediately after, the incident involving my client and Mr. Hafiz. Am I right?"

"Yes, you are. And Miss Rommel . . ." A look of anguish appeared on his face, but he didn't seem to have the heart to finish his sentence.

"That object in your hand," Frankie said, helpfully. "Is it the videocassette that shows all of this?"

"Actually . . ." He gave an embarrassed shrug. "Yes ma'am."

"It needs to be marked for identification." Frankie glanced at the judge. "Approach the witness?"

"You may."

Frankie took the cassette from Gleason and gave it to the court reporter, who stuck a blue label on it and marked it as Defendant's Exhibit A.

"Ms. Rommel," Gleason blurted before Frankie could get back to the lectern. He leaned forward with agonizing sincerity. "I don't know how to say this without you thinking 'Watergate' or trickery of some kind."

Frankie tethered herself to the lectern with one hand. "What are you saying?" she asked. "Has it been altered?"

"It got recorded over." He looked helplessly at the jury. "Just a real blunder, for which I take full responsibility. I should have secured it better, made it very clear to all concerned that there was something on it. See, what happened—"

"'Recorded over,'" Frankie said. "Was it erased?"

"Well, no. There's a difference. A tape is erased when somebody runs it through to erase it, like on purpose."

"So this was erased, but it wasn't done on purpose. Is that what you mean?"

"Except it wasn't erased. Only recorded over." The agony of confession etched his face. "Corporal James Terry—he's here, I brought him—he can tell you what happened."

"If it's only been recorded over, is there some way to bring it back?"

"No, Ms. Rommel. Once it's been reused like that, the new images are printed on top of the old ones, and . . ." He sagged with hopelessness.

"If we play it, what will we see?" Frankie asked.

344

Gleason wiped sweat from his forehead. Not a bad act. "The interior of the Laotian Embassy, September eighteenth, which we were requested by their security personnel to record with multiple cameras."

"The previous recording, of the Rashidi Embassy on July twenty-fifth and twenty-sixth, is gone forever. Correct?"

He was ready to cry. "My information is possibly parts could be recovered. But what you'd find, which would be bits and pieces, is subject to interpretation and speculation and not reliable. I really don't know what to say."

Frankie stormed back around the lectern. "We're very fortunate, aren't we, that you had a chance to look at it first?"

He nodded. "I'd say so." There was some laughter, and Gleason smiled ruefully. "I guess there could be some disagreement."

"Because you found nothing of importance, correct? Those were your words?"

"Yes ma'am. Really. Just the kinds of things you'd expect." The lines in his forehead crinkled with sincerity.

"It did not show Mr. Adamson inside the embassy or anything like that, did it?"

"Oh no. Nothing like that."

"You would have considered that important?"

"Oh yes. Very much so."

Frankie angrily bit her lip. "Officer. Isn't it true that you saw Mr. Adamson on that tape, running through the halls? And that he didn't have a pistol in his hands, or on his person?"

Gleason's expression was of a man who wanted to be helpful but wouldn't lie. "No I didn't, Ms. Rommel."

Frankie blew a wisp of hair off her cheek. "What about Mr. Hafiz, Officer? Isn't it true that you saw him with a pistol in his hand, chasing after Mr. Adamson?"

Gleason leaned back in his chair, totally mystified. "Mr. Hafiz was just checking rooms and halls. He wasn't running or anything like that."

"A night watchmen, making the rounds, and that was all. Right?" Frankie asked in angry frustration.

"That was all."

"And we have your word on the subject, just as we have it on this recorded-over business. Correct?"

"You've also got Corporal Terry, Ms. Rommel. Ask him."

Frankie glared at him with contempt. "I don't think so," she said, retreating to her chair. "I don't think he can add anything of importance. No further questions."

Clardy frowned slightly and shrugged. Frankie knew that Clardy wouldn't have let him off so easily. "Mr. al-Din?"

Husam stood up. "No questions."

"Your next witness, Ms. Rommel?"

Frankie had her back to the jury and her head turned away from the bench. She looked at Rick and winked at him. "The defense calls the defendant, Richard Adamson."

Rick pushed away from the table and stood up. The jurors watched him walk toward the witness box, examining him critically. In a soft brown coat and tie, his size alone projected an aura of strength. But his confidence deserted him as he was sworn in. Swallowing nervously, he sat down.

"Your name sir?"

"Richard Adamson Junior."

"Mr. Adamson, as honestly and directly as you can, will you answer my questions?"

"Yes. I will."

She glanced at the clock: eight-twenty. Hold on to your hat.

Yes, he'd worked at the Rashidi Embassy for five months, until July 21. He'd been the chauffeur for Princess Sahar bint Rashid. Frankie located a black-and-white photograph of Sahar, showing her stepping out of a limousine. It had run in the *Washington Post*. Rick's eyes touched it with longing as he made an identification, and the photograph became Defendant's Exhibit B.

In a low, sincere voice he answered Frankie's questions. He'd been a Marine, stationed in Qahtan, the capital of the Kingdom of Rashidi. He'd served as an embassy guard for the United States. He met the princess in Qahtan, at a State Department function. But in August 1990, after Saddam Hussein invaded Kuwait, he was transferred to Saudi Arabia. He got two letters from her, but couldn't produce them. They'd been in his apartment before his arrest, in a desk drawer that he kept locked at all times. But Mr. Daven, the investigator, couldn't find them.

The jurors leaned forward in their chairs, checking him out for signs of falsehood. They saw his steady gaze, the way he touched his cheek, shifted his weight, leaned forward, sat up straight, slumped. They heard his voice, which vibrated with—what? The conviction of truth, or the desire to beat the rap? Frankie liked its easy intensity. She even liked the hesitations, studded with occasional eloquence. Do you tell the truth, or do you lie? She knew the strength of the jury system and believed in the collective wisdom of twelve minds. They were rarely fooled, even by the cleverest lawyers. But will they fool themselves? How skeptical will nine blacks be of his story? She decided not to think about it.

Rick was not allowed to testify how he knew the princess was coming to the United States. To recite the contents of letters he couldn't produce would be hearsay on top of hearsay. He told of his discharge immediately after the war, applying for a job with the Rashidis, and getting hired. Sahar arrived a few days after he did, and Rick became her chauffeur.

There was tittering in the spectator area, which Clardy stopped with a bang of her gavel. It had not come from the Rashidis, who sat in a clump and glared at the witness. It came from the row of media people. In a low, expressive voice, Rick spoke of his love for Sahar, and hers for him. Husam objected heatedly to evidence about conversations with Sahar, interrupting the testimony with shouts of hearsay and relevancy. But Frankie wedged in much of it, citing exceptions to the hearsay rule and promising to connect it up. During Ramadan, they prayed; she more than he, he had to admit. When Ramadan was over, they married.

Clardy had to gavel down the Rashidis, who errupted with anger. She promised to eject them from the courtroom if there was any further disturbance. Rick's voice and manner grew larger, as though to meet the challenge of fear and doubt. The marriage was a contract between them, he said, that turned the two of them into one. They were one cell, and he felt it then, and felt it now. She was him and he was her, just the way the Koran said it was supposed to be. It hadn't been formalized by a government, but it didn't need to be. Husam blasted with a new objection. "Marriage" was a legal conclusion which the witness was not qualified to give. Clardy cautioned the jury that the witness's use of the term didn't necessarily mean they were married, and let it in.

On July 21 four Rashidis broke in on them at the Pembarton Oaks Hotel. They took Sahar—he couldn't stop them—then beat him up, questioned him, beat him some more, and let him go. Frankie hurried on, hoping the prosecution would miss the obvious: no evidence to corroborate his story. No hotel registration card for him to identify, no clerk waiting in the wings. Daven had tried to line it up, but the card and the clerk had been bought.

"The night of July twenty-fifth and the early morning of July twenty-sixth, this year, did you enter the embassy of the Kingdom of Rashidi?"

"Yes. I did."

"You've heard the evidence of the Government. Is that the way you went in?"

"No."

Frankie picked the metal hook off the exhibit table. "Until this trial started, had you ever seen this bit of equipment?"

"No I hadn't."

"Have you ever known an individual named Abdur Yusuf Rahim?"

"No. He was before my time."

Frankie glared at the prosecutor and let the hook clatter on the table. "If you didn't climb the balcony, what did you do?"

He always lost things, and had made an extra sets of keys to Sahar's limousine. He told of the extraordinary care the cars were given. He'd waited across the street from Herman's Texaco, near Dupont Circle, on Thursday afternoon. About four o'clock a new driver brought it in for its daily checkup and polish. When he got the chance, he hopped in the trunk. Later it was parked in the basement of the embassy.

He remained hidden until 1:45 A.M., then opened the lid. Some of the jurors were still on the edge of their chairs, but others had settled back and watched with frowns or smiles. He made his way through the parking garage to a staircase that led to the main floor, down a hallway, up to the second floor, and down another hallway to the office of the deputy ambassador, Faris abu abd al-Rahman. "Did you know you were being watched by an internal surveillance system?"

He smiled. "No."

The only weapon he carried was the plastic knife. He'd been nervous about metal detectors and had even taken the eyeholes out of his shoes. The only metal on his body were the parts in his watch.

"The prosecution claims you broke into the embassy for revenge. Is that why you went in?"

"No."

Look at him, Frankie thought, trying to send a message to the whole world. He does not lie. "Why did you go in?"

"Sahar was there. I had to get her out." His eyes fastened briefly on one of the jurors. "They were going to take her back to Rashidi and kill her."

Husam jumped up. "Object and move to strike!"

Frankie glanced at her watch: nine o'clock. They had a long way to go. The argument took place behind the sound screen, interrupting the narrative flow. They argued with typical emotionless civility, then reappeared on the other side of the sound barrier.

Rick was not allowed to state that Sahar would have been taken to Rashidi and executed, only that he believed she would. The defense would have the right to prove the reasonableness of his belief. "We'll take a ten minute recess," Clardy said, smiling at Frankie.

The jurors were back in their seats two minutes early, as though they had great seats to the best show in town. The contingent of Rashidis buzzed in low voices in Arabic, and the spectator area had filled. When Clardy came in, it was as though the curtain for the second act went up. "Please continue, Ms. Rommel."

Frankie had Rick tell the jury of his Marine Corps experience. Husam objected, but the judge allowed the evidence to prove the reasonableness of his belief. He didn't mention his world-class pitching arm, or the situation at home; only that he was eighteen and wanted to see the world. After boot camp he was ordered to the Marine Security Guard school at Quantico. His first duty post was the United States embassy in Costa Rica. From there, in the summer of 1989, he shipped out to Rashidi.

A spit-and-polish post, it was where he met Rory Bern, a black kid from Maine. Each knew he was better than the other, and they resolved the question in the approved Marine Corp manner: a fistfight. Husam objected for lack of relevance, so the jury never found out that Rory's kicks were better than Rick's chops, but not by much. Their competition continued. Others complained about the heat and sand and the rigidity of life, but Rory and Rick turned it into a game. They'd stand absolutely still for hours that seemed like days and have contests to see who could last the longest. The gunny would tell them, "No movement, no blinking of the eyes. I don't even want to see you sweat."

They knew they were different from the other jarheads, and a friendship grew. They were genuinely curious about Arabic ways and customs. They found English translations of the Koran, and books on the life of the Prophet Muhammad, and read them. Rick learned what he could of the language, but apart from a few expressions, didn't get very far. "I'm better at it now. They call it the language of God, and the sound of it has power. It can knock you down."

He and Rory bought *thobes* and *ghotras,* and looked like pretty big Arabs—until they witnessed a public execution in the Qahtan square. It brought both of them down to size. Frankie asked him to describe it, and Husam objected, but Clardy allowed the testimony. If believed, it could establish the reasonableness of Rick's belief that he had to rescue Sahar. "The courtyard was packed," he told the jurors, with

350

men and their sons, dressed in white. A few women in black *abayas* and half veils were on the steps at the far end. "It was noisy and hot."

Then a large black man came in from a doorway, twirling a sword like a baton. "It got so quiet you could hear the whisper of the wind."

"Continue, please, Mr. Adamson."

He cleared his throat. "Two men in blue uniforms dragged in a thin copper-skinned man." His voice thinned out, like a partially filled balloon as someone stretched it. "He had high cheekbones and black hair. They made him kneel over a wooden block, kind of like an old butcher's block, and locked down his hands." Rick's eyes glittered with respect and horror. "The man prayed and cried and I wanted to leave, but couldn't. I could smell his fear."

"Then what happened?"

Rick wiped his glistening forehead. "An imam, in a very stern voice, read the charges against him in singsong, like the call to prayer."

"What was his crime?" Frankie asked.

"Murder. He'd killed a shopkeeper who'd cheated him."

"Please go on."

Rick's expression had opened wide and his eyes were nonfocused. "When the sword came down, his head squirted away from his body. When it hit the deck, it kept moving, like it was still alive." His tone became distant and objective, a news analyst describing the most recent international disaster. "They call it 'heads dancing.' It changes you. All those little kids, on their daddies' shoulders, it changed them too. I don't think many of them will commit murder."

Two of the jurors on the front row stared in fascination at Rick. Others looked at the floor. "Based on that experience, did you come to believe that Rashidi, or Arabic, justice, was severely and rigorously enforced?"

"Yes I did."

"Tell us the events that led to your first meeting with Princess Sahar."

As he talked he glowed. Frankie was afraid the jurors might think he was acting. It began with an invitation from

351

the Rashidi chargé d'affaires, asking him to attend a reception at the palace of King Nuri ibn abd al-Rashid. Embassy guards weren't invited to official functions, but a newly appointed ambassador, from California, knew who Rick was and got it for him.

"Who are you?"

He told the jury of middle-class blacks of his silver-spoon heritage. He'd also been well-known as a high school athlete. He could have gone to college on a baseball scholarship, and might have made a good life for himself in the sports world, but didn't want to get trapped by a lifestyle of big bucks and glitz.

Frankie didn't try to read the jury. If they were outraged by his arrogance, or amused by his naiveté, she didn't want to know. They'd either believe him or think he was crazy, or both. It was during the reception, after meeting the king, that he met Sahar.

King Nuri rarely allowed Rashidi women to attend functions of state. "Their traditions don't allow women to mingle with men." But Nuri was different. "He wanted to bring his country out of the Middle Ages."

Objection, motion to strike, sustained, jury admonished to disregard. After the flap, Frankie asked him to go on.

Sahar was there with three women and perhaps a hundred men, in a huge room as perfectly furnished as anything he'd ever seen. She wasn't mingling, but they were in the same space. He didn't know how he wound up standing next to her. It was like a force swirled around, and when the currents subsided, that's where they dropped him. He was certain other people saw it, but no one did. She wore an *abaya,* the robe and cloak over the head that can turn a women into a lump, but she was too beautiful for that. "She wore a thin half veil, enough to see her face. Her eyes are hazel." He sighed. "Her skin is the color of soft wood." He blushed slightly, looking only at Frankie. "Her face is a perfect oval, like a falling tear."

There was movement in the spectator area as two Rashidis, with dark faces and heavy steps, stomped out of the courtroom. Frankie could feel their heat.

Later, Rick found she'd been as attracted to him as he was to her. "You have fill my heart with resonance," were the words he heard her say to him. No one was with them; there was no way to corroborate what she said, except through her. Clardy let it in at first because the words, though hearsay, described Sahar's state of mind. Then the judge changed her mind and the evidence was stricken from the record. Sahar's state of mind had no relevance.

"Your Honor, it *is* relevant," Frankie begged from behind the sound screen. "Her state of mind bears directly on the reasonableness of Mr. Adamson's belief!"

"I disagree, Ms. Rommel," Clardy said. "Too tenuous."

Nobody wins them all. Frankie wound Rick up again, having him testify that Sahar was all he could think of. The judge let *that* go in! She rushed Rick along. When they saw each other at embassy functions, he said—two more, before Saddam invaded Kuwait—they couldn't even talk to each other. But once—it could have been accidental—they touched hands.

Then in Saudi Arabia he received a letter from her. He couldn't tell the jury what it said, but it left him in a very happy state of mind. He replied with a letter addressed to "Dawn on the Desert"—a reference to the Arabic meaning of Sahar—which he sent to an address in Switzerland. It took him two days to write it, even though it wasn't very long. He told her what California was like, his impressions of Rashidi, and whether or not he believed in God. Three weeks before Desert Storm, he received another letter from Switzerland. This one left him ecstatic. He felt so good he barely noticed the war.

His hitch was up in March. Frankie offered a copy of his honorable discharge in evidence to prove the date. He was mustered out in the District, and immediately hired by the Rashidis. In less than ten days Sahar arrived in the United States as a fledgling diplomat.

Frankie asked the Government to stipulate that Princess Sahar bint Rashid had arrived at the embassy of the Kingdom of Rashidi on March 15, 1991, to take up duties in the Office of Information. Husam reacted angrily until she showed him newspaper clippings from the *Washington Post* and told him she would call the reporters who had covered the story. He agreed to the stipulation.

It was eleven. Frankie smiled at the clock, trying to get it to run backward. Clardy ordered another recess so the court reporter could rest her hands.

As Frankie arranged her notes on the lectern, she told herself to keep it short. There wasn't time to tell all of it. "Mr. Adamson," she said cheerfully. "You testified that you broke in to 'get her out,' because you believed she would be taken back to Rashidi and killed." Not her most elegantly phrased statement, but good enough for government work. "Do you recall that testimony?"

"Yes. I do."

So did the jury. In spite of the formalized setting and the dry exchanges and the breaks in the action, they seemed eager to hear the rest of it. "You've also described an execution you witnessed in that country. But the person involved committed a murder. Why did you think the princess would be killed? Wouldn't she have to commit a crime first, and if so, what was her crime?"

Rick let his gaze wander toward the knot of Rashidis, and when he spoke, it was with understanding. There was no denial in their attitude, which some of the jurors could see. Frankie could not have planned it better. "Sexual misconduct is *haram*. It's forbidden by Islam." Husam al-Din looked ready to leap to his feet, but stayed in his chair. "Honor and family are more important than the life of one person. When those bonds are broken or betrayed . . ." He looked at the jury, wanting all of them to appreciate the Arabic mind-set. "It isn't just the men. It's the women too. Sexual closeness and intimacy is encouraged by Islam, but only in marriage. It's too sacred to flaunt casually, as we do in this country."

"As I listen, I have the impression you agree. Do you?"

"I have respect for their attitudes and a lot of the results. Crime, for example. They hardly have any. It simply is not a problem in Rashidi." One of the reporters gave a short burst of laughter, then ducked his head. "But it has its downside too. It's very unfair to the women. This sense of honor is very macho, and—"

"Object," Husam said firmly. "This answer is not responsive, is opinion and speculation, and not relevant to any issue."

Frankie looked at the judge and said nothing. "Sustained," Clardy said. "The jury is directed to disregard the answer."

"Was it your belief, Mr. Adamson, that Princess Sahar would have been accused of sexual misconduct and executed?"

"That was my belief."

"You've told us how you got inside the embassy. When you reached the office of the deputy ambassador, what happened?"

He described going out on the balcony and climbing a vine-covered fire-escape ladder that could be reached from the balcony railing. Frankie interrupted and asked him to identify pictures Daven had taken from a distance with a telephoto lens. They showed the balcony depicted in government photos, but extended beyond it. The bare outlines of a ladder could be seen. The prosecution team, taken by surprise, asked for a recess. Ten minutes later they were admitted.

He was on the ladder when Abd al-Hafiz ran onto the balcony. The man had a gun in his hand. Rick did the only thing he could do: jumped on him. That's how Rick's scuff marks and blood got smeared on the balcony deck. But he didn't want to hurt al-Hafiz. They had been friends. He tried to wrestle him down, but the small man turned into a tiger. They fell against the brick wall and al-Hafiz started to scream. Rick didn't know he was killing him when the knife went in. Those thoughts were not in his mind. He acted, or reacted, out of his own instinct to survive, and to save Sahar.

It was almost noon. How had she ever thought she could do him in one morning? He finished his testimony with the rescue of Sahar and their dash through the grounds which activated the outdoor alarms. He put Sahar on Rory Bern's bike—you could see the relief on his face—which dissolved into a shrug.

Full circle, Frankie thought. "The rest of it you know," she heard him say.

Husam started his cross-examination after the lunch break. Frankie hadn't been able to eat. So what was new? As she listened she decided it could have been worse. At first Husam was flat, as though troubled, but he got into it later. He asked Rick if anyone from the Pembarton Oaks Hotel would testify to corroborate the supposed incident that took place there, and nodded ironically when he learned that Rick didn't think so. He spoke in arched and lofty tones of Rick's heroism, as the savior of this woman, then asked him if he knew where she was. Rick admitted that he did: Rashidi. Had she been dragged back there in chains, or did he know? He knew: she had not been.

He handed Rick the pistol and asked him to demonstrate the way al-Hafiz had allegedly held it. Prosecutors usually manage to get weapons in the hands of defendants, hoping they'll point them at someone. He also asked Rick to show the jury how he'd used the plastic knife. Rick cradled the blade in the palm of his right hand, with the butt of the handle resting against the heel. "So," Husam said. "Once it started its penetration, you simply pushed with the heel, using the large muscles of your shoulder. Is that correct, sir?"

"Yes."

"You are a person of great strength, are you not?"

Rick shrugged his wide shoulders.

"Perhaps also a person of modesty. How tall are you, sir?"

"Six feet three inches."

"And how much do you weigh?"

"A hundred and eighty-five pounds, the last time I weighed."

"And with a baseball in your hand, could you hit that clock on the wall?"

Rick smiled at him. Frankie let them play their game. "I think so."

"Are you a person of large imagination?" Husam asked.

"I read a lot."

Husam's eyebrows lifted. "I am not surprised. This adventure you describe. Is it out of a book?"

Frankie chose not to protect him. "No sir."

"Is it from your large imagination?"

"No sir."

Husam pursed his lips thoughtfully, and folded his notepad. "I have no further questions."

Frankie liked his style. With an ironic and understated touch, he'd laid the groundwork for a devastating argument. Where is the corroboration for this fanciful tale? he would ask them. You have nothing but the words of this man who is on trial. What would you expect him to say, that he did it? Or would you not expect a tale from him that rivals *The Arabian Nights?*

She wondered how Husam would argue after hearing the next witness. "Call Jamie Roon."

Daven brought a sandy-haired man in his thirties into the courtroom. His blue eyes and freckles would have been perfect for a Wyoming jury, but Norman Rockwell poster boys weren't that popular in the District. He wore a blue blazer with a crest of arms embroidered in gold thread over the pocket. Great. He dragged a large suitcase on a luggage rack behind him, and held a VCR cassette in his other hand.

Brooking Slasstein had slipped into the courtroom and stood along the wall. Frankie wanted him to see this. "Your name, sir?"

"Jamie Roon."

"Your occupation?"

"I'm a salesman and technician for En Guarde."

"What kind of business is that?"

"We provide electronic security systems for banks, businesses, hotels, homes, and so forth."

"Is the embassy for the Kingdom of Rashidi a client?"

"Yes," Roon said, making himself comfortable on his chair.

The skin in Gleason's face began to change colors. "Pursuant to a subpoena, did you bring records that show transactions with the Rashidi Embassy?" Frankie asked.

"I did."

Roon's testimony did not improve the condition of Gleason's complexion. He told the jury that En Guarde had put in the outdoor grounds security system in 1987, when the Rashidis bought the building. However, the internal surveillance system wasn't installed until May 20 and 21 of this year. Roon handled the sale and helped with the installation. A covert surveillance system, it had been put in place with great secrecy. The only Rashidi he had talked to—the only man in the embassy with knowledge of the transaction, as far as he knew at that time—was their head of security, Abd al-Hafiz.

Frankie selected a picture of Hafiz from the government's exhibits, showing him on the couch in the deputy ambassador's office. He appeared to be sleeping. "Was this the man you dealt with?"

He examined the picture. "Yes."

In early August—he wasn't sure of the date and had not made a record of it—he got a message to call the deputy ambassador for the kingdom, a Mr. Faris abu abd al-Rahman. Frankie turned to look into the spectator area. Rahman sat a few rows back, next to the aisle. Rahman thought there might be a videotape, Roon continued, but he didn't know where it was or how to unload it. "He said the police wanted it for their investigation."

Roon showed him the room in the Rashidi Embassy basement where the equipment was located: a video recorder, a monitor or view screen, and a control board. The room was locked, but Rahman had a card with all the codes and finally opened it. "He'd never been down there." The room was about the size of a walk-in closet, but well lighted and ventilated. The equipment sat on the table En Guarde had given them. The cassette in the recorder had been ejected, and the view screen—still on—showed Rahman's office. "What did you do?"

Roon pulled out a handkerchief and sneezed. "It was

obvious to me that Mr. Rahman didn't know anything about the equipment," he said, stuffing it in his pocket. "The cassette in the recorder had automatically ejected when it was loaded. I was afraid Mr. Rahman might lose what was on that last tape, by recording over it or any number of ways. So as I explained the control board and the system to him, I ran off a copy. As a courtesy. I thought he'd be impressed with the technology." Roon shrugged. "He wasn't. When I tried to give it to him, he didn't know what to do with it. So I kept it for him." He pointed to the cassette on top of the luggage. "There it is."

"Has the copy of the tape been exclusively in your possession, from that day to this?"

"Yes."

"Have you looked at it?"

"Yes."

"Has it been altered, modified, enhanced, or excised in any way?"

"No. It's the same now as it was then."

"Do you know what Mr. Rahman did with the original?"

"I know what he said."

"What did he say?"

"He said he was going to give it to the police."

Frankie turned toward Gleason and smiled at him. Then she offered the tape in evidence and requested permission to show it to the jury. The witness had thoughtfully brought with him the specialized equipment needed, she said. Judge Barbara Clardy glared at her with critical affection. Frankie had never been glared at like that by a judge. "Have you seen the tape, Ms. Rommel?"

"I have."

"Before we show it to the jury, I think we'd better give Mr. al-Din the same opportunity. Don't you?"

Frankie shrugged. "I suppose so."

Clardy announced a recess and the combatants trooped into her chambers. Husam brought Faris abu abd al-Rahman with him, as an adviser. As Roon set up the equipment, Gleason kept whispering in his ear, but Husam didn't appear to be listening.

Roon's running commentary, as he ran the tape, had the practiced sound of a sales pitch. The twenty-inch view screen could split into panels of twos, threes, sixes, eights, nines, twelves, and sixteens, he explained, demonstrating those capabilities. A time and date generator displayed the time and date across the top, in white numbers separated by colons. "Mr. Hafiz reloaded every morning at six," he said, freezing the screen, which showed 7:25:91::06:04:39. "That's July twenty-five this year, six A.M., four minutes, thirty-nine seconds." He punched a button advancing the tape. Seconds turned into a blur as the minutes rolled over in seconds, and the hours in tens of seconds. The activity on the panels displayed by the view screen speeded by like windows from a train going in the other direction.

"Mr. Rahman, we can focus in on your office and slow down," Roon said. Without being directed to, he punched buttons on the control board. The time and date display on top slowed so that the seconds ticked by as seconds. The picture showed Rahman standing with his hands behind his back, staring out the window. A woman with crossed legs and a stenographer's pad on her lap sat in the foreground. She smoked a cigarette, and her motions had an odd, jerky quality. "Mr. al-Hafiz had a time-lapse system, rather than an event recorder. The cassette holds six hours of actual time, but he expanded that six hours into twenty-four."

"What is the difference between an event recorder and this time lapse you speak of?" Rahman asked.

"The event recorder is motion sensitive. If nothing is going on, no pictures are taken." The sequence they watched had the quality of an old silent movie. "In actual time— that's the same as movie-screen time, or real time as it's called in our business—there are twenty-four frames per second. What we have here is six frames per second, which expands the time to cover a twenty-four-hour period."

"Mr. Rahman," Clardy said, "is there any question in your mind as to the accuracy of the picture?"

He sat near the screen, watching with fascination. "I am not so bald, am I?" he asked, feeling the top of his head.

Gleason alone was not amused. "If there aren't any questions," Roon said, "I can advance it."

After five in the afternoon, most panels stayed still. The exceptions would show a blur of motion which Roon would slow down and bring up. Rahman had worked until seven, and the cameras picked him up leaving his office, walking down the second floor hallway, and getting on an elevator. At ten o'clock—7:25:91::22:02:34, and rolling—Abd al-Hafiz could be traced stepping off the elevator in the basement. He walked into a room with no camera. "That is the barracks for the sentries on duty," Rahman said. Al-Hafiz walked out seven minutes later. He was tracked to another room with no camera. "That is the room with the movies. I remember now. My nephew calls this room his control center."

There were occasional blurs, which proved to be sentries—until 7:26:91::01:42:18, and rolling. "Here's where the action begins," Roon said. "I'll bring it up."

He made the camera shot in the parking garage full-screen. They watched the trunk lid of one of the limousines lift. A figure of a man emerged, carefully closing the lid. He turned around, full face to the camera. Roon froze it. "What have we here," Judge Barbara Clardy said, breaking the silence, "is the defendant, Richard Adamson Junior. In black face."

Triumphantly, like a Viking queen, Frankie showed the tape to the jury. They watched wide-eyed as Adamson worked his way through the embassy toward the office of the deputy ambassador. At various times Roon froze the picture, showing conclusively that the black-clad figure in running tights and bicycle shirt did not carry a pistol. He stealthily entered the door of the deputy ambassador and slid inside. His shadow could be tracked making its way to the doors that opened onto the balcony. He stepped out.

Two seconds later another panel exploded with action. The door to the control room in the basement burst open and the thin, intense figure of Abd al-Hafiz could be seen, dashing toward the basement elevator. The door clanged shut behind him. On the second floor a different panel showed the elevator door opening and Abd al-Hafiz storming into the hall toward the deputy ambassador's office. He carried a pistol high, in his right hand. He burst into the office, snapped on the light, jumped across the room to the balcony doors and disappeared outside. The time and date display showed 7:26:91::01:53:49, and rolling.

The seconds ticked by with no action on any of the panels, and Roon advanced the tape to 02:04:31. Clardy explained to the jury that the tape showed nothing in the interval; they could see for themselves in the jury room. Roon started it up. At 02:04:37 four of the panels showed activity as frightened, surprised men began streaming out of the barracks. No one seemed to be in charge until one of the sentries on the front door appeared and took control.

The sequence in the deputy ambassador's office showed the most commotion. The body of Abd al-Hafiz was brought in and laid on the couch. His coat flopped open, showing an empty holster.

At a quarter to four Frankie rested her case. She wanted Husam to give up. He was beaten, wasn't he? Didn't he know enough to lay down and roll over and stick his feet in the air?

He did not. He insisted on rebuttal, and asked for the weekend to prepare.

Judge Clardy granted his request.

# 27

It was after eleven when Husam opened the front door of his house. Abir had not waited up for him; he had told her not to. Sick in his soul, he knew he must first deal with his daughter, and then his wife. He peeled off his coat and hung it on the hook in the foyer. Looking around him at his possessions—the burnished hardwood floor of his spacious home, the fine old clock that ticked in the hall, the grand piano in the large living room—he knew he was seeing them for the last time.

He slipped off his shoes, so that he could move quietly about. His eyes adjusted to the darkness and he walked into the living room. He picked up an iron poker by the fireplace. The image of his father filled his mind, then seemed to fill his being. There was no question what his father would do, if he were alive. Husam didn't know if he would have the strength. He could barely breathe.

A light flicked on in the center of the house. Abir, in the kitchen? His stomach sucked into his throat. Kawthar. So be it. Husam's head became a balloon, floating across the floor, toward the light.

He stayed in shadow until he could peer into the kitchen. Kawthar stood by the open door of the refrigerator, removing something. A packet of cheese. Leaving the door open, she carefully unpeeled it, picked a large knife off the kitchen table and sliced off a chunk. She folded the wrapper around the cheese and leaned into the refrigerator to replace it.

"Kawthar!"

The girl spun away from the light of the refrigerator and stared toward his voice. "Daddy?"

He snapped on the light and advanced toward his degraded daughter, the poker held low in his hand.

"Daddy, I've missed you so much!" She rushed toward him, to embrace him.

Husam didn't know what to do. She wrapped her arms around him and started hugging him. The awful purpose in his soul drained out of him and he dropped the iron. But intense shame, humiliation, and anger remained. With roughness he pried her loose. "You refuse to live by the rules in my house," he said. "I ordered you to leave! What are you doing here? Where have you been?"

"I couldn't leave, Daddy." She put her face in her hands. "Please, Daddy, I'll do anything! You were so angry, and Mama said . . ."

She stopped, holding her arms around herself, biting her lip to keep from crying.

"What do you mean by this? That you could not leave?"

"Mama let me stay. In the basement. You never go down there."

Husam was stunned. How could Kawthar be a woman of the street, if she had lived in his basement from the day he ordered her out of his house? And how did Gleason know she lived there? Suddenly it was clear to him. "Your girlfriends," he said. "Have you told them of your problems, on the telephone?"

"Just . . . Mira. She wouldn't say anything."

Gleason, who must cover his associates with mud, to control them. Gleason had a bug on his telephone. A marvelous sense of relief washed through Husam. "Go to your room, Kawthar," he said, wishing time alone to enjoy the feeling. "We will talk in the morning." She started for the basement door. "No. Your room." Kawthar—in spite of her grown-up appearance—was a child. His child. "First, come here to me, and give me a kiss."

"My husband?" Abir asked sleepily.

Husam had not thought it possible to awaken his wife. "Yes." He felt tenderness for her. It had been too long since he had held her in his arms. "Who did you expect?"

# 28

**Monday, October 28, 1991**

Four lines of people stood outside the Superior Court
Building at 8:30 A.M., trying to get in. Many of those who'd
been turned away stood around in knots on the wide cement
veranda in front, like vigilantes, conspiring to take the jail
by storm. The guard at the security checkpoint recognized
Frankie and Arnie Daven and waved them through. "What's
all the fuss?" Frankie asked, afraid of the answer.

"They all think some Arabian princess gonna be here,"
she said, rolling her eyes.

The courtroom was packed when Frankie and Arnie tried
to push in. Every seat was taken except for a roped-off area,
reserved for the press. Spectators stood against the walls,
even though the show wouldn't start until nine o'clock.
Husam sat alone at plaintiff's table when Frankie and Arnie
struggled through the gate. "Do you see what you have
done?" he said, standing.

"Pretty exciting," Frankie said, plopping her briefcase on
a chair and opening it. She found her file labeled *Instructions* and pulled it out. "The judge told me she wants some
argument."

"Yes." Husam picked up a file and a legal pad. "I have
requested additional instructions. Shall we go in?"

"I'll stay, Frankie," Arnie said.

Frankie took a deep breath and tried to pacify the bees in her stomach. Husam obviously had been busy over the weekend. "Mix up his notes," she said to Daven, pointing at the papers on Husam's table.

Judge Clardy sat at her desk, wearing a white blouse with a bow in front, looking like a schoolgirl. The court reporter sat at the end of the table, filing her nails. "The media appears to have whetted a few appetites over the weekend," she said. "Sit down."

They did.

"Husam, do you have much in the way of rebuttal?"

"I have three witnesses, possibly four," he said. "It will be an hour."

"We could start final argument as early as ten, then. Ms. Rommel, let's look at yours first."

Frankie opened her file folder, prepared to do battle. But there was nothing to fight over. In addition to the standard instructions on reasonable doubt and presumption of innocence, Husam agreed the instructions on choice of evils and self-defense should also be given. "There is evidence to support them," he said. When she moved for the dismissal of the prohibited weapons count, Husam even agreed to that.

That frightened her. "So easy, Mr. al-Din?" she asked, trying to draw him out.

He did not look like a man who had given up. "You are not surprised, are you?" he asked. "Would you wish to draw attention to your mistakes?"

The shouting started when Husam gave Frankie copies of the new instructions he wanted: the gamut on the lesser-included offenses for murder. If the jury wouldn't go for first degree, he argued they should have the right to convict on second degree. If they didn't like that, they should consider manslaughter. Frankie begged and pleaded with Clardy, insisting that the right to a compromise verdict rested only with the defense.

She lost.

Frankie had known it would happen, and it had. Over the

weekend Husam had regrouped. He'd go for what he could get.

At ten minutes after nine the jurors filed in to the courtroom. Frankie was drained of energy. She pretended her feet were electric plugs and stuck them in the sockets on the floor. She barely listened as Clardy reminded the jury of what had happened and told them what was to come. The defense had rested its case and the next stage in the trial would be rebuttal evidence, offered by the government. "Mr. al-Din, you may call your first witness."

A small woman in an *abaya* with no veil moved shyly into the witness box. After giving her Arabic name, she told of seeing Sahar bint Rashid on August 14, at the legation for the Kingdom of Rashidi. There were no men lurking in the halls to arrest her, and she smiled and chatted easily with the women she saw. She had moved from the embassy to an apartment in town, and had come to the legation to pick up her clothes.

Frankie did her best. On cross-examination she asked the woman for details about Sahar's move. Why hadn't Sahar taken her clothes with her when she moved? The witness didn't know. The move must have been quite sudden, correct? The witness shrugged. The truth was Sahar had been held as a prisoner in the embassy, wasn't it? Frankie demanded. The truth was, an American—the one charged with murder—had freed her. One hears many things, the witness suggested. Husam objected, and the rumors she had heard were not allowed.

Husam took a long, careful look at Frankie, who had the sudden insight he was going to call *her* to the stand! Do it, she thought, putting on her most innocuous bimbo face. Then she could provide the jury with one-half of all the conversations she'd had with Sahar. The jurors' imaginations would make the other half. He seemed to recognize the danger and called a real bimbo instead.

Probably it was Frankie's mood. The woman on the stand looked exactly like Miss Black America, but might not have been a bimbo at all. She told the jury of sitting with the woman in the photograph—Sahar bint Rashid—at Dulles

International, on August 19. Sahar's state of mind bordered on exuberance, the witness said.

The next witness, a travel agent for Overseas International, also identified the picture of Sahar, as well as a copy of the ticket she had sold the princess. It showed her flight from Dulles International, with a change in Rome, then to Cairo, arriving in Egypt on August 20. Frankie nodded agreeably, as though she had expected it.

Oh well. In the great scheme of things, could the life of one Arabian princess make that much difference?

Husam sat down. Clardy solemnly declared that all the evidence was in, and that final arguments would begin after a short recess.

"So what're you gonna do, quit?" Brooking demanded. He bounced out of his chair in the witness room, his arms flapping like a turkey who needs to fly but can't. "Make up your mind."

"I just want to go to sleep."

"Frankie, it isn't over till it's over."

She looked at her tear-streaked face in the mirror of her compact. What a mess. "God, will I be glad when it's over."

Husam started his pitch at 9:45. It didn't take long for him to get serious. He picked up the CIA letter opener and held it with the butt against the heel of his hand. "More than six inches of this instrument of death was buried in the body of Abd al-Hafiz," he said, "by the defendant. He even showed you how he accomplished this feat of strength." Husam pushed the tip of the blade into the lectern, moving it. "The stomach, lungs, and heart of Mr. Hafiz were penetrated by this ferocious blow." He laid the weapon on the lectern. "The defendant claims it had to be done to save the life of this princess from Rashidi. You must answer the question with intelligence. Save her from what?"

He turned toward Rick. "On August nineteenth, 1991, she returned to this frightening land where she was born. This country, where she faces execution, according to the fantastic, *Arabian Nights* adventure story you have heard from the defendant." He shook his head in ironic disbelief. "Why does she go back, you may wonder? Does she willingly place her head upon a chopping block, so eloquently described by this man?" He showed them the palms of his hands. "It is not reasonable for you to believe such absolute nonsense."

He pointed at Rick. "This man is not a hero, except perhaps in his own eyes of himself. He is an intruder, a burglar in the embassy of the Kingdom of Rashidi, who invaded in the night. He carried with him a weapon of death, and used it to kill a human being. Do you let him walk away because he has such colorful imagination?"

Frankie made herself sit up straight as Husam launched into a discussion of the specific crimes Rick was charged with, starting with the burglary. She listened politely as he apologized for the mistakes of the prosecution. The burglary had not been committed by climbing onto the balcony. But did the action of the man in going all the way inside make him less of a burglar? "Of course not," Husam proclaimed. "It makes him more of one!"

To commit a burglary, one must also have the intent to commit a crime, Husam continued. Did the defendant have such intent? Of course! Why else did he take with him the plastic knife? The crimes he intended to commit were assault, and murder, Husam declared. And those in fact were the crimes he committed.

He asked the jurors to listen carefully to the instructions of the judge regarding the murder charge. Acting like the student in the front row who always took notes, Frankie listened. Judge Clardy would tell them that the defendant could be found guilty of murder in the first degree, *or* murder in the second degree, *or* manslaughter. What a peculiar animal was the law, Frankie heard her mind proclaim. First she strikes the jury with her right hand, then with her left, and the jury must decide which hand doth strike the hardest.

With care and sincerity Husam told them of his confidence in their ability to think clearly. Given that ability, he was certain they would agree that the elements of the crime of first degree murder were proved, beyond a reasonable doubt.

They could dispose of the first element. There was no dispute that the defendant caused the death of a human being. He showed them the letter opener. But there must also be a showing of malice, which he would return to, and a third element that required explanation. This third element could be accomplished in more than one way, he explained: either a killing by deliberate and premeditated design, or a killing in the commission of a burglary.

Holding the lectern with his hands, he leaned toward them with righteous zeal. He stood as tall as Brooking would stand, Frankie thought, if Brooking managed to climb on top of it. Frankie entertained herself with the image. She turned and found her compadre, smiling at her with encouragement from the front row.

What does malice mean? Husam asked. The judge will tell you it refers to a state of mind that has no regard for the life, or the safety, of others. Have we that in this case? Of course! We have an intruder in the nighttime, fired from employment, who carried with him a plastic knife. It was beyond conception that his state of mind had any regard whatever for life and safety. It will be interesting, he suggested, to hear how Ms. Rommel addresses this obvious fact.

As to a killing by premeditated design. Isn't that shown better by *their* evidence than ours? He picked up the cassette tape and asked them to view it in the jury room during their deliberations. "It will show better than a thousand words the premeditation of the defendant. Consider the planning demanded by this careful and secretive invasion." Nicely done, Frankie thought, watching him use the cassette tape to his advantage. "As a chauffeur, he had driven a limousine for the Rashidis, for which he made his own set of keys. Then he hid inside the trunk, like an assassin, to gain entrance into the embassy!"

Premeditation? Deliberation? he asked them, putting the cassette tape down. Remember too the wired gate in the

371

fence between the legation and the embassy, for which we have his fingerprints for proof. And his clothing and his blackened arms and face. And watch the stealth of his movements through the embassy toward—what? He claims not to have known of this internal surveillance. Do you believe him, this man on the security staff, who knew so much of the operations of the embassy?

Assume instead, perhaps, that he knew of this internal surveillance. Did he deliberately cast his line upon the water, and lure Abd al-Hafiz to his death? Surely that makes more sense of this brutal and wanton act than that he wished to save the life of this woman who obviously had no need to be saved.

First degree murder may be proved without this element of premeditation, when it is committed in the course of a burglary. Obviously, it was one or the other, he told them, or perhaps both. He asked them not to be misguided by the unfortunate mistakes of the prosecution. In spite of them, there could be no *reasonable* doubt that first degree murder was proved.

It occurred to Frankie that if Brooking got on the lectern, he could jump on the rail in front of the jurors. In her mind's eye she watched him do it. No wonder he won all the time. He could really get in their face.

But if for some reason you cannot agree that this killing occurred during the commission of a burglary, she heard Husam continue, or by premeditated and deliberate design, then your verdict should be guilty of second degree murder. It is a lesser charge, but is included within the charge of first degree. For the crime of second degree murder, all the law required was an unlawful killing, with malice. The force of this wound in the back of Abd al-Hafiz, Servant of Allah the Protector. Does not it alone prove malice?

But if you cannot agree as to this element of malice—if you conclude, for example, that he actually carried the CIA letter opener to open mail, and stabbed with such ferocity out of the goodness of his heart—then there is still the killing. In that case, their verdict should be manslaughter.

For the only way they could acquit this man, Husam declared, was to find him justified in his action. The killing—and he held the dagger in his hand as he spoke—must have been lawful! If they could agree by some stretch of the imagination that the killing was lawful, Husam said, then they should acquit. His manner did not indicate that he thought such a result was possible.

Frankie smiled. Lawyers were like wolves, and wolves were like mice, she thought. One shouldn't expect them to remain in corners very long. When one has them cornered, one should dispatch them quickly, rather than giving them a weekend to get away. She listened to Husam extricate himself from the position she'd worked so hard to put him in. "I do not apologize for the conduct of Lamar Gleason," he said. "But do two wrongs make a right?"

He continued with a sincerity that had to come from the depths of an honest heart. Who could understand why Lamar Gleason had acted in such fashion? There had been no need. The evidence of the defense was far more damning than that of the prosecution. But could they ignore or excuse the obvious fact that a vicious, brutal killing had been committed for no lawful reason, because of the wrongs committed by the Government's chief investigator?

He asked them not to punish the Government, by its verdict, for the conduct of an officer. "Let the Government take care of this man." He paused, conveying the unmistakable impression that the matter would not go unnoticed. They should accept the facts shown by the defense as they related to the commission of the crime, he said, thrusting the letter opener toward them. "Those facts do not excuse the intrusion, by this man, into the embassy of the Kingdom of Rashidi. They do not justify him in pushing this instrument of death into the body of the man he says was his friend!"

As Husam sat down the sound of a beeper in the courtroom could be heard. Frankie got up, her eyes drawn toward Brooking, who quickly made some hand movements that shut the noise off. He looked like an angel as he smiled at her and nodded. Very strange. The dwarf reminded her of her grandfather.

"As I listened to Mr. al-Din," she said from behind the lectern, "I was struck by two things." Her legs felt great. "First, he didn't even mention the real issues in this case: justification, choice of evils, self-defense." The charge she'd given herself by plugging into the floor had finally kicked in. "Was Mr. Adamson justified in what he did? *That's* the issue here." She reached as many faces with her eyes as she could. "Second, he said nothing—absolutely nothing—about the fact that Mr. Adamson has no evidence—none—to corroborate his version."

The jurors' expressions were wonderfully impassive. "Mr. Adamson told you of letters he'd gotten from Sahar bint Rashid, but our side couldn't produce them." She pointed at Rick. "All you have is Mr. Adamson's word. He told you they were at the Pembarton Oaks Hotel, but we can't prove that either. Not even a hotel registration card. As Mr. al-Din talked, I asked myself: Why doesn't he bring that up?"

Jurors were not noted for enthusiastic displays, but Frankie could feel a spark of interest. "Mr. al-Din hasn't forgotten," she said. "He's playing a lawyer game. He knows he'll have the last word here. If I'd said nothing about it now, bet your life savings you'd hear about it from him later. You will anyway. He'll tell you the defendant's story is a fairy tale. He'll tell you there is no corroboration whatever to prove it."

She glanced at Husam, hoping they'd see a glimmer of guilt in his expression. "He tells you two wrongs don't make a right, that the government shouldn't be punished for what Lamar Gleason did." She pointed at the unoccupied chair. "Where is Mr. Gleason, by the way? Under a rock?" She sipped from a cup of water. "I don't want you to punish the government for his inexcusable conduct. But I want you to think about it. If Lamar Gleason was capable of what we all know he did, he's capable of anything!

"He lied to you. He lied to his own lawyer. He deliberately destroyed evidence. How hard would it have been for him to destroy other evidence as well? I have no proof of it. But I have no doubt of it. There *were* letters. Where are they now?" She gestured toward the empty chair. "There were hotel registration cards too. They went the way of the cassette tape."

They were listening. Frankie could feel them respond. But she'd felt the same thing from other juries, and been wrong. "Why did Gleason do what he did? Mr. al-Din claims he doesn't know, but I have some thoughts on the subject. The morning this happened," she said, picking the grappling hook off the exhibit table and showing it to them, "his officers found this"—she waved it at them—"under a bush on the lawn." She put it down. "Later that day, they learned about the wired gate, with Mr. Adamson's fingerprints on it. They had their case!" She leaned toward them from behind the lectern. "It was perfectly clear what had happened. Reports were written, strategies developed, all going in the obvious direction."

There were some affirmative nods. "This isn't TV. There isn't always some deep, dark, devious reason for deception. It's life. Lamar Gleason didn't want the embarrassment that would go with a new development. He didn't want to undo all that paperwork. It's possible the answer is as simple, and as ugly, as that."

She opened her notepad on the lectern. "Let's look at the other point the government doesn't want to talk about: justification." She glanced at the words on the page. "Judge Clardy will instruct on choice of evils," she said, turning her notepad over. It got in the way. "What the judge will tell you is this: there are times when a person is justified in committing a crime."

Frankie moved around the lectern so they could see her, her body vibrating with intensity. She'd been told that, on occasion, she glowed, and it felt like she was glowing now. "Justified. Justification. Mr. al-Din tells you Mr. Adamson didn't have any. But he *did.*" She touched her stomach. "It's a gut thing, something you feel, as well as know. Do something for me." She found the defense cassette and held it up. "Be Rick Adamson for a few minutes. With me. Let's *be* him, and see what it feels like."

Some of the jurors looked frightened, but others appeared willing to try it. Frankie concentrated on the brave ones. "You have to get her out. Her life depends on it. This knowledge has been burned into every cell of your body. If you don't get her out, she'll be killed." With her right arm extended toward Rick, she brought him into the circle. *"Be* him, with that terrible certainty. Feel his fear, his desperation, his resolve. Are you justified in breaking in the embassy to get her? You bet you are. She is your wife! That is your reality. They were one person. You have no choice."

She walked slowly behind the lectern, the cassette still in her hand. "Now you're in the building. You don't know it, but Mr. al-Hafiz is watching you open the trunk lid and crawl out! He's sitting in his control room, watching you!" She held as many of their faces as she could. "What's he waiting for? Does he want to know what you're up to before he makes his move? You don't know, of course, because you don't even know you're being watched." She stepped over to the exhibit table and picked up the gun. "You slip into Mr. Rahman's office, carefully open the door, and go out on the balcony—and Mr. al-Hafiz can't see you!" She showed them the gun. "That's when Mr. al-Hafiz bursts out of the door of the control center and runs after you, with this."

There were some nods; more like blinks of the eye. That was all the encouragement Frankie could hope for. "When Mr. al-Hafiz charged onto the balcony, you were on the fire escape ladder. What do you see? A man, waving this!" She waved the gun at them. "Are you justified in doing what you do?"

Putting the exhibits down, she moved behind the lectern. "This man"—she gestured toward Rick—"had the life of Princess Sahar, and his *own* life, on the line. He did what he *had* to do. The judge will instruct you that a person is justified in acting to save his life, and that of another. That's self-defense."

A couple of jurors wore expressions that showed hope, but

others frowned. "Mr. Adamson has two defenses here. Take them in order. The choice of evils defense justifies the burglary, and self-defense justifies the killing. That is our law, and that is what Judge Clardy will instruct you. A break-in to avoid a killing, but then a killing to avoid being killed."

She thought she saw the lights go on in juror number five, but knew better than to believe it. She stopped, long enough to sip from a cup full of water. "The Princess Sahar bint Rashid is now in Rashidi. But does that mean Rick Adamson didn't rescue her from the Rashidi Embassy that night? Mr. al-Din scoffs at the notion. He tells you it isn't reasonable. But he doesn't deny it, and their evidence doesn't disprove it."

She saw questions on some faces, and kept talking, trying to answer them. The rebuttal witness from the Rashidi legation didn't contradict Rick's story, she said. What the woman told them was that the princess "had moved." Frankie asked them also to remember the demeanor of Rick Adamson, including what they knew of his background. Was he a liar, like Lamar Gleason? Did he fantasize the whole thing? Was he insane, or a monster? No! "He didn't make this up. He didn't lie to you."

Some of the questions may have been answered, but others seemed to pop up on many faces. Frankie knew she would never answer them all. "The fact that Sahar is now in Rashidi does *not* mean she didn't need to be saved from death on that night. It's a different culture. Many things could have happened after he got her out that made it safe for her to go back." Husam started to push out of his chair and Frankie knew she had to stop. The rules of argument kept her from bringing up anything outside the record. She switched to the law, and Husam sat down.

She took a swipe at the presumption of innocence and reasonable doubt. Mr. Adamson is the one who, under our law, gets the breaks, she told them. "You don't even have to believe he rescued her," she said. "All you have to decide is this: Did he reasonably believe she was in mortal danger?"

She looked at Husam, who sat in one position, as though posing for a painting. "Was there any denial from the Government that an Arab woman accused of sexual misconduct could be in mortal danger? No! The Government didn't deny that. It's as Rick Adamson told you. It's true!" The bastard didn't even twitch. "I'll be interested in what Mr. al-Din has to say on *that* subject."

Again she told them that under our law, the presumptions favor the accused. What did that mean? Among other things, it meant that—in order to convict—the jury must believe, beyond a reasonable doubt, that there was *no* justification.

"The first count is burglary, or the unlawful entry into a building with the intent to commit a crime. Mr. Adamson carried a knife with him, and according to Mr. al-Din, that proves he intended to do a murder!" She shook her head. "Come on, Mr. al-Din. He didn't want to kill anyone. His reason for carrying the knife wasn't that, and you know it. It was to save a life, the life of his wife, the woman he loved! But members of the jury, Mr. Adamson doesn't have to prove he broke in to save her. Mr. al-Din has to prove, beyond a reasonable doubt, that he didn't. Do you see the difference?" There were barely perceptible nods. "If you don't understand—and there's no disgrace in not getting it—*talk* about it. You owe it to me, the judge, the defendant, and yourselves!

"Rick—Mr. Adamson—told you the truth. I'm sure most of you know that. But some of you might not, and others may think he lied." She kept her eyes away from the jurors, not wanting any of them to think she really believed that. "But can any of you honestly say that you are persuaded, beyond a reasonable doubt, that he lied? Again, do you see the difference? All you need is the reasonable belief that he told you the truth. That's enough. Under the law that each of you has sworn to uphold, *he* is the one who gets the benefit of the doubt.

"The murder charges." She glanced at the clock, then back to the panel. It was almost eleven, and she didn't want

378

to give her opponent the lunch hour to polish his rebuttal. "Was there a killing in the commission of a burglary? No! There wasn't even a burglary." She held up one finger. "One. He was justified in breaking in, and"—up went another finger—"his intent was not to commit a crime." She tried to read their expressions, but saw nothing. "Was the killing premeditated and deliberate? No, again. He didn't know he was being tracked. He jumped on Mr. al-Hafiz because there was no way out. Mr. al-Din's suggestion that Adamson lured al-Hafiz onto the balcony is ludicrous!"

She saw some agreement. "Did he act out of malice? Again, no! That's when a person has no regard for the life and safety of others. Was that his state of mind? Members of the jury, that was *all* that was in his mind. All he could think of was the life and safety of another. Sahar." She walked over to Rick. "You've watched him," she said, inviting them to look at him now. "Did he want to kill Abd al-Hafiz, this man who had been his friend? Was that what was in his heart? Or did he want to save a life?"

Nobody was crying. Brooking wouldn't quit until there were tears, but Frankie thought it was time to wrap it up. "Choice of evils," she said, walking back to the lectern. "Lamar Gleason made his choice. Rick Adamson made his. Mr. al-Din wants you to make a choice in this case, and so do I. But your choice isn't really a choice of evils. It's a choice between right and wrong. The right thing is to acquit this man. He acted lawfully, with courage, and out of love. Follow our law," she said, drawing all of them into her soul. "Believe in the old lady, as I do. She won't let you down. She won't let Mr. Adamson down either." Her throat dried up. "Thank you," she whispered, sitting down.

Clardy glanced at the clock: ten minutes after eleven. "Mr. al-Din?"

Frankie hated listening to him talk, knowing she couldn't reply. But he didn't do anything she hadn't anticipated. He hit the same nails, only harder.

The judge instructed the jurors, all of whom listened as

though their own lives depended on it. Afterward the bailiff ushered the jury out, to deliberate. Frankie sagged into the table. "Hey babe," she heard Brooking say. He'd hopped over the rail and his face was practically in her ear. "All you needed was a pep talk. Great argument! Lunch is on me, why not? You won't eat anything anyway."

# 29

Frankie dragged through the afternoon in Brooking's office, hoping for and then dreading a call from Judge Clardy's clerk, telling them the jury had a verdict. Everytime the telephone rang, it felt like the touch of an electric cattle prod. At 5:15 P.M. they hadn't reached a verdict, and sat through the brief ceremony in the courtroom as the jurors were released for the night. They'd continue with their deliberations the next morning. The marshals let Rick talk to his mom, and Frankie got away as quickly as she could.

The walk to her apartment along Pennsylvania Avenue would feel good. If she got tired, she'd flag down a cab. But as she stepped on the sidewalk, a man peeled off the wall of the building. Something about his manner suggested he'd been waiting for her. She quickened her pace, then thought, the hell with it. If it's Gleason, let him take his best shot.

The man drew alongside. *"Is-salaam 'alaykum."*

Frankie turned toward him. "Prince Muhammad?" The facial bones were right—what she could see of them, behind dark glasses, a stubbly beard, and under a leather-brimmed hat—but the clothes were all wrong. *"Wa-'alaykum is-salaam!"* He wore a plaid coat over a turtleneck sweater, and a camera was slung over his shoulder.

"Very good, Miss Rommel. Will you join me for dinner?"

"I'd love it!" she said, holding out her hand. She realized she'd seen him in the courtroom. "You are a man of many faces, sir. I would not have known it was you."

He smiled with pleasure, bending over her hand and kissing it. "I dress as an American on vacation when I wish to keep my identity from others." He let go. "I am invisible even to my relatives in such attire. Ah!" His hand rose with the imperious gesture of an emperor. "Cabbie!"

Frankie allowed him to load her into the cab and take control. She liked it, in fact. "You are a compelling orator," he told her after ordering the driver to take them to the Punjabi, an Indian restaurant on Connecticut Avenue.

"It's easy when you believe in your case."

"So. The attorney does not stop representing the client, I observe." She started to answer, but the prince shook his head and motioned with his eyes toward the driver. "Let us continue this conversation in the restaurant."

There was hardly anyone there when he ushered her inside. The maître d' examined the prince for signs of solvency, but dropped his eyes when faced with a royal glare. They were seated in a booth at the rear, with high walls and privacy. "Mind if I smoke?"

"Not at all. Allow me." He pulled a jeweled lighter out of his pocket. "You are brilliant attorney, Miss Rommel."

She inhaled gratefully as he snapped the lighter shut. "I think crafty might be a better description."

"You are too modest. I enjoy the American trial. There is much"—his hand rolled around in the air—"interpersonal dynamic. It is amusing to watch the combatants reach for advantage."

"It isn't what you have, is it?"

"The systems of law hardly compare." A waiter appeared. "You will permit me to order?"

"That's fine." Frankie didn't care. She wasn't sure if she'd be able to eat.

He ordered quickly, including a carafe of red Italian table wine. "I have the appetites of a peasant." He had taken off the glasses and looked at her sharply. "Do you believe in your justice?"

"Usually," Frankie said, knocking an ash off. A feeling of exhaustion crept back into her bones, and she looked forward to the wine. "It doesn't always work. Ours isn't a perfect system."

"But shouldn't law reach toward perfection, toward the will of God?"

Given her 'druthers, she'd have picked something else to talk about over dinner. "The problem with that approach, Prince Muhammad, is who interprets the will of God?"

"Jurists, trained in the law."

The waiter approached with a tray, holding the wine and two glasses. He poured enough in Muhammad's glass for a taste. After a critical frown, Muhammad nodded, finding it acceptable. Frankie didn't want to argue over legal systems. Maybe that too was just another choice of evils. "May I ask, sir, about Sahar?"

He surprised her. He smiled. "She is extended." He held his hands a foot over his stomach. "The child within her grows."

"How does she feel?"

He shrugged. "I don't ask such questions."

"What will happen to her, Prince?"

He tasted his wine. "It is in the hands of Allah."

"Did you hear Rick—her husband—testify?"

Muhammad smiled. "So. The representation continues. I do not agree he is her husband, but I hear him speak and am impressed with his sincerity. I reserve judgment."

Frankie put her cigarette down. Her hands were trembling and she imagined tics and twitches all over her body. "Would you care to meet him?"

"In due time."

How could she throw up? She hadn't eaten lunch; there was nothing in her stomach. "Excuse me," she said, grabbing her purse and hurrying off to the ladies' room. She couldn't be sick. She never got sick. She wretched into a washbasin, ordering herself to get a grip.

A few minutes later, her face together and her hands steady, and a Clorets like a wad of tobacco in her gums, she returned to the table. "I'm sorry. A little upset stomach."

She regarded the bowls of food on the table hopefully, but they didn't do anything for her.

"Ah." He heaped curry and bite-size chunks of lamb on her plate. "Perhaps this will help."

Frankie didn't think so. She sipped wine and toyed with her food, watching him wrap lamb in the bread.

"Do you remember standing in *my* courtroom, Miss Rommel, asking me to consider certain facts of which I might not be aware?" He had the ability to keep eating as he talked.

"Yes. You were very patient with me."

"I was tempted to stand in your courtroom and create a similar disturbance."

She saw a bit of mischief in his expression. "Over what?"

"The letters of Sahar to this Rick fellow, which you imply were stolen." That was the first time he'd called him anything but the American. "You accuse the wrong person of treachery." Frankie sat up, listening. "The records from the hotel, and the witnesses. Neither was that done by this Gleason."

She tried a few grains of rice. They went down with the Clorets. "Who, then?"

"I do not know names of these criminals. That is not important."

She shrugged. It was too late to use them, and she'd never get them anyway. "Your people?" He nodded. "Where are they?"

"Destroyed, as are the records from the hotel. To remove the stigma of shame. I have this question to you. Do you not agree that you should make public apology to this man Gleason?"

"No!" She put down her fork. "Absolutely not!"

"Then perhaps you have not so much belief in the need for truth?" he asked, still teasing.

She smiled and lifted her wineglass. "Maybe 'truth' means more in your court than mine. Have you ever seen two people more committed to each other, Prince Muhammad? More married?"

He tapped his mouth with a linen napkin. "You change

subjects quickly," he said, "which is the prerogative of your sex." He poured more wine for both of them, totally oblivious of the control Frankie pasted over her face. "There are other letters between the lovers that I do not destroy. No one knows of them but me, and you."

She pulled out another cigarette. The letters Rick had written from jail, and the ones Sahar had tried to send from Rashidi? The lighter was in his hand and he lit it for her. "Will you tell me about them?"

"They are curious. They answer one another's questions, without knowing they've been asked." He folded his hands and slowly rocked his head, then went back to his food.

It had a hopeful sound. "What will you do with them?"

He shrugged. "I will use them, perhaps. Will you bring your client a message from me?"

Don't push the man. They don't like to be pushed. "I'd be happy to."

"There will be a decision soon, am I correct? The jury now must reach its verdict?"

"It could still take a few days." She felt queasy in her stomach again.

"If your American justice results in freedom for this Rick, I will provide him safe escort to Rashidi—if he wishes to go with me to my country. But you must make him understand the danger to his life. He will first be examined by the Great Court of al-Rashid. He must also face the justice of my brother, the king."

"Does he have a chance?"

Muhammad shrugged. "In my courtroom, I will say he has a chance. As for the divan?" His eyebrows went up. "My people have great admiration for love, and courage. We are a race of poets. But the choice will rest with the clan of Abd al-Hafiz." He looked at his fingernails. "Sahar is a wealthy woman. As you say here, it is possible that the clan of Abd al-Hafiz could use the money."

As soon as Frankie pushed open her door, she suspected something was wrong. The hall light was off, leaving the room in darkness, and she distinctly remembered turning it on that morning before she left.

Switching it on, she shut the door, telling herself to stop it. She would not live her life imagining things. It created more stress than she needed, and if she got an ulcer and developed cancer and died, who would take care of her horse? The bulb had been flickering last night. It must have burnt out.

Then who put in the new bulb?

The bees crawled around in her stomach as she placed her handbag on the TV and kicked off her shoes. Gleason stared at her. She saw him in the kitchen, behind the service counter between the kitchen and the dining room. "Hello, cunt."

She glared back at him. The bees boiled into action—but not with fear. They stormed around with sudden rage. Frankie saw a bully, a bag of hot air, a sixth grade moron who liked to terrorize third graders. *"God damn you, Gleason!"* she screamed, searching the room for something to hit him with. A tong by the fireplace would work. She yanked it up, lifting it high with both hands and whirling toward him. "What do you *mean* breaking in here, trying to scare the shit out of me! God *damn* you!" She charged into the kitchen, after him.

Surprise flashed across his face. "Lady, I don't want to hurt you," he said, backing past the refrigerator. His coat opened, showing a gun in the holster. "Take it easy now." She stalked him, measuring distances and getting closer. He jumped up on the counter and crashed across it, knocking the toaster, a can full of coffee, and a lazy Susan loaded with spices all over the place. "Shit!" He tumbled on the dining room floor and got his feet under him.

"You son of a bitch!" She could chase after him through the door or jump over the counter. The counter, she decided, not wanting to lose sight of him.

"Damn you lady, *I* didn't steal no letters," he whined. What was *that* all about? "That wasn't right, what you said about me in court! I just wanted to tell you, damn it!"

"What you want me to do? *Apologize?"* She kept coming, freezing him with her heat.

"You stay where you are, lady!" He verged on panic.

"This is *my* house!" She took a swipe at him, missing. "You are an *intruder!*" She advanced toward his pasty white face. "You are a *coward*. A *miserable coward!*" She swung again, destroying a lamp.

*"Shit!"* he screamed, showing surprising agility for a man of his size. He vaulted over the couch, landing on the coffee table, flattening it. "I'm *leaving!*"

"Oh no you don't!" Frankie raced him for the door, but he skidded a chair at her and she fell over it. When she got herself back together, he was gone.

She sat down on the floor, surveying the wreckage. "That chickenshit!" She couldn't get her legs to move. "Look at this place!"

"Frankie!" She heard a commotion in the hall, then someone banging on the door. "Are you in there?"

Daven. "What do you want?"

"I want to know if you're all right. I got Gleason! What's going on?"

Wearily—bone-tired—Frankie struggled to her feet. She opened the door. "How did you get in the building?"

"Brooking. He gave me a key, told me to sit with you. What happened?"

Daven had a choke hold on Gleason. Frankie looked at the poker behind her, then at Gleason. "Kill him," she said. "Then let him go."


# Tuesday, October 29, 1991

"What's taking them so long?" Rick asked. He was on the other side of the plexiglass wall at the Federal Detention Center.

"Who knows?" Frankie smiled at him and lit a cigarette. She'd quit when she got back to Colorado. "I thought they'd get a verdict today. Shows how much I know."

"What do you think?"

She didn't want to tell him. If there were holdouts, one

way or another, they'd probably compromise. "I don't think, when it comes to juries. Big waste of time."

He looked at her as though worried by what he saw. "You've lost weight, Frankie. I can see your ribs."

"Bullshit." She inhaled, and coughed. Great. Lung cancer. "Look who's talking?" She dropped it on the floor and crushed it, then wished she hadn't. "What will you do, Rick? I mean, if they acquit you?"

"Go to Rashidi." He swallowed. "With Prince Muhammad. What a guy, right?"

Two wrongs don't make a right, Husam had argued. "Do something for me first, okay?"

"Depends. What?"

"Talk it over with your mom."

## Wednesday, October 30, 1991

"The bailiff informs me you've reached a verdict," Judge Clardy said.

The courtroom was packed. Frankie sat next to Rick, but Brooking and Daven were part of the crowd. Husam sat alone at the other table. "We have, Your Honor," Juror Seven said, standing. The others stayed in their chairs.

"Are you the foreperson, Mr. Markson?"

"Yes I am."

"Let me see the forms, please." The clerk took them from Markson and handed them to the judge.

There were four verdict forms. Clardy read them over, frowning. Frankie watched her face for some sign, then told herself: it doesn't mean a damn thing.

The judge handed the forms back to the clerk, who gave them back to the foreperson. "They appear to be in order," Clardy said. "Mr. Markson, you may announce the verdicts."

"You mean read them?"

"Yes."

Frankie shut her eyes. "We find the defendant, Richard Adamson Junior, not guilty of burglary. Like that?"

"Yes. Take them in order."

She heard the rustle of paper. "We find the defendant, Richard Adamson Junior, not guilty of burglary." The sound of a page being turned in a book. "We find the defendant not guilty of first degree murder." Another page. "We find the defendant, Richard Adamson Junior, not guilty of second degree murder." He cleared his throat. "We find the defendant, Richard Adamson Junior, not guilty of manslaughter."

Frankie opened her eyes. She saw the judge through a bucket of water, smiling at her.

## Thursday, October 31, 1991

"You look great, kid," Brooking said in the lobby of his office, surveying Rick. Frankie thought he looked terrible. The bones showed in his face, and his eyes peered around the room from holes drilled just below his forehead. "Maybe you lost some weight, get it back, won't hurt any." She thought he looked like a scarecrow in a tie. Dressed in a light blue summer coat, his shoulders extended beyond the pads. Light brown cotton trousers with tight cuffs clamped his ankles. "What's your plan?" Brooking asked him.

"I meet Prince Muhammad at the Rashidi Embassy in twenty minutes."

Frankie wanted to fix his tie, but restrained herself. She found a tissue in the pocket of her skirt. "Your mom and sister?" she asked him.

"We said our good-byes. They may be at the airport, though. I hope not."

Frankie blew her nose. "Write to me." She stuck a card in his pocket, identifying her as a lawyer with NASP. "Say hello to Sahar."

He put his arms around her and gave her a hug. She hugged him back, hard.

"Sure." They let go of each other, and he picked up the carryon bag that had been stacked against the wall, looping it over his shoulder.

"You gonna tell them your mom's a Jew?" Brooking asked.

"They already know."

"Oy vey." They watched him open the door. "Rick," Brooking said.

"Yes sir?"

"Ever hear the story about the golf game between Jesus Christ and God?"

# DIANNE G. PUGH

## Author of *COLD CALL*

# S L O W
# SQUEEZE

## AN IRIS THORNE MYSTERY

### Available in Hardcover

POCKET
BOOKS

1006-01